Stone Clock

The Spin Trilogy by Andrew Bannister

Creation Machine
Iron Gods
Stone Clock

Stone Clock

Andrew Bannister

TOR

A Tom Doherty Associates Book
New York

This is a work of fiction. All of the characters, organizations, and events portrayed in this novel are either products of the author's imagination or are used fictitiously.

STONE CLOCK

Copyright © 2018 by Andrew Bannister

A Tor Book
Published by Tom Doherty Associates
120 Broadway
New York, NY 10271

www.tor-forge.com

Tor® is a registered trademark of Macmillan Publishing Group, LLC.

The Library of Congress Cataloging-in-Publication Data is available upon request.

ISBN 978-1-250-17923-4 (trade paperback)
ISBN 978-1-250-17924-1 (ebook)

Our books may be purchased in bulk for promotional, educational, or business use. Please contact your local bookseller or the Macmillan Corporate and Premium Sales Department at 1-800-221-7945, extension 5442, or by email at MacmillanSpecialMarkets@macmillan.com.

First published in Great Britain by Bantam Press, an imprint of Transworld Publishers

First U.S. Edition: November 2019

Printed in the United States of America

0 9 8 7 6 5 4 3 2 1

To Lara

Peace Rift Plateau, *Sholntp* (vreality)

They made love on a deep bed of living moss on a flat rock on the Forward Peak of the Prow Formation – an impossibly slender projection of tufa that stuck out a hundred metres over the sheer drop of the Peace Rift.

Hels had grinned and turned around before she straddled him. She was in determinedly basic Human form, and the view of her body from this perspective should have been enthralling, should have gone straight to his hind-brain without bothering with a hundred million years of humanity as a higher species.

It was – fine, yes, he had to admit. She looked great. Primitive. Animal, even, and maybe just a bit disgusting, not that he had any problem with that. And it felt good. Not great, but certainly good.

It was just that she was in the way. He had to keep reminding himself not to twist to one side to see past her.

The Peace Rift was roughly square in cross-section, about two kilometres deep and the same wide. It was different in every way from the surrounding high country. It was tropical where the High was cool temperate; it was exotic where the High was uniform; it was vividly colourful where the palette of the High was all about muted blue and green and grey – heathers and blunt grasses and, close to the edge, a few tens of metres of soft, thick rust-coloured moss that lived in the warm, damp, slightly radioactive draught that rose from the Rift.

Hels was getting into her stride. He shoved his hips upwards and gave her an encouraging moan.

The Rift was the result of a very final attempt to end a war. He had never really decided whether it had been a success or not. Certainly it had ended the war, so in simple terms it had worked. In memory, too; after all, even a hundred thousand local years later it was still called the Peace Rift – even when everyone had forgotten everything else about it including the fact of the war itself.

That was one of his main reasons for visiting the place when he could. To remember. After all, he had watched it happen – watched the flaming ships fall.

Watched. He backed away from the word *caused*.

Something was peaking. He cleared his mind and arched upwards to match the urgent movements.

This was his hundredth visit, now he thought of it. He tried to come here about once in a thousand years, local. First, because he had promised, but then increasingly because he had quietly fallen in love with the place. He loved its bones – the unchanging parts – and he loved the changes that came to their covering during his thousand-year absences. He always told himself it had nothing to do with being addicted, because someone had to believe that and it might as well be him. Anyway, guilt was a good enough reason.

Speaking of coming, focus . . .

They orgasmed at the same time. He was rather proud of himself. Pretty good management, considering he hadn't really been concentrating.

Hels finished shuddering and collapsed forwards so her head was between his feet. The movement raised her hips, unplugging her from his body. 'Whoof! *Not* so bad.' She swivelled her head round. 'You?'

'Yeah. It was fine.'

'Fine?' She raised her eyebrows. 'Are you actually awake, Zeb?'

He thought fast. 'Sorry. I went pretty far away, just then. In a good way.'

'You must have.' She rolled off him and landed leaning on her elbow, her face close to his. 'Sometimes I'm not sure I have your whole attention, you know?'

'Really?' He studied her face. Smudged by recent passion, but questioning eyes. Rather to his surprise, his body seemed ready to answer the question. He sat up, took her by the shoulders and gently pushed her backwards until she rolled over on her bottom and landed on her back. He let himself fall into the junction of her body.

'Zeb! *Mmm . . .*'

That was better. Oh yes.

Now there was nothing to interrupt the view.

Hels moaned. At least part of this visit was going fine. For a while he actually managed to forget the scenery.

The road train lumbered down the unpaved track at a steady two hundred klicks, its fat tyres drumming and crunching on compacted gravel, pinging over the sharper rocks and squashing shallow grooves in the long stretches of grass that filled the spaces between the patches where the road had been maintained.

The road train had been built since his last visit. It was another of those superficial changes that made him smile. It, and the whole trip, had been Hels's idea. He had only been in the vreality a couple of hours, tops, when he had met her, and within another hour he had decided that she would be more than satisfactory company during his stay – and that she was in charge of herself enough not to take any harm from it.

'You *have* to see the Rift,' she had said.

'Rift?'

'The Peace Rift. Do you really not know it? Oh, it's beautiful up there.' She studied his face for a moment. 'And quiet.'

He had smiled at the implicit suggestion, and allowed himself to be shepherded as if he had never been there before – as if no one had ever insisted that he had to see it; usually within the first hour of meeting them.

Now they were on their way back down, heading to some party in a place he really hadn't visited before, for the good reason that it hadn't been there before. The green-grey landscape swayed past the window. They were off the plateau, and through the thick belt of evergreens that encircled the rising ground like a tonsure. Now they were in grain country – millions of hectares of variously seeded, variably edible grasses that had been grown since the prehistory of the planet. Originally they had been grown for food; now they were just grown. In his current incarnation here, Zeb had read a Planetary Gov paper which reported, in the driest terms, that the risk to health arising from ordinary consumption of grain produced within a hundred kilometres of the Peace Rift – grain that had been bathed in rainfall carrying the slight but undeniable load of radionuclides that wafted from the Rift – amounted to an overall reduction in lifespan of twenty-five days. Out of an average of two hundred and seven years.

Detectable – and therefore unacceptable. But the grains were still grown. It was about heritage.

Two days before, and only a day after meeting her, he had watched while Hels had free-climbed a two-hundred-metre rock face. Afterwards, they had both got professionally drunk on home-brewed spirit, renowned – almost celebrated – for its high level of impurities. No one had stopped them, so some self-inflicted dangers were apparently acceptable. They had set off for the journey to the Rift with professional-grade hangovers.

Probably no one would stop them when they did something similar tonight. Zeb did, and did not, understand.

The car rocked and threw him against Hels. She stirred and grumbled, then settled back to sleep.

He wasn't falling in love, that was for sure. It was his Rule One. Don't get entangled with the vreal.

The route down from the Peace Rift to the plains was determinedly rustic. In that, it matched everything on Sholntp. The radiation load of the planet was at maximum, went the logic. So no fissional materials, trans-uranic elements or other nuclear malarkey could be allowed. It was animal power, renewable energy, or nothing.

In this case it was renewable energy, but as long as he kept the windows closed the smoke couldn't make him cough.

The road train was made from five power-cars, each with a thrumming alcohol engine mounted beneath it. The alcohol was brewed from the grain that couldn't be eaten. Zeb assumed that made the exhaust fumes not only smoky, but a bit radio-active as well. The combination of ancient and modern pollution amused him.

He felt Hels's head lift from his shoulder. She blinked. 'Where are we?'

He glanced out of the window. 'Off the plateau; about an hour from Hamlet, I'd say.'

She nodded, and lowered her head to his shoulder again. He shifted himself to try to make a comfortable spot for her.

More than anyone he had ever met, she could sleep anywhere, on anything. He envied that. More and more, he couldn't sleep at all, no matter where.

Yes; his hundredth visit to this vreality. The first visit, a hundred thousand years ago according to the local timeline, had not gone well.

Never get entangled, indeed.

Sholntp System (vreality)

It had been the greatest space fleet ever assembled by the
Seven States. Eleven Dreadnoughts, their elderly flanks
streaked with the scars of thousands of engagements as merce-
naries; as many again Pocket Battleships, hovering nervously
with their heavy weapon loads close to overwhelming their
engines; fifty cruisers and frigates, and behind them a mixed
bag of tankers and behind-lines warehouse units. All hired by
the hour, except for the Dreadnoughts – four of those were
indentured to the States, with a status somewhat below slav-
ery, and the other seven were hired by the day on rolling
contracts that auto-renewed.

And, of course, a single Glaive Class Carrier – the only reason the whole enterprise had passed anyone's commercial due
diligence. The *Death Rattle* was somewhere north of twenty
thousand years old, but still theatre-relevant out here; bought,
not hired, and therefore a major weight on the rubber sheet of
the States' debt for at least a century, if they lasted that long.

It was a show of force calculated to reduce the opposition to
the role of spectator. What was going to happen, it said, was
going to happen – and that was that.

It was Zeb's first time in this vreality, but *fuck* it wouldn't
be his last. When people outside asked him why he visited the

vreal so often, this just *had* to be one of the answers. He had chanced on a war; not a little local one, but a proper, great big existential-threat war, and when did you ever get the chance to just plug straight in to that sort of adrenalin?

Watching from his role in the opposition, he had never felt more alive.

He leaned down so that his mouth was near the grubby mike. 'Ready?'

'No.'

'Good. Let's go.'

'I'm sure I just said no.'

'You know a better way to die? Right now?'

There was a pause. Then: 'Nope. Smug dung-sack meat-head mammal-fucker.'

He grinned. 'Ship? I love it when you talk dirty.'

There was no reply, but the bits of the display in front of him that still worked flickered and steadied. Behind him, a faint, troubled saw-tooth hum meant that the main drive had fired up, just once more.

They had already felt the weight of the *Death Rattle*'s hand, and that had been a pure accident; they had been manoeuvring casually into position, trying very hard to look like a piece of nothing at all, when the vast ship had carried out a trivial course change. The energy backwash from those ancient, brutish engines had blown the rear half of their tiny craft (only eight metres long – barely even there by Carrier standards) into mist. Most of the bits that mattered had survived, but they were hanging in tatters.

Speed built slowly – given the state of the drive, quickly was no longer an option – but it built. They were off, and that was that; no going back.

He focused on the display for a few seconds to let it key to his visual cortex, and then leaned back in the lumpy couch and closed his eyes.

For a moment nothing happened, and he wondered if yet another of the elderly ship systems had packed up. Then the red-green smudges inside his eyelids cleared and darkened, and the Model began to form. He braced himself.

The Model always shocked him with its perfection, with its vertiginous scale. It made him want to hang on to something.

It was better than being there. It was as far from a simple view of space as a multidimensional model of the universe was from a wooden model of a planet orbiting a star. It was like being a god, like being able to focus on a single rock and then to pull back to a panorama of a hundred planets without losing a pixel of resolution.

No, it was *better* than being a god. And he didn't believe in gods.

You had to wait until the Model was complete; if you tried to mess with it when it wasn't ready you could end up as an unzipped cloud of data. He sat still.

Then it was complete, and he was at the same time a soaring bird of prey, an infinitely subtle system of doubly enhanced humanity hovering high above the sparkle of a galaxy – and a lens focusing on the finest grain of the smallest image of the slightest molecule . . .

Yes. The Model. That.

He reckoned on about ten seconds of, basically, psychedelic intellectual conflict before his senses settled down. And he had the buffer of his innate Otherness to rely on. What it must be like for timeline-naturals, he didn't care to imagine.

Or, more accurately, didn't care. This time he almost persuaded himself.

Unbidden, the Model was pulling him in. He let himself fall through the flying layers of false reality until he landed where it wanted him. You were never completely in control of the Model.

A planet. Temperate zones lying between tropics and polar

coolness. Greens and blues and scudding white clouds. Unremarkable.

Still falling. Into the atmosphere; past the clouds. Down towards a landscape of green and brown, a world of heather and old grasses.

It looked too anodyne. He raised an eyebrow and did the Model equivalent of turning a little to one side. 'Is that really it?'

'It really is. Why? Were you expecting something else?'

'Not sure.' He studied it a little longer. 'Looks a bit – rural, if you get me. As a launch-pad for galactic conquest.'

'I'm sure plenty of people and machines would take that as the hell of a compliment. This is the most elaborate disguise ever constructed for a planet; even the clouds are story-boarded. And, of course, the Seven States would insist that it isn't about conquest.'

'Of course.'

He stared back into the Model. A blotched black-and-cream moon swung between him and the planet. He watched it until it had dropped back out of sight, then blinked the Model out of his vision and sat back in the couch. Briefly, he hoped the pose looked relaxed. Then he laughed to himself. The ship had a million sensory channels; if it pointed even a few of them at his body his physiological state would be as obvious as if he were a child's text under a searchlight.

But it would think it natural that he was nervous. There was no reason to assume it could guess why.

An alarm chimed and the ship said, 'Look, things are beginning to happen. We're off. Ready?'

He nodded.

'Let's go.'

He shut his eyes and sank back in the couch as the acceleration built. The Model re-formed in front of him. They were off – at the beginning of a journey that should end, as far as they were concerned, with the Seven States having turned into Eight States.

11

Should.

The ship had been right. He hadn't changed his settings just before he sent the file. He'd changed them a minute earlier, when it had asked him how he slept.

Sleeping was easy. Staying awake enough was sometimes harder, but he wasn't expecting any trouble on that front for a while.

In the Model, the accelerating Seven States fleet was forming into a Carrier Battle Group with the faster, lesser units nurturing the *Death Rattle* in the middle. It looked very late in the day to be doing that, but they were confident that the threat, if it could be called a threat, was at the other end. They knew there was nothing here to trouble them.

Meanwhile, for their different reasons he and the ship were both watching for something. The ship, with its raptor-like ability to spot the most trivial movement, the stiffened hair on the back of the neck of prey that was so far away as to be all but invisible. He, with his vastly inferior senses – inferior even when enhanced a thousand-fold by the Model – and his dawn-of-time processing speed, but even so, with his human basic ability to put a hunch and a pattern together to make an intuition. It was a skill you could measure, and they had measured his. He scored in the top micro-centile. That was why he was here.

Or, more accurately, it was why they thought he was here. Even the ship, apparently. He was surprised that it had been taken in.

Always remember, before you get too pleased with yourself – the problem you have correctly diagnosed may not be the only problem. Someone had said that, but he couldn't remember who.

Something caught his attention, and now, in the face of all sensible evidence, his heart was pounding. The *Death Rattle* – their last, desperate throw – was beginning to move into position, which was what the ship had been referring to – but that wasn't it.

There. A pattern. Hundreds of thousands of tiny vessels – yachts, holiday cruisers, vulgar shag-palaces and modest family run-abouts, casually moseying about and taking pictures of The Fleet Leaving For The Great Victory (or whatever it would end up being called) to show the kids – had moved just a little bit so that to his human senses they didn't look casual any more.

That was it. Right on time.

The ship didn't seem to have noticed, but there was still time to tell it. It would expect him to tell it. That was what he was there for, as far as it and the rest of the home fleet were concerned.

He didn't, because it wasn't why he was here at all.

Then the vast cloud of insignificant little craft, with their insignificant little biological inhabitants, flared bright violet.

He had been expecting it but the intensity still caught him out. He cried out and threw up an arm to cover his eyes – but as he did so the ship reacted, dimming the Model until the stars had vanished and all that was left was a fuzzy blue disc a thousand kilometres across, made of ships.

The ship had time to say '*What?*' and then a point of light fiercer than a supernova flared in the centre of the disc. It grew, elongated and became an intense beam that lanced from the centre of the circle.

It struck the *Death Rattle*. The old ship disappeared, replaced by a hazy ovoid that flared and shimmered as the beam sank into it. He held his breath. How effective was that twenty-thousand-year-old shield?

He didn't have long to wait. The combined energies of those hundreds of thousands of fatally overloaded ship's reactors were overwhelming; the ovoid flickered, and with each flicker the hull of the ship grew more visible. It was orange-hot, and getting hotter.

Briefly the beam itself flickered and he caught his breath – was that it?

Then he realized that one of the slaved Dreadnoughts had soared through an impossibly tight arc and placed itself directly between the beam and the *Death Rattle.*

In the time it took him to let out the breath and take another, it flared through yellow to blue-white and became vapour.

Another followed it. And a third.

Let it stop . . .

Then it did. With no warning the haze of the *Death Rattle*'s shields flicked out of sight and there was nothing but the hull of the ship itself, glowing the same violet as the sword of the beam.

For a moment they matched each other. Then the beam guttered and vanished.

The whole engagement had taken less than ten seconds.

The Model brightened again, revealing the *Death Rattle* as a glowing hulk. Behind it, the disc of ships was fading to a dusty grey.

The ship made a throat-clearing noise. 'Well, I should imagine that was the first crowd-sourced death-ray in the history of humanity. Not that "humanity" sounds like a good phrase at the moment. And it does me no credit but I've worked something out. You knew, didn't you?'

He nodded.

'I thought so. How many people died on those ships?' The disc of ship-corpses brightened momentarily in the Model.

'About two hundred thousand.'

'Do you care? No, don't bother answering. I don't want to hear your voice.'

He shrugged. The ship would be monitoring him. It knew well enough how he felt, or at least it could see the physiological consequences.

Therefore it must know he felt sick.

He stared fiercely into the Model. The fleet was coming apart. Acid blue tell-tales had appeared above the image of each of the surviving hired Dreadnoughts, meaning they were back on the market. They must have severed their contracts, presumably on the basis that there was nothing meaningful left to contract *with*. A moment later the remaining indentured ship joined them, freed by the death of its owners. Meanwhile something different was happening to the hulk: it too had a tell-tale but it was red, not blue, and bracketed by two columns of quickly changing figures.

He watched them for a moment. 'Ship? Another problem. The orbit's decaying.'

'Oh, the shit-sack still speaks. I thought I told it not to bother.'

'I'm serious. It's heading for the planet.'

'I'm serious too. Oh, so serious. I can see it. That happens to ships when you murder them. So?'

He thumped the console; some more lights went out. 'Stop fucking sulking and engage!'

'What, or you'll knock shit out of what's left of me?' The ship gave a stagey sigh. 'For your information, I have been monitoring the situation and there is fuck all we can do about it.'

'And the population of the planet?'

'About three billion.'

'Right. Is this you caring, or you not caring?'

'Neither. It's me being helpless. Plus, I'm still coming to terms with your astonishing duplicity. Is this you trying to make a legacy that doesn't include complicity in hundreds of kilo-deaths?'

'*No!*' He breathed in, out, in again. 'Look, I saw the Gaming. I assume you didn't?'

'Above my pay grade. Plus, I have other things to guide me. Like a conscience.'

'You're a battle craft. Spare me the lectures, okay? The Gaming said that was the low-impact option. There was no way of stopping the battle. There were going to be deaths.'

'Oh good. Glad to hear it. Does that make you feel better?'

He thought for a moment. 'Ship? How many AIs died just now, do you think?'

'I don't think, I know. Just under a thousand. Why?'

'And two hundred thousand humans. We're both mourning.'

There was a long silence. Then the ship spoke. 'Right. We can shift the decay. Maps say there's a more-or-less uninhabited area on some high ground. With some fancy steering we might be able to guide the impact. Zeb? I am still never going to forgive you.'

'Fine.' He wasn't sure if he would forgive himself, now the numbers were settling in. 'What do I need to do?'

'Nothing just now. When the time comes, take responsibility. Because I can't. Understand? This is going to have your name on it, not mine.'

'I understand. I'll be staying around.'

'Will you? Good, because I am probably going to melt what's left of my engines pushing this heavy bugger in the right direction. If I end up crippling myself, and if that means dragging you down to the surface in a flaming ball, that will make it all worthwhile. I hope that's clear.'

'Very.' He shook his head. 'Just get on with it.'

Then there was the howl of engines at the end of their life, and a jolt of appalling acceleration that seemed to bend his spine double.

He dragged his impossibly heavy head round far enough to watch the display. There were two lines plotted. One, in blue, showed the do-nothing prediction, following a straight orbital decay towards a populous area – towards kilo-deaths, mega-deaths, giga-deaths. Deaths. The other line, in violet, showed the plan: a series of nudges producing a final resting place on a high plateau, about as far from population centres as could be achieved.

At first his heart sank; the old warship was still following the blue line. Then, almost imperceptibly to begin with, its course shifted closer to the violet.

He tried to shout with triumph, but even if he could have drawn a breath against the vast force closing down his ribs, the shattering noise of the dying engines would have drowned it – was drowning everything; he could barely think.

Then, so suddenly it felt like a blow, the noise and the pressure were gone and there was – nothing. Not even artificial gravity. That was ominous. He cleared his throat.

'Ship?'

The answer seemed to take a long time.

'Were you going to ask how I am?'

'Yeah. So, how are you?'

'Broken.'

'Fixable?'

'No way. Engines are down to two per cent. That's just enough to keep the lights on and the shields up, as long as I don't do anything else. With the best possible luck, if nothing interferes, and if I fly like a genius – I'm still dead. We're going to join the hulk in its own personal geological feature.'

He chewed his lip. 'I'm sorry.'

'Of course you are. I can tell. You forgot to ask if it worked.'

He stared. The ship was right; he had completely forgotten. He shook his head. 'Did it?'

'Yes. The hulk will impact the plateau in eight minutes. We'll be with it a few seconds later. Is there anyone you should be making peace with, before you climb into what's left of the escape pod and I squeeze you out into space like the piece of shit you are?'

'Just you.'

'Really? I'm not sure you have long enough to do that. Seven and a half minutes is pretty short. Seven and a half life-times would still be pretty short to be honest. The best you can do, and the least as well, is to come and visit what's going to become my grave. You'd better promise to do that, understand?'

The air was beginning to smell of something burning. He looked round, trying to locate anything that seemed to be smoking. Several things were. He moistened his lips. 'I promise.' Oh yes, he thought. I promise, and I wish you knew how much that promise meant.

'Good.'

The smell was getting worse. 'Ship? You're on fire.'

'I know that, you idiot. Six minutes. Will you stay a while?'

He stared at the screen. Their own trajectory was aimed inevitably at the planet. 'Of course.'

'Good.'

'Ship, I . . .'

'I didn't say talk.'

He suppressed a grin. 'No, you didn't. Sorry.'

They kept silent station together, while the surface of the planet grew and gained definition in the display. Then the ship made a throat-clearing noise. 'So, three minutes. You can duck out now, if you want.'

Suddenly he didn't want to, not yet. 'I'll wait another minute. Bail out above the atmosphere.' And watch you the rest of the way, he added to himself.

'Okay. It's your funeral. The pod's on line; better get in.'

An aperture above him flicked open. He nodded, took hold of his seat frame and boosted himself upwards and through it into the escape pod.

'Ready?' The ship's voice sounded very close in the pod.

'Yes.'

'Okay. Separation in ten. A half-minute burn should put

you into orbit for a while.' The aperture closed and there was a faint *shush* and a quick sensation of cold as the pod's air system woke up. Then he heard a sharp crack of explosive bolts and the whistle of short-action engines, and he was jammed back into the contoured pod wall.

A screen lit up. The ship was a shrinking dot, already glowing a sullen red. Obviously it had given up on the shields. Ahead of it, the hulk of the *Death Rattle* was a yellow smudge at the end of a trail of hot particles.

He watched the dying ship follow the dead one. The course looked good; the hulk was heading for an unlit patch on the face of the planet. He wondered what it must look like to anyone who was watching down there, searing across their night sky like the end of everything.

Then it hit.

At first it seemed almost trivial, as if anything so big as to be observable from this distance could possibly be trivial – just a yellow-white flash, quickly fading. But then it brightened again, and spread like an incandescent cut across the surface of the planet. The ancient engines of a warship capable of destroying a moon were voiding their stored energies. Rocks would be melting, forest fires would be spreading . . . he wanted to look away, but he couldn't, not yet. He had promised.

The ship he had just abandoned was still hammering down through the atmosphere, a barely visible brighter streak against the angry ruin of the planet below it.

Then the comms spoke, just once more.

'Zeb? Honour me, you piece of shit.'

And before he could say anything, the tiny streak obliterated itself in an even tinier spark against the molten fury still spreading across the screen.

He watched the display, forcing himself to keep his eyes fixed on it even as it brightened to a glaring yellow. He wanted it seared into his retinas.

I'll come back, he told the inferno. *More than you could possibly know, I'll come back and honour you.*

A warning buzzed hoarsely. He sighed. Much earlier than he would have liked, the pod orbit was beginning to decay. He closed his eyes, focused his attention on a distant part of his mind and did the thing that bailed him out of the vreality.

But yes, he would come back.

Experiment, Ice Blade
Sector, Bubble

The parapet was thick with overnight dust, coloured a ghostly reddish-grey by the dawn light of the Second.

The dust fell all the time these days. Mostly it was the same neutral colour and the same fine rock-flour texture. Very occasionally a layer of a different colour would land overnight, and the worn stones would gain a brief mask of red, or blue; on one memorable morning, a rich violet. Skarbo had never worked out what had produced that. But the next day the dust had been back to normal.

He always thought it was a poor memorial. The slow death of a planet should somehow have been more dramatic.

A transient one, too. By the time the dawns were over, one of the Janitors would probably have cleared the dust – always assuming it hadn't undergone a religious conversion, or decided (in one particularly colourful piece of machine psychosis) that it was an antique atmosphere-flyer. That one had been messy. The blunt casing of a Janitor was badly suited for flight, even if it was flight straight down. Out of respect for the departed machine, Skarbo had refrained from dropping his usual offering over the Edge that day.

But today no machines had gone mad, thus far, and those that were already mad seemed no madder than usual, so he limped to the Edge, hefted the piece of basement junk, and got ready to send it out and down to join the heap of similar detritus kilometres below.

He couldn't remember how he had come to start his little ritual. It had been five lives ago, he was sure of that, and he was equally sure that he must have decided not to remember. Sometimes his former selves really annoyed him.

Swing; heave. There – down it went. He watched it disappear into the depths of the canyon. It took a long time; the view was unusually clear today. Not much dust and even less mist. He strained his optic muscles and managed to track the tumbling dot as far down as the Mantle horizon. Almost four kilometres. He was unlikely to see further than that until the next Core Event, and that wasn't due for another hundred and eleven days.

By which time he would have been dead – finally, permanently dead, not the other sort – for over twenty days.

He had watched all night. Increasingly he did that. Rest evaded him, and besides his body seemed to need less of it. Less of everything. His appetite was diminishing. His carapace seemed *loose*. It made little creaking and rustling noises when he moved.

At least his eyes still worked, even if everything else was falling apart. He had nothing to complain about – he had chosen this form seven and a half lifetimes ago, and he had always known that the choice had an end-point.

At the end of his first life – *iteration* was the correct term, but he had always disliked the formality – he had chosen to bury his basic mammal inheritance beneath an insectoid form. Against the advice of his family, his friends and more than one counsellor, but he had never regretted it.

The form was practical. Eight three-jointed limbs that could be used for walking, but tipped with complicatedly articulated claws that could perform all the functions of a hand, rather more subtly than most. A slim, flattish carapace over an elongated hourglass body; mouth-parts which, unless he really tried, were usually concealed, with enough external equipment to allow human-compatible expressions. Standing upright – which was most of the time – he was a bit shorter than human average. The wings didn't work any more, but then he had never really liked flying, and the tough carapace, compound eyes and radiation-proof genes were still as useful as ever. His one concession had been to keep the best of both dietary worlds. He could eat – had eaten, indeed – just about anything, living or dead.

Now that he thought about it, there was a lot of customization in there. He supposed he remembered doing it, but it had been a long time ago and he had forgotten so much. Built to last, that was certain.

There was a noisy flapping behind him. He sighed, as quietly as he could, and turned to face the angry bundle of feathers that flapped at head height.

'Hello,' he told it.

'You *vandal*!' It was a furious screech. 'Do you know what that *was*?'

'Three metal spheres joined by a sort of web. So?'

'Three spheres? *Spheres?* It was an antique, you lunatic. It was the giro hub from a Glass Freighter, it was a million years old, and you just dropped it into the core of a planet that's going to *fall apart* in a couple of years?'

Skarbo nodded. 'So what would have happened to it when the planet did fall apart?'

'I'd have saved it!'

'I doubt it.' He shook his head. 'Face it, bird. This planet's over, with all its ridiculous antiques, and so are you and so, goodness knows, am I.'

The creature narrowed its eyes. 'I am *not* a bird.'

'Whatever.'

He watched the creature that was sure it wasn't a bird flap away across the parapet towards the darkness of the outer Burrow. Just outside the entrance it wheeled round and hovered.

'Forgot; you've got a visitor.'

'Really?' Skarbo felt a stab of unease. Visitors were rare; he'd prefer it if they didn't exist. 'Who?'

'How should I know? Biped. Talks. What else do you need?'

He bit back his first response. 'Where is it waiting?'

'The Machine Room. I said you wouldn't mind.' It flapped forwards and regarded him with its head on one side. 'Problem?'

He nodded, not trusting himself to speak.

'Oh well. Better go then! Good luck, *insect*.' It wheeled round in a noisy bundle of wings and flew off, muttering to itself.

Skarbo watched it go and then forgot about it. He was trying not to panic.

The Machine Room was his. More: in some ways, it was *him*. Had been so for most of his lives, as The Bird knew perfectly well. And now someone else was in it, for the first time in all those hundreds of years.

He gave in to the panic and ran. The Machine Room? Why had the bloody *bird* told whoever it was to wait there?

Most planets were called what they were because they always had been, or because the name commemorated some glorious conqueror or other.

Experiment had neither of those problems, but it did have others.

It had been an ordinary-looking little planet, one of only two orbiting a middle-sized star that was far enough from anywhere pleasant to have been left alone for a very long time.

Then a survey ship had wandered past, done a few cursory surface assays, and stopped dead while it checked the results.

There was no doubt: the planet's crust contained as much heavy metals as a hundred ordinary planets put together, all the way from lead to uranium and beyond.

It was an unprecedented find. It was also rather embarrassing; the ship was not only off its official course, but actually outside the formal territory of its parent civilization.

The ship and her crew had consulted, a little guiltily. They had considered contacting the home planet but decided against it because such signals might be noticed and tracked. In the end they opted, in effect, to bank the find. They seeded the planet with a slow-acting mining fungus that would digest the crust over a period of a few centuries, concentrating the metals in its mass and making them easy to recover in a quick fly-by grab. Then they wandered off, looking as casual as possible.

After all, they reasoned, metals were still going to be useful in half a millennium.

It would have worked, except that some of that uranium was just sufficiently concentrated for it to start its own chain reaction – an irregular little blob of a natural geo-reactor puttering along at about a hundred kilowatts thermal, and giving off lots of interesting particles, rays and fission products.

The radiation-tender genes of the mining fungus had gone wild, zipping through a few million years' worth of mutations in a single decade.

It changed, and changed, and changed.

Then it ate the planet.

In an orgy lasting little more than a century it bred and bored and powdered its way through the whole of the crust and deep into the mantle, converting the metal-rich rocks into vast fruiting bodies that made the planet look from space as if it had broken out in warts.

Then it died, and followed what was left of its original genetic design by turning into a rich and conveniently processed metallic dust.

It took almost a thousand years for a specially formed corporation of local enterprises to harvest the planet. When they had finished, it had lost its warts and looked instead like a dried-up worm-ravaged fruit, scarred across by mantle-deep cracks floored with coughing lava vents. The fungus had been random in its attentions, leaving everything from vast collapse-prone caverns to areas of rock that looked undisturbed, but were actually bored out on a microscopic scale so they were as fragile as rotten paper.

Slowly, but faster as the years ran short, they too were collapsing to dust.

And the years were running short indeed. In more than one way, and in more than one place.

'So, tell me about these machines.' The being calling itself Hemfrets waved an arm round the room.

Skarbo suppressed the urge to throw himself between the arm and the mechanism it had almost hit. He breathed out carefully. 'They are all clocks. That is, they are all representations of the same clock . . .'

'Which you continue to call a clock. Everyone else calls it the Spin.'

Patience. Patience . . . 'I know that. I acknowledge the name, but that is all it is – a name. Names may mean anything and nothing. "Clock" is a description of a thing, and this thing is a clock, no matter what else it may be. Its orbits, its geometry, are neither natural nor accidental. I believe that one of its functions may be to keep time.'

Hemfrets nodded. 'And you made these – representations.'
'Yes.'

'And so they call you Skarbo the Horologist.' Hemfrets wandered over to a low pedestal and leaned down to inspect the thing that was suspended above it. 'You made even this?'

'Yes. That's one of the oldest. It's more schematic than accurate.'

'I'd never know.' Hemfrets leaned in closer. 'How many planets did you say?'

'Eighty-eight permanent planetary bodies and five visitors, in four concentric shells. This model doesn't show the visitors.'

'And twenty-one suns. It's beautiful. Very fine . . . What are they made of?'

Skarbo pointed. 'The inner-shell planets are hollow invar. The second, titanium with a filling of bromine, pressurized to a solid. The third, solid copper–tungsten alloy; and the fourth are gold.'

'What holds them together?'

'For this one, strings of woven carbyne threads. The suns are various gems. Diamond, sapphire. That one there,' and his finger hovered above a small sparkling blue-green sphere, 'is artificial trichroic tanzanite. It changes colour when you move.' He added apologetically, 'That one had to be imported.'

Hemfrets nodded. Then it – Skarbo was always bad at gender – straightened up and stared. 'Wait. Are you saying that everything else *didn't*?'

'Oh yes.'

'But the planet was mined out!' Hemfrets waved round the cavern as if presenting evidence.

Skarbo was beginning to regret the conversation. 'Yes, on the gross scale. But the fungus preferred low concentrations; it tended to ignore pure seams and intrusive veins. I think they were too rich for it.'

'Too rich . . . So there's resource left here?'

Skarbo said nothing. Hemfrets gazed at him for a moment, then shook its head. 'We live and learn . . . but, well, to live we must eat. I hope you don't mind, but I took the liberty of check-ing your metabolism. Despite appearances we are surprisingly

27

compatible, you and I – but then you seem to be compatible with almost anything. Was that deliberate?'

'Yes.'

'Fascinating. Well, forgive my presumption but I have had food brought into the next chamber. Will you join me?'

Skarbo nodded, and followed the beckoning limb – presumably a hand – towards what he would have sworn was his private laboratory.

Even if Hemfrets had been his only visitor, the laboratory somehow felt less private – there was something *entitled* about Hemfrets – but there was the other visitor, the one Hemfrets had airily referred to as 'my Companion'.

Skarbo didn't like the Companion.

Skarbo didn't really like anyone, of course. He was quite content with that self-knowledge. Why else had he spent nearly nine lifetimes tucked away on this crumbling shell of a planet with most of his attention focused on a stellar artefact so far away that to visit it on any affordable ship would take another lifetime?

The Bird didn't really count as 'anyone'. There were always exceptions. And he enjoyed having something to annoy.

But he really, truly did *not* like the Companion, for what he suspected were far better reasons.

It looked like something he would dearly like to throw over the Edge.

Happily, the Companion had absented itself while they ate. Skarbo preferred not to think about what it might be up to. Besides, he was finding Hemfrets more engaging than he had suspected.

His guest was an androgynous biped, a full head shorter than human average. It was dressed in a short, lightweight-looking jacket made of matt dark grey material, and a narrow wrap of the same material that covered it from waist to floor.

The jacket was open, showing hairless, uniformly ochre-coloured skin. There were no secondary sex characteristics Skarbo could see, without being intrusive.

At least it had an interesting title: Regional Representative of the Crown Nebula ('The Blade is Hidden' faction). Skarbo had never heard of either the Crown Nebula or any factions. Few news channels reached Experiment and he didn't bother consulting them, so his knowledge of sector politics was very slight, and Hemfrets didn't seem inclined to explain.

Something demanded his attention. He focused on Hemfrets. 'I'm sorry?'

'I asked if it was truly a clock?'

Skarbo shook his head carefully. 'That is just my shorthand for it. It functions as one.'

'By what definition?'

'A clock is an instrument for measuring and recording time, especially by mechanical means.' He shrugged. 'It does that, beyond any doubt. What else it does, I don't know.'

'I believe there is the small matter of people living on it . . . But if it does that, why do you need the machines?'

'They are models. Means of analysis.' He struggled. 'People have always thought the clock to be inexplicable. I sought to explain it.'

'And you succeeded, I believe. I have been shown your paper. *On modelling the predictable effects of multiple internal perturbations on the long-term periodicity of the object known as the Spin.* I was told it was a seminal work. I barely understood the title, I'm afraid.' Hemfrets studied the platter in front of it, reached out and selected a morsel which wriggled briefly between its fingers. Then it looked up, and its eyes were sharp. 'But that was two hundred years ago.'

'Yes. I used my calculations to produce the best models yet. I thought I had succeeded.' Skarbo sighed and stood up, with a little difficulty. 'Come with me. I'll show you.'

He walked unsteadily back into the Machine Room. He didn't look back to check if Hemfrets was following – he already had the impression that the creature was hard to shake off – and when he reached the end of the room and turned round, there it was, wearing an attentive expression. One with a hint of patience. 'You were going to show me something?'

Skarbo nodded. 'It's not in here,' he said. He swiped a hand over the wall and it opened. He made to go through, then hesitated. 'You are the first to see this. The Bird, the Janitors – they're all excluded.'

'Ah. So why do you honour me with it?'

Skarbo had been wondering that. He didn't have the slightest doubt, but equally he didn't know where the idea had come from.

Eventually he said, 'I receive few visitors. I will receive no more. My work is mature. And, as you probably know, my lives are almost over.'

'So you have decided to share your inner sanctum? It must be very precious to you.' Hemfrets laid a hand on his shoulder. 'If it helps you, I give you my promise that I will never breathe a word about what lies beyond this door.'

Still Skarbo hesitated. 'Nor write one?'

Hemfrets tightened the grip on his shoulder. 'Nor write, nor post, nor leave a glyph for my lawyers, nor whisper to a lover. I'll keep the secret, Skarbo, and more than that, I'll personally answer for every atom of the place. Is that enough for you?'

Skarbo nodded slowly, and stepped through the opening. He watched until he was sure Hemfrets had followed him, and made the signal that closed it. It took most of the light with it.

Then he waited.

Hemfrets obviously had good night vision. It only took ten seconds.

'Ah . . .'

Skarbo nodded. 'You see it?'

'Yes. You made this too?'

'I did.'

'How long did it take?'

'A hundred years. A little more. And fifty before that for the enclosure.'

In the dim false starlight he saw Hemfrets turning towards him. It raised an arm, stood for a moment with the limb upraised as if unsure what to do next, and let it fall. Skarbo thought he could make out a shaken head.

'That is an astonishing feat.'

Skarbo shrugged. 'Perhaps.'

They both turned back to watch. Skarbo found himself wondering what it looked like through the eyes of another; eyes that worked differently from his own. Eyes that were seeing it for the first time.

There was no theatre. Skarbo had decided that early. No exotic materials; he had got that out of his system, which was probably a sign (and about time, eight lives in) of being grown-up. The planets were made from a proper analogue of planet-stuff. Iron–uranium cores, silicate-slush mantles, rocks. He had only cheated as much as was needed to get the relative densities right.

The stars were *not* proper star-stuff because that wouldn't have worked, but they were correct as to relative mass and size. The twinkle had taken years to perfect; in the end he had settled on a bundle of phosphorescent nuclear reactions helped on their way by doses of high-energy particles fired at them by carefully programmed guns.

And that, of course, was less than the half of it. Far less.

But it looked realistic. He turned to Hemfrets, who was staring at the beautiful fake. 'Do you like it?'

'I think it's rather beyond my likes and dislikes. Beyond anyone's, perhaps.' Hemfrets pulled its attention from the sight with a visible wrench. 'There's a story here.'

31

'Not really. I just wanted to get the model right.'

'Just . . .' Hemfrets shook its head. 'What scale is it?'

'One to ten billion. It is a mechanically accurate model in an evacuated chamber. Air resistance would interfere with the accuracy, you see. I would have preferred bigger.'

'I'm sure. But if it did the job . . .'

Skarbo looked at the creature, then looked away. 'It didn't,' he said.

'No? And you still tell me there is no story?' Hemfrets watched him for a while, until he felt his face warming.

'Perhaps,' he muttered.

'Then tell me.' Hemfrets put an arm round his shoulder. 'But not here. I am too overawed by your achievement – even if it isn't quite the achievement you wanted.'

Skarbo let himself be steered back through the Machine Room. There was a long raised viewing platform at one end of it, with padded bench seats running down its middle. If you sat one way you looked out over the Machine Room. Look the other way and you were faced with the even bigger space that was the top end of the Great Vent – the path of one of the larger magmatic excursions that had resulted from the phase of excitable vulcanism caused by the fungus. It was about a hundred metres across, and its magma-gouged walls were striated and polished and squashed and carved into abstract shapes and caves and buttresses. Nearly opposite the Machine Room some inexorable eddy in the molten rock had drilled out a wide, shallow gouge with glassily polished walls. If you stood in exactly the right place, a flat, dry version of your voice came back to you just under a second after you spoke – but the place had to be exact to the millimetre and Skarbo had never bothered marking it. These days, it took him hours to find it. He had put the viewing platform in several lifetimes ago, before he had noticed the echo. It had been at the suggestion of The Bird, he could remember that, but he had forgotten

'Affordable . . .' Hemfrets looked down for a while. Then, without raising its head, it added, 'I'm sorry for the intrusion, but exactly when will you die?'

'Eighty-eight days from now.' Skarbo thought for moment, then let himself smile. 'I'm looking forward to it.'

'And afterwards? Your kind believe . . . ?'

At first Skarbo didn't understand. Then he laughed. 'Simple. I expect you know this is not my original form?'

Hemfrets nodded. 'I wondered why you chose it.'

'Several reasons. One of which was scarcity. I wanted to preserve something – these creatures were extinct in the Bubble. They, we, live long and breed little. That is a poor adaptation strategy for worlds that may change.'

'But a good strategy for,' Hemfrets nodded at the room, 'this.'

'Yes. Well, then. My original kind had hundreds of religions and philosophies. I was brought up with them, but I shared none of them. I believe there are no gods, no afterwards, but then I have already had nine chances at life – eight versions of afterwards, if you will. Besides, I am the last of my kind as far as I know. I think I have the right to make my own rules.'

'So you have.' Hemfrets stood up and stretched. 'The last of your kind? You are a creature of excess, Skarbo. Nine lifetimes? The last? Hundreds of years of craft? All to study a doomed collection of planets from a planet doomed itself? Forgive me; I need rest, and time to process what you have told me. But if you agree, I would like to talk more about this when we wake.'

Skarbo inclined his head. 'Sleep well, for as long as you need. For myself, I don't sleep, but I'll be occupied.'

'You don't sleep . . .' Hemfrets shook its head. 'Another wonder. Well, I hope you *occupy* well. I will be with you again in about five hours, standard.'

It walked slowly out of the room. A second later a disturbance at the edge of his field of view told Skarbo that the Companion had followed.

The Companion, he reflected, was probably the reason he had just lied.

It wasn't that much of a lie. He *could* sleep, if he chose, or rather he could enter a torpid state which was as close to sleep as his modifications allowed. But, even these days when energy seemed to be elusive, he didn't *have* to. He did so very rarely, usually after some major effort, and he hadn't the slightest intention of doing so now. Not with those two anywhere near.

So instead of sleeping the not-sleep he was frankly afraid to enter, he walked back through the Machine Room, barely aware of the soft, off-beat tattoo of his five functioning legs. He had started out with eight. One had been lost in an accident – his fault – one had failed to regrow at the beginning of his current life, and one had simply atrophied and dropped off, quite painlessly, a few hundred days ago. That was age for you.

At the far end of the Machine Room, the walls came together at a steep angle that looked like a sharp dead end, or an inverted blade. Skarbo stopped just before the walls narrowed too much for his size, and stood still for a second, remembering.

Like this, and then that . . .

His remaining legs tapped what he hoped were still the right places on the floor. It had been a long time, and it was harder with only five.

It seemed to take longer than he remembered. Then the walls in front of him split neatly along the corner, and he was looking into a grey space with a flight of stairs at the far end of it.

He hadn't done this for two lifetimes. He had been meaning

to do so before he finally died, but it hadn't been a priority. Now it was. He had seen the light in Hemfrets's eyes; he had seen the slight hesitation of the Companion. Something was coming. He doubted very much if he could do anything about it, whatever it was, but at least he wanted to have seen it.

The stairs led up to a landing, and narrowed into a ladder. He had always struggled with the ladder. By the time he was at the top his breath was wheezing.

But then he was there, and the sight he had not seen for two hundred years was still as he remembered. He let muscle memory guide him back into the couch he had made for himself when he had first come here.

It angled back so he was looking up through the vast transparent dome.

He assumed that the place had been given a name by earlier people but he didn't know it. When he had arrived the planet had already been an abandoned husk.

His own name for it was God's Eye.

As an ex-mammal in an insect form he had a complicated relationship with eyes, and he had told the truth when he said he didn't believe in gods – but he still couldn't think of a better name.

Tonight, the dust layer was at its lightest. If he pushed himself up and forward a little out of the couch he could lower his gaze far enough to see the horizon, and the view was clear almost all the way across the diseased-looking surface. Only a blurred, dull pink sliver clinging to the edge of the distant curve of landscape betrayed the fact that the atmosphere was full of powdered planet.

Skarbo sighed and let himself fall back into the couch. The view to the horizon was interesting but familiar – even comforting, in a way. Whereas the view straight up was striking and not comforting at all, even if it, too, was familiar. From a long time ago.

The ship was close, far too close for any pretence that it was in orbit. It was poised a few hundred metres up, well inside Experiment's degrading atmosphere, and presumably sitting on one local gee of thrust, which struck Skarbo as a very wasteful way of going nowhere.

It was close enough for him to see plenty of detail. At this distance the curved grey belly was just high enough to catch the last of the low-angle sunlight glancing past the planet. It was covered with bulges and pods, each one throwing a stretched-out shadow across the hull.

There were many, many shadows. Skarbo knew about such things in theory, if not much in practice, and he suspected that if even a quarter of the bulges were weapons, Hemfrets's ship was by far the deadliest thing he had seen in seven lifetimes.

Not eight, because he had seen something like this before. Just once.

He had forgotten many things on purpose and many more by accident, but not this. He closed his eyes.

He had been flat on his back then, too, he remembered. But absolutely everything else had been different.

Greater Bowl, Gannff Planet, Mandate (Original), Bubble

'D o you realize, we haven't been outside this year?'
Skarbo nodded, which made the coarse moss on the bank tug his scalp up and down. It tickled. 'I know. Work, though.'

'In your case, maybe. Some of us were looking for a chance. Man, don't you ever look up?'

'I'm looking up now.'

'You *know* what I mean. Sheesh, you've already got twice the credits of anyone else. You're going to pass, like, years early.'

Skarbo shook his head. 'A year. That's all.'

'And you wouldn't be out here now if I hadn't hauled you. The first time it's been safe for months.'

'I work, Fostees. That's what we're supposed to do.'

Fostees shook his head vigorously, making locks of curly greenish hair flick round his forehead. 'Not so, my serious friend. Work is *one* of the things we're supposed to do. We are also supposed to attend cultural events, keep abreast of current affairs and take advantage of the extracurricular experiences offered by our time on this first-rank planet close to the seat of the sector government.'

Skarbo closed his eyes. 'Yes. I read that pamphlet too.'

'See? Not just my opinion, although it seems to have omitted sex . . . and, come on, admit it – it's a great view.'

Skarbo had to admit that it was.

They were lying just below the top lip of the Greater Bowl, about a kilometre above the disc of cloud that presently filled the lower third of it. It was late evening, almost fully dark, and behind and below them the lights of the city were splashed across the valley like a broken chain between the two gaunt Watch Towers that marked, and had once defended, its eastern and western boundaries.

In front of them, the cloud was still luminescing softly with the last of the solar energy it had stored during the day. Skarbo had read that it was closer to photochemical smog than cloud, but that didn't stop it looking beautiful.

The upper edge of the cloud was licking at one of the ring lakes that broke the smooth downward sweep of the grass surface. The Greater Bowl hadn't always been ornamental. It had originally been a three-kilometre radio telescope, and as if that wasn't big enough it had been meant to be part of an array of hundreds of identical telescopes, a thousand kilometres on a side. The construction would, people had believed, boost the economy of a planet that was flagging at the time, and the revenue stream from hiring out the enormous instrument to wealthy academic institutions from all over the system would pay back the equally enormous loans needed to build the thing.

This would have worked beautifully but for the small detail of the election of a reactionary anti-science government just as the first bowl was completed. They declared that it was ridiculous to bankrupt the planet in the cause of the wasted science of astronomy, and repurposed the bowl as a waste disposal site.

Five years later they had bankrupted the planet in the more respectable cause of making war on the neighbours.

The Greater Bowl remained the only bowl. Ten generations later, in a more environmentally conscious age, it had been excavated. Once its scarred and contaminated surface had been seeded with a coarse grass that didn't mind chemicals, a series of annular lakes dug to control surface-water run-off, and an ornamental lake created in the bottom of the bowl, it became an unofficial monument to the damage that can be done by really stupid people.

The cloud was intermittent. The bowl was big enough to have its own rather simple weather system, producing slithering acrid mists, occasional rain, and the cloud. Once or twice a year the whole surface froze, becoming a lethal but popular sledding venue. The lake was full of pollution-tolerant insects, and even the locals didn't swim in it.

Fostees was still talking. Skarbo tuned him out. He was good at that.

The cloud-light wavered and died, and his heart jumped. He had promised himself something, and now was the time. He closed his eyes and counted slowly to a hundred under his breath to give his eyes time to resensitize. Then he opened them and let himself stare straight up at the stars.

He had never done this before. His family would not have encouraged it; did not encourage what they called 'playful things'. There was duty, and responsibility, and virtue, and work, and more work, and if the work was finished then other work could be found. And so Skarbo was still working. It had taken Fostees, who described himself as 'fun-loving' – and Skarbo automatically inserted the word *trivial* – several weeks of nagging to get Skarbo even to have basic eyelid displays fitted. He was glad he had them now.

They were useful for work.

The view is of an oblique cross-section of the Greater Spiral Arm, providing one of the most densely populated starscapes visible from anywhere within the Bubble of the Mandate . . .

That had been in the pamphlet too, he recalled. But the words were inadequate. The shocking blaze of stars was indescribable. No wonder they had wanted to build telescopes here.

It was too much for him, first time. After ten seconds or so he shut his eyes again, but his retinas were still glowing with after-images. He watched them, and found himself focusing on one area in particular – a group of stars that were definitely either brighter or closer than the others, and which seemed very close together. Still keeping his eyes closed, he reached out a hand and prodded Fostees.

'The group of stars that make a rough circle,' he said. 'Close to the horizon. What are they?'

'Where? Oh. That's the Spin, of course.'

'What's the Spin?'

'Good grief. Where have you been?'

Skarbo sighed. 'Remember about the work?'

'Even so. The Spin's a thing that shouldn't exist, is what it is.'

Skarbo opened his eyes again to let the real starlight erase the fading blur behind his eyelids. 'Why?'

'It's impossible, or something. The orbits are wrong; the planets ought to smash into each other.'

'Why don't they?'

'I don't know! No one knows, I expect. It's pretty, right?'

Skarbo nodded, and closed his eyes again. One day, he thought, he might be able to gaze at the Spin without stopping. One day. He wanted to blink a search, but smearing the inside of his eyelids with glyphs would have destroyed the beauty, so he would make do with the little Fostees could add, letting his mind process and paraphrase.

There were eighty-eight planets and twenty-one suns in the cluster that shouldn't exist. Some were inhabited – perhaps most, but there was no contact with them. There had been, in the half-forgotten past, but the walls were going up all over the sector. People kept to themselves, including the people in the Spin.

He opened his eyes again and looked for the group of stars. There; or, now he looked again, not there. At first he thought it had changed shape, had become somehow flatter? But that was nonsense.

Then he realized some of the stars were missing. He could remember the image, and, compared with the memory, three bright points of light at the top of the group had gone.

So had some of the stars near them. And as he watched, a couple more winked out. He reached out and nudged Fostees. 'I think it's getting cloudy.'

'Can't be.' Fostees sat up and peered. 'There wouldn't be clouds at this season. It must be something else . . . Oh . . .'

There was a buzzing rustle from below them in the bowl. Skarbo glanced down towards the cloud, which looked unchanged, and then at Fostees.

'What's that?' he asked.

Then he frowned. He couldn't see the man's face but Fostees was sitting bolt upright, his palms pressing into the ground by his hips, and he looked as if he was staring down at the slope of the bowl.

'Fostees?'

The name seemed to penetrate. Fostees turned towards him, and there was enough starlight to see that his eyes were wide. 'Lie down!'

'What?' Skarbo shook his head. 'Why?'

'That way they'll pass over. If you're standing they'll build up against you and take you down with them.'

Skarbo looked at him. 'I don't understand—'

'Just do it! Face down!'

It was an urgent hiss, and as he spoke Fostees was already turning over and flattening himself against the grass. He had his hands covering the back of his head.

For a moment Skarbo stared at him blankly. Then he looked downhill.

The rustling was louder. As he watched, the edges of the cloud rippled and a blackly iridescent tide flowed up the slope towards him. It wasn't water; it was *things*.

He threw himself to the ground, buried his face in the grass and covered his head.

For a moment there was only the growing buzz and the scratch of the sour-smelling grass against his face. Then he was covered, by something that scratched and pattered and skittered in waves of hardly detectable weight; something that creaked and clicked and gave off a sweetly acrid smell that made him want to retch, and he knew without being able to see anything that this was insects – millions, billions of insects.

The inhabitants of the bowl had abandoned their home.

He lay, trying not to move, not even to breathe, while the countless pin-pricks danced up his body and his reflexes howled at him to jump up and run.

Then it thinned out and stopped.

His back felt wet. He unclasped his hands, raised his head and took a shuddering breath.

An irregular black circle was flowing up the bowl. As he watched, it crossed the highest of the ring lakes without even slowing.

He rolled on to his side and looked for Fostees. The man was standing, swaying a little and wiping a hand across his mouth.

'Shit,' he said, softly.

Skarbo nodded. 'Why did they do that?'

Fostees shrugged. 'No idea. I read about it once; they have some sense or other that detects when something is threatening them. Smells, vibrations, whatever – but why they did it just then? No idea.' He sounded shaken. He wiped his mouth again. 'That was disgusting. Are you okay?'

'I think so.' Skarbo wasn't sure he could stand. He rolled on to his back and looked for the Spin, and then froze.

There were no stars. Instead, there was a grey shape moving

across the sky – the blurred belly of something vast, barely lit by the lights of the city behind them.

Skarbo's mouth dried. He heard Fostees say, 'Oh, fuck.'

Somewhere in the city a single siren howled up the scale and then down, then fell silent. The lights of the city flashed once and then died.

For a moment there was complete darkness. Then, from dozens of locations across the bowl surface, shafts of angry violet light stabbed upwards, converging on the thing above them. They lit up a curving belly, rich with blisters and bulges.

Skarbo had read that the city had its own ancient defensive system, reserved as a desperate last throw when everything else had failed. Presumably, then, everything else had indeed failed. He half-closed one eye and tried to lid a news menu, but the links on the landing page were dead and the audio sounded like some sort of martial music. Nothing helpful.

He heard a wordless shout. He tore his eyes away from the huge ship – surely it had to be a ship, nothing else could be so big – pushed himself to his feet and looked for Fostees, but the other man was already over the lip of the Bowl and running down the long slope towards the city. The light from the old energy weapons had bathed the slope in a shifting glow, and by it he could see other people dotted around the bowl. Most were running towards the city; a few were standing, transfixed, like him.

For a while the ship seemed simply to ignore the fact that it was under attack. There was no sign it was affected – the beams simply stopped at its surface as if switched off. But then an irregular patch on the hull glowed briefly a dull orange, and the glow somehow detached itself and began to float downwards, gradually resolving into a gently fluttering mesh that stretched and tightened as it fell until it formed an expanding square. It was hard to judge the size or the height; at first Skarbo guessed it was a hundred metres on a side. Then, as it drew nearer, two hundred. Then three.

It was falling towards the city, he realized. Where Fostees had gone. Where many people had gone . . . he lidded and looked for the man's ident, but none of the screens were working and the music was irritating.

Then the mesh reached the level of the Watch Towers and, with a shock, he got the scale of it. It encompassed both towers easily; enough to overlap by what must have been hundreds of metres – and they were ten kilometres apart.

Where it brushed them, they flared yellow-white and evaporated. In ten seconds they were demolished to ground level – and the mesh went on falling towards the city below them.

Just before it touched, Skarbo shut his eyes, but the flare still printed bright smudges through his eyelids. There were screams, and he slammed his hands over his ears. Then a scorching wind crashed into him and he was thrown backwards down the slope of the Greater Bowl.

He remembered lying on his back. He couldn't close his eyes because there was something wrong with the lids, and he couldn't feel for them because his hands didn't work, but it didn't matter because the huge ship was sliding across the sky, uncovering stars as it went.

The last thing he saw was the group of stars called the Spin.

Sholntp (vreality)

To Zeb's wondering envy Hels slept through the whole of the road train journey to Hamlet – the sleep of someone completely at peace. The narrow polished-wood tube of the car could seat twenty, in five rows of four, but they had it to themselves so there was nothing to disturb them.

Most of the way, there had been nothing much to look at. He let himself zone out for a couple of hours, half-hypnotized by the gentle swaying of the car, its resin-and-oil smells and the regular breathing of his sleeping companion.

Then he began to see yellow glimmers dancing outside. Not Hamlet, yet, but the outskirts; the Skin Beetles never went more than about half a kilometre from their home.

Hamlet was built on, and in, and sometimes underneath, a single organism that, as far as he knew, was not only unique in the vrealities but had no counterpart in the real. It was one of the main reasons for the obsessive preservation of the planet.

Zeb had heard of primitive creatures that protected themselves within the shells of other creatures, or that accreted grains of rock around themselves as they grew. He had never heard of a plant doing the same – insofar as the Rockblossom *was* a plant, of course; even that wasn't really settled despite it being the most studied thing on the planet. It had things in common with fungi and with single-celled animals as well as plants, and its DNA was usually described as 'peculiar'. Shortly after it had first been discovered someone had called it 'the weirdest vegetable in the universe', and no one had ever really improved on that.

The glimmers were getting denser. Skin Beetles were about the size of a child's fist, with bioluminescent wings that were dark when closed but which cast a shimmering yellow-white light in flight. During the daylight they sheltered in burrows bored in the outer skin of the Rockblossom. At first people had assumed that they were parasites, because the burrows certainly looked invasive, but gradually it had dawned that something more complicated was going on.

In short, to metabolize their primary diet of smaller insects the beetles needed an enzyme found in the Rockblossom's skin – and only there; it was absent from the rest of the structure – and the Rockblossom, in turn, needed the minerals in beetle-shit.

The car was slowing down, and the glimmer from the beetles was picking out a bulbous form up ahead. Zeb nudged Hels gently. She stirred, and opened her eyes halfway.

'We're there.'

'Oh.' She sat up. 'Did I sleep all the way?'

'Yes.'

'I owe you.'

'I'll collect.'

She grinned lasciviously.

Then the car bumped gently to a stop. The internal lighting flicked on, and double doors halfway down the tube opened shakily. Cold air smelling of forest washed in. Hels stood up, stretched, and walked out of the car. He watched her appreciatively for a few paces; she was a more than acceptable view when there was no competition. Then he smiled at himself, and followed.

The Rockblossom's internal structure consisted of chambers, basically spherical but squashed together and linked and conjoined so that sometimes they formed caverns fifty metres across, and sometimes intimate spaces just big enough for two. It was the ideal setting for communal living. Hence Hamlet, which had no permanent residents but anything up to a couple of hundred transient ones.

Hels thumped her fist on a section of skin. Nothing happened. She tutted, and thumped again.

'Go away!'

It was many voices, raggedly out of sync and muted by the skin of the Rockblossom. The words ended in laughter.

Hels half turned towards Zeb and gave him an apologetic smile. 'They'll pay,' she said. Then she raised her voice. 'Guys? Open the door or I'll carve a new one.'

There was more laughter. Then Zeb heard a mechanical *snap* and a section of skin swung outwards. A cloud of smoke and vapour rolled out and up the side of the huge plant. He followed it upwards, watching as it dimmed a couple of stars on its way.

Hels was watching too. She grinned. 'I don't know how the thing lives through all the pollution.'

Zeb shrugged. 'It's lived through plenty. I think it's pretty robust.'

'Really?' She raised her eyebrows. 'I thought you were new to the place. Are you a Blossom scholar?'

'Scholar?' He thought fast. 'No, not that. I'm just interested in things.'

It seemed to be enough. She nodded, and walked into the smoke. He followed, resisting the temptation to hold his breath. After all, he was going to have to inhale sooner or later, and he couldn't see any obviously dead bodies.

He was expecting something harsh, but instead there was just a sensation of warmth and thickness. It felt a bit like he had always imagined breathing underwater would be. It didn't sting his eyes, either. He took another breath.

He realized Hels was peering at him. She looked amused. 'First time?'

He nodded, and she raised an eyebrow. 'You've lived a pretty sheltered life, for someone who is interested in things.'

'I guess so. It never really occurred to me.'

She laughed. 'Well, it's occurring now! Enjoy it. And, if you hang around, later on maybe I'll show you something else interesting.' She leaned in close to him and whispered, 'Some things are even more fun under the smoke than they are on the edge of the Rift.'

She let her lips brush his. Then she stood back and grinned.

He grinned back, meaning it. 'While I'm hanging around, are you going to introduce me to some people?'

'Nah. Going to keep you to myself.'

And he heard himself say, 'That'd be good.'

For a moment they locked eyes. Then, without anyone having planned it, they were leaning towards each other and somehow he could catch the scent of her breath through the smoke.

'Hey!'

They both snapped upright. A tall, thin, ochre-skinned creature was standing beside them, head a little to one side. It was naked except for a minimal wrap around hips so narrow Zeb could almost have closed his hands around them, and its torso was covered in pale blue stubble. Its eyes were half closed, showing a hint of purple irises, and it was the first obviously non-basic life-form Zeb had seen this visit. The wrap didn't look big enough to be concealing anything much.

It extended both arms and pointed a slim finger at each of them. 'No public mating, please.'

Hels waved dismissively. 'That wasn't mating.'

The creature folded its arms. 'It was precursor activity. You ought to thank me; a few minutes of that and you'd have been well on your way to being thrown out for breaking party ground-rules.'

'No we wouldn't. Besides, you're just jealous.' She pointed at the wrap, nudged Zeb and whispered loudly, 'It doesn't have any genitals.'

The creature smiled thinly. 'Correction; I don't have *external* genitals. Under the right circumstances I have all the genitals I need, thank you.' It turned to Zeb. 'You look unfamiliar, but there is something ... I imagine she's your latest?'

Zeb opened his mouth but Hels got there first. 'No. He's mine. *As* you ought to know, Keff.'

'Oh, I do know. But does he?' Keff eyed Zeb. 'You look to me as if you are new to this ... planet. Welcome. Let me know when you need a head-to-head.'

Zeb nodded. 'I will. Is that something we're allowed to do in public?'

Keff smiled, and it was like watching cords tightening across a carved skull. 'It is. I promise you, there is nothing I presently wish to do with you that cannot be done in public.'

Hels laughed. 'Manners!' She pushed Keff sharply in the chest. It took two steps backwards before regaining its balance and standing for a moment like an accusing statue. Then it shook its head slightly and walked off into the smoke.

Zeb watched the skinny figure disappear. 'Who was that?'

'You care?'

'Sure.'

She smiled. 'It's what you call for if you think you might be having too much fun.'

'Are you having too much fun?'

'Not yet.' And their eyes locked again, and they leaned towards each other, and this time no one interrupted.

*

The population of Hamlet varied. It could peak at nearly a thousand, but rarely for long, and it occasionally fell below fifty during rare periods when seasons and weather patterns combined to make it too cold, too windy or too radioactive for comfort. At the moment it was around its long-term median of two hundred.

People tended to know each other, and if you were new it made for a pretty intense party. Zeb had lost track of time.

'What do you mean, it's not smoke?' He waved an unsteady hand through the stuff, watching it curl round his fingers. 'Looks like smoke to me.'

The thin male with the finely wrinkled face shook his head. 'No, you see. It's supposed to look like smoke, but it isn't smoke. That would be, um, smelly. And dangerous.'

'So what is it?'

'Ah. It's very clever.'

Zeb waited. There was no rush. Whatever the stuff in the not-smoke was, it was relaxing.

'See, it's specially blended. Different every time, because every party's different? This one's pretty special.' He leaned carefully towards Zeb until their faces were only a hand's breadth apart. 'I was on the smoke design group. Four of us. It took days.'

Zeb nodded politely. He had the feeling this might take days too. Apparently the smoke that only looked like smoke was a complicated blend of gases, droplets, vapour-phase compounds and nano-particles, blended with a very small amount of real smoke for the sake of it and custom designed every time.

People in Hamlet obviously had plenty of leisure.

Hels had been edged away from him a while ago by a stand-ard party process, moving from friend to friend until he couldn't be bothered to keep up. Knowing no one, he had drifted between groups, exchanging variations on *hello* and running a competition with himself to see how long he could keep conversations going before things got awkward. About three minutes seemed a good benchmark.

Then he had washed up here, and three minutes was just a fond memory. His new acquaintance was called Retslamb. Or something. They were in a bubble-shaped space deep inside the Rockblossom, lounging in a complicated web spun out of ropes twisted from Skin-Beetle thread. There was a smoke brazier on the floor below them, and they were stoned to the wide.

Definitely relaxing.

He blinked. 'I'm sorry?'

Retslamb grinned. 'It's pretty dense here, huh? Listen, take a drink.' He held out a slim flask and shook it from side to side.

'Really? How will that help?'

'It's complementary to the smoke. Didn't I say? We designed the two together. The smoke takes you down,' and one hand described a lazy fluttering descent, 'and the drink lifts you back. You choose how up or down you want to be.'

Zeb took the flask, unstoppered it and sniffed carefully. It had a clean scent that, although faint, seemed to cut through the sweet clouds. 'How much should I drink?'

'If you want to get to a balance, about half of that.'

Zeb nodded and raised the flask to his lips. It tasted clean, too.

He handed it back. His head was clearer already. 'The rest is for you.'

But the other man shook his head. 'No way. I'm staying down.'

'Why?'

'Just stuff.' The grin was gone, and the thin face looked older.

Zeb studied him for a second, then shrugged. 'Okay. Your choice.'

'S'right. Choice. Look, it's been fine.' Retslamb swung his legs out of the ropes and pulled himself upright. 'Have a good party, all right?'

'Sure.' Zeb watched the man walk slowly out of the chamber. As he reached the entrance he stopped and stood aside, and Hels looked round him. 'Ah! Found you. Can you stand up?'

'Sure.' He demonstrated. 'Retslamb gave me something.'

She laughed, and nudged the thin man. 'I bet he did. Listen, come with me, okay? If I stay here any longer I'll need a drink myself. I want some fresh air. Oh – see you, Retslamb . . .'

With a twitch that looked ostentatious to Zeb, the other man had turned sideways and eased himself through the gap between Hels and the door. He paused just outside, gave an awkward wave and walked off, disappearing quickly in the dim smokiness.

Hels watched him go. 'What did I say? Or what did you say, if it wasn't me?'

'I don't think it was you.' He told her about the other man's change of mood.

She nodded. 'That explains it. He doesn't do sober, doesn't do straight. I think it hurts too much.'

'Why?'

'When he sobers up he remembers he's an Illusionist. I think he'd rather forget. Now, are you coming?'

She turned without waiting for an answer. He shook his head and followed.

He had no idea what she was talking about.

Hels led him through the elaborate vegetable intestines of the Rockblossom and along a low tunnel that he guessed was a Skin-Beetle boring, and then to his relief they were outside. He stood up straight and took a few deep breaths, expanding his ribs as much as he could to cram in fresh air instead of party smoke until points of light flickered in front of his eyes. When his vision cleared he saw Hels looking at him.

She smiled. 'Better?'

'Yes, thanks.'

'Feeling energetic?' She raised an eyebrow.

He laughed. 'I guess . . .'

'Good.' Her smile broadened. 'Let's find somewhere . . .'

Somewhere turned out to be a clearing a few hundred paces from the Rockblossom. Slim trunks curved inwards to form a tall arched roof; Skin Beetles glowed.

As it turned out, he was indeed feeling energetic. The fumes had cleared, and the glow from the insects was kind of romantic, and when Hels pulled him down to the ground the undergrowth was soft.

They were busy for a while.

Later, they rolled apart and lay looking up at the arching trees. It was beginning to get light. The beetles had dropped to the forest floor where they lay like fat, fading lanterns, and the forest had turned from glowing to grey. Zeb studied the shapes of the trees. Now they weren't oddly lit by the shifting glow of the beetles they looked very symmetrical. He pointed upwards. 'Is this natural?'

'No.'

It was Keff's voice.

They both sat up. The being was sitting cross-legged on the other side of the clearing.

Hels took a deep breath. 'What the fuck?'

Keff waved round the clearing. 'He asked if this was natural. Well, it isn't. As you know.' It gave Zeb a thin smile. 'She made it, as a matter of fact. I always assumed she had in mind the sort of thing you have just been doing.'

Hels stood up. 'Keff, that is *it*. I am so going to complain to someone about you.'

'Why? I waited until it seemed reasonable to engage with you.'

'You waited? Meaning you actually watched?'

'Not really. I kept out of it after you started eating each other's faces, right up to just now. I didn't want to intrude.'

'Oh good.' Hels looked down at Zeb. 'I'm sorry. Like, really sorry. That *thing* has so gone too far. Come on.' She reached out a hand. He took it and allowed himself to be helped upright, but then pulled gently free.

'Just a minute.' He walked over to Keff. 'What are you actually doing here?'

Keff moved slightly and was suddenly upright, as if it had been kept in a sitting position by some invisible tension that had just been abruptly released. 'Waiting for you. She has certain patterns of behaviour. I felt sure you would end up here sooner or later.'

Hels sighed. 'Right, well, I'm beyond offended so I'm going inside before I try to *hurt* something. Zeb, I hope I'll see you when you're done. Keff, if I see you, you're in trouble.' She turned and walked out of the clearing.

Zeb watched her go, then turned to Keff. 'I expect you don't have many friends?'

'No. You met Retslamb earlier.'

The abruptness made Zeb blink. He stared at Keff. 'What are you?'

'You're finding out. You met Retslamb earlier.'

'You said. Are we having that head-to-head you mentioned?'

'What did you think of him?'

Zeb paused before answering. The afterglow of sex had faded and the fuzziness of the party smoke was long gone; his instincts were awake and prickling. Eventually he said, 'I gather he's suffering from ingrowing Illusionism.'

To his surprise Keff laughed, a short explosive bark that sent the Skin Beetles whizzing up through the trees in a startled swarm. 'Very, very good! I admire you, among other reactions.' It looked around, then gestured towards the edge of the clearing. 'Shall we walk?'

The forest surrounding the Rockblossom was close to a monoculture. Slender trees with grey-blue limbs dropped fine, hair-like needles that formed peaty stratified drifts. If you walked very carefully you stayed on a soft covering with a

springy layer beneath it, but if you let a foot fall too hard you
went through the top layer and into older leaf-fall which made
a noise halfway between a crack and a squelch, and which
gave off a thick, tarry smell when your foot sank into it. Zeb
was breaking through with every other step, but Keff walked
quickly without even indenting the top cover.

It was hard to keep up, and Zeb was beginning to fall
behind. He paused to catch his breath.

Immediately, Keff stopped. Without turning, it said, 'Tired?'

'No. I'm just not playing games.'

'Really? Not mine, perhaps.' Keff turned round. 'You have
no idea what an Illusionist is, have you?'

Zeb met the alien gaze for a moment. Then he grinned.
'Okay, fine. So I'm from out of town.'

To his surprise, Keff grinned back. 'I know that. It's something we have in common. More than you guess, I should
think. We'll stop here while I tell you about Illusionists. Feel
free to lean on a tree.'

'Thanks, I'll stand.'

'Fine. They're recent. I first heard of them two hundred
years ago.' The pale eyes rested on him. 'Maybe that's why you
don't know about them.'

The implication hung in the air. Zeb shrugged. 'I told you.
I'm from out of town.'

'Yes . . . well, while you were – out of town, some people
started to believe a thing. A bit of philosophy, if you like. That
the world they live in is an illusion.'

Zeb raised his eyebrows. 'So what? Everyone wonders about
that sometimes.'

'They do, but a few people took it further than just wondering. They really believed it. And you know what happens when
you humans start believing something?'

A shape began to form in Zeb's mind. He leaned against a
tree after all. 'Go on.'

'You test it. Monkey curiosity, Zeb. You take the idea and you pull it and twist it and rub it and taste it and hit it against the rocks until it breaks apart and you can see inside it; what it's really made of.' The being paused, looked around and leaned back against a tree. 'But this idea didn't break.'

'Uh-huh?'

'Uh-huh. It got stronger.'

Zeb studied his hands. 'So? Everyone believes it?'

Keff laughed again. 'No! Most people don't believe anything, most of the time. A few, though, yes. They truly believe they live in an illusion. More than that – a simulation. I suppose you can work out what that means.'

'No, I can't.' It was time to stop this. Zeb pushed himself away from the tree. 'And I don't intend to try. You know what I think? We all hallucinate. All the time. It's how we perceive things, how we process them, how we make *sense* of them. And you're doing it right now—'

'I'm not—'

'—because the world makes you angry. You think the world's senseless and that makes you angry. Right?'

Keff looked at him, and then past him. 'I see the world exactly as it is, Zeb. Most of the time I'm the only one. Right now I might not be. I have the impression that you have been seeing things *for a long time*.'

It was still gazing past Zeb's shoulder. He turned, and realized that someone was watching them.

It was Retslamb. He looked uncertainly from Zeb to Keff. 'Uh, sorry. I went off, before, and I felt, you know. Then Hels said you were out here somewhere. Is this a bad time?'

Zeb shrugged and gestured over his shoulder. 'Ask that.'

The barking laugh came again. 'It's probably an ideal time. I'll leave you to it, shall I? I'm sure at least one of you has plenty to talk about.'

Retslamb grinned uncertainly. 'Sure. Thanks. So, uh, I'm not good outside, you know. Can we . . . ?'

The man needed help, almost as badly as Zeb needed not to be near Keff. Zeb stitched a wide smile on to his face and strode forward, one arm outstretched to sweep the other man into a hug. 'By all means. Back to the Rockblossom, and tell me about stuff.'

He didn't look back to see what Keff was doing. And he didn't take his arm from Retslamb's unresisting shoulder until he had walked the man safely back to his smoke – and when they were both inside he allowed himself to take several deep breaths of the soothing, stoning stuff.

But he didn't forget the emphasis Keff had placed on the end of that sentence.

It was time to get himself out of this vreality. Discreetly, for sure, and without pissing people off as far as that was possible. Especially Hels, not that either of them had promised long term.

But soon.

Experiment

Something woke Skarbo. Something very familiar and at the same time altogether wrong.

He prised open most of his eyes and looked around. He shouldn't have slept, needn't have slept. Why had he?

Then he remembered Hemfrets. *I took the liberty of checking your metabolism.* And if it can select food for me, he thought, it can select soporifics . . .

His eyes felt scratchy and his vision seemed blurred. He closed and opened them a few times but the haze persisted.

Then he saw the shaft of sunlight glancing down across the room – a shaft marked by a restless pink swirl.

Not haze, then. Dust.

The familiar smell of dust had woken him. It shouldn't be dusty in here. The place was sealed.

He was on his way to the stairs before he knew it, turning his awkward body around because descending them forwards was no longer possible – not with his legs in their current state – and taking one shuddering step after another, all the time trying desperately not to fall down because he was panicking, far worse than he had when The Bird, may it moult, had announced his visitors.

At the bottom of the stairs he turned round. The dust in the air was thick enough to blot out the dim light almost completely but he didn't need to see it; he could feel it.

He could hear something now, even through the heavy door. An urgent rattle, with a background that sounded like high winds.

He opened the door. The rattling grew much louder, and then something was battering him and shrieking.

'Tried to tell you! Tried to find you! And you choose now to disappear? Now? *Idiot!*'

'I didn't disappear. What's happening?' He couldn't see – the wretched creature was in his way. He tried to bat it aside but it was too fast. It flicked away from the blow and then flew even closer.

'Not happening – happened! Everything going. All ground to powder, all your precious toys, while you hide and snore! All. Look!'

At last the thing moved out of the way and Skarbo could see into the Machine Room.

It was like looking into a dust storm, a whirl of smoke and haze and debris spiralling in towards something in the centre of the room.

It was the Companion, and it was no longer hiding. Through the storm Skarbo could see a lumpy grey casing covered with blisters and bulges. Through a mist of horror and rage he realized it looked like a miniature version of Hemfrets's ship.

He heard himself shout something incoherent, the sound snatched away by the raging wind. He tried to take a step into the Machine Room but the force of the wind caught him and threw him against the open door. He felt, rather than heard, part of his carapace crack.

Then, quite suddenly, the cloud formed itself into a neat sphere which collapsed to a point centred on the Companion and vanished.

There was a faint *pop*. A layer of dust fell from the Companion's surface, collected itself into a tiny version of the whirlwind and disappeared into the grey casing without anything seeming to have opened to let it in. The machine was on its own. There was a second of clanging silence and then a flat voice that seemed to come from nowhere said:

'Processing complete.'

Skarbo looked around the room. It was empty – the models had gone, and the walls and floor had a smoothly scoured look. He looked at the Companion. 'Processing?' His voice sounded scoured, too. 'Processing what?'

But the device flicked out of sight.

Skarbo stared in horror. Then his fury boiled and he launched himself at the space it had occupied, his claws scrabbling at the floor.

He was less than halfway to it when The Bird slammed into him, knocking him to the side so that he had to brace his legs to stay upright. He glared at it.

'What?'

'*Not safe!* Not for you. Look . . .'

It wheeled round in the air and flew straight at where the Companion had been. When it was about a metre from the spot, it froze in mid-flap; there was a soft, almost soothing hum, and the air around The Bird seemed to flicker for a moment. Then the hum stopped and The Bird dropped to the floor and landed in a messy heap.

Skarbo stooped down and made to reach out for the body, but stopped as an acrid smell rose to him. He placed it immediately, although he knew he had never smelled it before. It was burnt feathers.

He watched the motionless sprawl for a while. One of the wings was sticking out at an odd angle. He thought of straightening it but it seemed – disrespectful. But he went on watching. The thought was growing that this was probably the last link to his old world. Besides, he didn't want to look anywhere else, and he was suddenly too tired to stand.

It occurred to him that in all the hundreds of years it had been here, he had never asked The Bird its name.

A while later he heard footsteps, and looked up. Hemfrets was standing a few paces away, looking down at him with what might have been sympathy. 'I'm sorry,' it said.

Skarbo looked away. 'Is it all—' He couldn't bring himself to finish the sentence.

'Processed? Yes.'

Skarbo nodded. 'You lied.'

'I did not.'

'Yes, you did.' Somehow he found the strength to rise. 'You said you would tell no one. You said you would keep it safe!'

'I did tell no one, but things changed. And to live, one must eat.'

Standing had been a mistake. Skarbo felt his legs weakening, and looked round automatically to find something to sit on. There was nothing – all processed, he told himself and felt dizzy at the thought – so he let himself fold down into a crouch on the floor. 'What changed?'

'Everything. We're at war, Skarbo. Have you heard of the Warfront?'

'No. What does it matter?' Nothing mattered, nothing.

'It matters because it is coming. It will sweep across the Bubble and burst it.' Hemfrets squatted down next to him and looked at The Bird. 'That seems to be taking a long time to recover.'

For a moment Skarbo imagined lashing out – sending a limb round in the fastest arc he could manage. Opening the face of a claw. Raking through flesh. The expression on Hemfrets's face as it fell back, wounded, with its tasteless remark punished.

But imagination was all he could manage. He sighed. 'It's dead.'

'I'd be amazed if it was. It wasn't last time.'

'Last time?'

'Yes. It became rather – defensive, when the processing began. Ah. See?'

There was a faint crackle. Reddish light flickered across the feathers, and The Bird raised its head.

'Ow.'

Skarbo sat back from his crouch. 'You're alive?'

'Must be. Hurts too much to be the other thing. Wing bad.' It scrabbled with the good wing until it could get its feet under it, and stood. 'Ow ow ow. Very bad.'

'You were burnt, too.'

'Yes. Ow.' It rounded on Hemfrets. 'Still here? Told him what you did, have you?'

Hemfrets stood up. 'I think he can see. Skarbo, I am truly sorry, but as you see there's nothing left here. You will come to my ship with me.'

'For what? You've destroyed my life. My *lives*. I'll be dead in eighty-seven days. Can't you leave me here in peace?'

'No, I can't.' There was something different about the voice that made Skarbo examine the creature properly. It looked different too, somehow stiffer and more upright, and he realized it was wearing different clothes: a dark-coloured close-fitting thing like a tunic with insignia down the centre.

Like a uniform.

Skarbo stood up carefully and faced it. 'Why not?'

'Because you'll be dead a lot sooner.'

Skarbo shrugged. 'So what?'

'And it won't be peaceful. Look, I *can't* leave you here. I have orders. We're at *war*, Skarbo. Do you understand? That is what changed. War has broken out, and everyone is grabbing whatever valuable assets they can before the Warfront gets here. Your planet was a valuable asset. You are a valuable asset. You have been grabbed, by me. You may just live long enough to be grateful you weren't grabbed by someone else.'

'And my models? Were they valuable too?'

'Yes. Too valuable to leave for others. I'm sorry they had to be destroyed, but I had no choice. And now I'm afraid you have no choice either.'

'Ah. Take me or kill me?'

'Just take you. We didn't discuss doing any killing.'

Skarbo looked at the creature. Its face seemed set. 'All right. Should I bring anything?'

Hemfrets shook its head. 'As I said, there's nothing left. Apart from that.' It gestured at The Bird.

Skarbo nodded. 'If it wants. Do you?' He addressed the last two words to The Bird.

It wagged its head from side to side. 'Want? No. But choice? No. Coming.'

'I feel the same.' Skarbo sighed. 'Very well, Hemfrets. Do whatever comes next. I don't much care what it is. Where's your pet?'

'Pet?'

'That Companion. You're responsible for it. Aren't you?'

Hemfrets laughed. 'You think? Something that powerful, and you think I'm in charge?'

'Well, what are you then?'

'Just a tool, Skarbo. Like all of us. Just a tool.'

It had been seven and a half lifetimes since Skarbo had made a surface-to-ship transfer – or any kind of journey at all – and he had no memory of it. Hemfrets went ahead to make whatever arrangements needed making for guests, and Skarbo and The Bird were left standing in the eerie silence of God's Eye. The place had been completely conquered by dust. It covered every surface and more was settling out of the air like heavy smoke.

There was no sign of the Companion.

After a while Skarbo turned to The Bird. 'Thanks,' he said.

'What for?'

'Attacking that – thing.'

'You were going to. Bad plan. Get yourself fried in your own shell.'

'It's not a shell. But thanks; especially when you already knew what would happen.'

The Bird was perching on the edge of the couch. It extended its wings and flapped noisily upwards for a few beats. Then it dropped again. 'Ow ow ow. Yes. Better, but not all better. Lucky you. Would have let you get on with it, if I hadn't already seen it before.' It swivelled its head on one side and glared up at him. 'Besides, got a guess about that. Reckon you've seen a ship like this before. Yes, yes?'

'Yes. How did you know? Had I told you? I don't remember.'

'Ha! No. But you aren't watching it. Biggest thing in the sky and you don't look? So maybe you don't need to. Maybe seen it before, see?'

'Well, yes. You're right.' Skarbo told it about the ship above the Greater Bowl. It listened, still with its head on one side. When he had finished it snapped its beak.

'The net thing. Whole city? In one go?'

'No. Not the whole city – the whole Mandate – in those days almost one per cent of the Bubble. There were seven planets. They destroyed the biggest city on each of them.'

'Not you though?'

Skarbo smiled. 'I was lucky.'

'That when you changed?'

Skarbo nodded. 'The ship recovered me. The Baschet were going to re-body me anyway, so I decided to be – different. Insectoid looked like a good option.'

'Why?'

'Because.' Skarbo smiled to himself. They had revived him

enough for him to be able to make his own decisions, and then let him wander round the huge ship while he made them. Once, he had chanced on somewhere that probably shouldn't have been open, and which contained a viewing system that probably shouldn't have been working. He could still remember looking down at a magnified view of the smouldering city, and seeing clusters of black dots flowing purposefully across the scene, and realizing that the insects from the bowl were making themselves at home.

He had been interrupted, and politely removed, and as he had gone he had looked down at the burnt ruin of his fragile mammal body and made a decision about durability. They had gone along with it, to his surprise.

But *because* was good enough for The Bird. He smiled again. 'Funny. For the second time in my lives, the Baschet destroy my world and then rescue me.'

The Bird gave a sharp cackle. 'Funny for you. Not for them. Last time they won.'

Skarbo watched The Bird for a moment. Then he said slowly, 'What do you mean?'

'First listen, then think, then speak if needed. Huh! Last time they won. So this time they lost! Fleet blown out of the sky or captured. Not even in this war – years ago.' It cackled again. 'Serve the bastards right. This one got captured. Not even sure who owns it.'

Skarbo looked up at the ship that still loomed over them. Similar, but different – the ship that had murdered the capital city of the Mandate had been featurelessly pristine. Now this one was lit up by the reflected daylight he could see it was shadowed across by streaks and scars. 'You might think it's funny. I'd rather be rescued by something in better condition.'

'So what? Dead in eighty-seven days. What do you care?'

It had a point. Skarbo looked down at his body. The leg he had injured when The Bird had shoved him aside was showing no signs of healing. It would probably drop off before he died. Down to four, but at least he would end up symmetrical. He sighed. 'I wonder where they'll take us?'

'How should I know? Ask; coming back. Look.' It waggled its head towards the entrance.

Skarbo followed the gesture, and felt the dizziness grow much worse. Hemfrets was indeed coming back, and this time it was flanked by two Companions.

'Sorry for the wait.' The voice was breezy. 'If you're ready, we'll be off.'

Skarbo pointed. 'With those things?'

'Yes.' Hemfrets shrugged. 'I sense your discomfort but I'm afraid there's nothing I can do about it. I'm just—'

'—a tool. Yes, I know.' Skarbo pulled himself upright. 'Where are you going to take us?'

'At the moment, let's get you as far as the ship.' There had been the slightest pause before the sentence, and there was another after it. 'Please obey all instructions.'

The Bird gave a couple of noisy flaps. 'Not good at that.'

Hemfrets glanced at it. 'Get good. Follow me, please.'

They followed through tunnels that Skarbo remembered as being full of junk, but which were now picked clean of everything except dust. The Bird scuttled along the floor grumbling to itself. Every now and then it gave a few experimental flaps and then swore. Obviously its wing was still an issue; Skarbo found himself wondering how fast the thing was expecting to heal. It was just as well the junk had gone, otherwise the creature would have taken forever to hop over it.

Gone. He blinked, and stopped dead. Something that felt like a bundle of rags wrapped round a sharp stick bumped into his legs.

'Ow! *Fuck* . . . what?'

'Sorry.' Skarbo turned round and looked down at the angry

eyes. 'But, it wasn't just my models? Did they process the junk as well?'

'Yes. Ancient things. Rare things. All dust. Thought you realized.'

Skarbo shook his head. 'No . . . but there were thousands of cubic metres!'

'Were. Still are. Just different shape. Useless shape! Vandals.'

From ahead they heard Hemfrets. It sounded testy. 'Follow, please! No waiting.'

They followed. The Bird was still complaining, but now Skarbo barely noticed it.

His horror at the destruction of his lifetimes' work was too big to feel. He knew he would feel it, maybe soon, but for now the numbness was the best he could do. But the basement junk, that was different. Even when he was selecting pieces to drop into the core of the little planet, even when he was teasing The Bird about it, he had really felt proprietorial; almost caring. Consigning things to the core had almost been his way of showing respect.

Now, he realized, he was mourning.

Well, he had to start somewhere.

The corridor ended abruptly, in a rough opening in a rock face. The edges of the opening looked fresh, compared with the eroded roundness of everything else, and so did the shuttle pad it led to – a simple, sharp-planed plateau fifty metres across, which had obviously been formed by just cutting off the top of a rounded hill. A bulbously ugly little ship squatted in the middle of it, its ovoid body supported on an asymmetrical tripod of legs that looked too thin for the job.

It was comprehensively battered, even more than the ship that hovered above them.

The Bird made a spitting sound. 'Trust that? Pah. Worse state than Skarbo!'

Hemfrets stood still for a moment. Then it turned round. 'Creature? I don't have time for this. Be quiet, or I will request one of the Companions to heat your beak until your tongue cooks in your head.'

Skarbo looked down at The Bird. Its beak was closed.

Hemfrets walked over to the shuttle, stopped a few paces from it, and raised a hand. The ship dipped on its legs until one end was against the rock, and a hatch opened. Hemfrets turned.

'Come on. Quickly, please.' The breeziness had gone. Now it sounded tense.

Skarbo walked up a roughened metal ramp that made faint scratching sounds under his claws. Behind him The Bird's feet clicked evenly, and he smiled to himself. The thing was calmer than it seemed.

Inside, the ship was utilitarian. There were metal bench seats that would do for humanoids but not for him, and the only light came through the open hatch. He looked around, and then shrugged and hunkered down on the floor. The Bird hopped about, swivelling its head and studying things. Then it settled by Skarbo's head, briefly flexing its wings. The movement looked natural.

Skarbo watched it. He had never been good at deciphering its expressions, but then he had never seen much sign of anything to decipher; it had mostly seemed angry or impatient. Now it looked – watchful.

He looked away. Behind him, he heard a mechanical groan and clang, and for a moment there was darkness. He felt his eyes trying to adjust, but either there was so little light that even he couldn't see anything or, more likely, age had caught up with his optics.

Then there was no need. Light flooded in. With no warning,

the hull had become transparent. Below, the pad was already receding, although he had felt no acceleration, and above him the belly of the vast ship was expanding to fill the view. He looked round and saw Hemfrets sitting on one of the benches. Its eyes were closed and it didn't seem to be doing anything.

He couldn't see the Companions.

Then they passed to one side of the ship, and he stared down in shock at its upper surface. Beside him, The Bird let out a soft croak.

Half the ship was missing.

It was as if some huge serrated blade had been dragged across it, tearing a rough-edged wound hundreds of metres across that ran almost from end to end of the hull. The gash was deep, with torn canyon edges. As they flew over it they looked into dark hangars, saw glimpses of twisted structures that could have been engineering spaces, and flicked through plumes of crystallized vapour leaking from the exposed entrails of the ship.

Skarbo found he was shaking. Without taking his eyes off the ship he said, 'Hemfrets? What did that?'

'A weapon, obviously.'

'But, we can't . . .' Skarbo stopped, took a breath. 'It's a wreck. It's going nowhere. What are you doing? You destroyed my life to put me on this?'

'The ship is fully functional.'

Skarbo stared at the carnage for a while. Then he shook his head. 'Well, I was going to die anyway.'

Something sharp tapped his leg. He looked down and met the eyes of The Bird. It shook its head very slowly.

Skarbo couldn't be bothered working out what it meant. He looked away.

They were closer to the ship and he could see deeper into the gash. There was movement in there. Things flickered at the corner of his vision, and every now and then something larger happened; the torn edges were busy with blocky devices that seemed to change shape as they moved, like clumps of rectangular pixels that were constantly reorganizing.

Then his brain processed the image properly and his eyes widened. The pixels were Companions, in flocks of – what? Thousands? And then, as he watched, one of the flocks spread itself over part of the gash. The pixels brightened, blurred, and coalesced and then there was just ship. A hundred-metre length of the gash had been healed, leaving an irregular strip of bright clean hull where there had been mortal damage – and another group of Companions was already gathering next to it.

At this rate the whole tear would be closed in minutes.

'Impressed?'

It was The Bird; either it had forgotten about Hemfrets's threat or it didn't care.

He nodded.

'Huh. Ask where it got them.'

'What?' Skarbo didn't understand.

'The Companions. Ask it!'

He half turned towards Hemfrets, but the creature spoke first.

'The Bird knows. It can tell you, if it's feeling so casual about the state of its tongue.'

Skarbo sighed. 'One of you? Please?'

'Ha. From you! Got them from you.' The Bird hopped from one leg to the other. 'Your stuff! All the play planets, all the junk.'

'*What?*'

'Forgotten already? Senile? Processed, remember?'

Skarbo stared at it. 'And made all those? Overnight?' He turned to Hemfrets and took a breath, but the other cut him off.

'No, not overnight. And I didn't make them. They made themselves. It took a couple of hours. Now will both of you please be quiet?'

They had passed over almost the whole width of the huge ship. The gash was half healed now; just before it passed out of sight, another section knitted itself together.

Skarbo shook his head.

The last time Skarbo had been on a ship like this – the only time – it had seemed, if not new, then sleek and purposeful and full of people. They had been triumphant, of course, fresh from their murder of seven planets.

This one looked empty and half demolished. The corridor walls were heavily scarred as if massive things had been dragged along them, and there were many empty spaces that looked as if they shouldn't be empty.

Then the word came to him. Not demolished – *cannibalized*. And his mind leapt the rest of the way.

He turned to Hemfrets. 'Who does this ship really belong to?'

They were in a control space, a twenty-metre hemisphere walled by screens, half of which weren't working. The ones that were showed enhanced views of the outside. Skarbo searched for his planet, and found it. It looked forlorn, and fuzzy-edged through a halo of dust. He sighed, and said, 'Hemfrets?'

'It belongs to me, currently.' Hemfrets didn't turn round. It was standing in front of a console that looked much newer than the rest of the ship, and its shoulders were rigid.

'Have you stolen it?'

'Not exactly.'

'What does that mean?'

'Nothing that you need to understand. We're at war, Skarbo. People at war don't give things away. You told me you hadn't heard of the Warfront.'

'Yes.'

'You have been very remote – but also very introverted. I will explain.'

And it did.

The Warfront had started as a collection of ideas that had coalesced into a movement. There was nothing much to unify it at the beginning apart from general discontent, but that had provided enough impulsion for the movement to become organized.

Then the first planetary military had lost patience with what it saw as a group of unruly kids and unleashed a messy coup d'état that had left a million casualties on the home planet and a lot of angry survivors.

Suddenly the Warfront had a sense of purpose. It was anti-commerce, anti-establishment (to begin with, until it grew enough to become a sort of establishment itself) and generally anti-status quo. It was ecological, preferring real worlds to virtual ones, with a muscular back-to-basics ethos. It excelled at attracting the shy, the angry and the excluded, and it was sweeping across the Mandate, gaining numbers as it went.

Skarbo stared at Hemfrets. 'It sounds like a big protest march.'

'That might have been how it started out. Skarbo, the Warfront was – *was* – a few million angry kids and some adults who should have known better. Now it is much more than that. It is an opportunity, you see? A thing within which all kinds of political ambitions can be played out. There are proxy wars within it, and factions, and an emerging leadership with a new focus.'

'Which is?'

Hemfrets smiled. 'The same as yours. The Spin. The Warfront is coming, Skarbo, and it is already hundreds of thousands of ships strong.'

'I see.' Then something struck Skarbo. 'We're at war, you said. Are you part of the Warfront, then? Or part of something else?'

'I'm not part of anything. I'm hoping never to be. Now please excuse me. And watch, if you like.'

'Watch what?' But as he spoke Skarbo caught a movement on the screens. He peered, and then moved closer.

Something had taken off from his planet – a fierce speck climbing on a short needle of light.

Hemfrets nodded. 'Good.'

'What?' Skarbo had meant to say more but before he could the little planet flared white, incandesced for a searing moment, and then simply collapsed to a point and disappeared.

From somewhere he heard a quiet croak. He looked down and saw The Bird watching him steadily.

'Sad,' it said simply.

He nodded. 'Sad.' The word seemed utterly insufficient, but he couldn't think of a meaningful improvement so he simply repeated it. 'Sad.'

Hemfrets turned from the display. 'I'm sorry. Do you need time to grieve?'

Skarbo stared at the creature. 'Time? Time before what?'

'I don't understand.'

'No, I believe you don't.' Skarbo walked back to the seats that were suitable for humans and perched himself awkwardly. 'You have destroyed my home, and my work, of nearly eight lifetimes. I will die in eighty-seven days. Do you think that leaves me long enough to grieve for what you have taken?'

The words had come out calmly. He was surprised at himself. He didn't feel calm.

Hemfrets shook its head. 'Probably not.' It took a few steps towards Skarbo and halted. 'Look, I'm sorry about your planet. Would it help if I explained things?'

'Possibly.' Skarbo shook his head. 'Although I doubt it.'

'Let me try.' It walked over to the bench and sat down, somehow managing to look as uncomfortable as Skarbo felt. 'You've been researching the Spin for hundreds of years. You watched it – running down. Yes?'

'Yes.' And added to himself, *a metaphor for my own decline.*

'So you saw it dying but you said nothing. Why?'

Skarbo blinked. 'I don't understand.'

'It's clear enough. You were able to predict the death, to put it that way, of a whole cluster of civilizations. Trillions of people. You had an audience – you were published, you were read – but you said nothing.'

'But that was . . .' Skarbo paused. He had been about to say that it had been private, but as the words formed he knew they were unsayable. He gathered himself. 'It was unproven.'

Hemfrets shook its head. 'You know that isn't how science works. You form a theory, and you expose it to challenge. But you kept yours in the dark.'

Skarbo shrugged. 'Why should I do different? What difference would it have made?'

'I don't know.

'Because it was *hopeless*!' The words were out before he had thought about them. '*I* saw it, *I* modelled it, and *I* knew no one could stop it. Is that enough for you?'

The silence seemed long.

Eventually Hemfrets squared its shoulders. 'Enough, indeed. But now the question is different. Will it be enough for others?' It stood up. 'There is a new focus on the Spin, Skarbo, and therefore there is a new focus on you. There are quarters for you. Follow me.'

Skarbo followed. He barely registered the regular click of The Bird, following him.

The quarters were in better condition than the rest of the ship – just. There were two adjoining spaces – one plain grey-walled cylinder a couple of metres high and a bit less across, and one flattened sphere the same height but several paces across. They were softly lit, although Skarbo couldn't see any light source.

They both seemed empty. Skarbo looked at Hemfrets. 'Quarters?'

It smiled, the thin lips making a hard line. 'The ship will adapt things when I leave. I advise you to stand in the middle of the larger space, without moving. You might find it more comfortable to shut your eyes until it's finished.'

It gave a shallow bow, and left. A section of wall healed itself seamlessly after it.

The Bird clawed briefly at the floor. 'Know what I think?'

'No.'

'It's scared.'

'Really?'

'Yep. Scared shitless. Scared like prey.' It wagged its head. 'Know what I'm talking about!'

Skarbo stared at it, and shuddered. For a moment he had imagined the creature with a beak full of wriggling insects.

Then the light blinked twice. He looked at The Bird. 'Time to shut our eyes?'

'Pah. Stare down anything.'

'Your choice.' Skarbo shut his eyes.

There was a busy hissing, just above the limit of his hearing, and air currents wafted over him. It went on for about a minute.

Then it fell silent. There was a second's quiet before The Bird said, 'Oh very funny.'

Skarbo opened his eyes.

The plain walls had gone. They were now covered with something like a very fine dense moss that changed colour depending on how you looked at it. It extended up and across the ceiling in a gently iridescent curve that looked blue near the floor, and merged into a dull sandy orange above his head.

There was a couch covered in the same stuff. The design was unfamiliar but it looked usable. Even comfortable. Something in front of the couch looked like an entertainment unit.

Skarbo glanced towards the smaller room. The same moss, and species-appropriate sanitation. He looked back at The Bird. 'What's funny?'

It flapped up from the floor and circled a tall pole with a bar across the top of it. 'See that? Bloody *perch*? Oh yes. Thank you very much. Speciesism, that is. Perch. Huh.'

Skarbo blinked. It had never occurred to him to wonder where and how, or even if, The Bird slept. 'What would you prefer?' he asked.

'Doesn't matter! Rest anywhere. Sleep flying. Don't care. Just not a bloody *perch*.' It hovered next to the perch and pecked it sharply twice, making a quick high *click* each time, then flew off across the room and disappeared into the smaller chamber. The door snapped shut, but Skarbo could still hear angry muttering.

He shrugged and settled down on the couch. Then something occurred to him. He stood up and wandered over to the perch. The surface of the bar was smooth, dull metal and it only took a few seconds to locate two fresh pock-marks where The Bird had pecked it. He extended a claw and dragged it across the surface. It left no mark at all. He tried harder with the same result.

Interesting.

But he was tired, in a way that his younger self could never have imagined. He settled back down, arranging his damaged leg carefully in an attempt – vain, he knew – to keep it as long as possible and, for the second time in only a day, tried to compose himself for sleep.

And failed, utterly.

He wished his leg would heal as quickly as The Bird's wing. Because it hadn't seemed troubled at all by flying, and that was interesting too.

He stared at nothing for a while.

Almost eight hundred years. He had rejected the world – all the worlds except one – for that long sweep of time, his focus far away on a distant object he would never visit. An object that he had thought, and feared, was proving him wrong over

and over. He felt almost cheated that it had after all been proving him right.

And for all that time, while his back had been turned, the
real universe had been full of events he had never seen.

And there stood the entertainment unit, if that was what it
was.

He pushed himself forwards and reached for some controls.
A few nervous minutes later, he had news channels.

War had indeed broken out – but that seemed too rapid a
description. Fostees, who had been studying politics, and more
specifically had been drinking at the time, had once said to
him there was a threshold of conflict above which wars became
general.

Skarbo had sighed, and asked him to elaborate because he
knew he was going to anyway.

'Simple.' Fostees put the wide, shallow cup of hot spirit
down on the low table. 'Lots of people fight for some of the
time, agreed?'

'Yes. I can't see the point of it, but yes.'

'Of course you can't. You're splendid, you know that? But
they do. And some people fight for lots of the time. But if you
have lots of people fighting for lots of the time, then war
becomes the paradigm, you see?'

Skarbo thought about that. 'How do you define lots?'

Fostees picked up the cup. 'Depends. In a single country, it's
very variable. With the right background you can have half the
population bashing each other but the wheels stay on, the
economy functions, everyone happy. Except for the half that
are bashing. Although they might be happy too.'

He drank, noisily, and then dropped the cup. 'Fuck . . .'

Skarbo sighed and gathered the shards of ceramic. 'Go on.'

'Thanks. So, the bigger the setting the better the maths
work. Anything bigger than a decent planetary system is
homo-thingy enough. Ten per cent.'

'Homogeneous? Yes. I see.'

'Very well done you. So if ten per cent of everyone is at war, then sooner or later everyone is at war. My head hurts.'

'You deserve it.'

But Fostees had been dead for hundreds of years, and the war was now. It had been brewing for centuries – longer indeed than Hemfrets had suggested – and the ten per cent had been passed, and was growing to encompass almost everything.

And was called the Warfront.

The Warfront was a permanent war economy. It assimilated, it coerced, it ate, and it grew. And it was indeed coming.

Wall Energy Collective

Zeb opened his eyes, looked around to confirm that he was where he had expected to be, and then closed them again, his chest falling in a deep sigh. To tell the truth he hadn't really needed to open his eyes to know he was back in the real; other senses could do the job for him just as well.

Waking from the vreality tasted of regret. Every time, no matter how hard he tried to persuade himself.

More specifically, on this occasion it tasted of frost and wood-smoke. He didn't really understand how frost could have a smell or a taste, but it did – a distinct, unique clarity on the palate that was quite separate from the collateral sharpness of burning fuel.

Once, when he awakened, there would have been other smells. Food, certainly; the sweetly starchy smell of grain broths, with acerbic overtones from mugs of hot infusions. Even longer ago, there might have been other things to notice. Sometimes even the softly musky scent of Aish's body, and a warmth next to him. She had disliked being with him when he was virtual, but she had stayed even so.

But that had been many, many awakenings ago. These days, Aish had pretty much given up on him. He had tried to explain a couple of times, but he must not have done it justice, and besides, her own responsibilities had grown so much since those early days.

But to be fair, he had trouble explaining it to himself sometimes. It was always easier when he was in the vreality, but then *everything* was easier in the vreality. Aish had called it addiction.

He reached up to his head and peeled off the close-fitting wire mesh skull-cap that was his connection into the vrealities. It snagged in his hair and he swore quietly and fiddled it loose.

It had been a while since he had cut his hair.

He opened his eyes and pushed back against the cot to shove himself upright. The thick cover fell away, and he grabbed at a robe. The temperature in the room was just on the wrong side of freezing; he guessed it was still well before noon.

His room was four metres square. One wall was transparent, a single sheet which had once included sophisticated insulation – but 'once' was hundreds of years ago. Now it was just basic glass, slightly dimmed by the huge lead content needed to stop it shattering on really cold nights. It leaked heat.

The view was almost worth it.

The room was two hundred metres up the Wall, part of a narrow inhabited band that separated the machine deck below from the solar wall above. The Wall was really the northern edge of an ancient quarry, about half a kilometre deep. The floor stretched away southwards for several kilometres, ending in a shallower cliff which you could see, on clear days, as a sharp line because of the pool of shadow at its base. He could see it now – the sun was still at a low angle, glancing across the plain and glittering off the hundred thousand or so solar panels they had mortgaged themselves to install at Aish's encouragement.

They would glitter, and the sun would trickle into his room, for another two hours. Then the sun would climb above the Skylid and that would be that until early evening. Their panels, and the strip of cold-hardened crops at the base of the Wall, would have to do without.

He sighed and turned away from the view. And then jumped. His door was open, and someone was propped in the opening. A young woman, frowning.

'Back with us?'

Zeb spread his arms. 'Hi, Shol. As you see.'

'Aish wants everyone. She's been waiting for you.'

'That's good of her. And thanks for coming to glower at me. I guess she's too busy to do it herself.'

Shol kept up the frown for a second longer. Then she looked down and shook her head, and Zeb guessed she was hiding a smile. 'C'mon, Zeb. You know how she is. Especially these days. She wants a meeting.'

'Well, she'd better have one. What about?'

Shol looked up. 'What do you think? Get dressed, mate.'

There were forty of them. There had been more at the start, when everything had seemed like a good idea. There had been more last time they had gathered.

Zeb shook himself. That was not a helpful state of mind. On the plus side, it meant there was more food to go round, when there was food. On the other hand, downward trajectories only end in one place. He shook himself again. Then a knot of people at the front of the group parted and a woman held up her hands for quiet. She got it, after a moment, and nodded.

'Meeting of the Wall Energy Collective, called to order.'

Aish looked tired. He wasn't surprised. But she still looked good, and she could still command a room.

'Okay. The general reports are uploaded. Did everyone go through them?'

Most people nodded.

'Any comments?'

A thin grey-haired male near the front raised a hand. 'To state the blindingly obvious, the power output's dropped.'

Aish sighed. 'Yes, Harmity, that was blindingly obvious. Thanks.'

'But why?' Harmity's voice was as thin as he was, with a whining overtone. 'In my view—'

But Aish cut him off. 'We'll come to the output in a moment. And, if we live to be very old, we might have time to come to your view.' Some people laughed, but the laughter was nervous and at least as many again didn't share it. Zeb raised his eyebrows.

Aish waved the laughter away. 'Look, I won't keep you waiting. The power is down because Orbital Joule has extended the Skylid. Not very much: about one per cent. Wait; hold on!'

The last word was barely audible; everyone was shouting. Zeb looked round the room, and then met Aish's eye. For a moment she held the look. Then her lips tightened, and she looked up and filled her lungs. 'Hey! Everyone! Quiet down.'

The noise subsided to a mutter. Aish nodded and opened her mouth, but Harmity beat her to it. He was shaking with anger.

'By what right?' He jabbed a finger in the air. 'By what *right* do they do this? Taking away our light?'

'*We* don't *have* rights!'

Zeb rocked back on his heels; Aish had shouted, not merely raised her voice but shouted. He couldn't remember her doing that before.

She stood still for a moment. Then she went on. 'Sorry. But you know it! We're just a bunch of Suncroppers grubbing away. They don't care what we do down here. Orbital got the rights to Lid all the planets in the Cluster and the only condition is they have to let enough light fall on the surface to maintain what life is there. And guys? We're down to forty. In their book that doesn't need too much light.'

A hand went up at the back. 'Aish?'

She looked, and smiled a little. 'Yes, Iverrs?'

The thin young man gulped. 'If, if there's not enough sun we can't be Suncroppers.'

She nodded. 'Good, Iverrs,' she said gently.

He gulped again, actually audible across the room. 'But, but, what else will we do?'

Aish glanced at the people standing next to the young man. One of them reached out a hand to him. 'Don't worry, Iverrs. It won't come to that. Look, come with me.' And the two of them left, with Iverrs's body language radiating anxiety.

Harmity watched them go. When the door had closed he turned round. 'Iverrs may be simple but he has a point!'

Aish sighed. 'Orbital doesn't care about Suncropping. Neither does the Cluster. We're not efficient; we just mop up what's left.'

'Which we then plug straight into the servers! No transmission losses! That makes us efficient.' Harmity glanced round the room, eyebrows raised. No one spoke. The silence seemed to embolden him, and he turned back to Aish, jabbing a finger. 'The bigger Skylid shades us more. Our own solar output goes down. Our crops grow less! What do we do? What are *you* going to do?'

Several people stood up, but Aish held up her hands. 'Before you all start? Last time I checked we were a "we", not a "you". Let's hold on to that.'

People nodded, and most sat down again. Only Harmity was left standing, with his arm still extended like an angry signpost. 'Very well. But *we* still need to decide what *we* are going to do about this.'

Aish nodded. '*We* do. And we will.'

The room was silent for a moment.

Zeb raised a hand. 'Have Orbital said anything about this? Or the Cluster?'

'If you mean, have I asked them, then yes. They haven't answered yet.' Aish sighed. 'Look, I'd be lying if I told you everything was decided, but I figure there are still some efficiencies we can go after. Look, you've all got stuff to do. I want a meeting of the Engineering group in three hours, guys. Can you make that?'

Half a dozen people nodded.

'Good. I'll keep on to Orbital, and meanwhile we'll get something sorted out. Thanks, everyone.'

It was dismissal and they knew it. Zeb watched for signs of resistance, but after a few seconds people began to stand and move away.

He nodded. Aish still had her authority. For the moment.

He waited until the room had emptied. Then he walked over to where Aish was still standing. 'Nothing personal, but you look knackered. You still trying to do this on your own?'

She gave him an impatient look. 'You had your chance to join in.'

'Had? Past tense?'

'It looks that way, unless you've changed. How many hours did you spend in vreality this last week?'

'Like you don't know the answer.' He looked away. 'Look, it's all on my free time.'

'It's *all* of your free time. You barely eat.'

They stared at each other for a moment. Then Zeb felt himself grinning. 'I used to enjoy these arguments when we were together, too.'

'You know, I sometimes think you truly did. I didn't. It's not good, Zeb.'

'Me or the solar?'

'The solar. I've given up worrying about you.' Aish shook her head, turned and walked off. He watched her cross the room, her back straight. Then he let his own back slump, wincing a little – maybe the immobile hours in vreality were catching up with him after all. He rolled his shoulders, causing a few clicks. Then he sighed. Aish was right. There was stuff to do.

At sundown, and even more tired than before, Zeb headed for the roof.

If the view from his room was good, the view from the roof was – astonishing. For a start, you could see the whole of the Skylid from here. At this time of day, with the sun below the horizon, you could see it even better. Given everything the thing meant to their lives it felt wrong to think it was beautiful, but, well . . .

It just was. Maybe that was why people mostly didn't come up here at night.

He had heard plenty of comparisons. Rainbows, flames, sunsets watched through a distorting chemical kaleidoscope. For his money they all fell short.

A Skylid was a layer, a film, a sheet, halfway between a vapour and a solid, one complicated molecule thick and as long and wide as you cared to make it. This one was quite small, as suited the planet beneath it: a disc a mere five thousand kilometres across. It probably weighed a couple of kilos.

Skylids were ancient technology. Zeb had heard that they had originally been made as an answer to the planetary overheating that had once been a widespread problem because of atmospheric pollution or just too much heat-generating stuff.

Richly ironic, these days.

Every molecule in the hazily diaphanous extent of a Skylid was a solar generator. Sunlight struck a Skylid, had the life sucked from it, and emerged as a pale ghost. The already cool planet beneath it got cooler. The waste heat from the huge server farms where most of humanity now lived in the vrealities was not enough to make up the difference.

But still – beautiful. Its orbit intersected the planet's

ionosphere, so that winds of charged particles played across its semi-conducting surface, giving up their energy to the power-hungry molecules with tiny bursts of coloured light.

Zeb had watched solar auroras on three real planets and a dozen virtual ones. There were no colours, no patterns, like it.

At the moment it looked like a code – vivid blobs stuttered across the sky so quickly that his eye could barely register them. The night before it had been as if the sky was a fractured mirror reflecting the birth – or death – of a star.

You could lose yourself in the sight. When the touch came on his shoulder he didn't know how long he had been there.

He tore himself away from the view, turned towards the direction of the touch, and sighed.

'Hi, Shol.'

She looked insulted. 'Hi yourself. Is that the best you can do? Sigh, and hi?'

'Sorry.'

'Don't apologize. You don't mean it.'

They watched the display in the sky in silence for a while. Then Zeb looked away from the shifting colours. 'Did Aish send you?'

'Did she fuck. I sent me. Zeb? Sometimes you can be a massive idiot.'

'But you and she?'

'Sure. Me and she. No change.' She watched him. 'Is that a problem?'

'No. Of course not.'

'Good. So, any intention of helping her out?'

'If I'm asked.'

She stared at him for a moment. Then her face darkened and her lips compressed. 'Oh, get over yourself. This is not about you!'

He shook his head. 'When did I say it was?'

'Well, you never behave as if it wasn't. Look, I haven't got time for this. You can add up as well as anyone here, so you know we have a major problem. One that could put us out of this business and right off this planet, Zeb.'

'Yeah, I know.'

'So? Get involved with it!'

'In what way am I not? I helped out today, didn't I?' Then he shrugged. 'Oh, don't bother. This is about vrealities, isn't it?'

Shol looked away, pointing her gaze at the lightshow that was the Skylid. Strobing colours flicked across her face. 'A bit. Aish thinks that's more of a symptom than a cause. That you're disengaged; maybe even depressed.' She turned back to him and rested a hand on his arm. 'You'd hardly be the first person in history to retreat to the virtual spaces to get away from the problems of the real one.'

'Well, thanks.' It was getting colder; he pulled away from her hand and wrapped his arms round his chest.

She took a breath, began to speak, stopped, and tried again. 'What is it, in there?'

He shook his head. 'I can't explain.'

'You need to. Look, people say you have a problem. That you're addicted. Zeb? I think they're right. People get addicted to vrealities just like they get addicted to anything else.'

The word stung. He waved a hand to bat it away. 'You're wrong, but even if you're right, so what? Where's the harm?'

'Ask Aish. Remember her? You used to be lovers.'

'*Fuck* you, Shol. We didn't split up because I went into the vrealities. It was the other way round. Things were bad between us, and I needed somewhere to go.'

'That's not what she says.'

'No shit.'

They were silent for a moment. The tight ball in Zeb's stomach was mostly anger, he told himself. Because there was no way it was going to be guilt.

Then Shol looked down at her hands. 'I can't protect you if you won't open up.'

'Protect me from who?'

'Everyone else. Zeb? How can you be so, so *dumb*?'

'I don't understand. I thought Aish was on side.'

'Oh for *fuck's* sake!' She threw her hands in the air. 'Aish *is* on side, just. But it's getting to the point where it doesn't matter if she's on side or not. And *I'm* getting to the point where I don't care enough about whatever it is you've got going on in there that I'm ready to see you drag her down. Get this: I care more about Aish than I do about this Collective, and believe me, right now I care a fucking sight more about this Collective than I do about you. So *give*!'

'Okay!' He realized he had shouted, and forced himself to pause, to breathe. At least to *act* calm, while he found the words.

She was watching him with waiting eyes. He sighed. 'Right. First, tell me this: when did you last visit a vreality?'

She shrugged. 'I don't know. Months ago. Why?'

'Humour me. Which was it?'

'Some gaming deck. You know? Some R 'n' R. I was in there a week, v-time.' Her expression hardened. 'I was back in ten minutes local.'

'Yeah. Same as everyone.'

'Everyone except you.'

He shook his head, ignoring the implied criticism. 'That's it. Drop in to the top level, fool around, game a little, maybe fulfil a few fantasies, and bounce out. That's all we do.'

'Sure it is. What else should we do?' Then she bit her lip. 'Oh, man . . . tell me you don't go into the full sim. Zeb?'

He said nothing.

'That's not our world, Zeb. You go right in, don't you?'

'Yeah.'

'Shit.' She looked down, and spoke at her feet. 'Why?'

'Why not? There's no law.'

'Oh, sure, and that makes it fine? It's just so, so . . . *intrusive*. Just wrong.'

They were both silent for a while. Then Zeb sat up straight. 'No,' he said. 'I'll tell you what would be wrong. A few lousy million of us, out here, burning up the last of our little lives feeding the servers and scratching a miserable living out of the bits of the planet that ever see the sun; half the planets in the Spin mined out or sucked dry, the other half fighting each other to death, actually killing *stars* for energy just so they can have another stupid war over the bones of some moon; the Cluster sitting up there counting their money and grinning their fat asses off – all for people who outnumber us a billion to one and live fifty generations in one of our days and don't actually fucking *exist*, and we never even get to *see* them? Find out what we're supporting? Feel something for them? Oh yeah. That'd be wrong, Shol.'

He found he was breathing hard. He lay back abruptly. A nub of rock dug into the small of his back. He ignored it, and turned his head a little so he could see Shol out of the corner of his eye.

She was looking at him sourly. 'You're talking like a Switcher.'

'No! No way.' He sat back up. 'The opposite. Isn't that obvious?'

'No. You said they don't exist. Isn't that what *they* say? Switch them off, they're not real?'

'They do. Not me. I care about what happens in there.'

Her eyes narrowed. 'More than you care what happens out here?'

'Not more. Different, I guess. And I have obligations, Shol. Obligations *to* the vrealities, and obligations *in* them.'

She sighed. 'Damn, Zeb, how stupid can you get? That's the addiction talking. You *can't* have obligations *in* the vrealities. It's philosophical nonsense. They're a simulation for a start. They're not real.'

'And we are?'

She gave him a level look. 'Just don't. Okay? And, your only obligation *to* them isn't to them at all. It's to the Cluster. They're the ones who keep the servers running, remember?'

'Yeah. And their friends Orbital Joule. The ones who just extended the Skylid? And all the other orbital companies across the Spin? They care so much about these not-real people that they're prepared to turn the so-called real worlds to bones and dust to keep them going? And I dunno, Shol. That sounds like a pretty major responsibility to me.' He looked at her. 'Maybe you could share it? You know – get involved?'

'Fuck you!' Shol got to her feet. For a while she stood like an angry pillar, silhouetted against the Lidlight. Then she looked down at him. 'I am not going to watch Aish work herself to death for you, you hear me? She can't run the place alone, and she can't fight off Orbital Joule alone either. I am going to drag your miserable hide into this no matter what you think. If the rest of you is still attached to it, fine. That's your choice.'

Zeb felt a grin breaking out. He stood up and turned to her. 'You mean, this is really about people after all? Well, shit, I'm in. You only had to say.'

For a moment he thought she was going to hit him; tension rippled through her in a human-scale reflection of the pulsing lights overhead. Then her shoulders dropped. 'I do *not* know how Aish put up with you.'

He laughed. 'In the end she didn't. You should thank me.'

'Patronizing is never good. She still wears that pendant thing you gave her.'

Zeb nodded. It had been a joke, almost: a dark red mineral sliver with the image of a star on it. He had meant it to remind her that there were still suns up there. He hadn't expected her to take it. Especially, he hadn't expected her to keep it now they weren't – whatever they had been. He knew that annoyed Shol.

He reached out a hand to the woman. 'Sorry. I'll do my best.'

'Does this mean you're going to spend less time in the vrealities?'

'No.' She stiffened, and he held up his hands, palms outward. 'You think I'm addicted, and I think I'm not. We aren't going to agree about that. But I'll lean into this one. Deal?'

She hesitated. Then she nodded. 'Deal.'

'Okay, good. Now, tell me something. What happened, that meant Orbital got permission to expand the lid?'

'How do you know they got permission?'

'How do you think they did it without? Orbital construction needs authorization from the Cluster, therefore they must have permission. Come on, Shol. Tell.'

'Okay. So, you're right that they got permission, but we don't know why.'

'Did anyone ask what we thought about it?'

'Kind of.' She sat down and rested her elbows on her knees. 'We were consulted, and we objected.'

'I take it we were ignored?'

'Yeah.'

'I don't remember hearing about this?'

She frowned, and the Lidlight made deep shadows in the furrows on her face. 'Yes, well, you were probably . . . busy.'

He stared straight ahead.

After a moment she sighed. 'Actually I was being unfair. No one heard about it, except Aish and me. People are feeling a bit unsure of things at the moment. We've lost numbers, everything seems hard going. You know?'

'Yeah. There was an atmosphere at that meeting.'

'I know. So we thought it was better to keep the problem quiet, until we were sure it was going to be a problem.'

He shook his head. 'I think that's a mistake, Shol. You don't get buy-in to anything by shutting people out of it. Seems to me you and Aish maybe need to climb out of your silo, before the rest of the team decide to drop a bomb in it.'

'Maybe. Aish has been very – strong. But she needs help, Zeb. We all need help, and since for some reason you seem to be still here, and although I *really* don't know why, Aish has some faith in you . . .'

She tailed off. He grinned at her. 'You know, for the first time I actually believe that she didn't send you.'

'Why, thank you.' Shol stood up, shivering. 'It's too cold for me. I'm going inside.'

'I'll stay out for a while.'

'And stare at that thing?' She gestured upwards.

'Yeah, well. Know your enemy.'

'Whatever. But Zeb? Don't forget your friends.'

He nodded. Then he said, 'Shol? Why does this matter so much?'

She smiled, a little sadly. 'It matters to Aish. You get that? And she matters to me. So I can't kick you off a cliff or drop you into a solar, much as I'd like to. Simple.'

This was getting too serious. Zeb mimed a sob. 'Oh, Shol. I thought . . .'

'Fuck off.'

He was going to say something else, but she had already turned and was walking away across the roof. Her boots crunched faintly over the frost-fractured layers of rock-flour and gravel. He listened until the sound faded, then lay back with his hands behind his head and gazed up at the Skylid. The air was freezing, and ice-haloes were beginning to form around the edges of the light. It was even more beautiful.

He barely noticed.

Freelance Charter (unnamed), Ice Blade, SCIOR

Experiment and its guttering little sun had lain just inside the edge of a constellation called the Ice Blade. When Skarbo had first arrived it had been newly won Baschet space, but it was nothing they much cared about and he had been allowed free choice in where he settled.

Since then it seemed to have changed hands, often. A resurgent Mandate had won it back, and then lost it, and then won it, and then lost it for the last time. It had briefly been owned – or claimed – by empires, collectives, industrial combines and, most recently, by a thing called the Sesqui-partite Council for the Improvement of the Outer Regions. But SCIOR, as it called itself, never met as a Council and did no improving, and Experiment went on being left to itself.

Now the Council was gone and the Baschet were back – again. And so was something calling itself the Mandate, which didn't look at all like the last Mandate, and so were a dozen others, and they were joining together, and hundreds of years of inert watchfulness had flown before them, leaving armed ships to fill the void.

The ships of the vast, combined fleet calling itself the Warfront.

*

95

Sleep had come for Skarbo in the end, but it was full of noise and the smell of burning. Now he was jolted awake. Alarms were blaring, a multitonal wide-spectrum noise that would have worked on any ear. He was trembling. He looked round, blinking. The soft light was gone, replaced by an unpleasant sharp blue that seared the eyes, and the mossy decoration on the walls and ceiling was swelling into something bulbous and squashy-looking. It was swelling quickly; already it had reduced the width of the space by half.

'Waaaark! *Fuck . . .*'

Skarbo's head snapped round. The cross-bar perch was encased in its own swelling balloon. The Bird's legs had been engulfed as well. It flapped furiously.

'Get off! Filthy . . . get o*ff*!'

There was a tearing sound and the legs came free. The Bird shot upwards, disappeared briefly into one of the growths on the ceiling and was expelled downwards like a surreal birth. It dropped to hover next to Skarbo. 'Bastard stuff! Don't need protecting.'

'Protecting?' Skarbo looked around. 'What's happening?'

'Ha! Miserable prey was right to be scared. Under attack! Ship's gone into impact mode.'

'Attack?'

'Must be. Serve them right.'

The trembling was worse. Skarbo tried desperately to calm down but the light and the alarm made it impossible. He gripped the side of the couch and hoped he didn't end up pulling his own claws off. 'Who?'

'How should I know? Might be a good thing, might be bad. Can't tell.'

'What should we do?'

'Wait it out. Nothing else to do. Probably won't take long.' The Bird dropped to the floor and let itself settle into a hollow in the soft stuff. 'Ha. Pretty comfortable when it's not trying to eat you.'

Skarbo sat back and closed his eyes. He was trying to be philosophical, but fear and anger were winning.

Then the ship shook, very gently.

The Bird looked up. 'Was that it? Think that was it.'

'That? How can that be it?' Skarbo glared at The Bird.

'Easy. Know how much energy it takes to make something this big wobble that much? That was plenty.'

Then there was another, slightly stronger shock.

The Bird wagged its head. 'Ah. Maybe not quite over? Could be another—'

It never finished the sentence. The ship seemed almost to hesitate, and then an appalling force took Skarbo and smashed him into the wall. Even with the soft covering, he felt as if the blow had crushed him – was still crushing him, holding him jammed so hard that he couldn't draw breath.

Another hesitation. He fell to the floor and lay winded. He had just long enough to hear The Bird saying something about field weapons before the force seized him again, wrenching him across the room. He crashed into the perch and swung round it, feeling his damaged leg tear away, and slammed into the far wall.

This time the force didn't stop. The room shuddered and there was a sharp groaning which vibrated him even through the deep covering.

The shuddering built in a crescendo that blurred his sight and hammered at his hearing. Then it stopped. There was a fraction of a second of breathless silence followed by a shattering concussion that seemed to crush Skarbo flat. For a long moment he had no sensation at all.

Then he was floating.

It was completely dark; he strained his eyes to the limit of their gain and detected nothing, not even the grey graininess of normal darkness. And quiet, too, but not totally so. It was a restless quiet, underlaid by a queasy rustle that sounded like something barely hanging together.

'Bird?'

There was a long pause. Concern; he got ready to try again. 'Yes.'

Skarbo breathed out. 'What happened?'

'Everything. Something. Something very powerful. How should I know? Stupid question. Better to ask what happens now.'

The concern was gone, replaced by a mixture of annoyance and relief. The creature sounded normal.

'Well, what does happen now?'

'Don't know that either.'

'No. I suppose not.' Skarbo explored his body cautiously. Apart from the missing leg, he seemed in one piece – even if most of the piece hurt. 'Can you get to the wall?'

There was a faint slur of air, like wings moving slowly. 'Yes. Not built for zero gee. But yes. Why?'

'To find a way out.'

'Out to what?'

Skarbo shook his head. 'The ship . . . what else?'

'Know what state it's in, do you? Know who's out there?'

'Well, no . . .'

'Bad idea. Not many possibilities. At worst, a hulk full of vacuum, or a ship full of hostiles. I'd prefer the hostiles. Unless you can exist in hard vacuum?'

Skarbo thought for a moment. 'I don't know,' he admitted. 'I've never tried.'

'Save it for emergencies then.'

He wanted to laugh. 'So what's this?'

'Don't know yet. Situation unknown, until someone opens the door. Get some rest.'

'Maybe.' It was unlikely. Zero gee and darkness were

disconcerting, and the site of his lost leg was painful. It helped to be thinking of something.

Then he opened his eyes wide. There had been a noise – and there was light, a slim, widening crescent. There was a quick hiss, and he felt his carapace flex a little. Pressure equalizing. At least that meant there was air.

'Ah!' The Bird clicked its beak. 'Answers! Wonder who?'

Skarbo didn't respond. He watched the crescent widen until it became the doorway. The light beyond it was dim, as if someone had turned the illumination in the ship down. Then his brain processed what his eyes had already known, and he felt himself go rigid with shock.

What was outside wasn't the inside of the ship.

He was close to one of the walls of the room. He reached out a claw and caught at the surface, moving as gently as he dared so as not to shove himself away. Then he pulled himself towards the opening.

The view expanded, became – vast.

They were inside a space. Shape and distance were difficult to judge. The far wall was a hazy violet blur that gave no clue to the eye. Stars shone faintly through it.

Skarbo felt something bump into him. There was a soft curse, and then claws walked up his back.

'Can't see through you. Oh . . .'

There was nothing to add.

The space was full of ships, stretching off towards the violet wall until they became too small to see properly, and between the ships were smaller things: pods and pieces of debris. Hardly any of them looked intact, and most were hideously damaged.

Skarbo found his voice. 'Bird? Where are we?'

For once the voice sounded subdued. 'Containment, maybe. That colour? Could be a field. Don't know. Don't know why it's full of air, either. Maybe it isn't. Maybe an oxygen bubble round us? But why? Don't know. Don't know anything.' It made a flapping noise. 'Don't like not knowing. It's about your turn to know something.'

'I'll do my best.' Skarbo stared out across the huge space. It wasn't completely still, he realized. In among the big things, there were signs of movement. Tiny stabs of light flickered, and here and there he caught a slight shift in a vast hulk, giving him a sudden mental image of the bloated corpse of some great sea creature, turning over uneasily in the surf. He shook his head and refocused on his immediate surroundings.

Then he startled, and almost lost his grip. Something was silhouetted in the doorway – an irregular mass about a metre across, with bumps and stalks and antennae. It was holding on to the edges of the opening with four flexible-looking legs.

It spoke. 'Life-form?' The voice was flat and metallic.

He peered at the thing. 'I suppose so,' he said.

'Are you tradeable?'

Skarbo was nonplussed. 'What do you mean?'

The thing bounced a couple of times. 'Tradeable, unit of exchange, perceived or actual value. Are you?'

'I don't know—' but then Skarbo felt claws digging sharply into his back.

'Yes!' It was The Bird. 'Definitely tradeable. The insect has high potential value. Strategic! Expert! What are you offering?'

The thing bounced again. 'Evidence. Require proof of worth. May take form of . . .'

There was a flash that seared Skarbo's optic nerves. When his vision cleared, he saw the remains of a couple of legs still gripping the edge of the opening. The rest of the thing was gone, and there was the sharp smell of complicated molecules burning.

The Bird floated round in front of Skarbo, its wings moving slowly. Despite what it had said, it actually looked very much at home in zero gee; Skarbo filed that thought away.

'Ooops,' it said, quietly. 'Wonder what did that?'

Skarbo gestured with his free claw. 'There's a choice,' he said, equally quietly.

There was. Things were approaching – a wild range of things, from centimetres to metres across. A few looked a bit like their first visitor, but as well as that there were featureless spheres and complicatedly aerodynamic-looking things and organic-looking things and – *things*. Most of them looked damaged.

A small dented cuboid shoved its way through the crowd. 'Apologies! The last machine was presumptuous. Also apologies for the abrupt removal from your last ship. To confirm – you are Skarbo?'

'Um, yes. Who are you?'

'Skarbo the Horologist?'

'Yes. Well, possibly ex-horologist. I don't really know. Again, who are you?'

'All.' The machine swivelled through a full turn. 'We are a collective. The other machine was a maverick. We don't tolerate privateers.'

The Bird clicked its beak. 'Who do you represent, then?'

'Ourselves, this place, and someone who would like to meet you.'

Skarbo looked at The Bird. It raised its wings at the shoulder. Shrug. He turned back to the little machine. 'What if I don't want to meet them?'

'Oh, you do. You just don't know it yet. Let's turn you round so you can see the rest of the view, shall we?'

The cloud of things dispersed, zipping back out of sight to leave just the little machine framed in the middle of the opening. There were busy clanks and scratching sounds through the walls and then the view began to move. Ranks of ships and wreckage circled past.

Then the movement stopped.

It became evident that they had been looking outwards

from their position in the vast space. Now they were looking inwards, towards the centre, and the light was much, much brighter.

Skarbo caught his breath.

The space was a sphere, and the centre of the sphere was on fire – a pulsing, flickering ball of yellow that fell just short of being unwatchably bright. It was surrounded by a cloud of wrecked ships and debris, dots to its fist, and as he watched a group of dots fell into it, leaving a brief, dirty red smear on its surface.

The machine started talking again. 'That's the other option. About twenty gigatonnes of molten metal, growing at one per cent a day. That's what this place mainly is – a furnace with a field round it. It's a crude way to recycle things, but it works.'

The Bird was keeping quiet. Skarbo found his voice. 'Everything in here goes in there?'

'In the end. Unless it's worth more sold than melted. That brings us back to you. Are you?'

'Worth more? I don't know.' The sight of the fireball was simplifying him; he couldn't think of anything more elaborate to say.

'Never mind. Why don't I turn off your anchor field and get the guys to give you one good push? Off you'd go. You'd be there in a few days. You're in an atmosphere bubble at the moment. We could leave that in place so you'd arrive with just enough oxygen to burn properly.'

Skarbo shook his head. Then something occurred to him. 'You said everything ends up in the furnace?'

'That's right.'

'But you don't. Why not?'

The machine didn't answer. Skarbo went on, 'I don't think you own this, and I don't think you started out here. Did you?'

He felt The Bird's claws tightening on his carapace. The machine floated a little closer and said, 'One good push, remember . . .'

'You aren't going to do that.' Skarbo felt his confidence growing. He looked round the group of ragged devices that had collected behind the little machine. 'I think you're scavengers.'

The Bird let go and swung itself round in front of him. 'Ha! Parasites. Skarbo's right. That's what you are! Ticks and fleas.'

'We prefer the word *symbionts*. Now, are you coming?'

Skarbo nodded. 'I suppose so.'

The journey took a while. The sphere was a hundred kilometres across, tiny by space-going standards, but the longest straight-line path anywhere inside it was the distance between two hulks, and the hulks were pretty close together, and the gaps between them were full of junk. Getting up any serious speed would have been suicidal.

Serious speed would have been disconcerting almost anywhere. They were in a kind of hemispherical basket made of metal strips, streaked black and brown with alternating bands of rust and burn. The strips were crudely fixed together with actual welds that had left lumpy beads along the joins. Skarbo scratched at one of the beads. His claw left a lighter brown streak in the rust. Real welds. Real rust.

The Bird watched him scrape. 'Just as well we're in a field bubble,' it muttered. 'Wouldn't trust them to make anything else airtight.'

Skarbo said nothing.

They had left their quarters behind, having watched the Factors give it the promised one good shove. Now they were edging between and around the motionless hulks and the unrecognizably twisted debris. Meanwhile their companion filled in the missing bits.

A Converter Sphere was basically an analogue of a very big single-celled organism. The outer field was the cell wall, the blob of molten ship in the middle was the nucleus. Charged particles in the outer field could store and change electrical

patterns just fast enough to imitate a primitive electronic pro-
cessor, well short of AI standards but good enough to count
ships. They changed their emissions spectra as it happened.
From the outside, a Sphere thinking hard looked a bit like coloured patterns on a soap bubble.

Spheres didn't think, or move, fast enough to be a real threat
to anyone, and what they did naturally was basically useful, so
people had left them to it for a hundred thousand years. No
one knew how many there were.

They existed to melt down dead spaceships, for money.
Mostly, Converters spent their time wandering round the
edges of mature civilizations browsing on the trash. Occasionally they were commissioned to do a specific clean-up job: if
the low orbit of your planet got too full of dead satellites for
comfort, and they were getting in the way of the yachts, you
called in a Converter. It gained the rights to the scrap metal
and maybe a small fee; you gained clear skies.

Most Converters worked more or less for themselves, most
of the time: every now and then, when the ball of molten metal
in the middle got too big, they would calve a huge blob, neatly
stratified by molecular weight, and sell it to someone.

But this wasn't most of the time.

This was war, and the war was about resources. Not just
raw materials, or water, or food, like the good old wars – this
war was about absolutely any resources at all.

Suddenly, Spheres and their contents were very valuable. So
much so that this one had been approached by no fewer than
eleven governments, armies and consortiums.

The Bird laughed at that. 'Do they all know about each
other?'

'Not my worry.' The little machine bobbed up and down. 'I
only live here.'

'Ransoming people, I suppose?' Skarbo frowned at it. 'Or is
that not your worry either?'

It bobbed again. 'To be honest, I don't worry about any-thing, but if you like worrying think of this: would it be better if I let every life-form that entered here end up as impurities in a ball of metal?'

Skarbo thought about that for a moment. 'I don't know,' he said. 'It depends what happens to them instead. But I assume that's not your department?'

The machine was quiet for a while. Then it said, 'This is a war. I'm not an expert, but it seems to me that the war was started by biological beings, like most wars. But for every tonne of biological stuff that ends up smeared across the ball, we send a gigatonne of metal into it. Some of that metal used to think. Do you worry about that? Or is it not your department?'

The Bird muttered, 'Ouch.'

Skarbo stared at the machine for a while. Then he turned and watched the hulks drifting past.

He wondered what they had thought about, and if they had been afraid.

Wall Energy Collective

'Zeb!'
          Something was digging into his ribs.
'Wake up!'
Digging in hard. He tried to turn over.
'Shit! Zeb, wake *up*, dammit!'
Something hit his shoulder. It hurt. He opened his eyes and managed to focus on a figure he recognized.
'Hey, Shol.'
'Oh, thank fuck . . .' She pushed her hair out of her eyes and he saw dark rings round them.
'What is it?'
'Trouble. Two sorts. Zeb, I'm sorry I hit you but you took so long to wake, I thought you'd got stuck somewhere.'
He shook his head. 'Just sleepy.' It was true, he was very sleepy. It felt wrong. He screwed his fists into his eyes and then levered himself up to a sitting position. 'Sorry, Shol. What time is it?'
'Daybreak plus two.'
He blinked. 'Then why's it dark?' The room was in half-light.
'Lens trouble. Three failures.'
'You're kidding.'

'I wish. We've lost twenty per cent of the total light in the last five hours.'

He stared at her. 'But that's crazy. Lenses don't fail. They just float there. Unless someone messes with them.'

She nodded.

'So someone *did* mess with them?'

'Aish thinks so. We'll find out when we look. Zeb, that means you. I need someone atmos-trained and you are. Were, at least. I'll be banksman.'

He swung his legs off the couch and stood up. 'Well, sure. But it's been a while since I went up. I'm kind of stale. Is there really no one else? What about Gesh and Xi? Or,' he paused, and sought names, 'ah, some of the others?'

'Geshwith and Xiparanafy were here last night. They're not here this morning. Nor are ten others – including Dekefstiel and all the recent atmos guys.' Her lips pursed. 'They all have names too but I guess you've been busy. It's been a while since you did much interacting.'

He ignored the comment. 'So where are they?'

'We don't know, yet. Still working on it.'

'Oh, shit . . .' He looked at her for a while. 'This is big, right?'

She nodded.

'How's Aish taking it?'

'Keeping calm. Making me proud. We owe her some of that back. Zeb? You gotta go.'

'Yes. Okay.' He straightened his back. 'Let's.' And followed her to the door, trying not to notice the weariness in her step.

They found Aish sitting in an alcove at the back of the room that multitasked as function space, meeting room and mess. It was the closest thing she had to a private office, and the impro-vised desk in front of her was usually littered with the paper notebooks which were her one real affectation. Once, while they were still an item, Zeb had suggested to her that the archaic devotion to paper was part of a rejection of the virtual.

It had been around that time that the relationship had taken a downhill turn, he remembered.

Now there were no notebooks. The place had a swept-clean look, as if Aish had subtracted her personality from it.

Tiny alarm bells sounded in the back of Zeb's mind. He sat down on the edge of the desk. 'Hey, Aish. I hear we've got to go atmos?'

She looked up, nodded, and looked down again. The alarm bells got louder, and Zeb glanced at Shol. She was biting her lip. He looked back to Aish, and forced himself to sound cheerful. 'That's fine. Is there any back-up or are we solo?'

She gave him a slow half-smile as if to say, *I know what you're doing.* 'Solo,' she said, and the smile faded. 'The others left. I found a message.'

'Left?' Zeb glanced at Shol. 'Left why?'

'Resigned. Gave up. They think there's no point. We should just switch everything off.'

Zeb and Shol exchanged looks. Then Shol let out a breath. 'Oh, Aish. They were so wrong.'

'Were they? Are you sure?' Aish gazed up at her with bleak eyes. Then she shook her head and did the half-smile again. 'Okay. Yes, I guess. Guys? There are three lenses out of place. Zeb, you get your arse up the Lines and fix them. Shol, you stand banksman.'

Zeb stood up and gave a stagey salute. 'Yes, ma'am.' He saw Shol open her mouth and kicked her softly. She closed it, and they left.

Outside the hall they stopped. Zeb looked at Shol. 'You ever seen her like that?'

She shook her head.

'Me neither. We'd better do what she says, Shol, but the difficult bit's going to be deciding what to do *next*.'

'Yeah. Zeb? Even more, you've got to stay engaged. You hear me?'

'I hear you.'

The tiny spartan capsule *bump-bumped*, and rose, and *bump-bumped*. Zeb gripped the frame of his seat and tried not to bang into things. He managed to open the comms.

'Shol? I think there's something wrong with this one.'

Bump-bump.

'Why?'

'It's really uneven.'

'Could be, yeah.'

He raised his eyebrows. 'Should I be concerned?'

'Don't know.'

'Okay, thanks for that.'

Bump-bump.

Shol was not feeling sympathetic, which was understandable. Maybe if he admired the view instead?

It was pretty good. Nearest the window, the segmented prehensile claws reached upwards, closed around what looked like nothing at all – *bump-bump* – and hauled the little capsule another two metres upwards.

The nothing at all, if he moved so the angle was just right, became visible as a fine, bright filament. It was actually not one but two parallel ancient-tech fullerene tubes bonded to each other to make a flat cable just under a millimetre across – and therefore colossally over-engineered – one of a narrow tripod of guy-wires ten kilometres high.

At the top of the tripod eight lenses formed a slowly rotating circular array, held taut by their rotation against their own much thinner tubes. From close up the array looked a bit like a flower. From down here it was still a dot, getting very slowly brighter.

It took a Tower Bug about two hours to climb to the array. Zeb was one hour into his journey, and the uneven motion was making him feel sick.

A Bug was a pressurized pod, just big enough to sit in, with three articulated claw-tipped hydraulic arms. It could use two together to haul itself up a cable, sticking the third out for stability and using it to swap to another cable if one was near enough to reach. It was a slow but safe way of accessing guy-wire structures, avoiding the potential damage from using heavier-than-air craft with their hot engine exhaust and their cable-knitting propellers.

Safe, that is, as far as the wires were concerned. Zeb had never felt sure about the safety of the passengers.

Two team members at a time, but only one in the air: wire-climbing was done by two trained people at once, but one of them always stayed on the ground, and only left it if the other needed rescuing. This time he was in the air and Shol was on the ground, and she hadn't needed to explain to him why that was the right way around. So, concentrate on the view.

Beyond the guy-wires, the world was divided into three horizontal bands. Below, the Plains, blurred by freezing fog that shone a little in the twilight. In the middle, blue-black sky, growing darker by the minute as he climbed and as the day drained away. Above, and a kilometre off ahead of them, the line of the Skylid.

It looked beautiful from this angle, too, and Zeb felt even guiltier at the thought.

Bump-bump.

Bump.

Zeb pulled his eyes away from the distance. The Bug had stopped, its upper claw frozen in the act of clamping round the guy. It swung a little, which somehow felt much more sinister than the jolting of the climb.

He hadn't stopped it. There was a basic display panel in front of him. It should have been alive. Apart from a single, lonely tell-tale, it wasn't. The little light blinked slowly – back-up power was available but not much else, apparently.

He cleared it and opened the comms. 'Shol?'

Nothing.

He tried again. 'Shol?'

The comms fizzed. 'Yeah. Sorry. I was running a few tests. Well, trying to.'

'I lost power. I'm on back-up.'

'We all lost power. That's what I was testing.'

'Oh.' The two tubes were conductors; smart pads on the gripping surfaces of the Bug's claws picked up power that was fed into the system at the base. Except now it apparently wasn't.

He waited. After a while Shol was back. 'Okay, our problem just got much bigger. Someone told Orbital Joule we lost half our remaining people, and they unfurled another big section of Lid.'

'Shit. How big?'

'It takes us down another twenty per cent – and we don't have twenty per cent. Not with those lenses down. Zeb? This is bad.'

'Yeah.' He thought. 'Listen, I have to go on up.'

'Yes, I think you do. How do your batteries look?'

He glanced at the tell-tales. 'Okay, but they could be lying. How long should they last?'

She paused. 'If the cells are in good shape there's enough for a full ascent plus fifty per cent. Getting back down's easier, of course.'

'Yeah. Easier.' It was: in an emergency you just unclamped from the guy and fell, trusting that the parachute was still working, and assuming there was anything left to get back down to. Zeb looked round the worn surfaces inside his Bug. 'How old are these cells, would you say?'

'As old as the Bugs are, I guess.'

'That's what I thought.' Zeb looked down at where the Base should have been glowing below him. It wasn't, but his imagination filled in the picture of Shol sitting in semi-darkness in the comms room. It suddenly seemed very important to know that there was a human being somewhere near him.

He cleared his throat. 'Shol, I need you to stay on line.'

'Will do.' She hesitated. 'As long as the power lasts. We're in trouble here.'

'Yeah. But not just us. I've been thinking, Shol. A bunch of people left in a huff, right? Saying it's time to switch off?'

'So?'

'So, what's the best way to switch off the vrealities? Take out the power supply. That's us.'

She was quiet for a moment. Then she said, 'Zeb, we're only a few per cent of the local grid, tops. Taking us out doesn't change the vrealities.'

'Yeah, but maybe it's not just us. Hang in, Shol. I'll see you down there.'

He waited for the *okay*. Then he breathed out, checked his display and tried to remember what the tell-tale was really telling him about the state of the back-up power. Healthy, probably – and misleading, very possibly.

Whatever. He powered up the controls and let the Bug resume its hesitant journey.

Bump-bump.

That much hadn't changed.

The tower didn't finish at the lens array. Above it, a single rope twisted from three more nanotubes extended another ten kilometres out, above the atmosphere and beyond the Lagrange point. On the end of the rope was a bob weight, whirling round the planet like the stone at the end of a slingshot, which kept the whole structure in tension. It was mathematically elegant, but technically crude – the sort of thing you did if you were improvising from a centuries-old parts bin.

Bump-bump.

The guys were getting closer together. Above him the lens array had turned from a dot to a circle, and then to a ring of circles which expanded until it was wider than his field of view.

When he was just metres below the array he stopped. The cell read-out hadn't changed, which made him trust it even less, but for the moment he still had power. He spoke to the comms.

'Shol? You okay?'

There was a pause. Then a voice, sounding distant as if he was at the far edge of its range.

'Not much to report. Power's running down. You?'

'I'm nearly there.'

'Can you see anything?'

'Nothing to see. The array looks fine, but I'm a hundred metres below it. Going to creep the rest of the way and then take a close look; plug into some diagnostics.'

'Okay. Be careful.' He could hardly hear the voice.

'I will.'

He took hold of the climb-handle and set the Bug crawling upwards on its slowest speed setting so that the arms reached and hauled barely half a metre at a time. He wasn't quite sure why, but it felt right.

Five minutes later the Bug snuggled up against the bulbous structural joint where the guys were tied to the delicate metal-and-glass flower of the array, and stopped. The Bug was quite capable of climbing round the joint and heading further up, but there was no need because the bit Zeb was interested in was at array level.

He woke the part of the board that handled diagnostics and let it look for a connection to the A-sub-I that ran the system.

A short pause. Then a couple of lights blinked once, and settled down to a sullen purple glow. Zeb pursed his lips. The little machine was alive, but not talking – the equivalent of the lights being on, and someone home, but definitely no visitors please.

It *could* just be a regular failure, he told himself. As well as being nearly mindless it was very old and very second-hand: it had been running various kinds of remote energy plant for thousands of years at least, switched from job to job by whoever chanced to own it at the time. And after all, everything the Wall Collective built, owned or managed to steal was second-hand, lashed together to last for just one more job. It was a metaphor for something, and not just for the Collective.

But the old A-sub-I was also very tough. Simple meant strong, especially if the simple thing was in a radiation- and debris-proof casing, had no moving parts and used a baby closed-loop fusion reactor that was almost everlasting. Therefore he didn't believe himself. It shouldn't go wrong.

He tapped his fingers on the console. Then he sighed and switched the comms from pod-to-pod to general broadcast. He thought for a while, then took a breath. 'Okay,' he said. 'I'm up here. From the state of the array control I guess you are too. I can find out what you've done here, and I reckon in a while I'll be fixing it, but I'm guessing it didn't break itself – so for now, let's talk instead.'

Nothing. He tried again.

'Hello?'

And waited, counting heartbeats.

He had got to a hundred, in what felt like a pretty short time, when the comms spoke.

'Hi. It took you a while.'

He stared at the display. 'Bugs aren't that fast. Especially if someone cuts off their mains power. Who is that?'

'Dekefstiel. Hello, Zeb.'

Zeb breathed out. 'Just you, or others as well?'

'Just me. The others have gone on. I thought I'd wait for you.'

'Me especially? How did you know it would be me?'

'It was easy to guess. You're the vreality addict, and you and Shol are the only atmos-trained people left down there. And Shol was always going to stay on the ground. Hence, you.'

At the mention of Shol, Zeb reached out and quickly toggled the comms to ground. Nothing; not even pilot tone. Shol had faded out. Suddenly he wanted very much to be down there.

That wasn't an option yet. He switched back to broadcast.

'—going to ask what's going on up here?'

'Okay – what?'

'We took out the array. Obviously.'

'Are you going to take out the rest?'

There was a pause. 'No. Not yet. We want to talk before we do that.'

Zeb felt his heart racing. *Not yet.* That meant *some time*, and without the arrays there would be no *down there*. He forced himself to sound calm. 'Talking to me isn't the same as talking to the whole Collective.'

'I know. But people listen to you. Aish listens to you.'

'She used to.'

'Don't piss around.' The voice was sharp. 'You haven't got time and neither have I.'

Zeb raised his eyebrows. 'You're starving the Base of power. People are going to die if that doesn't change. What do you want?'

'Well, long term, a real civilization with a proper stakeholding in real planets.'

Zeb laughed. 'I could have guessed that. Shit, I could have *written* it. And I'd have ignored it. Try again. Start with the bit where you want all the vrealities switched off.'

There was a laugh in the voice. 'Okay, fine. We want all the vrealities switched off.'

'And I don't. If that's all there is this won't be a long conversation.'

'Zeb, I could just take the whole array down.'

'Yes. And the Lid. And everything else. And kill all your friends. And see how long it takes for the Belt to catch up with you.' And, he thought, we're using up some more of that time you haven't got.

Dekefstiel didn't sound concerned. 'With respect, I don't think they're my friends, and you're the one hanging by one claw ten kilometres above the ground. Look, this is me being reasonable. We don't just want to shut everything down, you understand? We want a compromise.'

Zeb laughed. 'What kind of compromise? Like, just kill off a couple of trillion and leave the rest in peace?'

'Just killing them off isn't what we want.'

'The fuck it isn't. You're Switchers.'

'And you're oversimplifying. You know the vrealities better than anyone, don't you?'

'I don't know. Possibly. So?'

'What's the speed ratio?'

Zeb shook his head. 'It varies. Where are you going with this?'

'Roughly?'

'Couldn't we have discussed this at ground level?'

'We're discussing it now. Come on.'

'Well, okay. A few hundred thousand to one. So?'

'So, let's agree a time.'

For a moment Zeb didn't understand. Then he said, slowly, 'Are you talking about a deadline?'

'Call it a lifetime. Many, many lifetimes – say, half a million years?'

'Or half a year, as I call it. And then?'

'And then, we power down. Respectfully, if you like. We could even have a ceremony.'

Zeb stared at the comms. 'You have to be fucking joking,' he said eventually.

'Why?'

'Where do you want me to start?' He shook his head. 'Okay, forget that you think it's okay to kill a trillion people. Forget you think waiting six months before you kill them makes a difference. *Seriously* forget that you just suggested a ceremony. A ceremony! With what? A respectful speech and some sad music? Forget all that. But suggesting it to me? Me? Really?'

He had tried to sound calm but by the time he got to the last word his throat had tightened and his voice was rising. He reined himself in and waited.

Dekefstiel sounded amused. 'Yes, you. Really. If you want someone to make a difference, start with someone difficult. I'm starting with you. Tell me something – why do your friends down below want to keep the vrealities running?'

Zeb felt himself growing wary. 'Because they – we – have a contract.'

'Yes. Simple enough for them, isn't it? They do the day job in the real world and stay out of the pretend one. But you don't care about contracts, Zeb.'

Zeb didn't answer.

There was a long silence. When Dekefstiel broke it, he sounded brisker. 'Whether you like it or not, the future of intelligent life lies out here, Zeb. Not in there.'

'Fine. You think that, and I think that makes you less like intelligent life than the people in there. So what? Just kill me. That ought to do it.'

Dekefstiel laughed. 'If you were the only obstacle? Certainly. We might even give *you* a ceremony. But you aren't. There are whole planetary systems with entrenched economic models that have only one purpose, and you know it. We're growing, and we'll get there, but we need people behind us. Not in our way.'

'Join your movement. Is that it?'

'There's no movement to join, as far as I'm concerned, and if there was I doubt if you'd go that far. Not publicly.' Dekefstiel paused. 'But privately, maybe? You wouldn't be the only one.'

'Oh, I bet I wouldn't.' Zeb felt anger crackling inside him. 'Same as I bet that the guys who abandoned us down there didn't just have an overnight conversion, right?'

'You'd need to ask them.'

'I won't bother. They're probably too busy listening to you whispering in their ears.' Zeb shook his head violently. 'This has gone on long enough. I'm going to fix this array, and if I ever meet you, I'm going to fix you too. Got it?'

He had shouted the last few words. It felt good.

'Okay, whatever you say.' The voice was regretful, though still a little amused. 'But you might find that some things are harder to fix than you think – and much harder to get down from, afterwards. And Zeb? We are going to win.'

The signal cut before Zeb could reach the comms to kill it. He stared at the board for a moment, while all the things he still had to say to Dekefstiel bounced round his head. Then he let out a growl and flicked back to downward comms – still nothing.

He compressed his lips and turned to the array and its unresponsive A-sub-I. He had projected plenty of certainty at Dekefstiel, but that hadn't left much for himself. He had no idea what they had done to the system.

Well, it was time to find out. He fired up the full diagnostics suite, enabled the forced-entry function and set it loose on the sullen patient. The board display lit up to show a pool of rapidly changing numbers and symbols which Zeb couldn't read, but which he knew was a mind-map of the little machine.

He watched them, imagining that the diagnostics was some ancient cutting tool in the hands of a barber-surgeon, slicing down through skin and bone and muscle tissue and gristle to expose the heaving guts beneath . . .

The diagnostics gave an assertive buzz. The randomly wandering symbols flashed once and became a uniform pattern.

They were in. Zeb rubbed his hands and reset the diagnostics to 'investigate'.

The board flashed again, and this time it didn't dim; the symbols brightened through the spectrum until they were a glaring blue. Zeb raised a hand to shield his eyes and craned back in his seat.

Then the board began to smoke.

'Shit!' Zeb fanned away the smoke and, when more joined it, edged himself sideways off the seat and shrank back against the wall of the Bug, as far as he could get from the flaring device. As he watched between carefully parted fingers there was a sharp buzz like an old-fashioned electrical circuit shorting and then a *crack*. The whole board jumped a few centimetres upwards and then settled back on its pedestal.

The glare was gone. The smoke drifted upwards and formed a hazy disc in the curve of the ceiling.

Zeb lowered his hand slowly and got ready to move forward. Then he stopped. There was something . . . He pressed himself back against the wall of the Bug, tensed, and recoiled.

That was it. The wall was getting warm. He tried again. Definitely. And warmer now – becoming hot.

His stomach leapt. Batteries. The fucking *batteries* were behind that wall.

There was nothing he could do. He moved away and waited. He could feel the heat radiating off the metal, and the already smoky interior of the Bug was beginning to smell of hot structure.

There was a soft, almost disappointing *boom*, and the Bug

119

wobbled, just hard enough to make Zeb stagger backwards and bang his head on the wall.

'*Ow!*' He rubbed his skull. Then, as the pain faded, he let himself slide down the wall until he was hunched on the floor.

Without power – and he definitely *was* without power, because he could feel the Bug cooling down already – that was it.

He couldn't even release the claw from the guy and fall because the claw release was on the control board, and everything on the board had an unhelpful melted look. He reached up and prodded it anyway, just to make sure, and nodded. Completely fried – geriatric plastic welded to more geriatric plastic. One more prod, and a big piece of the corner of the board fell off and clattered on the floor.

It had been a hack, and an aggressive one. They had used the old A-sub-I as a conduit for an attack that had completely overwhelmed whatever passed for the brains of the Bug. It seemed to be over; he assumed that there wasn't anything much left to hack.

He laughed. Game over, basically. Time to wake up. Except that he was awake, and there was nowhere to go. He wondered if dying of cold was better or worse than asphyxiation, and which would come first.

'Ah, fuck it.' He repeated the words, much louder, so that they bounced round the inside of the metal coffin. 'Fuck it!'

Then he froze. The Bug had moved – a definite sideways jink. He stood up, and by the time he was upright there had been another, and another – a little kick every couple of seconds. He glanced outside but there was nothing there except the milky film of the Skylid, now just below him, and the midnight blue-black of high-atmosphere near-space above it. But the Bug kept twitching, as if someone was gently plucking the guy.

Then he felt his eyes widen. Not plucking – climbing. That had to be it. Another Bug must be coming up the guy to rescue him.

He grinned. There was only one other Bug and only one person left down there who could work it. He grinned wider and spoke the name out loud to help make it true.

'Shol.'

Well, he couldn't contact her; even the bits that weren't fried had no power. He just had to wait. He sat down again and began counting twitches.

He had never bothered working out how many times a Bug had to extend and grab and pull to haul itself up this far. Now he did, and came to around five thousand.

It was definitely getting cold. A Bug in motion was heated by the waste energy from the crude hydraulics of the arms. Now the only source of heat was Zeb. Not enough. He wrapped his arms around himself and went on counting.

The first thousand seemed to take a very long time. At fifteen hundred he began to count out loud, and the words came out on curls of mist, but by three thousand his throat was sore and he seemed to have trouble getting enough breath to push the long strings of syllables out.

'Three thousand, one hundred ... and ... twenty ... three ...'

He made himself count aloud as far as four thousand. Then he gave up. There wasn't enough air (and the bit of him that was still thinking clearly said no, that wasn't right, it wasn't air, it was the other thing and there was too much of it, not not enough) and he was shivering too much to form the words.

And then he lost count, and it didn't seem to matter.

He hoped Shol would be there soon ...

His eyes snapped open. There was a *clang* and the Bug jumped sharply.

She was here.

Something was bothering him. What did you do, now? There was something. If his head would just stop aching for a minute he could *think*. He shuffled his hands along the floor to prop himself up, and one of them found something hard. It was the broken-off piece of control board.

Ah, yes. That was it.

He picked up the board, selected a spot and whacked it, corner downwards, against the floor. And again.

The noise rang round his skull. He waited for it to subside, and listened.

Bong.

Yes; an answer. Shol knew he was in here and alive. Now it was over to her to do whatever she was going to do.

He hoped she would be quick.

His hope was justified. Even as he propped himself against the wall to wait, he realized that the air didn't seem quite so cold as before. He swirled the palm of his hand around in widening circles on the metal above him; then, at the limit of his reach, yanked it away sharply with an exclamation.

That patch was too hot to touch. As he watched, a circle a bit smaller than the palm of his hand began to glow.

Fuck, she was burning her way through. He backed as far away from the spot as he could, his heart clattering against his ribs, as the circle brightened to a vivid yellow. There was a sputtering noise. Then the incandescent metal bulged upwards and outwards in the middle and disappeared.

For a second, air roared out through the hole. Then there was a hollow, echoing *pop* and the roaring stopped.

His ears hurt. And his throat. And, still, his head. But breathing seemed easier. He shuffled over to the hole and called through it.

'Shol?'

There was a pause. Then a voice said, 'No. Sorry. I'm not Shol.'

The voice sounded as if it was talking through a gulp.

It couldn't be . . . Zeb swallowed. 'Iverrs?'

'Yes.' Another gulp. 'Sorry. Shol said you were up here but then she went somewhere and I couldn't find her and everyone was busy because the power was draining. So I came. I thought you would know what to do. Zeb? I think something really bad has happened.'

Zeb shut his eyes for a moment. The boy was right about everything except for the bit about *has happened*. It was still happening – and now he had another responsibility.

He took a deep breath of the air that Iverrs had brought with him, not daring to think about how long it might last, and said, 'What about Aish?'

'She went to talk to Orbital Joule. No one knows when she'll be back. I was worried. Sorry.'

'Okay.' Another breath. 'Iverrs? First thing. I'm really glad you're here, so you can stop saying sorry. Yes?'

'Yes. Sorry.'

'That was a start. Now, we have to get back down.' Translation – I have to get both of us back down. 'How much power have you got?'

'I can link with your system, then you'll see—'

'No!' He balled his fists. He had shouted. He mustn't shout, and also he mustn't do anything to worry Iverrs. He chose his words carefully. 'My turn to say sorry – but don't try to link. My system had . . . a failure. It could compromise yours.'

'Okay. I won't.'

Zeb waited for the *sorry*. It didn't come, and he nodded slowly. 'Fine. Now, how's your power? The three lights on the top of the board. Can you see them?'

There was a pause. 'I know where they are. Two greens, one amber.'

'Good. That's good.' It *was* good, but it could change. Would change, unavoidably, because those reserves were now trying to heat and recycle air in two Bugs not one, and would be doing even more double duty soon.

In other words, get on with it.

'There's no way to get me into your Bug, so we need to think of something else. Is your mobility okay?'

'Yes.'

'Right. I've got no power, Iverrs. Nothing – so if anything's going to happen it's going to be through you.' Something occurred to him. 'Ah, how many times have you worked one of these things?'

'This is my first time. The others would never let me.'

'Yeah. That's what I thought.' Zeb stared out and down over the Skylid. Expertise wasn't on offer, then.

'Zeb? I can help. They wouldn't let me really do it but I studied. I remember the whole manual. It's easy.'

'Oh good.'

'No, sorry, I mean it.'

Zeb shook himself. He was tired, that was all. 'Okay, Iverrs. I've got an idea. With your knowledge, we'll give it a go.'

A couple of hours ago he had been certain he was dead. Now he was just nearly certain, which shouldn't have felt worse but did.

Of course, the trouble was that he was nearly certain Iverrs was dead, too.

That felt lousy.

An hour later they were ready to try. Either way, it would be the first and last attempt.

'How's your power now?'

'Three amber lights. According to the manual that means half-reserve.'

'Good.' It wasn't, particularly, but the boy's voice was brisk with tension and Zeb really, really needed him not to panic.

He cleared his throat. 'So, let's go.' And held on tight.

'Yes.'

Nothing for a moment, and then the pod gave a tiny lurch to one side. Zeb braced himself for more, but that seemed to be it. He slowly unclenched his hands. 'That felt fine from here. Okay down there?'

'Yes.' Still terse – but phase one had worked. Iverrs's pod had inched upwards far enough to lift Zeb's slightly, so the strain was off the one claw Zeb was hanging by. Now he had to rely on the boy's photographic knowledge of the instruction manual. He had been right so far – under his guidance Zeb had already levered off a cover plate near where the arms sprouted from the outside of the pod. The arms were hydraulic, a technology even older than the fullerene ropes they clasped, and behind the cover was a knot of curling pipes and squat little valve things.

Zeb had located the flat stud that bled off pressure from the claw circuit. In his mind he had pressed it a dozen times – as briefly as possible, Iverrs had said. Enough to loosen the claw, without opening it so far that it lost its hold on the guy.

Now he steeled himself. 'Okay, Iverrs. Here we go.'

And pushed his finger against the stud.

At first it didn't move, and he pushed harder. Then it gave suddenly, and he jerked his hand back from it in a panic.

Nothing seemed to have changed. He swallowed. 'I did it. Not sure if anything happened. Can you tell?'

'No. Sorry.'

'That's what I thought.'

'Zeb? One red light.'

Zeb shook his head. They were out of choices. 'Okay, then. Time to go, I think. Iverrs? Nice and slowly, please.'

He held his breath. For a few very long seconds, there was nothing. Then the pod lurched a little to one side – and dropped smoothly through a metre or so before coming to a halt with a metallic clang.

It had worked. Zeb's pod was resting on the one below it, steadied by a loosely sliding claw on the guy above it. He realized he had expected any one of several possible sorts of failure, but not success.

He let out the breath. 'Okay, we're in business. Down we go.' And, with a flash of shame that it was an afterthought, 'Well done. I think you saved both of us. Now we'd better get back down and save everyone else. Did you read any other instruction manuals?'

'No. Sorry.'

'Well, we'll work it out when we get there.' He thought for a second and added, 'Trust me.'

'Of course.'

Of course. Zeb nodded. Iverrs had run out of people to trust down there. That's why he had come looking. It wasn't a good thought.

The pod twitched, and then again. Iverrs had started them heading downwards. He didn't seem to need to talk, which was just as well because Zeb needed not to. If he'd had any comms he would have had another go at raising the Wall, but the comms was as dead as the rest of the pod, and he didn't want to ask Iverrs. So instead he stared out over the pearly mist of the Skylid, and listened with his muscle-memory to the half-new, half-familiar bumping of his pod against the one below, and worried. At least the Skylid looked serene. He wondered why the Switchers hadn't interfered with that instead.

The movement was almost relaxing, and he was beyond tired.

'Zeb?'

He levered his eyes open. He must have slept – the Skylid was above them instead of below.

'Zeb? Are you okay?'

The voice sounded sharp, like someone keeping a lid on panic. The sound hot-wired Zeb to alertness. 'Yes. I'm here, I'm fine. What's the matter?'

'I can see something.'

'Where?'

'Outside. Towards the Skylid. I don't know what it is.'

He blinked, and tried to focus but the featureless surface of the Lid was hard to fix on. Then his eyes did the job for him and he realized that the thing Iverrs had seen was nearer – much nearer. Without looking away from it he called out.

'Iverrs? Like a fat black line?'

'Yes. I saw it first as we passed the Skylid.'

Zeb glanced upwards. That must have been a while ago. He chewed his lip. 'Has it done anything?'

'Not at first. Now I think it's getting bigger.'

Zeb watched the thing. 'So do I.'

'Do you know what it is?'

'No.' Uncertainty was probably not a good idea. Quickly he added, 'How are the batteries?'

'One amber. Two red.'

'Uh-huh.' The thing was definitely getting closer, but not close enough to resolve detail. Then it dropped below the background of the Skylid, and suddenly what had looked like a black line against the light background morphed into a chain of dots, silver in the Lid-light, growing larger. Then it – they – tipped forwards and became three featureless discs. They were closing fast.

'Do you know what it is now?'

The voice sounded flat.

Zeb shook his head. 'No, I still don't.' He watched the things for a moment. Whatever they were, they didn't look friendly.

He fought to sound calm. 'Listen, you've still got power enough to disengage, right?'

'Yes, but you'll fall if I do—'

'I'd be okay. Look, be ready just in case?'

The discs were losing height as they got closer. They were heading underneath the pods, and the thought crystallized in Zeb's mind.

Three discs. Three ropes.

They dropped out of sight, and the words were out before Zeb had time to think about them.

'Iverrs? Disengage. Now!'

'But—'

'Now!' He searched desperately for something to make it happen. 'I don't want you! *Go away!*'

There was something like a sob, and then the slap of a hand on a control, magnified by the echo of the metal pod. Zeb squeezed his eyes shut and waited for the jolt and the fall. He hoped Iverrs's chute was working.

And there was the jolt – but not the fall. Instead, the pod slewed into a violent launch upwards that threw him back against the side wall, then crushed him to the floor. And then, a sickening, spinning free-fall.

He flailed both hands and felt his fingers closing around the base of the console. Then he opened his eyes.

Motion. Black sky, and then a gently turning Skylid, and then the thin silver-grey curl of a severed cable, and then something he couldn't make out. It was like a shell, a scooped-out hemisphere, spinning towards him. There was something in it . . .

Then it tumbled past him and he saw. It wasn't a shell. It was half a pod, and the something was Iverrs. He had been cleanly sliced in two.

It must have been the cable. And the last thing he had heard would have been Zeb, telling him to go away.

The half-pod whirled away, and now he was falling faster. He didn't care.

Time to go away.

The impact was an instant, timeless white explosion behind his eyes. Then nothing.

Brasedl Space, ex-Mandate, Sphere

Without really knowing why, Skarbo had expected the wreckage to thin out as they approached the edge of the Sphere, but if anything there seemed to be more of the stuff. It was smaller, too, and increasingly densely packed together so they had to nose through, using the bubble-field to push things out of the way, which made the craft wobble uneasily. But for the field he could have reached out and grabbed pieces of debris from the hollow sphere of junk that was closing in around them.

He turned to the machine. 'Why is it so thick? We can hardly get through it.'

'Exactly.'

He waited, but it didn't seem inclined to say more. He looked down at The Bird, which was perching on a bit of metal that stuck out a little more than the rest. It was staring forwards, its eyes fixed. Then it snapped its beak. 'There. Thought so!'

'Thought what?' Skarbo looked up, following its gaze. 'Oh . . .'

The dense mass of junk in front of them had parted and they were in clear, black space – a bubble with walls of close-packed debris. He turned round to look at the section where they had just burst through; a dim back-scatter of light from their craft showed pieces slotting themselves back into place until there was no sign of a hole.

He looked at the machine. 'Very clever. What do you keep here?'

'Keep, that's not quite the right word. Curate, perhaps. Or tend. How good are your eyes? Can you see anything yet?'

'My eyes are eight lifetimes old, machine. They're nearly dead.'

'But they started from a high baseline, I believe. *Much* better than human.'

The Bird laughed. 'Little thing's been checking you out, old insect. Nothing to hide now.'

Skarbo gazed at it for a moment. In the dim light all he could see was a tiny glint, reflected off a round, black eye. 'What would it find if it checked you out, *bird*?'

'Ha. Not a bird. Nothing to check. Feathers and wings and fuck all else. You going to do any looking?'

'Yes.' He gazed forwards, and then to the sides, but he didn't know what he was looking for. Then, at the limit of his vision, the darkness began to resolve into shapes, and he saw it.

The darkness in front of them and above them and below them and to both sides wasn't empty darkness. It was full of ships.

He watched the grey shapes slide past. They weren't all the same, but they had certain things in common: blocky, brutal designs with no ornamentation, no concession to grace. Some were like cones joined back to back, and others misshapen cuboids. One was an elaborate cluster of different-sized spheres, each a very slightly different shade in the faint light. They were closer together than the hulks outside had been, and many of them were elaborately scarred and streaked with what he assumed was weapons damage – but they all looked whole.

There was something about them that made him feel uneasy. He turned to the machine. 'How many are there?'

It didn't answer immediately. Then it just said, 'Many.'

'And they are?'

'What you can see.'

He nodded. Many ships. He was still feeling uneasy. He had felt unease out in the main sphere, among the wrecks, but that was the unease of being amongst death and silence, if vacuum could be silent. Here was silence, yes, but not death. He searched for the word.

Yes: watchfulness. And he thought, *They're not dead.*

'Machine?' he said. 'Where did these all come from?'

'All over the place. This is one of the oldest Spheres. It's been around for a very long time, and it's lived through dozens of wars in dozens of sectors. Do you know how many ships it has processed, in those thousands of years?'

He shook his head.

'Nor do I. But hundreds of thousands, at least. Most of them didn't amount to anything, but once in a while the Sphere would find something . . . interesting. It has a most unusual mind-set, for a Sphere. It kept them. One day it found something *really* interesting.'

The Bird wagged its head from side to side. 'Interesting? Kept? Certainly unusual for a Sphere. Had help, did it?'

The machine laughed. 'It does now.'

'You?'

'Peripherally. We're nearly there.'

Skarbo stared forwards. It looked as if there was a kind of clearing in the ships – a larger black space between the grey masses. Then he realized it wasn't empty, not quite. In the middle was something . . . odd.

It was another ship, much smaller than the massive warships around it. It was longer and slimmer than they were, almost streamlined, like something that had once been meant to skim atmospheres, and there was something – he searched for a word – *baroque* about it: it had too many external

132

features, too many pods and deck lines and antennae. At one end were two splayed cylinders that looked like prehistoric engine nacelles.

It reminded Skarbo of something he had once found amongst the basement junk on Experiment, lifetimes ago. It had been a model of an ancient spaceship. He had kept it for a while.

He nodded towards it. 'Is that where we're going?'

'Nearly. See the thing just this side of it?'

Skarbo sighed, and strained his eyes. There was an irregular shape, slightly lighter in colour than the ship, passing slowly across it.

'It doesn't look very big,' he said.

'It's big enough. Look, matching paths with it is a bit fiddly. Do you mind if I go quiet for a while?'

Skarbo glanced down at The Bird. It was shaking its head, very slowly. 'Be my guest,' he said.

The irregular thing was in orbit around the waist of the old ship. Without the machine seeming to do anything much, their basket nudged a little hesitantly towards it. When they were a few metres above it a hatch slid open beneath them, letting out a little puff of ice crystals that fluttered past them. They dropped through the aperture and came to rest with a faint *click*, and the hatch closed over them. Air hissed in, and their bubble-field disappeared with a popping noise. Then a thick door squeaked open.

The machine had been – Skarbo wanted to say *perching* but that didn't seem right – on the end of the basket. Now it rose. 'Shall we go?' And without waiting for an answer it floated through the door.

The Bird swivelled its neck so it was looking sideways up at Skarbo. 'Well, shall we?' it asked, in a fair imitation of the machine's voice. Then it hopped up into the air and flapped slowly after the machine. Skarbo heard it mutter, 'Low gravity. Makes a change . . .'

He shrugged and followed. Then he came to a halt while his mind adapted. He was surrounded by trees.

The inside of the object was just that – the inside of an irregular shape a few hundred metres across, as if the thing had simply been hollowed out, and then the inner surface planted with forest. Or, he corrected himself – forests: a tessellation of patches of different greens, blues and browns, lit from above by a blue-white orb in the middle of the space.

He heard a croak overhead and looked up. The Bird was perching on a branch just above head-height. It pecked at the wood. 'Is this real? Looks real. Feels real. What kind of lunatic plants the inside of an asteroid full of trees?'

The machine rose until it was level with The Bird. 'That lunatic would be your host,' it said.

Skarbo blinked. 'You?' he asked.

'No. Your ultimate host. Come with me. I'll explain.'

It led them through the trees. There was space between the trunks, but no real path, and the ground was uneven with leaf drift and roots. Skarbo guessed that large creatures that walked didn't visit often; he trod carefully.

After a few hundred paces the forest changed. The trees around the airlock had been short and twisted, with deeply grooved blue-black bark that gave off a sour smell. Now they were taller – maybe thirty metres, Skarbo guessed, with straight slim trunks that seemed to have almost no bark at all but just a smooth pale-brown skin. There was more space, and the ground was even. He relaxed a little.

Then the machine stopped. 'This will do,' it said. 'Skarbo? Please stand a few paces further back.'

Skarbo blinked, and shuffled backwards. 'Here?'

'Yes. Thank you. Now . . .'

A puff of displaced air flicked Skarbo's face, and a platform appeared, floating a few centimetres above the ground just where Skarbo had been standing.

'Please stand on the platform. Bird? You may use it too, if you would prefer not to fly?'

The Bird hopped on to the platform and scraped at it with a claw. It trembled slightly. 'No thanks! Rather trust my wings.'

'As you wish.'

The Bird flapped off to one side and hovered. Then Skarbo felt the platform pressing upwards against his claws, and he was rising slowly. The platform was almost close enough to the nearest tree trunk for him to touch it. He watched it, frowned, and turned to look at another, a little further away. Then he looked round for the little machine.

It was floating level with his head, a metre or so away. He pointed to the tree trunk next to them. 'That one looks different.'

'Yes. It's not a tree. Look up.'

He craned his head back, feeling his neck creak. Most of the trees tapered with height until they spread abruptly into neat round crowns that looked like the tops of very tall thin fungi. This one continued straight up without thinning, past the forest canopy up into the clear air above before dividing into five symmetrically splayed limbs that cradled a broad inverted cone made out of dull stony-looking stuff.

Skarbo eased his neck back to the horizontal and looked at the machine. 'And this is?'

'Water tank. Used for irrigation in the wet season and fire safety in the dry. There are a couple of hundred of them in here. They're recycled – they used to be used as microwave antennae.'

The platform was still rising, floating slowly outward to match the splay of the limbs holding the cone. Then they were above the lip of the cone itself and looking down into it.

It was full of water, almost up to the brim. The cone was bigger than he had thought, and the surface of the water made a circle about twenty metres across. In the middle of the circle there was a floating object – a black sphere about half the width of the water. There was something rough and organic-looking about it; its surface was pocked and rippled, and there were orange spots that looked uncomfortably like mould.

The Bird flew over it and circled. 'What the *fuck*? Think this is a seed! Tell me it's not a seed?'

The machine laughed. 'It's a seed,' it said. 'The biggest seed in the known bubble. They grow over there.' It made a darting motion upwards and to one side, towards an area of forest halfway across the space.

'Well this one won't grow. Hollowed out!' The Bird dived towards the top of the thing and disappeared. Skarbo heard a couple of echoey squawks.

The machine floated over to him. 'So, the flying creature . . . How long have you known it?'

Skarbo sighed. 'Centuries, but it seems longer. Do we follow it?'

'Yes.' The platform was already floating towards the upper surface of the huge seed. The very top had been sliced cleanly off, leaving a circular entrance just big enough for the platform, which dropped neatly through.

Skarbo wasn't sure what he'd been expecting. The inside of the seed was a curved space, with the walls panelled in smoothly jointed wood – different sorts of wood, in a riot of different shapes and colours. He turned round slowly, trying to see if any of the shapes repeated. They didn't seem to. He looked at the machine. 'Who did this?'

'The ship. I think it was bored.'

Skarbo thought about that. 'The ship – the one this asteroid is circling around?'

'That's right. It liked the idea of having a moon.'

The Bird had been flying slowly round the perimeter of the space. Now it dropped to the floor. 'A bored ship that wants a moon, eh? There are names for that sort of thing.'

There was a slim column in the middle of the floor, spreading into five arms in an imitation of the pretend tree that supported the tank. The machine settled into the space between two arms. 'We need to talk about the ship. We need to talk about many things, including you. And you are Skarbo the Horologist?'

'We've established that.'

'As far as the ship is concerned that makes you another of the interesting things.'

Skarbo looked at it. 'Does that mean I've been collected?'

'You have.'

'I see. I suppose this wasn't an accident?'

'No. And, if I may ask, your remaining life? I hesitate to be indelicate . . .'

Skarbo was going to answer but The Bird saved him the trouble. 'Old fool's for the shredder. Eighty-three days and counting.'

The machine made a clicking sound. 'That is tight. Very tight . . . but possible. Possibly possible.'

'What is possible?' Skarbo felt himself beginning to lose his temper. 'My planet has been destroyed, my life's work has been obliterated, I have been kidnapped. I will die in weeks. What is possible, and why should I care?'

The machine made its sighing noise. 'Apologies. Yes. You have been roughly treated, although most recently you were not kidnapped. You were rescued, by us, from a privateer who had kidnapped you and destroyed your planet.'

'Hemfrets?'

'Yes. The thing called Hemfrets.'

'But how?' Skarbo remembered the weapon blisters on Hemfrets's ship. 'How could anything attack it?'

The machine made a sound that might have been a laugh. 'Do you think all the ships this Sphere ever collected are inside it? But it doesn't matter really. The main thing is, your life's work was not obliterated.'

'Yes it was. I watched it.' Skarbo felt bitterness rising to his throat.

'Only the physical part. And, if you're interested, it isn't over.'

Skarbo stared at the machine. 'Not over? How? I have been studying something which will destroy itself in a few hundred years. It took me hundreds of years to set up equipment. How can I start afresh, and to what end?'

After a short pause the machine said, simply: 'Who said anything about starting afresh?'

There was silence. Then Skarbo shook his head. 'No,' he said.

'No?'

'No. A universal no, if you like.'

'Universal?' The machine laughed. 'That's ambitious.'

'Yes would be ambitious. No is realistic. There is nothing you can suggest that would be feasible.'

'Fine.' The machine turned slowly through three hundred and sixty degrees, stopped, and sank into the cradle. 'I'll tell the Orbiter you don't want to visit the Spin, then.'

Skarbo sat down, very slowly. 'Visit? But that's impossible . . .'

'Yes, but clearly you don't want to. Don't worry about it. So, given that you're *not* going to the Spin, where would you like to die instead?'

Thinking was getting difficult. Maybe he was getting ready to die now, right here in the middle of a web of impossible promises – but he wasn't ready to accept that just yet. From the chaos he heard his own voice. It sounded calm. 'How can I reach the Spin? I would like to go.'

The Bird laughed. He ignored it.

'Well, now.' The little machine rose from the cradle again. 'The Orbiter has a plan.'

Skarbo looked up at the machine wearily. 'What's an Orbiter?'

Then he jumped, and The Bird fluttered quickly upwards and back, as if retreating and gaining height both at once. Someone had spoken.

I am.

It was a scratchy whisper like blown leaves – barely a voice at all – and it sounded old. Not just old in the way that Skarbo was old, and presumably The Bird as well (and that was yet another thought about the creature that he examined and filed away), but *old*.

The machine made a throat-clearing noise. 'Ah. That's our host. It doesn't speak much, do you?'

No.

'No . . . but, well, here is Skarbo the Horologist.' It paused. 'And companion.'

Yes.

The Bird dropped to the floor and scraped at it. 'This is going well. Senile, is it?'

Skarbo looked sharply at it. 'Enough,' he said. 'For once, enough.'

It scraped at the floor again. 'Agreed. Enough! Enough of everything. This is madness. I want out.'

The machine dropped on to the floor in front of The Bird, making a sharp *click* at which The Bird jumped back. 'Feel free to leave,' it said quietly. 'The core's still alight.'

The Bird looked steadily at it, then turned its head away. 'My choice, if I take it.'

'Yes.' The machine rose off the floor. 'The Orbiter is my friend. Yours too; and you're going to need one. Skarbo?'

Skarbo nodded. 'Yes. Erm, Orbiter? Hello.'

Hello.

'Yes.' The taciturnity of the thing was almost harder to deal with than silence. He looked round the room, at the expectant machine and the sulking bird. Then it occurred to him.

'Orbiter? Can I come on board? I'd like to meet you properly.'

The machine floated quickly upwards. 'I don't think ...'

Yes. That would be better.

There was silence for a moment. Then the machine said, 'Well, well.'

'Well, well?' The Bird wagged its head. 'You deserve each other.'

Skarbo ignored it.

Skarbo hadn't seen inside many ships in what he knew to have been a sheltered life – but the interior of the ancient Orbiter was unlike any of them. Where the inside of the moon, if that was what it should be called, was forested, the Orbiter was completely overgrown, to the extent that the mechanism of the airlock had had to grind vegetation out of the way to open fully. The airlock itself sounded like something that hadn't been used for a while.

The machine hadn't come with him. 'I've never been on board,' it had said. 'I don't think anyone has, certainly since it's been here. It likes privacy.'

Skarbo had thought about that. 'How long has it been here?'

'About twenty thousand years.'

'Twenty *thousand*?' Skarbo had shaken his head. 'How old is it?'

'I've no idea. It's an old design, certainly. I've never seen one like it.'

And now Skarbo was pushing through stands of gnarled bushes that could easily have been twenty thousand years old. Or millions, for all he knew.

The ship hadn't spoken yet, and Skarbo was in no rush to start a conversation. He wanted to understand this thing better, and he had the feeling that it was telling him things all the time, speech or not. He pushed forward through the damp vegetation. It smelled mouldy, and angular branches hooked at his legs so that he had to lift them in high steps to avoid tripping – or, worse, losing another limb.

After a while he reached a point where the bushes stopped. He walked through a faint violet shimmer and into an overgrown clearing. It was much cooler and the air felt dry and mobile; he looked round and realized that the shimmer was some kind of field. The place seemed to be divided into different habitats. He grinned; perhaps he had found a fellow obsessive.

There was a flat rock in the middle of the clearing that would do for a seat. He lowered himself on to it. 'Well,' he said. 'Would you like to talk?'

Yes. That would be good. The voice was even drier in here.

'Would it? I had the impression you preferred not to.'

It depends on the audience.

Skarbo nodded. 'I can understand that.'

You have spent eight lifetimes studying the Spin.

'Nearly, yes. Have you followed my work?'

From the beginning.

'I'm . . . flattered.'

I share your special interest.

There was silence. Skarbo waited. Was that it? Did ships get senile? Or had it simply forgotten how to talk to people?

Then the old voice said: *You researched, and you published, and then you fell silent.*

'Yes.' Skarbo felt uncomfortable.

I assume you had discovered that the destruction of the Spin was inevitable?

Skarbo nodded. 'Did you hear of that from Hemfrets?'

*No. Hemfrets chose not to cooperate. It died in the fur-
nace, in the remains of its stolen ship. I have studied too. I can
see what you saw.*

'Ah.' There was a little cloud of black dots, dancing in the
air close to the rock. Insects, presumably. Skarbo watched
them. Out loud he said, 'I tried to prove myself wrong. I built
better and better models . . . but I wasn't wrong.'

I followed a similar process.

Skarbo looked up sharply. 'Have you built models too?'

Some physical ones. But mainly in my mind.

'Oh. Well then.' Skarbo sighed. 'It seems we are both going
to lose something precious. But I will die before then.'

*Some things are not inevitable. Would you like to visit the
Spin?*

'The machine mentioned that. Yes, very much – but I don't
see how it can be done. There isn't time.'

*Again, some things are not inevitable. I will be leaving the
Sphere.*

'Why?'

*They are long-lived, but not immortal. This one is dying. It
has made certain . . . decisions. There is the matter of its
legacy.*

Skarbo watched the insects. 'The ships?'

*Yes, among other things. Most of them are antiques, but
they are still potent. At the moment they are hidden. When the
Sphere dies they will become known, and this in a theatre of
war with many participants. You are aware of the Warfront?*

'Yes.'

*It represents an existential threat to almost anything it
might encounter. The Sphere has discussed this with them,
and with me. I shared an idea with it, and it agreed.*

The voice fell silent. Skarbo waited for a while but it didn't
seem eager to add anything. 'Is this the plan the little machine
mentioned?'

The machine is called Grapf. I have told it as much as its little mind needs. I suggest you go back to the moon. I have preparations to make, but they will not take long.

'How long?'

Not long. Things are moving.

'I see.' Skarbo stood up. 'Um – this feels like an intrusive question, but what happens when a Sphere dies?'

The inner field fails, leaving the furnace uncontained.

Skarbo blinked. Uncontained . . . and suddenly he had a mental image of the incandescent ball of metal plasma raging outwards, consuming everything.

'I see,' he said. 'Yes. I would like to leave before that happens, please.'

I will call for you.

Wall Energy Collective
(unavailable)

Zeb didn't remember regaining consciousness. It might have been a while . . .

He was sitting among the remains of the pod, which was smashed open like a hollow fruit. He must have hit the planet hard.

He couldn't move his legs. He looked down and saw that he was encased in soft, off-white stuff. It had a dry, chemical smell.

Crash-foam. Someone had told him once that it was chemically triggered. He didn't remember it happening, which struck him as odd, but maybe it was just very fast.

He decided not to get hung up on that.

He needed to pee. For a second he wondered if the crash-foam had any negative interactions with human urine. Then he shook his head, and shoved his hands down into the stuff.

It tore easily. After a few minutes he had dug himself free. He pulled himself upright and stood, swaying, while he mentally explored his body. Mostly good, to his surprise, but one ankle didn't want to bear weight. When he looked, he found it extravagantly swollen. The chemical foam hadn't been quite fast enough, then.

He took a cautious step and bit his lip at the pain – but he could move, if not fast. He climbed awkwardly out of the pod and leaned against it while he peed. Then he limped a few paces further, to get away from the smell – of chemicals as well as his own urine – and sat down on a rock outcrop while he looked around.

He had crashed on a shallow mound a couple of hundred metres across, surrounded by short trees with blue-green leaves. Bare, eroded rocks poked up through a covering of thin grasses, with patches of grey heather straggling over them. He moved his good foot a bit to one side and squashed it down into the heather. It gave reluctantly, and sprang back the moment he lifted his foot.

A tough environment, by the looks of it, but it didn't look like anything he had seen down here before. He must have been thrown a very long way from the Wall – maybe down towards the equator?

'Hello, Zeb.'

Someone had emerged from the trees, off to his right – a thin figure, too far away to be distinct in the dim light.

'Feeling okay?'

He filled his lungs. 'Fine! Who are you?'

There was a laugh. 'You'll recognize me in a while, although I don't intend that you should get used to me. Are you sure you're okay? You're favouring your left leg. A broken ankle, perhaps?'

Zeb gritted his teeth and forced himself to take a step forwards. Pain shot up his leg but he managed to complete the step with his feet planted. 'Fine! See?'

'Don't contradict me.' The figure waved a hand, and Zeb felt his ankle crack as if something had struck it. His leg folded under him and he fell sideways, clamping his lips against a cry and catching his fall clumsily on one hand.

He looked up, and saw through a haze of pain that the figure was much closer. And familiar; yes, definitely familiar.

It leaned a little towards him. 'Yes, obviously a broken ankle. Is there anything you want to say?'

Zeb took two breaths through his nose. 'Keff? What are you doing here?'

Keff nodded. 'I knew you would . . . but I'm not here. Nor are you, in the way that you mean. Tell me, where do you think *here* is?'

'I don't know. Somewhere near the Wall Collective, I guess.'

'You're wrong. And you know you are.' Keff made a show of looking around. 'It's a pretty characteristic place, I'd say, even if you haven't seen it like this. Try again.'

'Fuck off.'

Keff laughed. 'I will, in a moment. But you won't. You're going to be around for a while yet.' It sat down next to Zeb. 'You see, *I found you.*'

Zeb stared at the creature.

'I knew there was something when I saw you at the Rock-blossom. It took me a while to make a guess, and another while to check out the guess. And then I *found* you. Have you worked it out yet?' Keff watched him for a few seconds, and then shrugged.

'I looked back along the timeline from when I met you, Zeb, and I saw a line of dislocations. Like spikes on a graph. Like footprints. Like little impact craters, each one surrounded by a spreading network of cracks. Every thousand years or so someone dropped into the vreality, hung around for a while, did pretty much the same sort of things each time and then left. And they always did it in pretty much the same place, Zeb.' Keff waved an arm around. 'They always did it here, on a planet that had been half destroyed by the fall of a ship called the *Death Rattle*. So I traced the footprints back to their origin – here – and so I found you.'

Zeb's heart was racing. He pulled himself upright and leaned back against the rock, ignoring the stabbing in his ankle. 'Here? But—'

'Yes, here. You're in the vreality you like so much. I thought that was obvious?' Keff stood up, looked away, spoke without turning. 'How could you be so stupid? Everyone else is happy to splash around in the virtual shallows, but not you. You could have done all the *fucking*' – the word was bitter with distaste – 'you wanted up there. That's what the top levels are designed for, even if everyone pretends it's something more profound. What else does recreation mean, to you lot? But you had to come down here. Every time you planted your idiot self in here, and even more, every time you just vanished when things got difficult, you set off another ripple of doubt. What possessed you?'

Zeb shook his head. 'Nothing possessed me. I promised—'

'You promised?' Keff spun round and held out a hand towards Zeb's good ankle. He felt a wrenching crunch, and appalling pain shot up his leg. There was a roaring which was half him and half the blood hammering in his ears, but he could still hear Keff.

'I know about your *promise*. I told you, I followed your clumsy trail back to the start. You promised to honour a machine that was about to die because you had already interfered, but all you did was to go on doing the stupid thing you had already started doing. You're a tourist, Zeb, nothing more, and like any tourist you fuck up the place you visit.'

The voice stopped, and so did the pressure on his ankle. The pain subsided, a little. Zeb felt his breath rasping against his scoured throat. He swallowed. 'What do you want?'

'Nothing you can offer.' Keff spread its arms. 'You've contaminated trillions of life-equivalent years. You can't give that back.'

'So, what then?'

The creature grinned. 'Amusement. You're stuck with me, and I can go anywhere and anywhen I want in this vreality. I'm a response to you. Think of me as an immune cell, if you like. I'm going to have some fun with you, and it starts now.

You're going to live through every – single – year – of the chaos you caused. You know where you are, but can you guess when?'

Zeb shook his head. He didn't trust himself with words.

'Well, you're back at the start. Just before it, really. Up above you, the Seven States are about to go into battle, and you're in a small crippled spaceship that's about to crash on this spot, followed by a big, dead one.' Keff grinned. 'And here's you with two broken ankles. What are you going to do?'

It turned and walked away.

Zeb stared after it. He almost called out, but stopped himself. He had no breath for word games and the only other option was begging. He'd given it enough fun already.

He looked round, feeling his eyes stretched wide with pain and adrenalin. He was in the middle of the wide mound – probably ground zero. In here, he would die instantly if he stayed put, and merely fast if he moved. Out there, outside the vreality, he had no idea. Keff had brought him in against his will, so he had to assume it was making the rules . . .

While his mind was racing, his body made a decision. He turned over on to all fours and began to crawl, away from the crash site and down the slope where he thought the forest was nearest, keeping his calves bent upwards so that his worse-than-useless feet dangled off the ground. Even so, his ankles lanced agony with every movement – but it was better than the alternative.

At first sight the rock looked smooth, but it sparkled with tiny off-white crystals which stood proud of the surface, so that after a while his knees began to bleed and he reflexively let his feet drop.

His bellow of pain brought blood to his mouth. He spat pink, and forced himself to start moving again.

By the time he began to lose the skin from the palms of his hands, he had no idea of distance or duration. There was only the next movement and the next growl of pain. Sometimes he tried to follow the occasional streak of grass that clung to low points in the surface of the rock, but they soon ran out, and he quickly found that the grass was almost as abrasive as the rock, and bled a stinging sap when it was crushed.

So he gave up, and just crawled, until every movement was a howl that begat another howl.

And then the rock beneath was gone and before he could catch himself he was falling, rolling down a steep slope off the edge of the mound and into the wiry forest, and the pain of his flayed body was multiplied by the tearing of his ankles against branches and boulders.

There was no way to break his fall. He went limp and waited for the end.

There was a *crack*, and a pause full of dreams. Then, voices.
'Whoa! Look . . .'
'What? Oh, shit. Where did he come from?'
'Don't know. He looks pretty damaged. Hey, friend . . .'
Hands on him, turning him over. One of his ankles caught on something and he tried to scream, but only heard a whimper.
'Hooo, fuck. You are so bust up. Can you talk?'
He tried to nod, but even that didn't want to happen. He moistened his lips. 'Crash.'
'Yeah, I bet. What were you in?'
He tried again and this time the words were easier. 'No. Crash – there's going to be a crash.'
Silence. He looked up and tried to see whoever it was. Two silhouettes against low sunlight, with heads turned sideways as if they were looking at each other.
Low sunlight. Nightfall – he had watched the ships go down into the twilight band, hadn't he? It must be soon; maybe very soon.
He managed to raise his arms and grab at one of the silhouettes. 'We need to leave! Now! Please . . .'

Hands took his and gently pressed him down. 'Sure. Sure. We'll leave. Just rest a moment.'

The silhouettes moved away and he heard low voices but couldn't distinguish words. He must have slept, because with no transition he was being lifted on to something, and then into something, and then there was the sort of fast, smooth movement that meant flying.

He wondered how fast they were going, and if anything that flew in an atmosphere could ever possibly be fast enough.

It was out of his hands for the moment.

He slept again.

Orbiter 'Moon', Brasedl Sphere

Skarbo spent the next two days wandering through the more accessible of the forests of the moon. He preferred his own company. He had things, as the little machine Grapf had said, to process.

Starting with his whole life's work. From the moment he had first seen the Spin, and watched it being smudged out by a Baschet ship, he had *known*, with a certainty beyond any logic, that he was going to spend the rest of his life observing it. Against everyone's advice he had chosen his insect form because it offered almost certain longevity, just to make sure he could – what? Complete his observations? Hardly; that enterprise was doomed to be unending.

What, then?

A few days before Hemfrets had arrived in his little world to annex it and powder it and do whatever else it had done, Skarbo had decided to acknowledge failure. Now, even with everything behind him shattered and very little in front of him, he was less sure of his decision.

After a day of wandering he had discovered that forests were not the complete rulers of the inside of the moon. A few hundred metres from the old water tower, the trees thinned out and gave way to a sort of sculpture garden – or that was the best

151

description he could come up with; he had asked the Orbiter, through Grapf, but it had taken its usual course and said nothing, and the little machine itself had said it didn't know.

There were twenty-two objects, all dull white ovoids mounted on slim columns that ranged from less than a metre to more than ten in height. The objects were different sizes too, but not so great a range: the biggest was about ten metres across and the smallest about half that. Their long axes all pointed in different directions, and from time to time, if he looked away and then back, one of them had moved a little – but he never caught one in the act.

The ground around the columns was covered in a very fine, soft black sand that held the heat of the sunlet for a long time. It was good to sit on.

The Bird was enjoying itself too. From a position of initial dubiousness it had now discovered the pleasures of the near-zero gravity conditions at the centre of the moon, and was trying to set speed records for power-dives from there to the forest. Skarbo watched it fly in a tightening spiral up to the centre, where even to his eyes it became a fuzzy black dot against the background of the forests. It would play at the centre for a while, tumbling and flapping in the directionless gravity-free space, and then launch itself randomly downwards in a streamlined, back-swept black blur, pulling out of the dive in a tree-brushing display of aeronautics. From time to time Skarbo heard a faint *haaaaaa!*

The Orbiter hadn't wanted to be precise about how long the Sphere had to live – but not long. It wasn't a random thing, apparently; the huge entity had some choice in the matter.

The Bird was back at the centre, spinning. Then it fired itself down, this time more or less towards Skarbo. He fought the urge to stand up, move away from the clearing and take shelter among the trees. He wasn't sure how good the creature's steering was.

The dot grew quickly.

Then Skarbo felt the ground move, and suddenly he was sitting down much harder than before. He forced himself to stand, feeling his legs creak, and took hold of a column to support himself.

There was a shriek from somewhere above.

'Gravity!'

He looked up, and then ducked reflexively as The Bird corkscrewed over him. It half recovered, stalled, and disappeared into the trees. He heard a distant *'fuuuuck!'*, and then nothing.

He followed. There was definitely something wrong with the gravity; it was stronger, and it kept changing so that his legs buckled and swayed as he walked.

As he arrived at the edge of the clearing, The Bird hopped out of the trees, shaking its wings.

'Are you all right?'

It shook its head. 'No! Not right at all. Big problems. Gravity gone wrong. Don't know why. Probably means something very bad.'

Skarbo nodded. He was trying to convince himself that this was all part of the preparations the Orbiter had mentioned – but it wasn't working. 'Let's get back to the tower.'

'If we can . . . gravity still wrong.'

It was, and walking was difficult. Skarbo moved from tree to tree, using the trunks as props; The Bird hopped ill-temperedly in front of him, swearing under its breath every time the ground jinked.

Then they were among the slim trunks of the trees near the tower. Skarbo looked up, and saw the inverted cone sticking out above the leaf canopy. He looked round for any sign of the machine.

Then the ground kicked and swerved beneath him and he fell, landing heavily. The Bird made an inarticulate squawk and shot up into the air. It hovered for a second, swinging from side to side, staring upwards. Then it dropped until it was just above Skarbo. 'Run!'

He stared at it. 'What?'

'Run! You deaf as well as senile? Tower's falling. Run!'

The ground kicked again, and Skarbo looked up.

The tower was swaying, swinging through a widening arc.

He levered himself to his feet and ran, or tried to. The ground was no longer jinking, but there was something seriously wrong; something was making what should have been a straight path into a curve that kept slamming him into trees, and he didn't seem to weigh as much as he had before.

Then he heard a drawn-out tearing sound that ended in a deep, concussive crash.

Instinct threw him to the ground before he had time to think. He hooked a couple of legs into some roots, and flattened himself as much as he could.

Something roared behind him. Then the water hit. He felt it trying to tear him loose, to blind him, to force itself beneath his shell and peel him open. Something heavy battered into him and wrenched him away, tumbling him over in a chaos of limbs and bubbles. Then he crashed into something, and for a while there was just blur.

Then the water had gone. He didn't remember it going. He was lying on his back, staring up though unable to focus – but at least he could breathe.

His sight cleared and he was looking up at the canopy of leaves, but now there were ragged holes in it, and the light looked different.

Something appeared in one of the holes. He squinted, and then sighed. It was The Bird. It flapped down and perched on a broken branch by his head. 'Still alive, are you?'

He managed to nod. 'And you.'

'Seem to be. Huh. Stupid questions.' It hopped along the branch, and then back. 'Might not be for long. Seen the light?'

'Yes.' He stared upwards. 'It's different. Less intense. And less steady.'

'Clever. Yark! You fireproof, insect?'

He stared at it. 'What?'

'Not so clever. Gravity went mad and I fell out of the sky. What else fell? Eh? Eh?'

Skarbo shook his head. Enough; it was enough. Everything was. He levered himself up into a half-sitting position that emphasized every ache, and spoke slowly. 'I don't care, bird. I might not be alive for long? Fine. Now feels like a good time for it to end. But please? Let me go in peace? Shut up?'

'Fine! Cook in your shell if you want to.' It flung itself into the air and hovered over him so he could feel the gusts of its wingbeats on his eyes. 'Fire, insect! The sunlet fell, that's what. The forest is burning.'

Skarbo thought about that for a moment. 'So? Where should we escape to, do you think?'

It paused, and wagged its head. 'Don't know. Might fly to the centre.'

'Well I can't.' Skarbo lay back. 'Enjoy your trip.'

'Oh for fuck's sake . . .' It wheeled round and disappeared upwards. Skarbo had to admit that the downdraught it left smelled smoky. He shrugged. No Spin, perhaps – but then he had never really believed he would get there.

He shut his eyes, and promised himself there would be no dreams.

The smell of smoke was getting stronger. He felt himself beginning to curl up into what he sensed would be his last position. Perhaps it would be quick.

Then something knocked against his shell. He opened his eyes, and saw Grapf. It pulled away.

'Are you hurt?'

'No.'

'Good. The Orbiter says we need to evacuate. Please follow me.'

It floated off a few metres, and waited. Skarbo hauled himself upright and followed. The ground seemed steadier, but there was definitely something odd about the gravity – an uneasy sensation of motion that didn't stop if he stood still.

The machine led him back to the clearing where he had found the ovoids. He had expected to see them scattered around, but somehow they were still on their columns. He shrugged. 'What now?'

'The Orbiter's breaking the moon open.'

Skarbo blinked. 'Breaking?'

'Yes. Ah – here's the pod.'

A white sphere about four metres across floated into the clearing and lowered itself to ground level just in front of them. The machine positioned itself over the top of the thing and dropped sharply on to it. There was a dull click, and the side of the pod split into slim segments that floated out of the way. The machine bobbed inside. 'Come on. The Orbiter can't wait long.'

Skarbo climbed warily into the thing. The inside was plain and there was nothing to sit on, so he stood. There was a rattle of wings and The Bird skidded to a stop on the floor next to him. It looked around, and then turned to the machine. 'Looks new. Out of character. Why?'

'It's not new. It's as old as the Orbiter. It's just never been used before. Please keep clear of the entrance; we're about to leave.'

The Bird hopped a few steps further into the pod. 'That old? Untested? Not reassuring.'

'I'm sure it works very well.' The machine swung gently sideways until it knocked into the wall, and the slender segments fitted themselves back into the entrance, knitting together with long seams that glowed briefly blue and then vanished. There was a faint smell of ozone.

For a moment the inside of the pod was dark. Then the walls flickered and disappeared, and suddenly they seemed to be standing in nothing. The forest floor was dropping away fast, although there was no sense of motion – they were already a hundred metres above the treetops. Not far from where they had been, the forest was burning, and Skarbo could see the bright spreading smudges of other fires further off, with columns of smoke rising and swirling in spirals towards the centre. Other sunlets must have fallen. The forest wouldn't last long.

He turned to the machine. 'You said the Orbiter was going to break open the moon,' he said. 'What does that mean?'

'Exactly what it says. Watch.'

And as it said the word *watch* the moon split itself neatly in two – a line appeared round its circumference and spread quickly into a black chasm. The forests next to the split leaned almost horizontally into the gap, and Skarbo imagined screaming winds as the moon's air was sucked out. The fires all flared a hungry yellow as the air whipped them, and then just as quickly subsided to angry red glows.

Then the two halves of the moon were apart, and Skarbo could see the old Orbiter, framed slightly off-centre between them.

Again without any sense of motion, the pod flicked neatly through the gap and came to a halt still some distance above the Orbiter.

For a few breaths everything seemed still. The Bird made a creaking sound somewhere at the back of its throat. '*Yaw.* Fire's out. Moon's wrecked. And?'

'Ssh.' Skarbo tapped it with a leg. 'Look. Something's happening . . .'

Something was. A section of hull at the back of the Orbiter had opened – just a pair of doors hinging outwards, looking very old-fashioned but somehow very purposeful. Then a pale pink haze appeared between the doors, expanded to become a bubble, and elongated itself towards the split moon, weaving a little, in a way that made Skarbo think of the questing limb of some blind sea creature. When its tip was between the two halves it opened into a wide funnel shape.

Skarbo squinted. There was a grainy shadow across the outer end of the thing . . . Then he realized. It wasn't a shadow. It was trees.

The forests were flowing out of the halves of the moon, down the funnel and into the body of the ship.

Skarbo found his voice. 'Is it saving the trees?'

'No.' Grapf sounded breezy. 'Most of them won't live through the vacuum. Too much cellular damage – but it will record their genes. And it never wastes biomass. The trees would have been worthless as soot and charcoal.'

They watched the silent procession of dying trees for a moment. It was already tailing off; the process had been very quick. Skarbo wondered how many megatonnes of wood had flowed through that tenuous link. He glanced up at the shadowy ranks of warships; they looked as if they were watching too. He smiled at himself.

Then the great harvest was over. Skarbo had half expected the funnel to withdraw, but instead it was tilting upwards and the pod was dropping towards it. Then they were in it, and the haze closed around them.

Skarbo was getting ready to ask when they would be on board the old ship, when the floor kicked softly under him and the haze vanished. The pod made a *click* and the side opened.

The old dry voice of the Orbiter said, *Welcome.*

Skarbo looked around. 'Oh,' he said, and his voice echoed.

He was standing on grey stone flags, flecked with blue and

gold. Each one seemed to be a different shape, and they were tightly jointed along fine black lines of mortar. They looked flat but weren't – the surface curved gently up, becoming walls that disappeared upwards into mist a hundred metres or so away so that he felt as if he was standing in a cupped hand.

In the curve of the stones, there was something he recognized – an intricate cluster of spheres, some shining and some dull.

It was a model of the Spin.

He found his voice. 'Did you make this?'

It isn't exactly made. But yes, I caused it. I said we had something in common.

The Bird rustled past him and flew a circuit of the model, spiralling upwards to hover directly above it. Its wings made faint swirls in the mist. 'Very good,' it said. 'As good as anything the insect made in eight hundred years! You can talk about planets together.' It glided down and dropped to the ground next to Skarbo. 'Now where am I going to be?'

Here.

'Oh, no. Not here. Somewhere with trees. You're full of trees!'

Yes. And other things. But I want you here.

Skarbo fought back a smile. 'Why?'

I am busy. The Sphere was attacked – is still under attack, by an outlier of the Warfront. I have had to bring forward some plans. This has killed approximately a megatree, which I regret. Now I am needed. You may watch.

The mist around the edge of the stones darkened and became space.

Skarbo caught his breath.

The view was of roughly what they had seen from the mouth of the tunnel that had brought them into the ship – but at the same time very, very different. Before, the great ships had been shadows and silhouettes and grey shapes. Now they stood out as bright, sharp-edged monsters against the fuzzy sea of junk behind them. And, he realized, they were moving. With the delicacy of dancers and far too quickly for their size, they slid round each other, leaving behind their uneven rows and forming themselves into a sphere within the larger sphere of debris. And with the old Orbiter in its own hollow at the centre of the sphere, Skarbo noticed.

The voice of the old ship broke in on the thought. *Please prepare for a bright light* – and as it finished saying *light*, the sphere of ships flared a harsh, nerve-burning white.

He had shielded his eyes just in time. Fierce after-images smudged across his vision even so.

He heard The Bird say, 'Shit . . .'

He cautiously unshielded an eye. The ships were still there, but the debris had gone. All of it – he could see all the way to the little molten star in the centre of the Sphere and, in the other direction, all the way to the gauzy outer field.

There was something wrong with the field. Even though he had never properly seen it before, he could tell that without doubt. Most of it was still the shifting, multicoloured veil he had expected but there were ragged patches of plain colour – sullen reds and blues, and here and there a nauseous yellow. They were spreading. He pointed at them.

'Orbiter?'

Yes. The attack has damaged the outer field. Those colours mean that sentience has ceased in those areas. The Sphere would have died in days. Now it will die in hours, if no one intervenes.

'Oh.' Skarbo watched the patches. Two were growing towards each other, one red and one blue. When they touched, they snapped together into one. The colour flickered harshly for a second and settled into red. It looked unpleasant, and he dropped his gaze. 'Is it in pain?'

Yes, in its own way. But we have an agreement.

The ships were moving again, undoing the globe as if it was

a puzzle and instead forming a hollow cylinder. Not quite hollow, Skarbo realized – there was one ship in the middle of it. It looked bigger than the others; he hadn't noticed it before. It also looked more battered, like one of the hulks he had seen on the way here.

The hollow cylinder was pointing towards the centre of the Sphere, and suddenly Skarbo had a vision of what might be about to happen. 'Is the old ship part of the agreement?' he asked.

Yes. That was the vessel that overwhelmed Hemfrets's ship. It volunteered. It was damaged. Now it, too, is choosing to die.

Skarbo nodded.

Beams of light leapt from the surrounding ships, lining the cylinder with a complex latticework that flexed and shrank until it was a close fit round the old ship in the middle. The light flared, just once, and the old ship was gone, launched like a spear towards the centre of the Sphere.

By the time it reached the molten core, it was an orange speck against the yellow-white incandescence. It disappeared.

The core convulsed, shrinking for a second. Then expanded, almost too quickly for Skarbo to follow, into a vivid globe of flaming plasma. Even as he began to turn away it reached them, streaming past the ships in writhing gouts of bright gas. He flinched, but then saw that the inferno was parting as it reached them; against its brilliant light he could see a faint translucent cone. Some sort of field, then.

And then the gas was past them, and pouring into the outer field.

The field flared, came apart like paper, and swirled away in dying shreds.

Skarbo took a breath. 'Is that it?'

Yes. The Sphere is over. I am sorry.

'Now what?'

Watch.

'What? Oh . . .'

As he watched the formation broke up. The movements were different. Instead of being graceful and sinuous, they were jerky – almost brutal. Then half the ships flicked out of sight completely. The view zoomed out, making his head swim, and he was standing on nothing, apparent kilometres above an Orbiter that had become an elongated dot.

Ahead of him there were more dots. Many, many more – a fleet, at the least, and a smaller group that he guessed were the old ships from the Sphere, squaring up to them.

He pointed. 'Is that the outlier?'

Yes. They have exposed themselves.

The old ships were outnumbered tens to one – hundreds. More. It was impossible.

Then, too quickly to follow, the formation of the old ships blurred and stuttered. Patterns formed, changed and vanished, and with each movement it seemed to Skarbo that the numbers of the enemy – he heard himself use the word, and almost laughed – were reduced.

And then it was over. He hadn't counted the numbers of the old ships but there didn't seem much change. The other ships were gone.

He breathed out. 'Orbiter? Did we win?'

That battle, yes. But they were mainly Baschet Clients – privateers and chartered yachts, never more than half-integrated into the Warfront. They stood little chance against professional warriors.

Skarbo nodded. 'I didn't think of you as warlike.'

I am not. But when you are as old as me, it pays to have warlike friends.

There didn't seem much Skarbo could add to that – but he found himself agreeing with it thoroughly.

The thought made him look for The Bird, which had been

uncharacteristically quiet. It was standing next to him, its eyes bright in the darkness. Its head was a little on one side, and its expression was quite unreadable.

Skarbo smiled to himself.

Then the ship added, *And now, we are at war, too. Even if that was just an outlier, it was Warfront.*

Skarbo stopped smiling.

Sholntp (vreality)

The high square window was plain glass. There was a diagonal crack in it, and the blue-white beam of the street lamp outside threw a slanted square of light across the face of the woman sitting on the other side of the table. The shadow of the crack looked like a scar.

The woman was thin and elderly and pale, and her voice sounded thin and pale too.

'You must understand,' she said. 'You said there would be a crash, a short time before the two ships impacted. What happened may well wipe out life on this planet. How did you know?'

It was Zeb's third day in the cell. He had woken there, they had treated him there, and now they were questioning him there. Politely, but insistently. He was answering – uselessly.

They told him it was a miracle that he had survived. His rescuers had not, and nor had ninety million people so far. The count was rising, they said. He must be able to shed some light, they said.

It wasn't in their nature to resort to indelicate methods, they said, when he continued not to help. And paused just long enough for him to imagine what they meant.

The thin woman was a recent arrival. He suspected she was their last throw, before they overcame their natures and got indelicate with him.

'I'm sorry,' he said, for the hundredth time. 'I can't help you.'

They had dragged him, in a charred medical pod, out of the remains of the low-atmosphere flyer that had somehow made it nearly two hundred kilometres from the crash site before the plasma storm of the old warship's dying engines had whipped it out of the sky. They had told him it was by luck that he had been found in the first place; it was luck the pod had protected him; it was luck that someone alive had been close enough to the wreck of the flyer to find him over again. He had been luckier than his rescuers, who had not survived.

He didn't feel particularly lucky.

Eventually the thin woman seemed to run out of different ways of asking the same question. She sat frowning at him, and he returned the frown as levelly as he could until she shook her head slightly, stood up and left. Zeb watched the door close behind her and listened for the quiet snick that meant locking. Then he stood up himself, stretched, and winced as the movement tightened half-healed skin. His ankles were encased in cylinders of barely yielding foam-heal, which meant that he walked stiffly but without pain. The foam would be removable tomorrow, they had told him.

Apart from the table and two chairs, the world of his cell contained an electro-san that was the highest-tech thing he had seen here, and a cot which was much more primitive. He had little idea of the world outside his cell, except that it often contained sirens and sometimes the sound of crowds. He lowered himself on to the cot, pulled the discoloured cover over himself and got ready to wait.

Then he sat up again. A siren had wailed, but it was different. The others had been classic way-clearers – sharp,

Doppler-shifting tones that swelled and faded as they passed. This was an urgent, rising howl that spoke directly to the part of the brain that said *Run*.

The crowd sounds had paused when the siren started. Now they were back, with an edge that hadn't been there before.

It sounded like panic, and it didn't stop. It almost drowned out the snick of the door opening.

Zeb had expected the thin woman, or a medical orderly, or any of the anonymous questioners he had met over the last three days. He got Keff.

The thin creature was dressed in military drab. As much to gain time to think as for any other reason, Zeb pointed at it. 'What's that all about?'

'Things are getting pretty official out there. I'm blending in. Someone might even ask me to do something useful. I'll tell you what that feels like, shall I, if it happens?'

Zeb sat down again. 'Fuck off, Keff.'

'No. I'm enjoying this too much already. Do you have any plans?'

'Beyond staying alive? No. I was supposed to die up on the plateau, wasn't I?' He glared up at Keff. 'I bet it really cooks your shit that I didn't.'

'Not really, given that I had to intervene more than once to get you out in one piece. How interesting do you think you'd be to me dead?' Keff walked over to the cot and stood over Zeb. 'I am in charge here, Zeb. *I* am in charge, and I have some games to play with you. The next one starts now – well, started ten minutes ago, really. The wind has changed, and the dust cloud from the ships is blowing this way. Did you hear the sirens?'

Zeb nodded.

'Well, they're radiation alarms. Stay outside, here, and you'll get a lethal dose in a day. Inside it'll take longer. Someone once said that panic is worse than radiation. I don't know about that, but it's definitely quicker.' It shook its head theatrically and then knelt down by the cot, reached out a hand and laid it on Zeb's shoulder. 'People are being simultaneously crushed and irradi- ated, and you did it. Don't you feel just a touch of pride?'

Zeb turned his face away.

'Well, whatever. Three things you need to know now. One – the government has run away, starting from when the sirens started. Two – your image, and a version of your part in this, has been on news channels for the last twenty-four hours. And three – the door to this cell no longer locks.' It stood up and rubbed its hands together in front of it. 'Good luck.'

And then it turned its back and walked out, leaving the door half-open behind it.

Outside, the crowd sounds became louder. Zeb looked up at the window. It was too high for him to see anything but sky and the street light. The light had been on for some hours. How much more night was there? He needed the night.

Something crashed against the glass, and again. It rang harshly with the blows but didn't break. Zeb waited for more, his hands half raised to cover his face, but nothing else seemed to be coming. The crowd had quietened, too.

It was a watchful quiet. Patterns, patterns . . .

Zeb threw himself at the cell door. He was halfway through it when there was a dull orange flash and a hot concussion that emptied his chest. A gust of searing air crashed through the doorway, slamming the door violently closed behind him. He bounced off the opposite wall of the corridor, and staggered crabwise until he fetched up, wide-eyed and panting, at a turn in the corridor with his back against the wall.

There was a long, still moment. Then the building shook, and the cell door and a section of the wall around it exploded out- wards on a blossom of flames and crashed across the corridor.

Zeb was turning by the time the blast hit him.

He became conscious of noise. His lips were pressed against something cold and his mouth was full of dust. His shoulder hurt.

He lay still, listening. There was nothing but the slow, surging sub-noise of blood in his ears. Each surge throbbed painfully through his head.

He raised himself cautiously on to all fours and waited until his head stopped swimming. He wanted to spit, to clear the harsh grit from his tongue, but that would be noisy and anyway he had nothing to spit with. Instead he wiped a finger on his shirt and swept it round his mouth, flicking the biggest crumbs of building away.

Then he stood up.

There was still no sound. There was light, but not much; dull yellow ceiling globes flickered uneasily every few metres, but their glow barely reached the floor. Towards where his cell had been, they were broken and dark.

His first thought was to prefer light, even if it was grudging. He turned and began to follow the corridor away from his cell. He had no idea where he was going. They had brought him in half conscious; the building could have been all corridor as far as he knew.

The walls were a bare grey material that glowed a sickly orange under the lights. No signs, no directions, no indication of a way out. No change.

After ten minutes he stopped.

He could blunder round the place for ever. And the longer he was in here, the more night he used up and the more likely he was to meet someone.

Of course, there was *one* way out. It might be full of people but then, it might not.

He turned and began to retrace his steps towards where his cell had been, navigating partly by the muscle memory in his legs and partly by the thickening dust and smells of burning. Not just burning building – there was a sweet undertone that he didn't recognize. At the last corner he halted and listened as hard as he could.

Silence, as far as he could tell. He braced himself and began to move his head a little out from the corner.

And froze. Not silence. There had been a soft rustle. He strained his ears – again; another rustle, and then a sound like a throat being cleared.

Zeb thought for a moment. Then he shrugged. It had always been possible. He scanned the floor at his feet, located a piece of wall-rubble about half the size of his fist and picked it up as quietly as he could. Ready to run, he lobbed it out into the open corridor and waited, his heart banging.

Nothing at first. Then the throat-clearing again.

Zeb crouched down and moved forwards very slowly until both eyes were clear of the corner. He paused for a moment, and then stood up. He had found the people after all.

It was difficult to be sure, among the demolition, but he could see at least five bodies. They were sprawled outwards from the blast hole as if they had been sprayed, and his mind filled in the pattern – they had been in the cell when the second explosion had happened.

That accounted for the sweet smell. He felt his throat convulsing.

The rustle came again, and he saw one of the bodies move slightly. He edged up to it and crouched down.

It was – had been – a young female. Short hair on one side of her head, but the other side was an ugly mat of blood and peeled skin and pale, shattered bone, and the pool beneath her was black and shiny in the dim light. One arm was twisted into an impossible shape, and her eyes were closed, but somehow she was still alive. For one breath, two breaths, three, her chest rose and fell, and from this close to her he could hear the bubbling and creaking of shattered ribs.

Then she took one more breath, and this time her eyes flicked open for a second, gazed sightlessly and closed. The breath left her and didn't return.

Zeb kept station with her for a moment. Then he shook his head, stood up, and picked his way carefully out through the rubble and the bodies, trying not to breathe in the smells of burnt flesh and burnt hair.

There was a ragged, roughly circular hole in the outside wall of the cell, about as high as he was. Humid night air drifted through it, and the hazy beam of the street light picked out swirls of dust disturbed by his feet. He stopped a couple of paces short of the hole and listened again.

Still nothing – no crowds, no sirens.

Zeb didn't understand. He took another step towards the hole.

Then something grabbed his ankle.

He went down, landing on his side on a pile of rubble. He had time for a single yelp of pain before someone was on top of him. He glimpsed a hand opening, and then his eyes were full of dust and he screwed them shut. Blows landed on his face, his arms, his chest. He tried to grab one of the swinging fists but found his own hand caught instead; he felt his thumb seized and forced back agonizingly.

It broke, and he howled with pain. There was laughter, and his other thumb was seized. He flailed desperately with his crippled hand, found a face and jabbed as hard as he could with stiffened fingers.

They sank into eye sockets. The laughter became a scream and the face was yanked back sharply. He followed the shifting weight, forcing his hips upwards and ignoring the harsh grinding of the rubble into his side, and suddenly the weight was gone.

There was a crash and a shout, abruptly cut off. Then nothing.

He waited – blinking reflexively, eyes streaming, his ribs grating with every breath – until he could keep one eyelid open for long enough to see.

Someone was sprawled between him and the hole in the wall. The head had landed on the jagged edge of the wall. The face was upwards.

What was left of the face. It looked as if it had been flayed, from the eyes to the lips. Blood was oozing from beneath the closed eyelids.

Zeb looked down at the fingers of his broken hand. There were wet, grey scraps sticking to them. The skin had peeled from the face like wet paper.

He threw up.

Shephhat City (vreality)

The big ferry gave three short blasts on its siren, and the blue haze hanging over its funnel thickened to a plume of black smoke. Even at this distance Zeb could feel in his chest the bass thrum of the engines.

Water churned under the vessel's stern and she moved away from the pontoon, forcing her sharp prow between the press of smaller craft that choked the harbour. Everyone was trying to do the same thing – leave.

The city of Shephhat was built on six big islands and a bunch of smaller ones that formed a roughly circular cluster in the mouth of a deep fjord on the coast of the southern continent, a third of the way round the planet from what would one day be called the Peace Rift. The normal population of the city was four million. Now, three quarters of those had gone and most of the rest were following them.

It was forty-one days since the crash. For half that time, the huge thermal updraught from the dying ship had carried radioactive, chemically complex ash most of the way round the planet on lethal, artificial trade winds. The winds had coincided with Shephhat's natural rainy season, dumping thousands of tonnes of slow death on the city.

The ash was everywhere. Most people wore close-woven

fabric masks if they could afford them. Fortunes had been made by suppliers, and for a while it had actually been a fashion statement to be seen with the expensive sort. But that had been before the first riots. After that, conspicuous consumption looked like a much worse idea, and soiled rags became the usual choice. By the second week of the ashfall, they were the only option left.

The riots had mainly been about food.

There was a drawn-out splintering crash from the harbour. The ferry had ploughed into a log-jam of old barges. Their flat decks were packed from edge to edge with people standing. The impact shook them to their knees, and hundreds fell or jumped into the water.

The ferry drove through them without slowing. Zeb watched people disappearing into its bow-wave and realized that in this restricted space the ship's propellers must be drawing tonnes of water down her sides to feed their hungry thrashing.

He turned away quickly, but not quickly enough to avoid seeing the first smear of pink foam on the ferry's wake.

'Quite a sight, eh?'

Zeb glanced towards the voice and sighed. Keff was leaning on the harbour railing next to him. The creature had turned up every now and then, choosing its moments carefully.

It turned to him. 'Proud of yourself yet?'

He said nothing.

'The numbers are rising. Almost two hundred million so far. You know the amusing thing? Only about half of those are radiation deaths. The rest are starvation, conflict, water-borne diseases, all that good stuff.' It nodded towards the harbour. 'And drowning and being minced by propellers, of course. Well done you.'

Zeb felt his lips twisting. 'Haven't you got someone else to bore?'

'Not really. No one that would be as much fun as you. You're a personal project. Almost a pet.' It straightened up. 'I'll be seeing you. Often.'

It sauntered away. Zeb watched it until it turned a corner. Then he sighed.

He had taken the decision to go nowhere very early. He had no faith in the idea of escape from Shephhat, and the only thing he wanted to escape from was Keff, and Keff would certainly follow him anywhere.

The ferry had crunched its way through the smaller boats. Wreckage closed behind it, covering the surface of the water. Another few thousand people off on their futile journeys. Most of them would be hoping to get down to the planet's southern pole, where people whispered that the isotopes didn't fall.

Within a few more days everyone that was going would be gone. Zeb had tried to remember if he knew anything about what had happened to them, from his past visits to the future of the vreality, but he couldn't. Either there had been nothing to remember, or he had been too busy enjoying himself to take any notice.

He shoved himself away from the rail and walked off the promenade. For the first few days he had tried to disguise himself but now there was no need. Starvation and ingrained dust made gaunt strangers of everyone.

He had decided to see if Keff would let him starve to death. There was no food; like many trading societies Shephhat grew little and imported much, and the much had become nothing on the day of the crash. It had taken a few days for warehouses to empty, many of them into the storehouses of the wealthy – and only a few days longer for the rioters to sack the storehouses. After that there was hunger.

Zeb rode the hunger like a discipline. He walked slowly, he rested often and he kept his breathing regular to avoid becoming light-headed. Now he was walking – slowly – up the long

174

shallow ramp from the promenade towards the tall buildings that lined the shoreline like monuments.

The defining feature of the city was new towers growing from old roots. Zeb had mentally divided them into three levels – the towers themselves, none of them less than three hundred metres tall, with the cost of habitation rising rapidly with height. They contained apartments and government offices and head offices and the best brothels. At their roots, nameless, powerless, luckless almost-people subsisted on the wastes that the wealthy let fall. In between, Shephhat's service sector hauled itself as high above ground as it dared, to be far enough from the poor without coming too much to the notice of the rich. The best of their homes were built in between the towers, not even reaching down to touch the ground. Connection rights to a tower couldn't be bought, but they could be leased, at an annual cost per square metre sufficient to feed and clothe ten families.

The middle levels were almost as crowded as the ground. Zeb had stayed at ground level, even though most of the towers were now vacant.

The tall buildings closed round him and the shorter ones over him, and the ground became damp. A few weeks ago it would have been soft and wet. The towers discharged their waste – *all* their waste – directly to the ground, where everything had once had a value.

But nothing had a value now except uncontaminated food and clean water, and since there was none of those things left in the city the rich had gone to shit on people somewhere else.

If other people didn't shit on them first, of course. Zeb's lips twisted.

Then someone tapped him on the shoulder.

His instincts, and what was left of his muscles, wanted to spin him round, but both were dull enough for him to ignore them, because spinning round would have meant falling over. Instead he took a couple of careful breaths and said, 'Yes?'

'Trying to starve yourself?'

Zeb felt his face draw into a harsh grin. 'It's worth a go.'

'No, it isn't. You can't die, Zeb, not until I say so, and I don't say so.'

Another breath. It didn't seem enough. 'Well done.'

'Sure. Now, a warning. If you try to die – *however* you try to die – I will know, and I will prevent it. And then I will reward you with a death, or maybe more than one death, of my choice. They won't last, of course. Sorry.'

'Right. Of course you are.'

And there were shouts behind him.

This time he did turn round.

There were four of them, all male, all young, and they were running towards him. They weren't saying anything but there was recognition on their faces. He put his hand up to his own face and felt smooth skin. The beard and the sores were gone.

He looked like his own picture again.

It was too late to run. The first man veered a little aside as he approached, swung out an arm and caught him on the neck. The force wrenched him round in a full circle, slamming him head first into a timber column. Green and purple lights flashed behind his eyes and he slumped to the ground with his face in the mud and his lungs empty.

The next kick killed him. With simple clarity he felt it land, just on his temple. He felt the bone of his skull give way, his face grind through the dried mud, the neat little *click* of something snapping in his neck, and then the sudden, complete absence of any feeling from his body and a draining of thought from his mind.

He expected – what? He didn't know what happened when you died, or how good an imitation of it a vreality could manage. He did know that they were still kicking him; he couldn't feel the blows landing but his head was wobbling and rolling on his limp neck as his body jerked.

Then they stopped, and for a moment there was quiet.

Fluid began to pool round his head. For a moment he thought someone was pissing on him, but even to his fading senses the stuff was pinkish and felt a little oily against his cheek.

Then he saw pale blue flames dancing above the fluid.

There was no pain, but he had just enough remaining sensation to know when his eyes began to melt. After that there were dreams.

At first he could guide them; he thought of Aish and saw her looking up from some work or other and smiling, and he smiled back, but she didn't respond and he realized she wasn't quite looking at him but slightly over his shoulder.

Then he pictured Shol and this time she was definitely looking at him, but not smiling; her brows were lowered and her face was flushed with anger. She was saying something but he couldn't hear the words.

He was about to picture something else when he felt control being wrenched from him. Images blurred. There were flashes of childhood, deep-buried but instantly recognized; there was an early lover but not his first, and there was half a pod tumbling slowly past his vision with the clean-sliced half-body of Iverrs leaking threads of blood that bubbled in the vacuum.

Then there was a hut, no, not a hut, bigger – a low wooden building, surrounded by birds that were books, flapping their pages slowly as they circled the place, and a voice he half recognized saying hello.

Then the dreams faded and he woke, with the memory of Aish and Shol and Iverrs and the others in his mind, all dead.

He wept helplessly from his melted eyes.

Handshake Space (neutral – disputed), Left Hand Stewardship

There was a read-out in his quarters. It showed a number which was an analogue of what their real speed would have been, across the ground, if there had been any way of expressing what was meant by 'real', 'speed' and 'ground' for something travelling as fast as they were.

The Orbiter had repeatedly tried to explain it to him, and repeatedly failed.

He allowed himself to understand that they were going very, very fast; that their speed involved the combined engine power of thirty-one remaining ancient battleships from the Sphere's cache, of which the smallest was two kilometres long – and that the Orbiter had never gone this fast either.

They were hanging between the ships in a latticework of fields that appeared red if he looked backwards and blue if he looked forwards. The red and the blue and to some extent even the ships themselves were illusions at this speed, but he didn't care. He had the impression that the old vessel was enjoying itself.

So was he. His quarters were odd, but in ways that pleased him – a series of rough chambers connected by sinuous tunnels, just big enough for him to walk upright. They were made of some stuff that looked like coarse grey concrete, but that was slightly warm to the touch. The Orbiter had said they were modelled on giant ant-hills. For a while he wondered if the ship was trying clumsily to make him feel at home, but he suspected it was much subtler than that. Or possibly it was just having a laugh.

Things settled into a routine. Skarbo found it at the same time healing and boring. He spent some time exploring. The old ship had told him there were other models of the Spin, but not how many. He was beginning to wonder if its reticence had more than one purpose, and that one of the purposes might be fun.

He had found six so far. A couple were nearly as big as the one he had seen first but one, hidden away in a damp forest glade, was small enough that he could almost embrace it. None were as elaborate as the ones he had made, but the Orbiter had plenty of other opportunities for elaboration – there seemed no limit to the variety of habitats it had managed to squeeze in, and he suspected it had other hobbies as well. One of which was reticence.

Grapf followed him around. He began to like the little machine, which seemed to know the Orbiter very well.

At least the old ship had relented from its original plan to keep him and The Bird in the model bowl. As well as his personal ant-hill, he had the use of a little hut in the corner of an evergreen area. It smelled good, and as a benefit it had a viewing screen which showed current affairs and, he discovered, entertainments.

In a moment of aimless fiddling about, he had discovered that the screen could be made to display 'time to destination'. Right now the figure shown was just over two hundred hours – ten days – but that, he had found, was not ten days to the Spin. Even at this unimaginable speed, getting there would apparently take longer than that.

We cannot approach the Spin like this, the Orbiter had said.

'Why not?'

The Bird had answered first. 'Because we'd look like a missile! Probably get shot out of the sky. Bang! Pieces.'

The creature is right. We could be taken to be a Dispersable Invasive Force. The Spin may have defences against such things. It used to.

The plan, then, was to pause and regroup about a light-week from where the Orbiter believed the Spin's sphere of influence probably ended. From that distance, the Orbiter could make it to the Spin under its own steam in about another thirty days, with some of the old warships riding cover at a discreet distance. Good enough.

But there was something else.

You will probably have to disembark for a few days.

Skarbo had paused at that. 'Really?'

I advise it.

'Why?'

I intend to reconnoitre. Spin space appears silent at present, but that does not mean that it really is so, or that it will certainly remain so.

'I don't understand. I thought the Warfront was behind us.'

It is. But is it only behind us?

The Bird hovered, canting its body up and down in a gesture Skarbo had decided was an avian nod. 'Who fights a war with only one front? Eh?'

Yes.

Skarbo frowned. 'Can't one of the warships go?'

It would be too noticeable. If I go alone I might still pass for an amiable geriatric.

Skarbo avoided The Bird's gaze. 'I see. Where will we wait for you?'

But the old ship said nothing.

This did not impress The Bird. Later it barged into Skarbo's quarters, already talking as it came through the door.

'It said where we're going yet? Eh?'

It meant the Orbiter. Skarbo sighed. 'No,' he said. 'I expect it will.'

'Expect? Ha. Know what I expect, do you? I expect it's senile. Or stupid. Both. Spent too long plotting in dark corners and remembering the good old days. Know how old the thing is?'

Skarbo shrugged. 'Old.'

'Damn right. Tens and tens and tens of thousands of years. AIs don't last for ever.'

'I suppose not.' Then something occurred to Skarbo. He looked sharply at The Bird. 'How old are you?'

It had been dragging a claw restlessly along the ground. Now it paused for a moment and looked up, twisting its neck to stare at him with one eye. 'Told me all your secrets, have you?'

Skarbo said nothing. It seemed to take that as confirmation. 'Course not. Why shouldn't I save a few?'

'As you please.'

'*Please* has nothing to do with it. Nothing *please* about what's going on now. Or what's going to happen. Senile.'

'You called me that, once.'

'Might have been right. Maybe you and it deserve each other.' It shook its wings and flew off.

Skarbo watched it go. Maybe we do, he thought. As for you and I? He shook his head.

The screen in his hut had been showing 'one day to destination' for a couple of hours when something pinged softly. He looked up from the old movie he was watching. 'Yes?'

We are decelerating – about to dock. It will take a few hours. Would you like to watch?

A few hours seemed rather a long time, but Skarbo didn't have anything else to do. He nodded. 'Yes please.'

Please come back to the model bowl.

He sighed. 'Can I see it from here?'

Not so well.

'All right.' He levered himself up on to legs that seemed stiffer each day, and walked slowly back through the forests to where they had seen the model of the Spin on the first day.

The model was still there, but the bowl had changed. The misty walled edges had gone, and now it seemed he was standing in space with the Spin below him and the network of warships all around. There was a fluttering behind him, and he half smiled to himself.

'Hello,' he said, without turning round.

'Hello yourself. Been having a good time, have you?'

'Good enough. You?'

The Bird flew past to hover in front of him. 'No.'

He was about to ask why when the old ship spoke.

Now.

And the lines of colour between the ships began to strobe fiercely.

Skarbo fought off the impulse to duck. 'Is that supposed to happen?'

Yes. Wait. You will see.

He waited – and then the lines vanished. He drew a breath. Above him The Bird made a clicking noise.

He was looking at two interlocking rings, slender and rough-textured. There was nothing to give away their size, but some sense told him they were very big indeed. 'Ah, ship?'

Two hundred kilometres.

He blinked. 'I hadn't—'

You were going to ask how big they were.

He heard The Bird muttering 'smartarse' under its breath, and ignored it. 'Yes, I was.'

Each ring is presently two hundred kilometres in diameter. This may change soon.

'How?'

The Left Hand Stewardship has authorized extensions. There is population pressure.

The old ship explained things.

It was called Handshake, which apparently referred to some arcane form of greeting from when everyone that mattered had hands. The galaxy was full of things rather like it, except for the shape.

It was a pattern which had been repeated uncountable times through history. If you had run out of space, or food, or money, or luck wherever you came from, you climbed into the least busted old ship you could find and headed out. When you ran out of fuel, you either bought some more, if you were lucky enough to have the means, or stopped if you were everyone else. Handshake was what happened to the kinds of people who stopped.

Ring-shaped structures weren't new, in space. You could make an airtight tube out of almost anything, and a circle was the most logical shape. The rings of Handshake were sectional – each ring was made of roughly six hundred sections, each about a kilometre long. The sections were isolated from each other: infectious diseases were common among refugees, but this way they could only spread so far. The same could be said of other passing issues, like insurrection or accidental vacuum.

Interlocking rings were more unusual. Skarbo watched them for a while. Then he said, simply, 'Why are they like that?'

As usual the ship didn't answer. He shook his head and turned to The Bird. 'Do you know?'

'Not know. But surmise. Peacekeeping.'

'What?'

'Peacekeeping. Obvious. Two rings, two governments. Redundancy, see? But they've got to cooperate. Got to keep the rings aligned, otherwise,' and it shrugged expressively.

'Oh. Does it work?'

'Suppose. The ship says they're at war with each other. Still seem to be floating around nicely.'

They were closer now. The space around the rings looked hazy; Skarbo realized it wasn't haze, but ships. 'There must be millions,' he said out loud.

'Maybe. Bad times everywhere. People running.'

'Where from?'

'Told you. Everywhere.'

Skarbo stared at it. 'From the Spin?'

'Maybe. Close enough. From the Warfront. From whatever the Warfront ends up fighting. Ask the ship.'

For once, the old ship didn't wait for further prompting. *Remember that Handshake sits at the point where several spheres of influence just fail to meet. It is, fundamentally, outside almost everywhere, so it is a natural point of exit for everyone.*

Skarbo thought about that. 'And afterwards?'

There is no afterwards. Handshake space is small.

'And therefore crowded.'

Indeed.

They watched Handshake growing larger until the whole of both rings no longer fitted within the hemisphere of display above them. The network of warships around them had disengaged and dispersed – less threatening, said the Orbiter – and they were creeping forward at a gentle thousand klicks through a cloud of local craft and space junk.

Then the Orbiter spoke.

I have accepted the hospitality of the Left Hand Stewardship.

Skarbo looked at The Bird, which shook its head. 'Meaning?'

As you look at it, the right-hand of the two rings has agreed to host us. They outbid the Higher Closed Loop.

Skarbo sighed. 'Which is the left-hand ring, yes?'

Of course.

The Bird hopped. 'I like outbid. Makes us sound valuable.'

They think we are. You have been invited on board. I will need a few days to do my exploring.

Skarbo watched the image. 'They're at war with each other. Is it safe?'

Everywhere is at war with everywhere else. I am reasonably confident that you will be safe here. I am not confident that you will be safe with me, which is why I am exploring. Besides, you may find it interesting.

The Bird leapt noisily into the air. 'May? Not in doubt! Bored, bored, bored. When do we go?'

They didn't mention you. But you can try.

Skarbo managed not to smile. And, with a corner of his mind, reflected that he had never heard the old ship make such a qualified statement. *Reasonably.* Well, well.

The Orbiter came to a local stop just under two tenths of a second from the Left Hand Stewardship, neatly aligned with its axis. One of the old warships was hanging around a second further out, just in case, and the others had made themselves scarce.

The Orbiter had given Skarbo something it called a beaconer – a flattened dull metal ovoid small enough to lodge under a corner of his outer shell. Once there it seemed to stick. The old ship had assured him it wouldn't fall out. A sharp tap, and it would call for help.

He wondered if it did other things, but the ship didn't say. It itched a bit.

He tried to ignore it while they watched the little shuttle creeping towards them. The Bird clicked its beak.

'Skarbo'll be dead by the time that thing gets here. If it ever does. Nervous, or slow?'

Probably neither.

It wasn't impressive, whatever else it might have been. There was something improvised about it – an unfinished-looking lumpiness and asymmetry which screamed home-made.

Then it had arrived, and docked with a series of scraping thumps.

Skarbo looked at The Bird. 'Still sure you want to come?'

It made a contemptuous whistling sound. 'Still sure. Anything's better. Come on.'

The inside of the shuttle was roughly functional – a stubby metal tube with rows of bench seats which seemed to be made of wood. There was nowhere for a pilot, so presumably the thing was automated. It felt somehow nautical, thought Skarbo, and it smelled of oil.

The Bird made a loud sniffing noise. 'Phaugh!'

Skarbo looked down at it. 'You don't have a nose,' he pointed out.

'So what? Still stinks.'

There was a mechanical clank and the shuttle jolted. Skarbo staggered a little and grabbed the back of a bench. 'We seem to be off . . .'

Then there was a hoarse buzz, and an electronic-sounding voice said, 'Welcome aboard. This is the charter shuttle *Son of Zephyr*. Our journey time to civilization will be ten minutes, Left Hand local. In the event of depressurization, air-breathing creatures will die. Please be ready for acceleration.'

Skarbo looked around, but apart from the benches he couldn't see any way of being ready for acceleration, or anything else. He shrugged and sat down. The Bird arranged itself on the seat beside him in what looked like a crash position, wings couched and head lowered.

For once it hadn't said anything. Skarbo found himself wondering if it was air-breathing.

Then, with no more warning, force slammed him back against the bench. It lasted about ten seconds and then stopped as fast as it had started.

He looked round, and saw The Bird extracting itself from the angle formed by the back and the seat of the bench. It stretched its wings. 'Acceleration? Don't think it did that on the way here.'

Skarbo was about to say something, but the electronic voice got there first. 'It didn't. But *Son of Zephyr* was learning the route on the way out. It knows the way back to civilization, now. We can go *fast*! Prepare for more.'

They prepared.

There were three more fierce jolts of acceleration, and then a nauseous series of blasts and skews as the shuttle matched velocity with the huge ring. Then there was another grating mechanical clang and they were docked.

The journey had taken less than ten minutes. It had felt like an hour.

'We arrive! *Son of Zephyr* is proud to deliver you to civilization and will be proud to return you when you are dismissed. Equalizing pressure . . .'

There was a hiss and a soft air current that smelled of something muskily organic. Then the front section of the craft split along a line that hadn't been visible before, and opened itself like a beak.

'Please! Step forwards. A Floater will be here shortly.'

'A what?' Skarbo looked out through the opening. It was poorly lit. He could just make out several big, vague shapes. 'Why is it so dark?'

'Sir, Floaters do not enjoy bright outside. Inside can be different. Here is yours . . .'

One of the shapes had drifted closer. It was bigger than he had thought – much bigger, at least fifty metres across and roughly spherical. As it closed with the entrance, a patch on its surface wrinkled and peeled open, starting as a dot and quickly growing to an orifice big enough to walk through.

The Bird hissed. 'What is that?'

'Floater. This is the Dirigible Fungus Fillpsps. For onward journey within!'

Skarbo stepped forwards. The musky smell was stronger, and there was a faint warm, slightly humid air current against him. It came and went, very slowly. He looked down to The Bird, which was standing next to him with its neck thrust forwards as if it was studying something. 'Is it breathing, do you think?'

It shook its head. 'Don't think anything. Dirigible Fungus? Nothing to think.'

Behind them the shuttle's voice said, 'Enter. Onward journey to greater things. I must go.'

The Floater had come close enough that there was almost no gap. A short step took Skarbo into the thing, and a rattle behind him told him The Bird had followed. The beak-doors of the shuttle shut behind them with a brisk clank, and the opening of the Floater wobbled closed in an uneasy pastiche of lips contracting.

The inside smelled of rot. It wasn't quite dark – the walls gave off a dim phosphorescence that made Skarbo think of small things squirming. It was enough to see that the space wasn't a simple sphere: there were lumpy protuberances and mounds sticking out at random. Skarbo sat on one of them. It gave a little under him, as if it was full of liquid. It was more comfortable than he had expected. He patted it, and looked at The Bird. 'Join me?'

The Bird shook its head. 'Not touching anything I don't have to. Might catch something. Pissed off with stupid games. You seem resigned. Can't think why.'

Skarbo watched it for a while. 'Maybe I just look resigned,' he said eventually.

The Bird said nothing.

Skarbo closed his eyes. Just for a moment, he told himself.

*

Not all Floaters were alike. Some were bigger than others, for a start. This one was three hundred metres across, and nearly five hundred long.

'They're all connected.' The small elderly-looking human male called Gorrif waved an arm in a circle. 'Hundreds of kilometres of micro-myco-fibres. The ones near here can't move about much, of course. The fibres are in the way. And this one's basically immobile. Right in the middle, you see? But the outer ones, like your friend Fillpsps and so on, can range quite widely if they're careful not to get tangled.'

Skarbo nodded. 'How long have you been collecting them?'

'Collecting?' Gorrif gave a high-pitched laugh. 'Oh, I don't really collect them. They wouldn't like that idea, I'm sure. I host them, I suppose. Peculiar things, aren't they?'

Skarbo nodded again, but said nothing. He wasn't sure what position Gorrif was in to call anything peculiar.

It had taken them a while to get here from the point where the shuttle had dropped them off. Fillpsps had drifted a few hundred slow metres before handing them on to another, slightly smaller Floater, and they had changed hands another six times by the time they had come to a stop against the dull-brown, warty hull of the biggest Floater they had seen.

Its size was the reason the Dirigible Macro-Fungus Gadaps had been chosen as a dwelling by Gorrif when he had arrived here a few hundred years ago – he was vague about time but then he seemed vague about many things; Skarbo had the impression that here was another creature who preferred his own company.

Gorrif had been hospitable despite that. Especially to himself.

The low table in front of them was loaded with little oval leaf-shaped plates that Gorrif said were made of shed fungus layers. They held snacks that Skarbo thought smelled like shed fungus layers.

He looked at them. 'Are these all edible for me?' He had played the phrase through in his mind a few times. It seemed blunt, but he had run out of any other way to put it.

'Yes, I believe so.' Gorrif waved the hand again. 'If you have any doubt, please feel free to pass. I won't be at all insulted.'

'Oh. Thank you.' Skarbo looked around for The Bird but it had wandered off, muttering darkly to itself, when they had first arrived, and he hadn't seen it since. He added, 'And I won't be at all insulted if you feel free to enjoy yourself.'

'Quite.' Gorrif spoke through a mouthful. 'And of course there's plenty to drink. I'm on firmer ground there, to be honest.' And, as if to contradict himself, he reached unsteadily for a flask, grasping it on the second attempt.

'Yes. Well, thank you for your hospitality.'

Gorrif took a sip from the flask. 'You're welcome. I was most excited to have won, I'm sure you will appreciate.'

Skarbo blinked. 'I'm sorry?'

'Are you? Why?'

'No – I don't understand. What did you win?'

Gorrif put the flask down carefully. 'Well, you, of course. The right to host you, at least. Didn't you know about the lottery?'

Skarbo stared at him. 'No,' he said. 'I was told that the Left Hand Stewardship had agreed to host us. That they had outbid the others.'

'Ah. Apologies! That's true, but it's not the whole of it. They needed to get their costs back, obviously, so they ran an internal lottery and I won. We do tend to monetize everything here.'

He paused, and looked at Skarbo as if he was expecting something. Skarbo said nothing, and after a moment the man blew out his cheeks. 'It was rather expensive.'

For a moment Skarbo couldn't think of anything to say. Eventually he settled on, 'I'm flattered.'

'Oh, no. The honour is all mine!' Suddenly Gorrif was on his feet. 'I've looked you up, of course. Such a history! All those years of study – lifetimes! And the models, oh, the models. Is it true that they were all destroyed?'

'Yes.' Skarbo was about to say that there were more models on the Orbiter, but then stopped. He didn't trust this creature.

'How dreadful. But of course, there's more to the story than that, isn't there?'

'What do you mean?'

The hand waved again. 'Well, obviously there is. All those rumours can't be wrong. Why do you think I spent all that money? Eh? Do have a drink.'

He shoved a flask forwards, but Skarbo waved it away. 'What rumours?'

'Oh, don't dissemble. I'm sure you know better than anyone.' Gorrif leaned closer and Skarbo caught the smell of many different substances on his breath. 'The Spin, of course. You studied it for hundreds of years. Obviously you didn't publish everything you discovered. Who would? I don't blame you. You'd be a fool not to keep something in reserve.'

Skarbo resisted the urge to take a step back. 'I'm a fool, then.'

'I doubt it very much.'

They stared at each other for a moment. Then Gorrif looked down, his face collapsing from eager to sulky. 'Well, if you won't tell you won't. Seems a shame. I daresay I'll find out. Perhaps your bird will tell me.'

Skarbo shrugged. 'I doubt it. And so you know, it's not my bird. I'm definitely not responsible for it.'

'Yes. I imagine that would be a burden . . . well, well. If you can't eat and you won't drink and you won't talk about your lifetime obsession, at least let me show you something more about mine. Gadaps? We'd like to see out. Will you dilate, please.'

There was a tremor beneath Skarbo's feet and the end wall of the Floater rippled and split, pulling apart along a vertical line until the room was completely open to the exterior.

The great dim shapes outside seemed closer, seen from here. And closer to each other, too, in a way that somehow made Skarbo feel tense. He walked towards the opening to get a better view. There was something . . .

Then he saw it. He turned to Gorrif. 'Are they *squaring up* to each other?'

The little man smiled. 'Well done. Your lifetime habit of observation serves you well.'

'But they're not going to fight?'

Gorrif spread his arms. 'Why not? I'd hardly be much interested in them if all they did was to float around, would I now?'

Skarbo stared at the man for a moment. There was something new in the eyes, or perhaps it had always been there and he had just noticed it? Something cold and hungry . . . Then he looked out towards the shapes outside. Two of them were definitely drawing closer to each other. Without looking away from them he said, 'Why do they fight?'

'Ah. They don't fight each other in the wild, of course. But this is a stressed environment. There isn't enough room, you see? Normally, if a colony gets too dense in the middle, there's space for groups to separate and drift off somewhere else. Not here.'

Skarbo looked sharply at him. 'Are you saying you do this deliberately?'

'It's a consequence of the environment.'

'But you determine the environment.' Skarbo looked away. As a human, he would have felt sick. That had been engineered out – but he could remember it.

'Yes, I suppose I do. And a bit of quiet bioengineering, if I must be honest. They have a natural defence mechanism – a layer immediately beneath the tegument is slightly corrosive. It makes them less likely to be eaten by things that move faster than they do, you see? But here, the effect is stronger. Much stronger, in fact. Strong enough to be used as an offensive mechanism. And the chemistry varies from one to another, so they aren't evenly matched. You never know which will have the advantage, but it's rather fun guessing. Watch.'

And Skarbo knew he was going to, and that made it worse. He tried to tell himself he was showing some kind of respect for them, but it lacked conviction.

The two Floaters were almost touching now. They were roughly spherical, rough-surfaced grey-brown masses that Skarbo guessed were about twenty metres across. Dozens of slender filaments radiated from each one to what Skarbo found himself thinking of as the watching Floaters – although whether they were really watching he didn't know. He didn't want to ask Gorrif.

Then the two touched.

There should have been a spark, thought Skarbo, or a gasp from a watching crowd. There wasn't – just two bodies pressing slowly against each other so that they visibly flattened at the point of contact, pausing for a long moment, and just as slowly bouncing apart.

But not unchanged. Even from here Skarbo could see an ugly blistered patch on one of them. It seemed to be spreading.

'Ah!' Gorrif was by his side. 'A good start, that. But just a start. Which one has your bet?'

'*Bet?*' Skarbo shook his head. 'Absolutely not.'

'A pity. It would have made things much more interesting. I was thinking of offering you the chance to win back your companion.'

The words sank in slowly. After a long moment Skarbo made himself turn to look at the man. There was no doubt about it – the eyes were definitely cold. 'What did you say?'

'Your companion. The avian creature. Friend, possibly. I did speculate about lover, given how you bitched at each other.'

'The Bird? What have you done to it?'

'Oh, nothing yet. Merely detained it. It is rather tiresome, isn't it? Honestly, I would understand if you decided not to win it back.'

Skarbo decided the man was serious. He wondered if he should ping the Orbiter; the beaconer was still itching faintly at his shell. He thought for a moment. He had no idea whether anyone here could do The Bird any serious harm. If he had to bet on anything it would be that the thing had allowed itself to be detained for its own reasons. He shrugged. 'You will need to release it when we leave,' he said, and turned away to watch the show outside.

But not so quickly that he missed the flash of disappointment that crossed the pudgy face. He smiled to himself, just a little.

The two Floaters had drifted apart and were now closing again. The injured one, if that was the right word, had managed to rotate a little so it was presenting undamaged skin. Skarbo wondered if that was it – the whole strategy? And how much skin could the thing lose before it did whatever they did? Died, he supposed.

But then he saw that the injured creature was gaining height – quickly, and the fine threads that joined it to the others were stretching and snapping so that it was trailing a gently waving clump of them like some sea creature.

'Ah.' Gorrif nodded. 'A high-risk strategy. Now we'll see.'

Skarbo couldn't see what the creature had gained. 'Won't it die, now it's disconnected itself?'

'Possibly. Not certainly. Watch.'

The injured Floater was almost directly above the other. It had stopped rising, but the other had started to gain height, presumably in response. As it rose it brushed a tendril, very gently.

It stuck.

Skarbo ramped up his vision as far as he could, until he had a grainy view of a few square metres of tegument. It took him a moment to realize what had happened – the tendril hadn't stuck. It had penetrated, and an ugly little raised crater was growing around it. As he watched the fibre began to thicken.

Then another touched, and another. Skarbo pulled back his focus until he had the two Floaters in his field of view, and already the view was very different.

The two were joined by a thickening bunch of the fibres that were pulling the skin of the lower Floater into an ugly peak. Then it tore, peeling away to reveal a dark pinkish-brown substrate that looked uncomfortably like exposed flesh.

The injured creature began to lose height. As it fell it pulled at the skin still attached to the bundle of fibres, and the tear grew, running around the body in a ragged fissure that started to drip clear liquid.

As Skarbo watched the thing seemed to shrink and shudder. He turned to Gorrif. 'Do they feel pain?'

The man shrugged. 'I don't really know. Who cares?'

Skarbo looked at him for a moment. Then he said, 'I'd like to leave now.'

'Yes, I expect so.'

'And?'

'That can be discussed shortly. Besides, don't you want to see the coup de grace?'

'No.'

'Feel free to look away.'

But Skarbo didn't.

The falling Floater was still turning, hanging off a lengthening strip of its own skin, and the victor was still rising, keeping the tension on the bundle of threads that maintained its death-grip on the other. The watching – if they *were* watching – Floaters seemed to be drawing away a little. Skarbo wondered if they had lost interest, now the spectacle was almost over. Hating himself for doing it, he asked: 'What happens to it now?'

'Keep watching. Ah! There. See?'

And he *had* seen something, but he wasn't sure what. Something had flicked across his field of view and stopped at the victim. He looked harder – there was another, and another, and now he could see.

He wished he hadn't.

There were carrion-eaters in this place, then. They were little black flying creatures, too small for him to see clearly even with his vision ramped up to the threshold of pain; but he could guess. They were smacking into the peeled flesh and disappearing. Burrowing. He imagined sharp mouth parts . . .

Next to him, Gorrif was smiling. 'You see? The thing is almost dead now, but nothing will be wasted. The Floater Mites will make sure of that. It will make the perfect host for their larvae. You should be proud.'

Skarbo turned to him slowly. 'I?'

'Well, yes. Of course! You and the Mites have some shared heritage, at least in spirit. Insects together!' He looked sly. 'Or do you propose to deny the choice you made, all those lives ago?'

Skarbo bore down on his anger. 'I deny nothing. I am not the perpetrator of this. And, I repeat – I wish to leave.'

'Ah, of course. As I said, that needs to be discussed.'

Skarbo shook his head. 'I have nothing to discuss with you.'

'Perhaps so, but I wasn't referring to myself. There are other interested parties. I assume the little thing concealed under your carapace is a signalling device?'

The anger ebbed, to be replaced by something else. For the

first time since Hemfrets had invited itself to his planet, Skarbo felt fear. He stopped the slow movement of his claw towards the device the Orbiter had given him. 'Supposing it is?'

'Would you gamble on your ancient friend being able to come to your aid unimpeded by some of those interested parties? Ah, but I forgot. You have already told me that you don't gamble.'

Skarbo forced himself to speak calmly. 'Are you going to allow us to leave?'

'Us? Well done for remembering. No, I am not. With apologies, I have already received nine offers for you. Do you know what's happening out there?'

Skarbo waited.

'You're in a war zone. I don't know what's going to happen to you after you're sold, but I'm not going to stay here. I wouldn't have done in any case. Have you any idea how bored one can become with Floaters? Stupid things. I've been ready to go for years. Any one of those offers would get me out and away, so I suppose you should be flattered by that. I will be accepting the highest – ah, now, as it happens. There. Done. And certainly it cannot be undone, in case you were thinking of asking. Your new owners have rather forthright business habits. Even my death would not be guaranteed to nullify the contract. And in case you're thinking of appealing to the Left Hand Stewardship, don't bother. They'd be breathing vacuum if they interfered.'

Suddenly Skarbo didn't need to force himself to calmness. It was happening to him anyway, the only sane response to a situation so far out of his control as to be almost comical.

Almost.

His claw had completed its interrupted journey. He felt it close on the beaconer, felt the little device scratch its way out into the open. He held it up.

Gorrif laughed. 'Gambling after all? A last desperate throw?

Well done. I'm almost relieved. There must be a bit of human left in you after all.'

Skarbo shook his head. 'You were right the first time. I don't gamble. But I don't think the Orbiter does either.' And he squeezed the little thing gently.

There was a faint *pop*. Then the beaconer shook itself free from his claw and flicked away to hover in the air halfway between him and Gorrif.

They watched it for a moment. Gorrif laughed again. 'Waiting for an answer, I expect,' he said. 'It will have to wait a long time. I told you, this is a war zone. Your mad old friend is probably a cloud of vapour by now.'

Skarbo said nothing.

Then the little speck began to move, swinging slightly from side to side and turning on its axis. It looked, thought Skarbo, as if it was searching for something.

The movement stopped.

Then it was gone.

A fraction of a second later the room exploded.

The blast threw Skarbo backwards towards the dilated opening. He landed on his side a couple of metres from the edge and desperately dug his claw into the floor. It yielded just enough to give some purchase and he managed to stop his slide.

The room was full of dust and swirling debris. His shell felt as if it had been squeezed in a vice, but by some miracle he had kept his remaining limbs.

He heard a cough, and looked up. Gorrif was lying near him, his confused face white with dust. A scarlet trickle from one ear contrasted starkly with the mask. He raised himself on an elbow. 'What . . .'

'I don't think it waited for a reply,' said Skarbo. He unhooked his claw from the floor and stood up, keeping the open claw pointing at Gorrif.

The man's eyes were fastened on the claw. He licked his lips. 'You're still sold,' he said. 'There's no point fighting.'

'There's no point me doing nothing.' Skarbo took a step towards the man. 'Maybe I have something in common with those mites after all.'

The eyes opened wide, and the man scrabbled backwards along the floor. 'Now, wait . . .' he said.

'I've waited.' Skarbo took another step towards him.

Then there was a furious screech and something burst into the room and hovered between them.

'*Haaaaa!* Where *is* the fucker?'

It was The Bird. It, too, was covered with dust. Its eyes were wild and its feathers were sticking out as if frozen in mid-explosion. It gave a few harsh flaps while it stared at Skarbo as if checking him over. Then it nodded, wheeled round, pointed itself at the prone Gorrif and launched itself downwards like a missile, screaming hoarsely.

It landed on his face, claws first. Gorrif yelped and thrashed his arms at the thing but it clung on, claws raking, beak stabbing. Now and then it made a '*ha*' noise.

Skarbo winced, and looked away until the howls and the wet noises had stopped.

After a while The Bird hopped round into his field of view. 'Ah! Needed that. Now, think we'd better leave.'

Skarbo allowed himself to stare at it. From the shoulders back it was still white with dust, but everything in front of that was slick and red. He didn't quite manage to quell a shudder.

The Bird met his eyes. 'A bit extreme, you think? Possibly. Sorry. Channelling the inner raptor.'

Skarbo nodded. 'Don't restrain yourself on my behalf. I didn't like him.'

'I could tell. You raised a claw. Never did that to me, no matter how I pushed . . . but take some advice? If what I look like bothers you, don't look at him.'

199

Skarbo held the gaze for a moment. Then, deliberately, he turned away and looked at the shape that had been Gorrif.

The body was quite still. The remains of the face were angled upwards. The skin had been peeled away in raking gashes. The mouth was open, and a section of what Skarbo realized was severed tongue lay across the lips. The eyes were red-blue holes. A cold, detached little part of Skarbo looked for any evidence of eyeballs, and found none.

He turned back to The Bird and drew a breath. Then he let it go.

It tilted its head. 'Decided not to ask something?'

He nodded.

'Wise. Ha! Rhymes with *eyes*. Shall we go?'

He nodded again. 'Yes. How?'

'Good question. Think things are in hand. Just not sure which hand.'

Then there was a distant bang and a high, moaning hiss. The floor quivered under him and he felt his carapace flex.

'Bird? I think there's a puncture . . .'

'Yes. Explain later. Think things are going to get busy. Remind me whether you can survive vacuum?'

'I don't know.'

It swivelled its head and glanced up at him. 'Better hope busy means quick . . .'

The pressure was definitely falling. He took a breath that seemed hard-won. 'Can *you* exist in vacuum?'

It didn't answer. Then there was a *pop* and they were surrounded by a hazy violet bubble. His shell stopped flexing.

Someone had generated a field. He looked round. At first he saw no one. Then The Bird said, 'Ah-*ha*,' and he looked again.

A few centimetres outside the field, and joined to it by a fine violet tendril, floated the beaconer.

The Bird gave a hop. 'Talented little thing . . . sorts us for the moment.'

Skarbo nodded. 'Do you know what happens next?'

'No.'

Skarbo looked from The Bird to the beaconer. It was just – hovering. He shrugged. It was worth a try. 'Um, beaconer? Can you extract us from this place?'

It didn't move.

He tried again. 'Have you signalled the Orbiter?'

Still nothing.

'Are you waiting for something?'

The little thing twitched.

The Bird clicked its beak. 'Better not wait long. Place is falling apart.'

Skarbo looked around. The Bird was right. Gadaps was not dealing with the reducing pressure. Nasty-looking bulges and blisters were swelling on the inside of its hull. The floor was rippling, and the opening to the outside was quivering and clenching as if in a battle with itself. Through it, Floaters, tangled in their own fibres, bounced off each other like executive toys.

Then the opening snapped shut. The Bird *yawk*ed. 'What's that mean?'

'Defence, I suppose.'

'And trapped! Didn't you notice? Your turn to think of something. Come on!' The voice was higher-pitched than usual.

Skarbo sat on one of the more stable floor projections. 'What do you want me to think?' he asked.

'Anything! Get on with it.'

'All right.' He looked at the creature for a moment. 'I think I can't imagine any way out of this that lies within my power. I also think that not only are you not what you seem to be, you are not even what you claim not to be. As I may die here, and you may do whatever it is that whatever you are does, it would be courteous of you to be honest with me.' He shrugged. 'You did say, anything.'

201

The Bird stared at him for a while, switching its head from side to side as if seeing which eye gave the best view. Finally it said, 'You choose unusual times for your confessional moments.'

'I'm not confessing. I was hoping you would.'

'I'm sure you were.' It went on staring at him for a while. Then it looked away and shook its head, the most *human* gesture Skarbo had ever seen it perform. 'I'm not a bird. I've been telling you that for hundreds of years. As for the rest? Some secrets are secret, and some secrets are other people's secrets, and many secrets aren't as interesting as you think. Take your pick.'

Skarbo nodded. 'That was as much as I was expecting,' he said. 'So, what do I call you now?'

'Stick with bird. I'm used to it.'

'And how do we get out?'

'I still don't know. It was your turn to think of something. Remember?'

The floor rocked. They looked at each other. Then the end wall dilated abruptly, as if the edges had been forced apart by something.

They had. The Bird stared, then turned away. 'Oh, shit. Again?'

Skarbo nodded. 'Again,' he said. 'Hello, *Son of Zephyr*.'

'Greetings! Sorrowful that civilization falls short. At your disposal!'

The Bird muttered, 'Disposal sounds about right . . .'

Skarbo prodded it with a foot, and it fell silent. To the shuttle he said, 'Can you get us out of this compartment?'

'Certainly. The hole will allow exit as well as entrance. Please: board.'

They boarded. The field bubble and the beaconer moved with them. As the beak thing squeaked closed, Skarbo said, 'Ship? May I ask something of you?'

'Anything! It is my pleasure.' And the voice sounded genuinely enthusiastic.

'Well, would you mind accelerating very gently this time?'

There was a tiny pause. Then the ship said slowly, 'Not go fast?'

'If you wouldn't mind.'

Another pause. Then, 'Very well. Slow. Uninteresting.'

Something struck Skarbo. 'Can we see out?'

The voice perked up. 'Certainly! I have full screen-through capabilities. Look!'

The walls blurred and vanished, and they were standing on nothing.

The little shuttle was shouldering its way through a throng of Floaters. The things didn't seem to be making any attempt to get out of the way, and he could see their skins stretching and grazing against the invisible hull as the ship pushed them aside. Smears of thick mucus with snapped fibres stuck to them fogged the view.

He wished he had allowed speed, now. Any acceleration would have been better than this slow-motion slaughter. He shook his head. '*Son of Zephyr*? Are these organisms common?'

'No. Dirigible Fungi are rare. One planet only.' It still sounded enthusiastic. 'Those in this compartment are unique! Genetically altered. There are none others. *Son of Zephyr* is glad to give you sight-seeing tour.'

'Or genocide, as we call it.' It was The Bird, and for once Skarbo found himself agreeing. 'Ship,' he said, 'can you disable the view, please?'

'Disable? But it is unique . . .'

Skarbo said nothing, and after a moment the view faded and turned back into wall. Now he could see the bench seats again he sat slowly down on one, and The Bird hopped up next to him.

'Don't think those things had much of a life,' it said quietly. 'Might be a relief.'

Skarbo stared at it. 'Are you developing sympathy for other creatures, bird?'

It *yark*ed. 'Only some of them. Don't assume it's universal, insect.'

Skarbo nodded. He was about to reply when the shuttle shuddered and then seemed to leap forward.

'We are out!' The ship sounded pleased with itself. 'Do you want to see now? It will be instructive.'

It didn't wait for an answer; the hull cleared, and they were looking back at the ring. The shuttle must have speeded up because there were already three segments in the field of view. It was easy to tell which one they had just left – there was a neat round hole punched in it. A cloud of ice crystals was dispersing, and if he looked closely Skarbo could see dots and blobs. Floaters, or what was left of them.

He shook his head. 'Ship? Did you make that hole?'

'No! *Son of Zephyr* has no capabilities of this nature.'

'Then what did?'

'The small device you carried.'

Skarbo blinked. 'Really?'

'Indeed! Many capabilities. Ah – there is a message.'

It stopped speaking, and after a moment there was a warmly human voice.

'Attention, shipping. In view of recent events, the Left Hand Stewardship of the Handshake has gained approval for the ninety-first segment to be excised immediately. The operation commences. To avoid field effects, withdraw to a distance of ten kilometres and stand by.'

The ship lurched violently, and suddenly the ring was much further away. The movement stopped, and just as suddenly the view zoomed back in, grainier now as if heavily magnified.

For a moment, nothing seemed to be happening. Then Skarbo saw a bright, fierce dot at either end of the segment, at the point where it joined its neighbours. The dots grew bigger, swelling into lurid magenta globes.

Then an arc jumped between them – a wavering red line that began to spread itself round the segment until the whole thing was surrounded. The intensity climbed to a peak, and then, so suddenly it made Skarbo's eyes flicker, the segment was gone.

He stared at the image. 'Is that it?'

The ship sounded edgy. 'For the present! The Stewardship will now be seeking bids from more suitable tenants to fill the vacancy. Meanwhile, fields maintain the integrity. See?'

At first Skarbo didn't see, but then his abused optics adjusted and he could make out a faint purple thread, joining the severed ring.

Next to him, The Bird said, 'Hm. Bit summary. Ha. No need for Gorrif to worry about his contract now.'

Skarbo looked at it, made to say something, and stopped.

He was sure The Bird hadn't been in the room when Gorrif had mentioned that. He nodded to himself. 'Where do we go now?'

'Alas, *Son of Zephyr* does not know. I am despondent.'

Skarbo looked down at The Bird. It shook its head. 'Despondent, fat lot of use.'

'Contrition. War reaches us. All things become unknowable.'

'So where *are* we going?'

'Wherever safety . . .'

Then the ship lurched. Skarbo grabbed at the back of a seat. 'Please go to safety gently!'

'No . . . that was not *Son of Zephyr*.' The voice managed to sound nervous.

The Bird jumped into the air. 'If not you, then who? *Son of Imbecile*!'

There was another lurch. Then the ship said, in a flat tone, 'The insult is unmerited. *Son of Zephyr* has been arrested. We are held in a restrainer field. Apologies.'

Skarbo looked up. 'I can't see anything.'

'The field is not visible. Please be seated and await information.'

Now the tone was dully mechanical. Skarbo thought about this. Then he gave in to instinct. 'Ship? Are you afraid?'

The ship didn't reply. The Bird dropped neatly to the back of the seat and made a pantomime of shielding its head under a wing. At some point, Skarbo noticed, it had managed to clean off the blood.

Then they both looked up sharply. Another voice had spoken – also mechanical, but harshly so, like buzzing metal components.

'Attention. Life-form indicated. Life-form respond.'

Skarbo looked down at The Bird, which had uncovered its head. 'Life-form, singular?' he whispered.

It shrugged.

Skarbo smiled to himself. In his normal voice he said, 'Life-form responds. Who are you?'

'Attend.' There was a pause, then a different, human-sounding voice. 'Hello? This is Left Hand Patrol, External. It seems there's someone alive in there. Is that right?'

Skarbo carefully didn't look at The Bird. 'At least,' he said.

'In that case, you're under arrest. We always check, when we take on a crusher. We'll bring you in gently. Stand by.'

'Crusher?' The Bird swivelled its head to glare up at Skarbo. 'Thought this was a shuttle.'

Skarbo waved it away. 'Arrest?'

There was a pause. Then the voice was back. 'Let me explain. A punctured segment counts as criminal damage, and your ship caused it. It will be taken away and crushed. You are under arrest, as of now. We'll formalize it when you dock. You are liable for the disposal cost of your ship, plus the cost of your transport, cell, rental, air and rations, from now until the end of your sentence. If you don't pay, the sentence doesn't end.'

'Wait!' Skarbo was on his feet. 'It's not my ship!'

The voice sighed. 'You are the life-form on board, correct?'

'Well, yes . . . but . . .'

'Then you're legally in charge of what the ship does within a kilometre of Handshake. The Left Hand doesn't recognize ship AIs as being responsible, see?'

'I don't see! No one told me that.' Skarbo wanted to jab a claw at something. 'I was kidnapped!'

Now there was a hint of amusement. 'Records say you willingly entered a commercial arrangement. You knew about the lottery, didn't you?'

'No! Not at first . . .'

'Sure you did. You can't smash your way out of a segment just because you don't like the bargain. Sit tight. You're coming in. You and whatever you've got in there with you.'

There was a faint *click*. The ship moved again, but more gently this time.

Skarbo thumped the floor. 'Ship! *Son of Zephyr*! Talk to me.'

There was a long pause. Then the ship said slowly, 'Nothing to add but apologies. *Son of Zephyr* will be crushed . . . end.' It fell silent, and nothing they tried changed that.

There was only waiting, as the ship closed with the segmented rings.

When they docked, Skarbo was met in the airlock by a polite but insistent floating machine that arrested him. It seemed bemused by The Bird, which thought it was funny to perch on top of it, and summoned human help. The human help declared The Bird to be an unlicensed weaponized entity and added possession of it to Skarbo's charges.

He looked round for the beaconer, but couldn't see it. He hoped it was somewhere, doing something useful.

He felt a little sorry about *Son of Zephyr*. But on the plus side, they took The Bird away with them.

Wiits Range (vreality)

He let go of sleep unwillingly – more unwillingly every day – and looked up towards the leaf canopy. Bright light above it; he had slept long, and his luck had held. No rain today.

He reached out a hand. The bundle was still next to him. More luck – no one had stolen it. Perhaps after all he still had enough reputation to be left alone.

He turned on to his side, pushed down with an elbow and hauled himself upright. The bundle was tied with a looped leather thong. He reached down, hooked it up with a finger and let the loop fall round his neck and one shoulder. It dropped into its natural place just above the indent of his waist, and he felt it and then forgot it.

It contained everything he owned, and he had been carrying it for (and his mind advanced the number almost as if it had been a mechanical counter, with a *click*) three hundred thousand days.

The round number made him blink.

Onwards. Yesterday, before he had slept, he had decided to move on down to the coast. It was autumn, and there should be good catches of fish, and the women would be too busy fishing to repair the small ailments that came upon boats and tackle late in the season, so there would be things for him to do, and reward to be had, and possibly warm places to sleep, better than a carpet of leaves when the rains came on and turned it into a sodden mat.

His feet knew the way. He had followed this route (*click*) eight hundred and eight times. For the first few hundred years there had been no settlement. Then it had gradually accumulated, like a callus on a tree growing round some tiny burrowing creature. Now there were hundreds of houses. Most of their inhabitants were just far enough above the poverty line that they could be sure of still being around to suffer next year.

He remembered numbers. He had died (*click*) nineteen hundred times, although not recently. He had forgotten many other things.

People called him whatever they liked. Now-and-Then was one name and Passthrough another. There were more. It didn't matter to him.

He left the trees behind and loped easily down the shallow hills towards the coast. He couldn't see the water yet – that wouldn't be in sight for a couple of days – but the bank of cloud that always built above the shore was visible at the horizon.

At midday he stopped to drink some water from one of the small streams that rose on the lower ground. He ate little – was rarely hungry, couldn't really remember being so, not properly – but thirst was never far away.

Something in his head was trying to catch his attention. He stopped for a moment and focused his attention inwards, searching for it. It happened occasionally, but only at very long intervals. The last time, within a few days he had found himself at war. Not part of a war, but actually, singly, all on his own, at war with a civilizational group called (*click*) the Zamphr.

The time before that, there had been about to be a plague. Plagues were frequent. The weather patterns of the planet were still disrupted by the updraught from the Peace Rift – although no one was calling it that yet. But then, it was only a thousand years old. The other him would be getting ready to make his first regular visit round about now.

The time before that . . . didn't matter.

Never mind. He would find out what it was when it became.

The land flattened out as it neared the Sea. The ocean had no name he had ever heard other than Sea; the people who had colonized the shore over the last few hundred years were literal-minded. By the second day the forests thinned and gave way to grassland, which itself gave way to a tough, wiry mat of bluish-green Sandcreep. The blades flicked and sprang under his feet, threatening to slice his ankles, and he remembered (*click*) to stop and pick a couple of the long, tough leaves from a Palmsallow bush to bind round his legs.

He was among the first houses sooner than he had expected. In the (*click*) eighty-one years since he had last been here, the town had grown – again. Back then, it had stopped at the Back Banks, a peaked arc of warehouses and slopshops and flophouses and smoking little workshops that stretched up towards the hills – and therefore away from expensive property owned by sensitive people – like the pulled-back cord of a catapult.

Now the Banks was enclosed by its own catapult-cord of something much bigger and newer-looking. Low, anonymous sheds with shallow-pitched roofs and bland grey walls of cement blocks lined fresh roadways paved with something flat and uniform that wasn't mud or cobbles. There were chimneys, but the word seemed too antique; they were tall, slim metal pipes, and they didn't leak the old-fashioned curls of blue smoke, but their tops were stained black and the air above them shimmered and hazed with a blue-grey mist that spoke of hot, chemical processes.

There was an elusive acrid tang in the air. He stopped and sniffed at it, as if daring it to show itself fully. Then he laughed.

'Progress? The fuck you say.' He laughed again, and added another 'fuck' for good measure. Then he reset the bundle at his waist and walked past the new stuff, towards the old stuff that had been new before. Progress, indeed. Pollution, as well as starvation.

The Back Banks seemed much the same, if older and more broken. Clay brick walls which (*click*) had been straight and fresh when he last came this way were now irregular, and it seemed to him that the ways were quieter. Less people, or less movement, or both.

Interesting.

His feet took him to the same old place without intervention from his memory. The same sign still creaked on the same iron chains, an oil-painted image commemorating the last time anyone had tried to declare any sort of monarchy over the coarse self-governing people of the coastline.

The Gutted Prince. The name always made him smile. The sign less so – but, give it that, it was hard to forget.

Inside, the single room smelled mostly of the same smoke and liquids, with a hint of something else he didn't recognize. There was no bar, just a wide table in the middle of the room, covered with bottles and barrels and bundles of leaves and stacks of the little pressurized metal canisters that contained whatever vapour was in fashion.

Last time (*click*) the canisters had been in the minority. Now they occupied over half the table. Add drug dependency to the standard problems. Interesting. And, more interesting, the place was half empty.

It was time to sample. He thumped the table. 'Shop!'

And turned round, and found himself looking into a half-familiar face – wrinkle-tanned, with wide-set grey eyes. He squinted. '(*click*) Lanceste?'

The face widened into a laugh. 'You're Passthrough, yeah?'

He nodded. 'Among other things.'

'I thought so. I've heard of you.' The laugh stopped. 'I'm Lancreasty. Lanceste was my grandfather, and he left you a message – pay your bill or fuck off.'

He nodded again, pulled the bundle off his shoulder and looked round for a flat surface. There was only the table. He shrugged. 'Do you mind?' And pushed the heap of canisters to one side.

'Hey! Don't do that.' Lancreasty made to straighten the pile but found a hand against his chest. Brace, and push, and the man was staggering backwards, two, three, four barely controlled steps until the rail of a long wooden bench met the small of his back. He went over, head first.

The man who was presently Passthrough shook his head. 'Sorry,' he said. 'I'm pretty sure I told your grandpa he should move that thing.' As he spoke he was placing the bundle on the table.

Lancreasty had made it back on to his feet. He took one, but only one, step forward. 'I'll call the Straights . . .'

'Sure you will. They'll be along in a while.' Two leather thongs were undone, and the outer flap fell open. He took hold of it and flicked.

The bundle unrolled across the table.

He reached along the row, sorting and discarding. 'Ah, sorry. No money. That's awkward. But I have got one of these.' He selected one of the small, dull metal things, pulled back sharply on a lever (another sort of click) and held it out.

The stack of razor-edged discs at the end of the thing glinted. The room went quiet.

He smiled at Lancreasty. 'Know what it is?'

The man nodded, without taking his eyes off the thing.

'Well done. Any time you decide you don't need your eyes, you let me know and I'll bring it back. Now, I want—' He paused. He had been going to try several things, because it had been a long time, but now didn't seem like the best moment to get wasted. 'I want a brew. What have you got?'

Still without taking his eyes off the cocked Springer, Lancreasty reached towards the table and patted along it until his hand met a barrel. He snagged a glass, held it under the spigot, filled it and held it out. The surface of the muddy liquid trembled slightly.

Even drained at speed, as a substitute for everything he had been going to do instead, it tasted thin and flat. Slamming the glass down on the table and seeing the flinch in the barkeep's eye went some way towards making up for it. But only some.

He narrowed his eyes and leaned towards Lancreasty. 'So, tell me something. If the Straights are still going, are the Measures as well?'

Lancreasty didn't answer, but his eyes widened a bit. The Straights were merely a semi-private militia, but the Measures were the enforcement arm of an organized crime syndicate; one of their income streams was providing a quality assurance service for the Town Fathers. If you were caught out by the Measures, they impounded your business and cut off one of your hands. It worked.

'Because if they are, I think they'll be interested to hear you're watering the brew. Want me to tell them?'

The man shook his head.

'Okay. Sounds like a deal to me. No Straights, no Measures. And do me a favour?'

An eager nod.

'Don't leave any stupid messages for your grandchildren.'

Still keeping the Springer cocked and visible, he rolled up the bundle with one hand, fiddled the thongs back into a knot and swung it over his shoulder.

Then he turned round, and grinned at the watchful eyes of half a dozen customers. 'See you in a couple of generations, then,' he said, and walked towards the door.

As he crossed the threshold a hand caught his sleeve. He

looked into an unshaven face with a pair of yellow eyes sunk deep into dark pits. 'Yes?'

'He waters the brandy too . . .' The words were slurred.

'The hell you say?' He sniffed carefully. The smell was unmistakable. 'But you still drink it, right? Seems to me it's not him that's the fool. You might want to think about that.'

The man sagged.

Outside, he paused. The sun felt welcome on his shoulders. He took a deep breath, emptied it in a single gust, and took another to flush out the sour air of the room from his lungs. Then he laughed. 'You drink too much, anyway,' he told himself. 'Still addicted to something. Whatever. Onwards.'

Onwards took him through streets that sloped mostly down and got narrower as they went. The acrid smell had gone, replaced by older scents – tar and timber and the smoke of non-complex things burning, and fish and things to do with fish, and cheap, poisonously adulterated weed and, increasingly, too many people. Even though the sun wasn't hot or high yet, children sat in pools of shadow as if they weren't going anywhere else that day. Some prodded listlessly at broken objects that shouldn't have been toys. Some scratched patterns in the dust, making a soft *shush-shush* noise like sleepy insects. Some did nothing.

He stopped at a crossroads, under an overhang where the corner of the street had taken a bite out of the ground floor of a leaning building. Someone had mended the wound with square concrete blocks that crumbled a bit under his fingers. He didn't remember any of this.

'You poor old fucking place,' he said out loud. 'What happened to you?'

Then he froze.

There had been a noise – the quiet tap of metal against metal, somewhere to the left and behind him.

And another, this time to the right.

And no other noises. The children were sitting rigid, their heads down.

Patterns again. Left, and right. At least two, then, and they had cocked their weapons. Whichever way he went, they would assume, he must cross one line of fire and run along another.

Was this what he had been waiting for? Another death? Keff had taken its time.

It was a long time since he had seen Keff, now he thought of it.

Well, then. A mental shrug, and another guess.

Left it was.

He braced one hand against the blocks behind him and shoved, hard, kicking himself out from under the corner of the building and skidding hard round to the left, his feet scrabbling up dust.

The man in the Measure guard's uniform already had his musket at his shoulder, but it was still pointing at where the oncoming body had been when it broke cover.

There was a whistling *bang* and a cloud of grey smoke.

Gunpowder smell. Something touched his shoulder, no harder than a flicked finger, and then he was diving through the smoke.

He slammed into the body behind it and they rolled together. One hand found the musket, wrenched it away, hurled it. Then he was up and running again. Somehow the Springer was still in his other hand but the children were still there too; seen from his slowed-down chase world they were little statues near the ground, and the Springer fired wide. It was no use yet.

There was a shout, and another bang somewhere behind him. He felt something hit his hip, low down on the right, like being kicked, and then he was round a corner and panting in the recess of a doorway.

He had been hit. The place on his hip felt hot and numb, but a sharp pain knifed outwards from it, down his leg, and his foot didn't feel right. Nerve damage, then, and maybe a lodged musket ball. By comparison his shoulder just hurt a bit.

Both wounds were bleeding. That might turn out to be his biggest problem later, but it wasn't now, and he wasn't dead yet. This was almost fun.

Patterns, patterns ... what pattern would he be making right now, if he was either of them? Always assuming they weren't pattern-blind themselves.

Yes. That.

He listened, hard. The street was quiet, with the watchful lack of noise made by a whole bunch of people trying to be silent. It was an excellent background for ...

There it was. To the right. A very quiet footstep, close. And another, closer. One man, then, moving carefully. You know I'm here somewhere, friend, but you just don't know where.

One more footstep should do it.

It landed. He took a deep breath, raised the Springer into a position which should put it in the face of anyone creeping along the wall, and spun out of the recess, his arm ready to fire at—

The woman?

He went rigid, mid-turn, lost his balance and stuck out an arm to steady himself against the wall.

She was tall and thin, and her clothes were definitely not the uniform of either the Straights or the Measures. She looked relaxed; amused, even.

He managed to get himself together enough to ask, 'Who are you?'

She smiled. 'Someone you weren't looking for. But since I'm what you've found, shall we get on with it?'

He shook his head, and the movement made his shoulder hurt. 'On with what?' Belatedly, he raised the Springer.

She frowned, and shook her head. 'Don't do that.'

And suddenly the Springer was red hot. He yelped and

dropped it. Then he glared at her. 'How the fuck did you do that?'

'Long story.' She grinned. 'So, yes. Getting on with it.' And before he could react, her foot pulled back a little and then blurred forward.

The first kick caught his knee. The second, as he collapsed forwards, his stomach. He was barely aware of the third, except that the impact flicked his head round and back.

A constellation of coloured lights, and then nothing more.

Handshake, Left Hand
Stewardship – Independent
Penitentiary Co.

S karbo had kept careful count of the days since his arrest. There had been twenty-nine of them.

Fights were common.

The weapon of choice was a nailblade: sharpened toenails set into a length of anything available. The toenails of elderly bipeds were prized for their toughness. Prisoners received an allowance of dried leaves that produced an acerbic infusion if left in the water ration for a day. It made the water merely bitter and tongue-drying, according to those who had tongues. It also hardened nails, if they were left to soak in it until they matched its off-greeny-brown colour. Skarbo thought the nails and the brew smelled similar to begin with.

The toenails of deceased, and sometimes not yet deceased, bipeds were not in short supply. Attrition was encouraged, as an alternative to both release and feeding. Gorrif had been right about the tendency to monetize: The prison was private, taking one global payment when each inmate entered – and that was it, unless and until they paid off their own charges. It wasn't a business model that incentivized the management to keep prisoners alive for too long.

Skarbo tried to stay clear of the fighting. It wasn't too hard. His form set him apart. Someone had swiped him experimentally with a nailblade a few hours after he had arrived. It had glanced off, leaving a faint scratch. Too much like the material of his shell, he supposed. After that the others mostly left him alone, but it was a watchful avoidance. One that could end at any moment.

Now he was wedged into a corner while the two males tried to kill each other. He wished he knew where the beaconer was. He hadn't seen it since the arrest.

'Ten on the Cutter!'

'Twenty!'

The tall male called the Cutter looked poised, relaxed. He was better muscled and better nourished than the other, and the long nailblade sat easily in the palm of his hand. Skarbo would have bet on him, too.

Except that he didn't bet. And besides, the other man . . .

Well, there was something . . .

Skarbo wasn't used to assessing mammals. He had been no good at it when he had been one himself, and the memories, for what they were worth, had all faded. But the short male made something in his subconscious twitch. He was breathing hard, but it didn't look like the breathlessness of exertion. A thread of saliva swayed down from one corner of his mouth, and he wiped it away on a filthy sleeve. The movement dragged his lips down and, just for a moment, Skarbo saw a yellow tooth that was too long to be called a tooth.

So, fangs, then . . .

The tall one made a quick feint forwards, and then danced to the side as the short man lunged. The watchers growled appreciatively. The tall man laughed. It looked like a game.

The prison had once been divided into cells by a grid of fields, but fields cost money to run and maintain. Now it was a single, huge, open floor, perhaps a kilometre long and half as wide. People slept where they could, if they could, but never for long; the ones who survived were those who skimmed the upper surface of sleep. Deeper could be lethal.

The floor looked open, but wasn't. It was divided into patches – areas with fluid boundaries that changed according to the results of turf wars, bribery or even marriage. He had had to have the concept of marriage explained to him three times before he got it.

The patches didn't reach to the edge. A strip all the way round them was empty, bounded by people on the inside and, in concentric bands on the outside, a warn field, a burn field and the wall proper. He had clipped the warn field once, only partly by accident, and the shock had knocked him off his feet. The burn field, if one had the strength to get to it, did what the name suggested.

The perimeter strip formed a circuit just over three kilometres long.

Skarbo had found out about the patches by accident. You couldn't see them – but he had been walking his usual circuit when he strayed a few paces inwards and suddenly found someone in front of him.

'Fuck off, beetle.'

Skarbo had looked at the squat figure. He guessed female, but wasn't sure. He was sure about the smell. Even in here it stood out.

'I'm not a beetle,' he said.

'Sure you aren't.' A broken-toothed grin. 'How about roach? So, fuck off, roach.' A slight pause. 'For your own good.'

'Yeah. This is our patch.' Another voice. 'Stray in here again and she'll tear your legs off. What's left of 'em.'

'Should do it anyway.' Yet another voice.

And suddenly there were several people forming a tight arc in front of him.

He took a step back, and ran out of room. So they were behind him, too.

'I didn't know,' he said, and heard helplessness in his own voice.

A tall male stepped forward from the group in front of him. 'Need teaching, roach? Bet we can teach you plenty.'

Laughter.

A voice behind him said, 'Looks like his legs'd come off pretty easy. What do you say? Take the lot, or leave him with just one?'

The tall male spat. 'The lot. And then turn him over. Maybe there'd be something soft to scoop out.' He licked his lips.

The group closed in. Hands seized him.

'Hey!' The voice came from behind the group. They hesitated, and then Skarbo saw their faces harden.

'Hey! Shitmeat! Leave the roach alone.'

The group paused. The tall man's face flickered, and he half turned to speak over his shoulder. 'Fuck off,' he said.

'Yeah, maybe. But not until you grow up.' The squat female who had originally confronted him shoved her way through.

The man she had called Shitmeat spat again. 'On his side now, are you?'

She shook her head. 'No way. But I founded this patch, remember? And I don't want to be slipping over in a mess of insect guts either. I said leave the roach alone.'

'And I said fuck off.'

The woman shifted her position just a bit. 'Really?'

The rest of the group stood back. Shitmeat grinned. Then he threw himself towards her, hands outstretched, fingers clawing towards her face.

She didn't move until he was almost on her. Even then she didn't seem to move much – but there was a wet-sounding thud, and Shitmeat was on the ground, curled around himself. His eyes were closed, and he was making a keening noise.

The woman walked up to him and leaned down. 'It's still my patch,' she said.

Then she kicked, twice, hard enough for the effort to lift her a little off the ground.

At the first kick, Shitmeat screamed. At the second he vomited.

The woman stood back and took a breath. 'Grow up,' she said. 'And clean up your puke. I don't want to slip over in that, either.'

The group dispersed. Skarbo gulped. 'Thanks,' he said. 'I owe you.'

She was turning away as she spoke. 'Fine. Maybe in another world you'll pay me. Now, you fuck off too.' And then she was gone.

Behind him he heard someone say, 'Roach', and another voice sniggered.

After that he preferred to keep to corners. And managed not to tell himself that that was what roaches did.

Someone now tapped him on the shell, and a hoarse voice said, 'Space for another?'

Skarbo blinked. Courtesy was rare here, and when it did happen it wasn't always what it seemed. He gave himself a moment to get ready for whatever reaction might be needed, then half turned.

He blinked again. The tapper was an elderly human-looking male, and old age was as unusual in here as politeness. He squeezed himself to one side and the old man slipped in next to him.

'I'm grateful.'

Skarbo nodded, and turned back to the fight. The two were circling; the Cutter still had his nailblade, but he was looking warier now. The other looked relaxed.

'I'll take fifty each way . . .'

'Fifty? Where'd you get that much? Suck someone off for it, did you?'

Laughter.

A tap on his shell again. He turned fully this time and looked at the old man. 'Can I help you?'

The mouth split in a grin. 'I doubt it. I don't suppose I can help you either, 'cept perhaps we can talk to each other? It's not a tradition hereabouts but you never know, we might start something.'

Skarbo shook his head. 'I'm sorry. I don't think I have much to say.'

'Fine. I'll talk.' The old man stared past him at the fight. 'If I had money I'd bet on the little one. You?'

'Neither.'

'Doesn't surprise me.' The man narrowed his eyes. 'I heard some things about you.'

Skarbo waited.

'I heard you know when you're going to die. Is that true?'

'Yes.'

'Uh-huh. When is that, then?'

Skarbo hadn't been thinking about that. How long had he been here? He had to count in his head. 'Thirteen days from now.'

The eyes widened. 'As precise as that? And as soon?'

'Yes.'

'I should call you the deathroach.'

There was a crash, and shouts. The old man's eyes widened. Skarbo turned his attention to the fight.

The two men had closed. The Cutter was still upright but staggering, with the short man's head buried in his midriff and his arms wrapped tightly around his opponent, locking the tall man's arms to his side. The nailblade swivelled uselessly in a pinned hand.

'Ten on Rask . . .'

'And ten . . .'

'Twenty here . . .'

The old man nudged Skarbo. 'Sure you won't?'

'Bet?' Skarbo shook his head again. 'Won't, and can't.'

'Fine. I would, but can't. Listen, deathroach, we have something in common. I know when I'm going to die, too.'

There were more shouts. The pair had separated. A broad gash ran down Rask's shoulder, but he looked poised and watchful. The other man was clutching his ribs with one hand, and his breathing was short.

'A hundred on the little Rask!'

'Fuck your money . . .'

And then someone was pushing through the crowd to the front – a slim female with clothes that were actually intact and almost clean. She held up a hand, filled her lungs and shouted, 'Five hundred on Rask to kill the next time they close. Who'll take?'

There was a breathless silence. The old man leaned towards Skarbo and whispered, 'Be impressed, deathroach. In here, people are bought and sold for less than that.'

For a moment he thought no one was going to take up the bet, but then a voice from the crowd said, 'Taken.'

The woman craned to see. 'Who's that? Are you solo?'

'I am so. Lift me, you.'

Bodies moved around, and then someone was raised on to a shoulder – a squat humanoid creature with huge eyes set in a flat, pale face. It raised an arm. 'I'm taking your bet, you fucking termagant. You still good for it?'

'I'll take your money, if it's there to be taken.' She laughed. 'If not, I'll take you.'

The creature raised a finger and twisted it from side to side. 'Like fuck will you. Let them fight!'

The crowd roared.

The Cutter licked his lips and took a half-pace forward. Rask watched him. Then, too fast for Skarbo to follow the movement, he charged forward and leapt, landing with his arms and legs around the tall man's torso. They crashed and rolled and Skarbo saw the nailblade flailing and slashing, and when the two stopped rolling the Cutter was on top, but something was wrong – he was howling, a high, sharp sound, and the nailblade was held out at an unnatural angle.

He was still held by Rask's legs and arms, and the short man's head was buried in his armpit, working and twisting.

Then the Cutter's howl changed note. Rask pulled his head back, and there was something in his mouth – something that stretched out from the ends of a ragged, bleeding hole in the Cutter's arm.

Sinews. No, wait. Tendons. That was the word.

Rask growled, his jaws working, and suddenly the tendons snapped and the Cutter's arm was hanging, the fingers of the hand now limp around the handle of the useless nailblade.

And then Rask's head dipped in again, but this time to the throat.

There was an audible crunch. The howling stopped. Rask rolled over and climbed off the limp body. He stood and bowed, once.

Then he swallowed.

There was a moment's dead silence. Then the crowd roared.

Skarbo felt the old man's hand on his shell. Very close to him, the old voice said, 'Let's go. Unless you're bidding for meat?'

'Meat?'

'Of course. Why waste the body?'

Skarbo shuddered.

The old man didn't seem to have a patch of his own. They ambled across several notional boundaries and stopped in a clear space close to the outer walkway, where the old man squatted down. 'Here'll do,' he said, patting the floor next to him. 'Join me?'

Skarbo folded his legs beneath him.

From this close he could smell . . . something . . . on the old man's breath. It was sweetly sour. A smell of corruption.

He decided to ask the question. 'When will you die?'

The old man smiled. 'Sniff it, can you? You got good senses, deathroach. Humans can't. It'll kill me in three months, if I let it. I'm not going to let it.'

'I don't understand. How will you stop—Oh.' He fell silent, and shook his head.

The smile broadened. 'I see you worked it out.' The old man took a breath, and Skarbo heard bubbling. 'I got a dose of Flakeworm. You know what that is?'

'No.'

'It's parasites. Little eggs, so small you can breathe 'em in, and they grow to worms and the worms grow to bigger worms, and then one day they all bust out and turn into Flakeflies and you breathe 'em out again.' He paused. 'Only, breathing 'em out isn't so easy as breathing 'em in, if you see what I mean, and you don't get to breathe them all out because they get stuck, and the ones you don't breathe out find other ways to get by . . . I'm not going that way.'

Skarbo nodded. 'What will you do?'

He got a sharp look. 'That's my business. Got plans.'

For a moment neither of them spoke. Skarbo watched the thin chest lift, pause, and fall, and listened to the faint catch at the top of each breath that gave away the effort it cost. After a while, as the old man didn't seem inclined to volunteer anything else, he said, 'Do you know where you caught them?'

'Know? No. But guess – I guess I got them on a freighter on the way out.'

'Out of what?'

'Where, not what. Out of the Spin, deathroach. That's where.' The old eyes narrowed. 'Got your attention, did I?'

Skarbo nodded, only realizing he had done so when the movement was finished.

'Thought I would. Want to hear the rest?'

This time the nod was conscious.

The old man was called Pathin. He talked, slowly, about the Spin.

The population of the Spin had peaked, at least in modern history, at just under a trillion formal inhabitants, and as many again who were anywhere between less formal and passing through – but that had been a quarter of a million years ago. A long time, but still modern by Spin standards.

Since then, the trend had been uninterruptedly down, and the curve had been steepening.

Pathin had lived on a planet called Zshifs. He looked up at Skarbo. 'Hear of it?'

'No.'

'Thought not. Outer Spin, on this side. Two suns, one of 'em red. Three planets.'

Skarbo half closed his eyes. He could visualize the models . . . 'Yes,' he said. 'Got it.'

'Good. Nice place. Farms. Pretty coloured shadows from the suns. People used to say if you got laid by the light of the red one, the child would be a girl. Could have been right.' The old man let out a sigh which tailed off in bubbles. 'Then the sun started failing. Less light for the farms, you know? Then people started sticking these big solar panels in orbit. Gather the energy high up, before it hits the atmosphere, that's what they said, and beam it down. More efficient.'

Skarbo stared at him. 'But how would anything grow?'

'You tell me!' Pathin shook his head. 'So things died, year by year. And I left. We all left. There was nothing else for the freighters to do anyway. No goods. No food. Just people, leaving. Know how many were on board with me, deathroach?'

Skarbo shook his head.

'Five thousand. And that wasn't one of the big ones. I heard a thousand ships left the Spin just that day.'

Skarbo looked at the old man for long time. 'How many?' he asked eventually.

'You heard.'

'Yes, but . . . that would mean five million people on the same day? Why that day?'

Pathin coughed and spat. He studied the streak of phlegm for a moment, then looked back at Skarbo. 'You don't get it, do you? Not just that day, deathroach. Every day. Millions every day. Hundreds of millions every year. I wasn't the first, and it got quicker after. You looked at the Spin from the outside and saw it was dying, right? Well we looked at it from the inside and felt it dying. What was there to do? Go virtual or get out. I got out.'

'And here you are.' Skarbo looked around the floor.

'And here I am, but that's not all my story. I've done plenty since. Got laid. Got drunk. Made money. Lived a life.'

Skarbo thought about that. Then he asked, 'How long since you left the Spin?'

Pathin smiled gently. 'I told you – a life. A long one. I reckon the Spin's about empty by now. I'd guess it's the first time in history a whole galaxy's been evacuated. If you're hoping to go there and meet living things, you're too late. They'll be gone, or virtual.'

'Virtual?'

'Of course. Living in the machines, deathroach. The vrealities. A lifetime in one of those takes a few hours in the outside. What do you think all that solar power was used for?'

There was a long silence. Skarbo felt a cold, quiet knot growing in his abdomen.

Then Pathin nudged him. 'Don't give up, deathroach. You're not done with your life yet, and nor am I – not quite! Neither of us knows the final score yet. I'll tell you mine at the end.' He looked up sharply. ''cept in your case, I probably won't. Not if you've any sense.'

Skarbo laughed. 'What choice am I going to have?'

The old man looked at him for a second, then looked away.

The crowd had dispersed. People were milling past, trailing muttered conversations. Some were carrying lumps of red flesh, none bigger than the palm of a human hand. A few were chewing.

The loser had not gone to waste. Nothing in here went to waste – and it occurred to Skarbo that here was another reason he was being left more or less alone.

Basically, he didn't look edible.

He shuddered, and reached out a claw to Pathin. 'These people from the Spin. Where did they go?'

The old man waved a hand vaguely. 'Everywhere. Anywhere. They're here, for a start.'

'Refugees?'

'Some. And some not. Plenty brought money. They're running businesses. Planets, some of them. This place, too. Brought their feuds with them, they did. That's why Handshake has two ends.'

Skarbo looked at him. The wrinkled face was expressionless. 'So, how did you come to be here?'

The old man turned and spat again. 'None of your business, deathroach.'

Skarbo nodded. 'Well, thank you,' he said. He stood up.

'Wait.'

The old man's hand was on his leg. He looked down. 'What?'

'Maybe I can help you after all. Haul me up.'

Skarbo held out a claw. He wasn't sure how much help he could be; even wasted as it was, the old man's body weighed enough to pull the limb off. But it seemed the idea of support was enough, and Pathin pulled himself to a standing position without more than a soft tug. Once upright, the old man leaned in towards him. His voice seemed hoarser. 'See where I spat?'

'Yes.'

'Tell me what you see.'

Skarbo frowned. He looked towards the streak of saliva.

Then he looked back at Pathin. 'I see flakes,' he said. 'Brown-coloured flakes.'

'Yup. That's the beginning.' The old man slapped his chest. 'I feel 'em. It's coming, and early. This is where you help me and I help you, deathroach. Come with me down to the far end. If I falter, drag me.'

Skarbo nodded, and began to walk alongside him. They went slowly, with Pathin pausing every dozen or so paces to draw a dozen rough-sounding breaths, but they went.

At the far end the floor narrowed. The bodies thinned out; this was the worst lit, worst ventilated part of the prison, and only the poorest, sickest or least mobile stayed here.

At last they were at the very end. The last occupied patches were behind them, and they were on empty floor. The walkway, and the field beyond it, formed a narrow arc-shaped barrier, partly enclosing the biggest empty area of floor Skarbo had seen here. Dark and remote and stuffy though it was, even so he didn't understand why no one had claimed it as a patch.

Then he saw a roll of stained cloth on the floor ahead of him. Pathin sighed, slumped down, and gathered the cloth under his head, and Skarbo got it.

'This is your patch?'

Pathin grinned, and even in the poor light Skarbo could see that there were brownish fragments on his ruined teeth. 'Yup. Home. Good place for a last stand, eh?'

'I suppose so.' Skarbo looked around at the empty floor and the stained cloth, and something in him broke. 'I'll stay with you.'

'Oh no you won't.' Pathin coughed, spat into the palm of his hand, and closed his fingers around the result. 'You may not be bothered by creepy-crawlies, deathroach, but that's not the half of it. Not even close. Besides, I'm giving you a job.

Much harder than watching your relatives fly out of my mouth. You up for that?'

Skarbo smiled. 'Yes,' he said. 'They're not my relatives, but yes.'

'Good. Here it is: get everyone, every living creature, away from here. Create a clear zone of at *least* a hundred metres. You got that?'

Skarbo stared at him. 'I heard it, but—'

'A hundred metres! Hell, deathroach. You were ready to watch me turn into a hatchery for flying insects. How is this worse? Sometimes you don't get to choose your challenges. Get on with it. And get on with it soon. You've got five minutes.'

And he turned his face downwards and buried it in the cloth. His body was shaking with coughs.

Skarbo looked around. The boundary of the patch was closer than a hundred metres – much closer. And there were people near by. They hadn't been there before, but the sight of an insect crouching next to an obviously dying human had piqued interest.

He had an audience.

He stood up and, bereft of ideas, began to walk towards the edge of the patch. The watchers stood up as he approached.

'Did you kill him, roach?'

'What's to see?'

He swallowed. 'Pathin wants to be left alone.'

Laughter. A young male pushed to the front of a growing group. 'An old weird man dies. People watch. You going to stop us?'

Another one joined him. 'Careful. The roach might wing you to death.'

More laughter.

Skarbo shut his eyes for a moment. Then he had the idea. He opened them, as wide as he could, and pointed back over the heads of the crowd. 'The doors! Look!'

They spun round and stared. Then the first youth turned back. 'What? Can't see anything from here. What's going on?'

Skarbo willed earnestness into his voice. 'You can't? Of course; you have mammal eyes . . . the field is down. I can see it.' He raised his voice. 'The field is down! Run!'

For a long moment nobody moved. Then someone started to walk. And then run. And then they were all running.

Skarbo heard bubbling laughter behind him. He turned to Pathin. 'This had better be good,' he said. 'Or I'm dead.'

The man laughed again, a stuttering rasp full of obstructions. 'You'll be dead either way, if you stay here. Run yourself.' He curled over and put his head between his knees.

Skarbo stared. Then he ran.

The moving crowd had gathered numbers as it went. The floor behind it was empty, and Skarbo's claws skittered over the surface. He had never been good at running; this form didn't suit it.

Then the room lit up. For a fraction of a second he could see his shadow, lancing out at a low angle for metres in front of him – and then he was blown violently forwards, and hot air was scouring his shell.

Drops of something pattered down.

He rolled to a stop and turned to look behind him.

Pathin was gone. Scraps of cloth lay at the centre of a flower of red on the floor where the old man had been.

And behind that, a ten-metre-long break in the haze of the burn field. And beyond that again, a ragged hole.

Skarbo began to walk, and then to run.

As he reached the place he hesitated, one leg over the torn threshold, as if to test its ability to bear weight – even, to be real. Then the rest of the crowd caught up with him, and he was shoved forward. Belated sirens began to wail, but they were coming from behind him.

It was logical to run.

He ran.

*

Skarbo woke slowly from a sleep he hadn't realized he was having. It was quiet, and the surface beneath him was cool metal. He opened his eyes.

It was dark, and the air was moving slowly and smelled industrial – oily and burnt, with a sour undertone which was gone almost before he had noticed it. He listened for anything. At first he heard only the noises of his own body: the subliminal creak of ancient, stiff carapace and the faint surge of body fluids, usually drowned out by background noise even in the quietest place. He listened to them patiently until he was so familiar with them that he could filter them out and hear past them.

There it was. A deep, slow pulse – and now he had fixed on it, he realized it was in time with the ebb and flow of the air currents. An ebb and flow that favoured one direction very much over another.

So that was where he was – but where was everyone else? There must have been hundreds in the crowd.

Well, it wouldn't be solved from a prone position. He lifted himself cautiously, and discovered that standing still worked.

Now, which way to go? There were senses he barely remembered having, that were all about echoes and air movements and how close things were, and they were telling him that walls on two sides were close and the ceiling was low. A tunnel, then. Or a duct.

And therefore only two choices. To where the air was coming from, or to where it was going.

In space, mechanical things created air but living things breathed it. Out loud he said to himself, 'I choose living,' and began to walk.

For a while he thought the duct was straight, but then he realized that he was unconsciously correcting his course in response to those senses, and always in the same direction. He was walking round a long, shallow curve, as if his environment was wrapped round something else. As he went, the echoes changed, as if the space was getting bigger. Or as if the duct was widening towards something.

Then he tripped over the first body.

He couldn't see it, even with his optics strained to the edge, but just from the length he guessed it was male.

He shook his head and stepped over it.

A few dozen paces further on he found another. Then two together, and then a tangle of them, difficult to count in the dark, and now there was a sweet smell in the air above them as if something caught in the fabric of their clothes was very slowly seeping out.

Then the duct turned a corner and he saw light ahead. He quickened his pace, stepping high to keep his body above the bodies on the floor.

Another corner and it was light enough to see. He stopped and looked, his breathing shallow.

There were hundreds of them, and they were piled up against the wall that closed the duct. It wasn't solid; it was made of a metal mesh with spaces big enough for a human arm to fit through. Many arms had fitted through it, and were frozen in the middle of their desperate gestures towards the other side. A few lay severed on the floor beyond. The sweet smell was very strong.

They had been trying to get out. Skarbo recognized some of them from the prison.

He was still staring at them when he felt a faint movement in the air beside him. He turned towards it, and as he did so a crisp voice said, 'You are dead.'

The voice came from above him. He looked up, and saw something like a dull metal bar about a metre long. It was floating, almost vertical but with its top angled a little towards him, so that he felt looked at.

'What are you?' he asked it.

'I am an Excrutor. You are dead.'

He felt like laughing. Instead he shook his head. 'No. They are.'

It leaned back as if surveying the scene. 'The procedure is successful. They are dead. Therefore you must be dead.'

Skarbo looked around at the bodies. He thought of the sweet smell. 'Was it gas?'

'Yes. Cyanide. Therefore you must be dead.'

Skarbo shook his head again. 'It seems not. What are your instructions?' And tensed.

It seemed to think for a moment. Then it swung itself horizontal, one end pointing at Skarbo. 'Amendment: insect form renders you anomalous,' it said. 'This is to be corrected.' And before he could react it had blurred through a flat arc and struck him like a club.

The blow connected with his head, hard enough to lift him off his feet. He landed on his back and rolled, thumping awkwardly into the pile of bodies at the end of the duct. His impact dislodged one of them and it flopped down next to him, one arm lying limply over his head like an embrace.

He didn't wait for the pain. From the corner of his eye he could see the thing that called itself an Excrutor bearing down on him; another blow like that and it would be right, and he would be dead.

He reached up the pile of bodies, grabbed at a protruding leg and pulled as hard as he could.

For a moment he thought it wasn't going to work. Then there was a little movement, and a little more, and one more desperate heave brought dead people rolling down on to him like an avalanche. More than he had thought – the weight thumped down through his shell and flattened him against the ground.

The thumping stopped, and there was quiet for a moment.

Then he felt blows, rapid and repeated, transmitted down through the inert flesh and bone, and the weight on him seemed less. The Excrutor was coming for him, and it was coming fast.

He had run out of ideas. He wondered what would happen if the thing broke his shell.

The last corpse was whipped away. He turned over, flailing limbs upwards as if they would have any effect against this airborne cudgel.

He was surrounded by smashed meat. Corpses lay around him as if they had been at the centre of an explosion. The Excrutor was poised above him. It was smeared red and flecked with shreds of skin and bone. It swung back.

He closed his eyes, waited, and then opened them again.

The thing was still motionless at the top of its backswing. He watched it for a long second. Then, panting, he scrambled backwards over the ruin of flesh, his claws slipping and scrabbling on the slick surface.

The thing still didn't move, but now he could hear a faint, harsh hum. It was getting louder.

The outline of the Excrutor blurred. Then it began to smoke. Skarbo backed away.

The Excrutor now started to glow, climbing quickly from sullen red to a sharp yellow. Drops of molten metal fell from it and sizzled on the flesh below. Then it simply dropped, landing flat on the body that had shielded Skarbo.

There was a loud hiss and a cloud of sweet-smelling smoke. Skarbo crept forward.

The Excrutor was half buried in the charred, steaming grave it had burned for itself in the dead man's flesh.

Skarbo sat back. He was breathing hard, and his head felt – strange. He reached up and touched the place where the blow had landed. He had expected to find himself split, to feel fluids leaking out. He supposed he *had* fluids? But there was nothing to feel; no obvious damage. Even so, he still felt strange.

'Took a hit?'

Skarbo jumped. The voice had come from the heap of bodies. Which was moving.

An arm extended up, a corpse rolled aside, and someone stood up. She wiped an arm over her face, and grinned. 'You should know all about burrowing into heaps of dead stuff – roach.'

There were broken teeth in the grin, and the breath stank, and as she said the word he remembered. She had called him that before. After the fight.

He breathed out. 'Is there anyone else alive?'

'No.' The word left no room for doubt.

'How did you survive?'

She shrugged. 'Good luck and good genes. I heard you talking to the old man.'

He waited.

'You're interested in the Spin.'

'Yes.'

'Want to go there?'

'Yes.'

'Forget it. You might as well burrow down into that lot,' she gestured at the heap, 'and wait for the juices to fall into your mouth.'

He suppressed a shudder. 'Why?'

'What the old man said? He knew less than half of it. He came from money, roach. He knew long words. He could pay for a freighter berth, when there still were some. He knew shit about where the rest of us came from.'

'You're from the Spin too?'

'Where else?' She frowned, cleared her throat, and spat. 'Ugh. Fucking cyanide. Not even imaginative. Yeah, I'm from the Spin. Everyone's from it, roach. No one goes *to* it, not any more.'

Skarbo sighed. 'Tell me about the Spin. And, please? My name's Skarbo.'

She watched him for a moment. Then she spat again. 'Okay. Skarbo. I'm Chvids. I'll tell you about the Spin, but I won't do it here. The management will be sending someone along soon and I don't want to meet the sort of people they'll send.'

Skarbo looked around. There didn't seem to be many options. 'Where shall we go?'

She grinned. 'Out, would be favourite. This way won't work, so I'd bet on that way.' And she pointed back down the duct.

They walked back through the darkness, past the point where Skarbo had woken. The breeze became stronger, and so did the industrial smell.

For a while neither of them spoke. Then Skarbo said, 'Why didn't you come this way in the first place?'

He heard a soft laugh. 'Think about it. There were hundreds of us. What happens if I'm the only one running this way? Pretty soon I won't be the only one. It's not the ones at the back of a crowd that get crushed. Plus, I guessed they'd gas. Better to run away from that stuff, even for me. If I lived? Then I could go back.'

Skarbo nodded. Then something occurred to him. 'What did you do to that – thing?'

'What? The Excrutor? Nothing. That wasn't me. Guessing that was you, my friend.' Another laugh. 'One more good reason to hang out with you.'

He shook his head. 'It wasn't me.'

'The hell you say.' There was a pause. 'Someone looks after you, Skarbo. I think I'll stick around.'

'You looked after me . . .'

'Yeah. But those shits are dead, same as all the other shits. It's just us.'

Skarbo said nothing.

They had passed the ragged hole back into the prison floor.

A hundred metres further, and the duct widened abruptly and split into three. It was still dark, but Skarbo's eyes had gone on adjusting, rather to his surprise. Now he had a grainy forward view, and Chvids was a swaying shape next to him. Her eyes shone faintly.

Skarbo stopped. 'Which way?'

Chvids paused, and he saw her turning her head from side to side. 'Not sure. I think there's more air coming down the middle; maybe that way?'

She took a step forward, but Skarbo reached out and stopped her. 'Wait,' he said.

'Why?'

He looked at her, surprised. He had known his eyes were superior to mammals', but he hadn't realized that his ears were too. 'Can't you hear it?'

'No. What?'

'Try, then. Just listen.'

They stood silently for a moment. Then she nodded. 'Like a rattling?'

Skarbo felt himself grinning. 'Like that,' he agreed.

'Which means what?'

Skarbo grinned wider.

Then it was on them.

'Haaaa! Found you. Alive? Alive! Ha. Who's this?'

Skarbo looked down at the woman, who had covered her head with her arms. 'This is Chvids. Hello, bird.'

'Hello yourself. Stupid!'

Skarbo blinked. 'How so?'

'Why didn't you wait?'

'Where?'

'The other end. Stupid!'

Skarbo sighed. 'How would I know to do that?'

'Thought melting that flying club thing would be enough of a hint. What else would it have taken?'

'I didn't know that was you.' Skarbo reached down and touched Chvids on the shoulder. 'It's—' He paused. He had been going to say *a friend*, then just *friendly*. He compromised. 'It's not an enemy.'

She uncovered her head. 'Really?'

'Really.' Skarbo hesitated. 'At least, I don't think so. I've known it for eight hundred years.'

She turned, slowly, and he saw her eyes open wide. 'The fuck you say.'

'Yes.' He shrugged. 'Bird? Where do we go?'

'Middle way. The Chvids thing was right. Tell her I'm not a bird.'

Skarbo laughed. 'I'm glad to see you,' he said.

It made a creaking hiss, and snapped its beak. 'That makes one of us. Come on. People are waiting.'

Chvids looked at it. 'What people?'

'People. Come on.'

Skarbo held out a claw. 'Wait a moment,' he said. 'Would these people include the Orbiter?'

The Bird paused. Then it tilted its head from side to side. 'Maybe. No sign of it, but it knows best. No other traffic either. War's coming, Skarbo. The Warfront's on its way. There's a no-fly zone for two hundred klicks around the Handshake now; agreed by both rings. We look stuck.'

'Right.' Skarbo stared at nothing for a moment. 'Well, we'd better think of something. Hadn't we?'

'I have. I only said we *look* stuck. Get moving.'

You couldn't see the Ringway unless you looked closely enough, and there wasn't any way of looking closely enough without getting close enough to be sliced in two.

It was quite a well-kept secret.

Skarbo held on to the grip in front of him. 'How fast?' he shouted.

The Bird swivelled its head so its beak was close to him. 'About a thousand klicks. Feels faster, yes?'

'Much faster.' It did; even with little surface detail on the connected pods of the Handshake, and nothing else close by for the eyes to fasten on, there was something urgent about the way the little capsule was moving.

'Is it fast enough?'

'Don't know. Hope so. Still accelerating a little.'

The Bird had certainly thought of something.

The Ringway was a circular thread-field that went right round the outside of the left-hand ring of the Handshake. A dumpy capsule big enough to hold half a dozen medium-sized humans hung off it by two rings of the same field type, one at each end, to give a sort of frictionless circular zip-wire. It only needed a small reaction motor at one end of the capsule for acceleration, and one at the other end for braking, and you had a fast, simple way of getting around the whole structure without having to bother about the internal doors – or, importantly, going through anyone's territory; by long agreement the Ringway was neutral, all the way round.

It was also very noisy. The reaction motors were antique pulse-jets and at speed they made an angry yammering noise which set the whole capsule vibrating in sympathy. The inner, relative to the Handshake, half of the pod was clear, meaning you could see the thin violet line of the thread-field, seemingly dead steady in the centre of the view, with the segments of the Handshake flicking by in the background.

Chvids was grinning broadly. It exposed eroded gums. Skarbo had expected to be bothered by this, but he wasn't. *I'm getting less human*, he thought. *Should I care about that?*

And knew that he didn't.

He cared less and less about most things. Food, for one. On their way here The Bird had asked, suddenly: 'When did you last eat anything?'

The question had made him think. 'I don't know,' he admitted. 'A while ago.'

'What sort of while?'

He thought harder. 'Ah, when we got to the Orbiter, I guess.'

The Bird glared at him. 'That's a long while ago. It's too early for you to be shutting down. You need fuel.'

'I feel fine.'

'That means nothing. Mammals feel fine while they're freezing to death. Some insects feel fine when they've got a brain parasite that makes them fly round in circles.'

'Really?'

'No, I made it up. Ha! *Obviously* really. Don't trust your body to make decisions for you, that's what I'm saying. But, presumably, that means if nothing has gone in, then nothing's come out?'

Skarbo stared at it, then shook his head.

Chvids tapped him on the shell. 'Ask the bird thing if there's any food,' she said.

Skarbo sighed. She didn't like talking directly to The Bird, and it in turn didn't respond to her third-party questions.

And in any case, he knew the answer. There wasn't any food. He wondered when *she* had last eaten. And, as an aside, if The Bird needed to eat at all.

Now it was speaking. He shook himself. 'Sorry, what was that?'

It raised its voice to a near-screech to cut through the noise of the pod. 'I said, we're up to speed. Are you ready?'

He nodded.

'Right. Let's get on with it.'

Skarbo turned to Chvids and motioned her to hold tight. She nodded and clenched her fingers on the rail in front of her. Her lips were compressed.

Skarbo nodded at The Bird, which was somehow managing to hang on to the vibrating rail above the control patch. It

243

seemed to take a breath. Then it loosened its grip and swung on the rail until it was upside down, its head level with the bottom of the patch. It glared at the patch for a moment, switching its head from side to side as if scanning. Then it made a quiet *ha* and stabbed its beak at the patch.

When it pulled back, there was a neat oval hole in the patch. The Bird regarded it for a second and then stabbed again, three times into the same spot.

On the third stab, there was a fizz and an acrid electrical smell.

The Bird swivelled itself upright. 'Think that's it. Might take a—'

The lighting flicked from neutral to a glaring blue and an alarm blared.

The pod trembled. It skewed violently round, slamming Skarbo against the side of his seat – and then the gravity was gone.

The motors fell silent. The light faded and died.

'—moment,' said The Bird quietly. It looked around. 'That did it. We're off.'

Skarbo looked towards what had been *up*. The thread-field was gone. So was the Handshake, and instead there were stars.

Chvids's face was pale in the faint starlight. 'What happened?'

Skarbo reached out a claw to touch her on the shoulder, and then thought better of it. 'We've broken away. We're free-falling out of Handshake space.'

'Flying away from the ring?' Her voice trembled a little.

'Yes. We should be picked up.' He didn't add the word *soon*. He assumed she was grown-up.

She nodded. 'Picked up by who? These people you talked about?'

Skarbo looked at The Bird. It shrugged. 'In the end. Probably. Tiny volume, Handshake administrative space. Once we're out of it they won't bother with us.'

Chvids nodded again. Then her face flickered. 'Um, I feel—'
She didn't finish the sentence.

Skarbo ducked, just in time. Obviously she had managed to eat at least something, fairly recently.

Fortunately The Bird hadn't vandalized the pod's housekeeping systems when it shorted out the field controls.

'And that?'

The Bird peered. 'Not sure. A nebula? Big cloud of hot gas. Skarbo? You're the astronomer.'

Skarbo shook his head. 'I was a horologist.'

'Well, you spent eight centuries staring through this part of the sky to look at your precious stone clock. You must have noticed something.'

Skarbo suppressed a sigh. He turned towards the thing the other two were looking at. 'Yes, it's a nebula.'

'Got a name, this thing?'

'I'm not sure.' He searched his memory. 'It might be the Flatfruit Nebula. I haven't seen it from this angle before.'

'Ha. Guess not.'

Chvids was staring at the view. 'It's beautiful.'

'I suppose so.' Skarbo looked again at the hazy streams of colour, and realized that she was right. It was beautiful. The benefits of fresh eyes, he thought – and once she had recovered from her zero-gee nausea, Chvids was looking at *everything* with fresh eyes.

They'd had time to talk, in the hours since they'd broken free from the Ringway. She had been born on a farm in the Spin, on a planet she couldn't even name. Sometimes, for a tiny proportion of her life, she had been allowed outside, working fields in the dying light of suns shielded by solar panels. But mostly she had lived and worked in the half-light of the kilometres of tunnels, tending the fat white grubs which probably had a better life than she did, at least up to the point where they were electrically stunned, mechanically skinned and minced.

She and another worker had stowed away in a mince tank. They didn't know where it was going, and they had no idea how long they would survive – if at all.

Chvids had survived until the tank was pumped down at what turned out to be the Handshake. The other had drowned. When they were found, Chvids was imprisoned on a charge of vandalism – the mince was condemned as contaminated.

She had never seen anything like stars before.

She had also forgotten her dislike of speaking to The Bird. To Skarbo's surprise, it was treating her with grave respect.

'And what's that?'

She was pointing back past the Handshake towards a faint, granular surface that covered the whole field of view. It seemed to curve over towards them as if it was reaching out to surround them.

'Ah.' The Bird wagged its head from side to side. 'Not so good. That's the Warfront.'

They watched for a while. Eventually Skarbo asked, 'Ships?'

'Yes. Ships. Many. Still a long way away.'

Chvids pointed again. 'They aren't all a long way off. Look.'

Skarbo followed her gesture. There was a bigger dot against the background. A moving dot; growing. He watched it for a moment. Then he turned to The Bird. 'Will that be friendly, when it gets here?'

'Not if it's coming from there.' The Bird lowered its head. 'This may not have worked.'

'Can we track it? Identify it?'

'No. Pod's only got a beacon. Can't even switch it off. Too late anyway. Shit. It's coming fast . . .'

Skarbo strained his eyes. He could already see details: a blunt, angular shape with business-like projections. 'It doesn't look like anything I've seen before.'

The Bird peered. 'It doesn't look like anything good. Wonder if—'

Then it stopped.

'Hailing escape vehicle. Answer.'

The voice sounded like hammered metal.

Skarbo glanced round the cabin and then at the others. 'We can't,' he said. 'There's nothing to communicate with.'

The voice came again. 'We'll worry about that. You talk. We'll listen.'

Chvids nudged Skarbo. 'They're vibrating the metal,' she whispered. 'Maybe they can pick us up the same way?'

'Well done.' The voice didn't sound congratulatory. 'Now stop whispering and identify yourselves. You've got ten seconds. Then we shoot you.'

The Bird opened its beak, but Skarbo made a sharp downward motion and it subsided. 'We are three escapees from the Handshake,' he said. And then, just in case, 'We're neutral.'

'The fuck you say. We escaped from the Handshake too and we ain't neutral. No one is, not with that pile of ships a day behind them. Names?'

Skarbo glanced at The Bird. It glared out towards the ship. 'You first.'

'We're the ones with the guns. Names! Ten seconds.'

The ship was close now. Skarbo guessed it was less than a hundred metres away. It didn't seem to be closing; it hung steady in the field of view. It had an improvised, theatrical look, like something assembled by a child to be frightening – some of the blade-like fins and riveted bulges were obviously false.

But then, it had subtle enough field control to be able to vibrate intelligible sounds out of their hull – and hear them replying.

At least five seconds had gone. Skarbo made up his mind. 'Chvids, Skarbo and companion,' he said.

The voice was quiet for a few seconds. Then it said, 'Skarbo is a name I've heard. Along with *wanted* and *dead*. But *companion* is no name at all. You didn't do what we said. Stay near the centre of that thing.'

And without any warning the image of the ship wobbled and disappeared. In its place there was something much smaller – a featureless flattened off-white ovoid about half the size.

The Bird made a harsh noise. 'Bad! They've dropped a field. Weapons . . .'

A spot at the front of it glowed bright yellow.

Skarbo had time to say, 'No, wait,' and then there was a crash, and suddenly the pod was spinning wildly. An alarm howled, and there was the screech of escaping atmosphere. Skarbo crashed into something metal and then into Chvids, who made an oddly hoarse, wordless growl and grabbed weakly at him. She held on for an instant and then lost her grip, whirling away and slamming into the wall.

Then there was a soft buzz and the spin slowed to a halt. The screech of the departing air died to a high whistle – but didn't stop. Skarbo looked towards the source of the sound and saw a little mound of self-seal foam mushrooming out from the wall. They'd been holed – were still holed.

The voice came again. 'Warning shot. To judge by the stuff squeezing out I guess your hull has not quite plugged itself. I don't care, and the next hole will be much bigger. Names.'

The Bird had sunk its claws into the edge of a couch to steady itself. It flapped its wings once. 'Haven't got a name,' it said sulkily. 'Can't help you. Stupid reason to shoot.'

The voice laughed. 'It might have been stupid yesterday but it isn't today. Right. I figure you're harmless where you are. I'm gonna take you on tow.'

Skarbo glanced at the foam plug. 'We're still leaking.'

'And I still don't care. If you're still breathing when we get back to the Handshake, let me know.'

Skarbo turned away, and closed his eyes. Then he opened them again. Something floated across his vision, a little dark sphere, and he waved a claw at it.

It shattered into hundreds of much tinier spheres. They were dark red.

He turned to Chvids, who was clinging to the bulkhead with one hand. A stream of the little spheres was coming from somewhere on her head.

As he pulled himself closer she turned towards him and smiled, and he saw the gash across her temple.

Then he corrected himself. Not across. Through.

Something had sliced deeply, neatly into the woman's head – a tidy black-edged ravine, wisping balls of blood.

Without looking away he said, 'Bird?'

Chvids closed her eyes and her fingers relaxed.

'Bird?'

'What? Oh.' It pushed itself off from the couch and drifted over to Chvids. One of the drops of blood burst against its head. It didn't seem to notice.

Skarbo felt anger rising in him. 'Ship out there? Whoever you are? Chvids is injured, maybe fatally. What are you going to do about it?'

There was no answer. Skarbo got ready to shout.

Before he could, the pod rang like a gong.

The white ship seemed to flicker. Then it became an expanding cloud of plasma.

Skarbo looked at The Bird. It raised its head slowly. 'Well now,' it said.

Then there was another voice.

My apologies. Are you well?

It was the Orbiter.

The Bird got there first. 'How well do you think? Skarbo was kidnapped, then imprisoned, then we were shot.'

And there are three of you. Who is the third?

'Female. Humanoid. Injured.'

I see.

Outside a faint haze flicked into being between them and the rest of the universe, and the pod jinked slightly to the side. The sound of escaping air ceased. The movement knocked Chvids gently against the bulkhead. She made no noise.

There is no time to bring you inside. Things have become – imperative. Treat her as best you can.

Skarbo stared out at the haze. He couldn't see the ship. 'Is that it?'

For the moment. Many apologies, again. I am less – able than I was.

'Able?' Skarbo shook his head. 'I don't understand.'

You should, of all people. But I have help. The old warships are not far away.

The haze deepened. The Bird nodded at it. 'Looks like a tow-field. Think we're going wherever it's going.'

Beyond the haze, the stars blurred. The Bird clicked appreciatively. 'Going somewhere pretty fast.'

Skarbo watched the haze for a while. Eventually he said, 'I see.'

They had done what they could with the pod's limited med kit. An uneven mound of gelseal covered Chvids's temple, and after some debate they had sedated her. Now she half lay, half sat on one of the couches, held in by a loose seat web. There was no gravity, so presumably they were within the inertial bubble of whoever it was who was towing them, but it might return at any time.

Skarbo watched her. He had known little about human anatomy even when he had had one, and now he knew nothing.

He hadn't even liked her. And now here he was thinking about her in the past tense.

He was roused by a soft peck on the shoulder. He turned and found himself looking into The Bird's eye.

It tutted. 'She chose to come,' it said.

'I know.' It didn't help. 'She should be coming out of the sedation now.'

'Be patient.'

Skarbo shook his head. 'I've *been* patient. I've been being patient for eight hundred years.' He stared at The Bird. 'And I have achieved nothing. *Nothing!*' He had shouted the last word.

The Bird pushed itself away from his shoulder and turned both eyes on him. 'You think?'

'What else should I think?' Skarbo shrugged. 'I spent all that time watching something dying slowly. Now here I am, watching—' He stopped, and looked at Chvids.

Her eyelids were flickering. Then they opened. Her eyes rolled, and focused. She took a breath.

'What's happening?'

The Bird floated over to her and stared at her for a moment. Then it performed an elaborate mid-air shrug. 'Oh, not much. You got shot. Skarbo's blaming himself. I'm blaming him too.'

She coughed. 'It's not his fault. Is it?'

'Who cares? Blame him anyway.'

Skarbo pushed it out of the way and it drifted off without protest. 'Hello, Chvids. How do you feel?'

She shook her head a little, as if testing something. 'Okay. Weak. Kinda sick.'

'Don't move.'

'I'm bored.' But then she sighed, and her eyes closed.

Skarbo looked at her, and then at The Bird. It shook its head.

It was two days before the Orbiter and its friends felt able to slow, briefly, enough to take them on board. The pod still smelled of vomit that the housekeeping system couldn't quite clear.

The Orbiter was indeed less able than it had been. It had been damaged, elaborately. From the front it looked fairly intact, but there were long, seared wounds down its baroque flanks. One of them broadened into a gash that showed the stars on the other side.

Two of the ancient warships flanked it, like bodyguards. Or carers.

Skarbo stared at the mutilated ship. 'What happened?'

I found something, and I was found.

When they were on board, the Orbiter explained. It had moved out of Handshake space towards the Spin, and for almost two days nothing had happened. Then it had run into a war.

Skarbo nodded. 'The Warfront.'

No. Not that; but a result of it. The Warfront can only move at the speed of the slowest vessels, but it can grow as quickly as people join it. I did not anticipate that. It has grown very much.

'How much?'

It is now half a million kilometres across. Look.

Air in front of Skarbo fuzzed, and became space. At first he thought it was space densely packed with stars, but then his mind completed the double-take.

Ships. Hundreds of thousands of ships; maybe even millions, forming a shape like an outstretched hand, curved and ready to close.

'Oh,' he said.

Yes. The Warfront has so far avoided the Handshake, but it has moved around it on all sides. It is entering the ungoverned space at the periphery of the Spin, and as its tendrils close in it is trapping things between them. Systems, small civilizations, and some pre-existing wars that are becoming more intense under the pressure. I got caught in one.

'I'm glad you escaped.'

I almost didn't. I had to be rescued.

'By these two?' Skarbo gestured to the left and right, pointing through the hull to roughly where he thought the flanking warships were.

Yes. And in the process they disclosed most of their capabilities, and therefore were noticed. And so we are now in a hurry; the Warfront as a whole will want them, and various actors within the Warfront will want to get to where they suspect we are going before we do.

Skarbo nodded. Then something occurred to him. 'Where is Grapf?'

Destroyed. I will miss it.

And the old ship fell silent.

Chvids was intermittently wakeful, to begin with. She even asked questions.

'Do you know where it's taking us?'

The Bird made a dismissive noise. 'Want to guess?' And then, without waiting for an answer: 'The Spin. Where else? That's where that lot are heading.' It wagged its head towards the wall of ships that was the Warfront.

They were getting closer.

Her face crumpled. 'I don't want to go back. I don't want to—'

She didn't finish. Skarbo's mind completed the sentence: . . . *die there.*

'Don't worry,' he said. 'It won't be like it was before.'

Which, he thought, was certainly true.

She seemed reassured. She closed her eyes. 'Tired. Head hurts.'

Later, she half woke, and was sick again. Then she didn't wake any more.

They watched her troubled unconsciousness.

Now, there was no doubt. Skarbo could see star patterns that he had last observed when he stared out into space from Experiment.

The Orbiter let him play with the viewing controls. In one direction, there was the advancing Warfront. It had washed over the Handshake as if the vast structure didn't exist.

Which it no longer did.

He had asked the Orbiter how many ships were following them.

Many hundreds of thousands of capital ships and far more smaller ones. It is one of the greatest collections of ships for half a million years, and the number is growing by assimilation. Those who don't join are processed. Listen.

There was a fizzing noise, and then audio.

'. . . latest to join the Warfront is the New Hanseatal Navy, and they didn't even wait for their government to agree. Join or die, was the message, and they joined. Now, our reporter Kalf Bbei was embedded with the Navy and we're hoping that means she's now embedded with the Warfront. Kalf?'

'. . . (*crackle*) . . . es, can you hear me? I'm still on the same ship; we've positioned ourselves within the Warfront fleet and we're heading past the outskirts of the Hans system.'

'We hear you clearly, Kalf. Tell me, are there any restrictions on you?'

'None. The attitude seems to be, the whole galaxy can see where the fleet is going so what's the point in secrecy?'

'And you are still going to the same place?'

'Yes we are. We are heading for the Spin, and it's hard to see what could stop us.'

'And, if you can tell us this, what does it feel like, being part of that?'

'I can't lie, it's exciting and terrifying, both at once. There's a sense, when you talk to people, of being involved in something huge, some great project like there's never been before. We don't know what we'll find when we get there; we guess there'll be competition. There's talk of another fleet, heading from the other side, but we just don't know about that. Why wouldn't there be? Everyone is positioning the Spin as some kind of prize. Meanwhile people are talking about a new beginning, but catch them off guard and you find some of them are afraid it will be an ending instead. I don't—'

The voice cut off.

'Kalf? Are you there?'

Silence.

'Well, we lost Kalf. That is, we lost contact. We hope we didn't lose her too. Kalf, if you can hear us, we'll stay—'

Then that voice cut off too.

Skarbo stared at the place the voices had come from. 'Ship?'

Gone. Everything is changing, Skarbo. I, too, have a sense of ending.

Skarbo blinked. He had never heard the old ship sounding so reflective. He thought about that for a while. Then he said, 'Ship? So have I. But I'm not ready to end yet.'

Yes. And, of course, endings often come before beginnings.

'And beginnings before ends.'

They stopped talking, and Skarbo went back to the viewers. It felt better to turn them away from the Warfront, which was out of his control or understanding, towards something which he at least understood.

Or thought he did.

Yes. The Spin.

He wasn't sure how he felt about that. With, he counted, seven days of life remaining, he was almost there. And somehow, he felt further away than ever.

'Orbiter?'

Yes?

'What is it like there?'

Quiet.

'Do you know where we're going?'

Only from memory. I have not been here for almost a hundred thousand years. The population centres were near the middle. But I would rather begin at the periphery – the Outer Rotate. There is – was – a transit station. I will head for that. There may be a shuttle. You will need one, if you want to land anywhere.

Skarbo blinked. He had thought his own life was long. A thousand centuries – and that was only the latter part. How old was this thing?

He shook himself. 'Is there a map? I would like to . . .' he hesitated. He wanted to say, *make it real. To put back the people, in my mind at least.* Instead he said, 'to learn it.'

I can project some images.

'Thank you.'

And the space in front of him was full of planets – a model, not a map, looking just the same as the many models he had made over the centuries. But not the same, because if he reached a claw into this model he could grasp it, move it. Go closer.

He lost himself.

The alarm sounded, and Skarbo realized it was the second time. He disengaged from the model.

He didn't know how long he had been Spin-gazing. The model was intoxicating; he could wander among the planets, watching clouds pass over continents he had never seen in eight centuries of observation, and then dive through the atmospheres to see cities, oceans, mountains.

He had hoped to see activity but the model seemed static. Nothing was moving.

The alarm had stopped. He looked round. 'Ship? What was that?'

We are slowing. We will dock shortly.

'Dock? Oh. Where?'

There. Look.

Skarbo looked. Next to him, The Bird was perched in its usual observation place on the rail. It was silent.

He supposed the thing he was looking at was a space station, but it was on an incomprehensible scale – far bigger than the Handshake.

If you took a few hundred spheres, each a kilometre across, packed them closely round a bomb, set it off, and then froze the whole thing a second after the explosion, then you would get something that resembled this. It looked as if it had only stopped moving for a fraction of a second – as if it was ready to start expanding again at any moment.

Skarbo found his voice. 'What is it called?'

It used to be called simply Terminal. Now it emits an auto-matic call-sign which says it is called Exeunt. I don't know why. I have hailed, but there is no response.

'Will you approach?'

Yes.

'Is it safe?'

There seemed to be a slight pause. Then the ship said, *Prob-ably. Remember we have back-up; my friends are not far away. And if you want to make planet-fall, we need to find an atmosphere-capable craft. There used to be such here.*

'I see.' Skarbo looked away.

The Bird hissed, 'You know what that is?'

Skarbo blinked. 'It's a space station; some sort of entry por-tal, I suppose.'

'Maybe that, but something else. It's the kind of really big thing you make to make yourself feel better about having for-gotten how to make planets.'

'Really?' Skarbo stared at the thing.

'Really. Showing off like that's a sign of decline. Proper advanced stuff doesn't have to be big and fancy. Ha. And the word Exeunt is about leaving, not arriving. Reckon they knew they were on the down escalator.'

The thing grew in the screen. Spheres drifted past. Close up, their surfaces appeared scarred and discoloured.

They nosed up to a sphere that looked fairly intact. There was a soft *clunk*.

We have docked.

Skarbo and The Bird looked at each other. Then The Bird raised its head. 'Any sign of life?'

There was a pause. Then, *No. Apart from an automated response, no one is talking to me.*

'Which means what?'

I don't know. It is interesting that my identification seems to have been recognized.

'Why?'

Because it was last used a hundred thousand years ago. That implies continuity of recollection. Possibly, of ownership or management.

The Bird gave an impatient hop. 'And? What do we do?'

I suggest you wait. I think it would be unwise to enter this place until we have more information.

'And this from the machine that sent us into the Handshake?' The Bird shook its head. 'Ha . . .'

I seem to remember you went willingly.

The Bird huffed. Skarbo watched it, then looked away. 'What about Chvids?' he asked.

There might be better medical facilities in there. There might not. There may be risks. Given her status I cannot recommend it.

'Status?' Skarbo glanced towards the woman. She was motionless, floating slackly within the seat restraints, and her face was grey. 'Is she dying?'

Close to dead. I am exploring one avenue.

'Which is?'

She would live out a normal life in a virtual setting.

Skarbo blinked. 'Only that?'

I cannot foresee another way.

'Virtual?' The old man had talked about the vrealities of the Spin . . .

People were beginning to matter. Chvids in particular. And that was why he had done what he had done. He promised himself that it made sense.

They disengaged, and spent an hour slowly nosing around and between the forest of spheres. The ship didn't suggest docking again, and Skarbo didn't need to ask why. Instead they scanned, and mapped, and watched.

There would have been little to dock with. Most of the spheres showed at least some damage; many were ravaged, with deep rips exposing twisted metal structures on the inside. Now and then the Orbiter extended a field and pushed a drifting piece of debris out of the way.

Then it stopped.

Ah. This is new.

Skarbo looked out. At first he thought he was looking at even more extreme damage; they were near the end of the great central shaft, and instead of a neat closure there was a rough stump, with broken stalks sticking out of it. One of them ended in a half-sphere.

Then his mind processed the word *new*.

'Under construction?'

Yes. At least, at some point it was. I assume the work has been abandoned for many years.

The Bird nodded. 'Explains the state of the place,' it said.

'What do you mean?'

'Half built? Bound to fail. Like a half-built nest – always falls apart.'

Skarbo nodded.

Then, so fast he felt dizzy, the world in his head rearranged itself, and he knew.

'Oh,' he said, and it seemed to take centuries just to form the syllable. And then, 'Ship?'

An hour later they found the shuttle. Skarbo barely heard the Orbiter announcing it. He had spent the whole time staring out sightlessly at the half-finished thing that was bound to fail, and wondering how it had taken him eight centuries to realize this one simple fact. And hoping, with something far on the other side of desperation, that the idea he and the ship had come to would work.

The ship had listened to his thesis. He hadn't been sure it would. When he had finished it had indulged in another of its increasingly frequent long silences.

Then it had said, *I agree. I am astonished. I congratulate you.*

He shook his head. 'There's no point in congratulations. It was a guess. You might as well thank The Bird for giving me the idea.'

Nevertheless.

Skarbo felt like hitting something. 'But it's too late! I should have thought of it lifetimes ago. Lifetimes! And I would need lifetimes to analyse it. Now I have no time at all.'

Another silence. Then the ship said slowly: *It may not be too late. I have an idea.*

Skarbo looked up. 'I have a guess about your idea.'

The vrealities. Is that your guess?

'Yes. There could be lifetimes.'

Are you ready to spend more lifetimes on a problem?

'Yes.' He looked at Chvids. And so is she, he thought.

And now he was staring out, and his mind was racing.

Skarbo?

'Yes . . . yes.' He pulled himself out of it and looked at the image of the craft. 'Is it – suitable?'

Approximately. I would not recommend high-gravity work . . . Are you still convinced you want to do this?

He nodded. 'Yes. All of it. For her,' he pointed at Chvids, 'and for, well . . . everything.'

Not for you?

'No. Or, not mainly.' To one side, he heard The Bird muttering something about a fucking saviour complex. He ignored it.

Indeed. I have selected a suitable planet.

'Good. Then we'd better go.'

Wiits Harbour (vreality)

Zeb woke from unconsciousness. It seemed to take centuries, and it hurt as much as waking from death.

He sat up and assessed his environment, because it seemed safer than starting with himself. That could wait.

He wasn't in the town. The smells were different, and so were the sounds. The last thing he remembered from the town was busy silence, but this was different – the natural quiet of a place being itself. Air movement, and distant sea birds. And along with those, a soft, deep, fundamental creak that made him think of trees.

The air smelled of sea, too. Not the industrial sea of the town, but something fresh.

He hadn't opened his eyes yet, but now he felt ready.

The first thing he saw was the woman. Her eyes were still amused. 'Hello again,' she said. 'Back with us?'

He gave himself a moment to recover. Then he said, 'I wasn't with you in the first place.'

'No. But you are now.'

He said nothing, simply watched her. She watched back, without wavering or changing her expression, which was the bare trace of a half-smile.

She was tall and slim, wearing loose trews and a simple shirt that emphasized her shape by hanging loosely. At first glance it looked like youthful slenderness but there was something behind it, as if the young woman was just an image projected on to an older background. Her face, too – it was smooth, but with a fragility which seemed heightened the more he looked at it.

Her eyes were deep brown, and gave nothing.

When he had finished his inspection, he looked away, thinking that if they had been playing a game he had lost it. The thought made him smile.

He wasn't ready to re-engage. He stood up and stretched, taking his time, and looked about him.

They were in a round chamber, no more than a dozen paces across. The walls and ceiling seemed to be woven, of some sort of thick vine laced through uprights in a complicated pattern that baffled his eye when he tried to study it. There were mats of something similar, but finer, on the floor, and there were tall narrow windows spaced evenly around the walls.

He took the half-dozen paces to a window and looked out. And down.

He managed not to catch his breath, but it was close. There was sea below them – a long way below – a grey-green crawling surface streaked with off-white.

He couldn't help it. He turned back to the woman. 'How high are we?'

The half-smile broadened. 'Only four hundred metres. This is the Lower Lookout.' He heard the capital letters.

'Lower? There are more?'

'Certainly. Look out this way.' She gestured to the windows behind her.

He walked over and looked, and this time there was an up as well as a down to look at.

Several ups, in fact. He could see several more . . . towers? No, not towers. More like stems – knotted, plaited, twisted

263

stems that thinned and bulged as they rose. At the base they disappeared into the ocean. At the top, they opened out into complicated latticeworks that flattened into platforms.

He shook his head. 'Are these what I think they are?'

'I suppose you think they're trees?'

He nodded.

'No. Even though people call them the Seatrees, they aren't trees. They're more like vertical corals. But they grow; about ten centimetres a year.'

'Barely enough to notice.'

Now there was no doubting her smile. 'That depends how long you have to do the noticing. When we came here they were only a few metres above the water.'

He did a quick mental calculation. 'But that means you've been here . . .' He fell silent.

'Yes.' She stood up, and became brisk. 'Something we have in common, I think. Tell me your name. Your *real* name.'

He stared at her. Then he said simply, 'Zeb.'

'Right. Well, come on, Zeb.'

He shook his head. 'Not yet. Who are you? Why did you attack me?'

She pursed her lips. 'The word you're looking for is *rescued*.'

'No it isn't. I was fine, then you kicked me unconscious.'

'You weren't fine. You had the Straights and the Measures after you. You were wounded. Or have you forgotten? You were going to die. Again.'

'Again?' He looked at her sharply. 'How did you know that?'

She laughed. 'There's nothing special about it. You have history, my friend. You have left traces. Legends, even. You are interesting. And you seem to be healed, by the way.'

'I . . .' He reached a hand to his hip, then his shoulder. No pain, and no blood. He looked at her, and felt his eyes widen. 'You did that?'

She watched him for a second. 'Problem?'

'No.' It was a lie. He had a problem with anyone who could mess with the vreality. He hadn't seen Keff for lifetimes, had almost forgotten the creature. Was she another?

She was still watching him. Then her lips twitched and she looked away. 'Your choice. So, are you coming?'

He shrugged. 'What's the hurry?'

She smiled, but now it was different – it was sad, and this time age shone through. 'For him, the hurry is – infinite. But I'm afraid you and I have no need to hurry at all. It's something else we have in common, Zeb, and it's why I was hoping you'd turn up.'

She walked up to the wall and pushed it gently. A section unravelled itself to leave a hole just tall enough for her to pass through it upright. She walked through, turned, and beckoned.

He followed. He was wondering what she meant by *in common*.

Spin, Outer Rotate

Skarbo was standing about five paces from the edge of the cliff. It was as close as he dared go; under its sparse layer of grey, dusty soil the rock was soft, and shot through with frost-fractures, and the land at the base of the cliff a kilometre below was strewn with fresh rock-falls.

The shuttle had worked. It was little more than a tapering tube with an elderly chemical motor at one end, but it had juddered down through the old, thin atmosphere well enough, and settled with a jolt and a creak on to the high plateau barely a hundred metres from where they had intended to land.

It was very cold, not that it seemed to bother him, but there was no frost. The air felt thin and old and utterly dry, and it smelled of rock-flour.

In some ways it reminded him of the last years of Experiment, but somehow worse – he struggled for a while, and then came up with the word *abandoned*.

Yes. Abandoned; that was it. But then Experiment had never really been inhabited, except by him – and this place obviously had.

The ship said that the rows of polished, tilted plates were

266

primitive solar panels, much lower tech than the vast, silent gauzy film of low-orbit solar array they had passed on the way down into the atmosphere.

Skarbo had caught his breath at the sight of the array. 'What is that?'

It is called a Skylid.

'It's beautiful.' It was – the shifting colours reminded him a bit of the surface of the Sphere.

Yes. It is a monomolecular solar collector. There is another name for them – I have heard them called Shrouds. Because in the end the planets beneath them die. As has this one.

Skarbo watched the beautiful, deadly thing rippling gently, and said nothing else.

Now he was on the surface he could see more than solar stuff. From what little he knew of agriculture this was an unlikely site for it, but someone had tried. Between the base of the cliff and the solar farms were the other sort of farm – a strip of cultivation a kilometre wide, with different-looking plants in different areas. Skarbo thought he could see the ghost of organization.

All dead, all dry.

He felt for the little comms bead that dangled from a fine chain round his neck – it was supposed to look unobtrusive, not that he could imagine anyone caring – and raised it to his mouth.

'How long has the place been abandoned, do you think?'

I don't know. There are no active records in any form I can read. Perhaps if you looked there would be hard copies, but there isn't time.

He nodded. 'How far away is the Warfront?'

Just under a day. Skarbo? You don't have to hold the bead up. It will pick up your voice from the resting position.

'Oh. Sorry.'

He looked out at the solar farms again. Old, and crude – but viable. The ship insisted they were generating, and so were the ones in orbit.

And that meant that the other things the ship had found should still be working.

The planet looked a bit odd, from space. When they had first seen it it had been just another chilly, bluish little ball orbiting a guttering yellow star. Old and cold, like almost everything else they had seen in the Spin, with darker patches marking the ghosts of oceans. Surface water was obviously a thing of the past. But as they got closer, more features came into view: networks of kilometre-scale striations, light grey against the dull blue of the surface, radiating out along the surface from both poles.

Closer again, and they became buildings – rank after rank of low, plain metal structures, half-buried in dust, linked together by tracks and lines of cables strung on pylons.

Skarbo had pointed at the cables. 'Are they real?'

Yes. Ancient technology, but simple and durable.

At first sight everything looked as dead as the rest of the planet seemed. But then the ship switched to infra-red.

The planet lit up. The dull striations became angry weals.

The structures were radiating multiple megawatts of heat into space.

The ship had dropped into a geostationary orbit and they'd watched in silence as the planet turned below them. From this close, they could see breaks in the lines of heat – sections hundreds of metres long which had gone dark.

The Bird had been very quiet. Now it clicked its beak. 'Some broken stuff.'

Yes. But mostly not. Over ninety per cent of the structures seem operational. Remember we are only seeing the surface. Most of the equipment will be at depth.

Skarbo blinked. 'Most?'

Yes. You are looking at the outward expression of ten thousand cubic kilometres of machinery.

'All running virtual realities?'

Yes, I believe so.

There was nothing more to say – but it meant that the other avenues the ship had talked about were still open. And, just possibly, the thing Skarbo had in mind was possible.

Possibly.

But now he was on the surface, far from the poles, and it was time to move. He said, 'Where should I go?'

Below, into the habitable spaces. I'll guide you towards where I think there may be an interface.

He nodded and turned away from the cliff edge. There was a low blockhouse a hundred metres in from the edge. The ship had said it was the entrance.

The sled carrying Chvids's motionless body floated after him. The grey of her face somehow suited the planet.

'Is she still alive?'

Barely.

That was the real hurry.

The entrance in the blockhouse faced the cliff edge. It was open; had obviously been open for a long time. There were drifts of dust inside, and the pale, low-angle sunlight picked out dancing motes as he walked through.

No sign of rain, he thought. If there had been rain the dust would look different.

The front of the blockhouse was a flat landing. Behind it, shallow steps went down in a wide spiral. There was no need to ask the question; there was only one way to go.

The stairs were dusty too, and within one full turn they were dark. He thought of asking the ship to find some systems and intervene, but it would be doing plenty of intervening soon enough. For the moment, they had planned for darkness. He flicked the little bead and it lit up, bouncing a diffuse yellow glow off the walls. Without him doing anything, a similar bead lying at the end of its slack chain on Chvids's chest began glowing too. They were slaved together, he remembered. It lit up her face from below, cancelling out the grey and making her appear almost healthy.

Three turns, four, five, and they were at another landing. He stopped, and the sled nuzzled gently into him from behind.

'Ship?'

Yes. This is the level. Follow the corridor.

It led away from the stairwell for ten paces, towards a square of light. Then he was through the square, and the world opened out in front of him.

He stopped, and looked. 'Ship? Can you see this?'

Yes.

There wasn't much more to say for the moment.

He was looking out over the edge of a chasm carved out of the grey rock, wide and deep but only ten metres or so across. The roof was far above his head. A ledge like the one he was standing on ran along the far side of the gap. Leaning out cautiously, he could see there were more ledges below, a few metres apart, and he realized they were other floors of the habitat.

Looking down, there were clearly many storeys. He could see at least ten.

A line of doors opened off the ledge opposite, and light was showing through them.

He cleared his throat. 'I'm in the living area. Where now?'

Cross the space. There should be bridges.

He looked to the side. There were. They were narrow, and there were no guard rails. He walked up to the start of the nearest and looked down at it.

'Ship? The walkway is broken. I can't get across.'

Yes. There has been a significant earth movement. I would advise finding another.

Skarbo nodded, and paced along the ledge to the next bridge. This one was missing, too – just broken stumps with a network of cracks radiating back into the ledge. Flakes of rock fell away as he approached.

He thought for a moment. 'Ship? How much weight will the sled carry?'

It is meant for one – but Chvids is less than average weight, and you have not taken any nourishment for fifty days.

'That's what I thought.' He pulled the sled towards him and pushed down on it, gently at first and then as hard as he could. It gave briefly beneath his claw before rising again, and he felt his feet begin to leave the ground.

It would have to do.

He reached over Chvids, took hold of the opposite edge of the sled, and pulled himself awkwardly on top of her. The sled swayed beneath him, but maintained its height. He extended a leg and managed to push it against the wall behind him.

The sled floated slowly forwards, out over the chasm. Skarbo concentrated on not looking down.

Then they were at the other side. He rolled off, keeping hold of the sled with one claw. He felt Chvids roll too, and realized he had dragged the edge of the cover with him.

He put it back. She didn't respond. Haemorrhage, the ship had said. Untreatable.

There was a door every dozen paces or so. Most were open. A few were missing. He looked along the row. 'Which one?'

Any. You should find units easily. They would have been widespread.

He left the sled and explored. The rooms were the same – square in plan, with full-width windows of slightly cloudy glass looking out over the plain. Some had hangings over the windows. There were sleeping pads of varying sizes, their fabric covers stiff with frost.

Then, in the next room, he found them. He nodded to himself. He should have expected that.

There obviously weren't many insects here. That, or the dry cold, or something else, had preserved the bodies fairly well. They were shrunken, desiccated, but recognizable. He guessed the choice he had made for Chvids, they had made for themselves.

'Ship?'

Yes?

'I've found some people. See?'

He held up the bead and swung it round.

Ah.

Skarbo looked closer. 'They have some sort of mesh thing on their heads. Is that what I want?'

The vreality interfaces. Yes. You could probably use those.

'Yes. I'd rather not.' Very much rather not, he thought. 'I'll look for others.'

But he watched the silent bodies for a while, as if keeping a vigil. Then he got ready to leave.

And didn't. He had noticed something.

He looked closer. Lying on the chest of one of the bodies, blurred by dust, was a rough-shaped oval of something, a bit bigger than a human thumb. He considered it, and then reached out a claw and very gently lifted it. It came up, pulling a length of fine chain that left a clean dark line in the dust on the faded clothes.

A pendant. He blew the dust off it – some dark red material, a little shiny, with the pattern of a stylized star etched into it.

He blinked. Someone had cared about this one. He wondered who, and what had happened to them.

He sighed, straightened up, and walked out to the corridor.

In the next room there was a cabinet by the end wall, with what looked like a little grey heap on a shelf. He chose one and shook the dust off it. It was halfway between skullcap and headset.

'Ship?'

I see it.

'Will it still work?'

Try. There was the hint of a shrug in the word, and Skarbo almost smiled.

Almost.

He picked the thing up and studied it. It was made of a fine grey mesh. As he took hold of it, a small patch near one end flickered and settled down into a steady orange glow.

It appears to be active.

He nodded. 'What do I do?'

Put it on Chvids's head. But make sure you have one ready for yourself first; you should not leave too long between her entry and yours.

He laid the thing down on the sleeping pad and walked out on to the ledge. This time the search was quicker; he found another, two rooms along. It glowed, too.

He took it back with him.

Are you ready?

'I suppose so.' He held up the mesh. 'It doesn't look the right shape for me.'

I believe they were meant to be universal.

'I hope so. Are you sure about the vreality?'

I have scanned it. It is functioning. The speed-up from here to there is approximately times one quarter of a million. On that scale, the Warfront will enter Spin space in roughly a thousand standard years.

He still hesitated. 'And you can do what you said? Project things in?'

I am fairly confident. The format of data may be altered, but the integrity should be preserved.

He had run out of questions, and Chvids had almost run out of time.

He studied her face. She was very pale. Her eyes were half closed, which was almost worse than being fully shut, he thought. Not sleep, and not waking. Not even the healing dormancy of ordinary unconsciousness, but some other state; only and forever accessible from inside.

And inside was all he had left to offer her.

It was time. He sighed, and picked up the mesh. He lifted Chvids's head a little so he could lay the thing beneath her, and then drew it round her skull.

The light brightened. The thing flexed under his touch and then tightened, fitting itself to the woman's head. For a moment he wondered if her eyelids had flickered, just a little. He looked carefully, but saw nothing more.

'I think that's it,' he said. 'I hope.'

Good. Now, if you are ready?

'I'm ready.' He looked round, and then lay down on the vacant sleeping pad. With the mesh held above his head he said, 'See you in a thousand years.'

Or a thousand minutes. Good luck.

Skarbo smiled. 'Point of view,' he said. Then he pulled the mesh over his own head, and felt it close like a caress.

The world faded.

The world faded, and then another coalesced. Clouds grew out of grey haze, limiting the view. A grass-covered slope solidified beneath feet that weren't the feet he had worn moments ago.

Of course, he wasn't really wearing them now ... but he would have to get used to that.

Behind him a voice said, 'Skarbo?'

He looked round, and smiled. 'You've changed.'

The tall female returned the smile. 'I've already been here a month. But you've changed as well, more than I have.'

He looked down at himself. Human, standard, more or less. A shape he thought he remembered. 'Oh . . . yes. Well, I'd say I have changed *back*.'

'Were you human once?'

'Once. And perhaps always. And perhaps I was always potentially an insect, at the same time.'

She laughed. 'There is something about you, now you say that.'

'Yes.' He flexed his arms, took a couple of strides. 'It's good. How do you feel?'

'Fine.' She looked at him for a moment. 'This is it, isn't it? I can't go back.'

His human lips made the slight sad smile without his permission. 'No. Not for long. You'll live as long here as you will there, but here is much slower. You will have time.'

'How much time?'

'I don't know. Many lifetimes, possibly. I hope—'

He stopped, and she reached out and took his hand. 'Are you just here for me? You don't have to be.'

'No. Not just. I would have come with you, but there's something else too, now. I have something to do.'

And he told her. It took a while, and when he had finished she was quiet for as long again.

Eventually she said, 'I'll stay with you. As long as I can.'

'Thanks.'

'So.' She looked around. 'Where do we go?'

'I don't know. The Orbiter should have sent some information; we need to find that.'

As if on cue, the clouds cleared.

They were standing on a wide, slightly rolling plateau. To one side, the land fell away down a slope that looked kilometres long, to a series of valleys that blurred into distance under low sunlight. Patches of forest competed with the bluish-green grass. To the other, a steep upwards slope, quickly exposing bare, shattered-looking rock that rose to a peak a few hundred metres above.

Without talking, they climbed up the peak. It took them half a day, and by the time they were standing at the top the sun was directly above them. Chvids squinted up at it, and then grinned at Skarbo. 'I've never felt that before. I like this dream.'

He smiled. 'It's not a dream. It's a future.'

'I suppose so.'

They looked about them, scanning the land. Up here, a steady wind brought an aromatic scent that Skarbo assumed was forest. Trees, he thought. The Orbiter would like it here.

There were no other smells – no trace of wood-smoke, and nothing that seemed animal – and no sound except the wind.

Chvids broke the silence. 'What are we looking for?'

'I don't know. I'll know it when I see it.' I hope, he thought.

She nodded. 'Fine. Well, if you can't see it from up here we need to be somewhere else.'

'Yes . . .' He looked out across the land. 'But I don't want to just head off at random.'

'Then don't.' She laughed. 'Forgotten already? Head towards the air.'

'What?' And then he remembered the prison on Hand-shake. 'But how does that help?'

'It gives a direction to follow.'

He looked at her, and then turned towards the wind. It seemed steady. In the far distance, he thought he could see a band of clouds. Possibly a coast? He remembered that coasts were supposed to be good locations, weren't they?

'Okay,' he said. 'That's what we'll do.'

Chvids smiled at him. 'One more thing. Do you know how to grow food?'

He shook his head. 'No. I need to warn you, there's hardly anything I know how to do.'

'It's okay. You only need to know how to do the one thing, here. If you get any spare time, you can learn.' She turned to face the wind. 'Right. New life. Let's go.'

Town (name unknown)

The towers were linked by a cradle of rope walkways that swayed gently under his weight. The ropes weren't level; as he followed the woman from tower to tower they gained height. There were more towers than he had seen from his starting point. They formed a straggling line that marched out to sea, getting taller the further they went. He had counted twenty-one before he saw the last.

Even though they had climbed – what? A hundred metres? – he still had to look up to see the top of this one. The rope didn't connect to a platform, as it had on the others. Instead it wrapped round the fat, grey column in a woven spiral catwalk, seemingly just wide enough for his feet, that climbed about twice his own height with every turn. At the top, at least another hundred metres above him, there was a broad platform that looked different from the others – not woven, but constructed.

As the woman reached the spiral she stopped, and beckoned him forwards. 'You go first.'

He paused, one hand knotted into the rope. 'Why?'

She smiled. 'It's not me he wants to see, and not me that wants to see him. Not principally, at least.'

Zeb sighed. 'Lady? Whoever you are? I'm not in the mood for games.'

She nodded. 'That's good, because he doesn't play them. I'll get out of your way.'

And before he could reply she had let go of her own guide rope and stepped off the walkway.

Reflex made him step forward but before he had completed the movement the walkway danced under him. He looked down and saw the woman hanging from it by one hand. She was grinning up at him.

'Go on,' she said. 'After you.'

He shook his head and walked on to the spiral. It felt firmer than the walkway, but there was no guard rail. He leaned in to the stem of the Seatree. He had expected it to be cold, like stone, but it felt slightly warm. A faint rustle behind him and a tremor under his feet told him that the woman was upright again.

The view of the rest of the Seatrees filled out as he climbed. From above, he could see the black dots of birds wheeling around the platforms. Now and then one flew close enough for him to observe properly – a dull black, compact bullet of a body with oddly slender wings the length of his arm, and a hooked beak. He hadn't seen them before, anywhere in this vreality or in any of the others.

He had climbed thirty-one turns of the spiral before his head was level with the bottom of the platform. The ropes angled up through an open hatch; another two metres and he was through it and standing on a floor of closely jointed timber.

He turned around slowly, trying to take the place in. It took more than one turn.

He was in a mechanism. It was the only word that would do; he had emerged in the middle of an intricate cloud of *things* – globes and dots and skinny connecting rods and complicated tracks that were only circular if he looked at them from a certain angle. It was big – the space was perhaps fifty metres across and the same high, and the thing filled at least half of it.

He heard the woman behind him. Without turning he asked, 'What is it?'

And then looked up sharply. Somewhere above him a male voice had answered, 'Think of it as a puzzle. Do you like it?'

'I don't know.' He felt a rush of impatience. 'I don't know anything, right now. In fact, if you don't start telling me things I might break something, just to see what happens.'

The voice laughed. 'That wouldn't matter now. But I'll answer your questions. Walk to the edge. I'll join you there.'

Zeb bore down on his temper. This doesn't matter, he told himself. Nothing in here matters, not now, not for the last thousand years.

He walked to the edge. When he was outside the mechanism he turned round and looked at it properly, and then he realized.

'Planets,' he said out loud. 'It's not a puzzle. It's planets.'

'It's both.' The voice was closer, but still above him. He looked up.

Now he wasn't surrounded by the planet machine, he could see the rest of the space. It was roughly hemispherical. There was an opening at the top, a few metres across, covered by translucent stuff that let a diffuse light through, and there were other openings set seemingly at random around the curved walls.

Everything else was shelves and pigeon holes and racks and circular walkways and ladders, with stacks and blocks and rolls of paper tumbling out of them.

Someone was hand-over-handing slowly down a ladder. They reached the floor, pushed aside a roll of paper with one foot, and turned to walk over to Zeb.

It was a tall, thin man dressed in what Zeb took at first to be rags. But they weren't, he realized. The man wore a long jacket and a kilt that came almost to the floor, made from sewn patches of some dark brown stuff that looked at the same time shiny and a bit hairy.

The light from above showed untidy brown hair, but hid the features.

The man nodded. 'Hello,' he said.

'Hello.'

There was silence again. Then the man said, 'Are you going to break something?'

Zeb looked around. 'Not yet. Are you going to tell me what's going on? She won't,' and he gestured over his shoulder to where the woman was standing.

'Yes. I'm going to explain everything. It will take a while.'

'I've got a while.' Zeb shrugged.

'And so has she, for the same reason. But I haven't.' The man smiled sadly and stepped forward. The light from another of the openings glanced across his face, and Zeb found himself looking into eyes which made those of the woman look new-born. There was something else about them, too: just for a moment he thought another creature was looking out through them, and his hind-brain filled in a slight chirrup, like hard wings.

Then the impression was gone. He looked away. 'Okay, then. Tell me.'

It was late, and the sky had darkened to purple.

They had left the place the tall man called the Second Machine Room, and were in something much more like living quarters – another hemispherical room, but much smaller. The top of the coral stem poked up through the floor and opened out into a shallow cup. A fire flickered in it, and the smoke drifted up and through a blackened grid of open-weave at the top.

The tall man's name was Skarbo, and he had told.

Now they sat in silence. Skarbo had cooked spears of meat over the fire pit and offered one to Zeb. A sharp flavour cut through the smokiness. He realized he was hungry.

'It's good,' he said, for something to say. 'What is it?'

'Did you see the black birds?'

'Yes. I've never seen them before.'

'I bred them.' He shrugged, and Zeb saw another flash of insect in the movement. Now, of course, he knew why. 'I needed a hobby, and it amused me. They serve to remind me of someone – some*thing*, perhaps – I knew for a long time.'

'And it amuses you to eat them?'

'Oh yes. Yes, very much. Immensely satisfying. You haven't said anything about what we told you.'

'No.' Zeb's back was stiff. He leaned back and rotated his shoulders. 'It's a lot to take in. Eight hundred years out there, and then all that time here . . . well, what do I say?'

'I understand. I generally don't think about it. Besides, the years out there, as you say, often seemed to me to be wasted. I was trying to work out something which proved to be wrong – utterly so. Whereas in here I began in the right place.'

Zeb nodded. 'And you have succeeded?'

'Yes. Quite easily. And I suppose the old work wasn't wasted. Those rolls of paper? That's it. All my models, rendered in ink.' He laughed. 'I expect it was the only way the ship could drop them into the vrealities. Either that, or it thought it would be funny. It took me virtual centuries just to read it all.'

'And then you knew?'

'And then I knew. Had known, really. It was a chance remark that made me realize what I knew.' He fell silent for a moment, and looked down at the spear of bird-meat in his hand. 'Just because they were powerful, why do we assume that our predecessors were perfect? Or that nothing interrupted them? The Spin was falling apart because it had never been finished. All those impossible orbits and peculiar force fields and things? They were just the scaffolding. It was the biggest building site in the galaxy, and it was – is – falling down.'

'And you think you know what to do about it?'

'Oh, I *know* that I know. I just don't know if I could. That would depend on others, if it came to it.'

'Would? If?' Zeb looked at the man. He was sitting, hunched forward towards the flames, his face flickering to the yellow glow. Now he looked up, and the dark eyes were pained. He drew a breath, but then the woman spoke.

'You should go. Nothing has changed.'

'Should, should . . .' Skarbo shook his head.

Zeb looked from one to the other. It felt like an argument that had been played out many times. 'So,' he said. 'What . . . ?'

The woman smiled. 'The old fool has convinced himself that he has to stay for me.'

'You?' Zeb stared at her. 'But wouldn't you go back too?'

'No.' She shook her head gently, but it was a very final gesture. 'There's nothing to go back to. I was fatally injured out there, and now I'm dead. I've been dead for a long time.'

Zeb wanted to ask how. *We have something in common*, he thought, and the words formed themselves into a baleful thought. He swallowed, and turned to Skarbo. 'So how long would you have to stay? If you did?'

The man shrugged. 'I don't know. For as long as the vreality lasts. Millions of years, possibly. I brought her, you see.'

'Yeah, it's all his fault.' She laughed. 'See, in his world *every-thing*'s his fault. Trying to hold up the world with your stomach muscles.'

'I wasted eight hundred years . . .'

'Oh shut up.' She was still smiling, but there was a serious edge in her voice. 'Get back out there and fix the thing you can fix. I'm beyond fixing.'

Zeb cleared his throat. 'And what does that make me?'

Her smile faded. 'Ah. Well, tell me. How long have you been in here?'

He thought for a moment. 'I don't know. I can remember some things, when I want to, but there are so many . . .' He stopped, and shook his head.

She nodded. 'Yes,' she said. 'That's how it feels. That's how you know.'

The baleful thought was ready to be thought.

I'm dead too.

He stared into the fire and watched the swell and fade of heat washing over the coals. The changing colours reminded him of something.

The Skylid, that was it. And there, between him and the memory of the Skylid, was Aish – and if he was dead, presumably so was she, and Shol, and all the rest.

The memories seemed suddenly very fresh. And too brief.

The price of addiction, indeed. He could almost hear Aish saying it.

The coals blurred. He dragged a hand over his face and looked up to see the woman looking at him.

She smiled sadly. 'I'm sorry, Zeb.'

He nodded. 'Thank you. Why were you looking for me?'

'Not so much looking, but I recognize a rumour when I hear it. Someone coming back after an absence of generations?' She shrugged. Then her mouth twisted upwards. 'And having left an unpaid bar bill the last visit made you seem interesting. You were both off the usual timeline and either forgetful or just naughty. I wondered if you were a kindred soul. I'm going to need one of those soon, Zeb.'

'Well, that's lovely.'

They jumped at the voice. Zeb saw Skarbo staring at something behind him. He got to his feet and turned round in time to see a thin figure walking into the circle of firelight.

It was Keff.

Zeb sat down again. 'Oh, for fuck's sake,' he whispered.

Keff sat down next to him. 'Sorry, what was that?'

Skarbo was on his feet. 'Did you bring – that – with you?'

Zeb shook his head. Keff giggled. 'Not exactly, but you could say I'm his fault. I've been following you around for centuries, Zeb, through all those different vrealities and all those lives and lives and lonely lives. I thought of weighing in sometimes, but you seemed to be having a pretty miserable time all on your own, so I left you like that. On your own. Oh fuck, this is so funny. All those crap lives and you're *still* here?' It looked up. 'Found some friends now?'

The woman walked up to Keff and stared down at it. It stared back, for a long moment. Then it looked away. 'I see,' it said. 'You think you can control things in here? I watched you heal his bullet wounds, but you're a long way from being in charge, I promise.' It nudged Zeb. 'Mind you, I watched her kick you in the guts, too. That was a lot more fun. I was hoping she'd kick you in the balls, but never mind.'

Zeb looked at the creature for a second. 'At least I've got balls,' he said eventually.

'Remember that, do you?' Keff stood up and turned to Skarbo and the woman. 'You were about to tell him the good bit, weren't you? Don't let me interrupt. I'll enjoy this.'

She shook her head. 'What are you?'

It laughed. 'I'm his personal pain in the arse. How does it feel, being dead? It's one way of being sure you have nothing to live for.'

Zeb felt something hardening within him and he looked up at Keff. 'So, if I'm dead, what does that mean for you?'

'I'm sorry?'

'Well, now I'm some kind of ghost in the machine, that's it, isn't it? You've won. I can't go back. And that means you've lost too.' He grinned, feeling air around his teeth. 'It's over, creature. End of your purpose.'

Keff's voice rose a little. 'Don't flatter yourself. You weren't my only purpose, and you still have centuries of misery and loneliness in front of you. So much to look forward to.'

The woman shook her head. 'I don't think so,' she said.

Keff laughed again. 'Oh really? Given that you're dead too? What are you going to do, whoever you are?'

'My name is Chvids.' She pointed at Keff. 'What's your name?'

It didn't answer. Zeb looked up and said, 'It called itself Keff.'

'Did it really? Was that your name out there too, creature?'

It still didn't answer. Suddenly Skarbo laughed. 'I begin to see,' he said.

Zeb looked from one to the other. 'Well, I don't. Someone explain.'

'It's easy.' Skarbo leaned forward and put his hands on the edge of the fire pit. 'Keff is dead too, aren't you, creature?'

It looked petulant. 'What if I am?'

Zeb began to smile. 'Ah,' he said. 'Three ghosts.'

'So what?' Keff's voice was almost a whine. 'I can still do what I like. I can make things happen! I can make his life shit. Shit! For ever! How does that sound?'

'I don't think so.'

Chvids glanced at him. 'You've thought of something,' she said.

'Yes.'

'What?' Keff looked genuinely confused.

Zeb spread his arms. 'Easy. If we're the same, then whatever you can do, I can do. Maybe I'll even do it better. Maybe I'll make your life shit instead. A duel! What do you say?'

'You wouldn't.' The voice was rising. 'You couldn't!'

'Oh yes he could.' Chvids sat down next to Zeb. 'You said I healed his bullet wounds, right?'

'You did!'

286

'No I didn't.' She took Zeb's hand. 'He did.'

'Did I?' Surprise flooded Zeb.

'Yup. Listen, why not? For however long you've been around here, you must have got hurt sometimes, right?'

'I suppose. I don't remember. Apart from the times I got killed.'

'Sure, but it must have happened. Same as it happened earlier.' She grinned. 'Try it now.'

'I don't know how.' He attempted to look inside himself, feeling almost as if there should be some sort of control panel.

Keff sighed theatrically. 'Well, while you try to work that out, shall we do something else?'

'Such as what?'

It looked around. 'Well, having a fight looks like a way forward just now.'

'Fight?' Zeb was on his feet.

'Yes. I would, if I was you. Or you could just give in.'

The room rocked slightly. Zeb looked around, eyes wide. There was a smell of smoke, and it wasn't from the fire pit.

Skarbo stepped forward. 'Is this you, Keff?'

'Nope.' It shook its head. 'Seems you might have enemies apart from me. I'll always be your *best* enemy, of course.'

Red light flickered through the walls.

Zeb stared at Chvids and Skarbo. 'Do Seatrees burn?'

Skarbo shook his head. 'No. But paper and wood do.' He nodded upwards and out. 'And they are.'

Zeb ran to the door and looked out. He watched the flames for a moment. Then he whispered, 'Oh, shit.'

A hundred metres above them, the Second Machine Room was blazing.

He turned round. 'What do we do?'

Skarbo and Chvids said nothing.

Desperation built. He felt like shouting. 'There must be something! That's your life – your lives . . .'

'There isn't.' Skarbo's voice was flat. 'Let it burn.'

'Oh, come on.' Keff looked from him to Chvids. 'Really? No fight? No fun?'

'There's no one I want to fight. The only person I could, I'm not going to.' Skarbo turned away and spoke to the fire pit. 'Chvids? Am I right?'

She nodded. 'I'm sorry. But it had to be done. You would never have left if I hadn't.'

Zeb felt his mouth hanging open. He closed it. 'You're kidding. *You* torched the Machine Room?'

'Yes.'

'Wow. I'm – impressed.'

Keff laughed. 'I'm more than impressed. I'm guessing it took a while to build that thing?'

Skarbo smiled. 'A thousand years.'

'Woah. *Go*, girl!' Keff made the trace of a bow towards Chvids. 'Wanna be friends?'

She didn't answer.

Zeb looked from her to Skarbo. 'What now?'

She shrugged. 'We should leave. Skarbo?'

He looked at her for a moment, then nodded slowly. 'Yes. Yes. You're right, of course. I would have wanted to stay. I still do, in a way, and you can't set fire to the reason for that.'

'But you're going?'

He smiled. 'Yes. I can take a hint.'

She seemed to hesitate. 'What do you have to do? To . . . go?'

'Nothing physical, I believe. But I'd rather not simply vanish.' He stood up and stretched. 'I've enjoyed this body. Goodbye, Zeb. I'm sorry not to have known you longer.'

Zeb looked down. 'Oh well, you'd probably have ended up hating me.'

'I doubt it. Goodbye, Chvids.' And that was it; he turned and walked out. Zeb watched him walk across the swaying

'I heard you. What?'

The Warfront has arrived early.

The old ship sounded . . . tense, if that was possible. Skarbo stood, thinking. Then he said, 'What does that mean?'

It means it is difficult to extract you.

'Ah. Difficult? Or impossible?'

Difficult. And provocative. I am under—

Then it cut out. Skarbo felt his heart speeding up. 'Ship?'

Silence. Skarbo's mind filled in a word – *attack*.

He was on his own, then.

He took a careful step. His legs held – just; there was a brittle fragility about them which made him suspect he would lose them very easily. He had once surmised, in a moment of morbid curiosity, that he could probably still walk, just, with only two limbs. Level with a human, in that respect.

He was getting steadier. He walked over to the sled that had held Chvids. It still held her body, but he didn't need to go too close to know that that was all it was now. The sled had settled to the floor, its energy cells drained. It seemed fitting.

The room lit up – a quick, harsh flash that left images on his optic nerves. And another.

Then sound reached him: a stuttering hiss.

Energy weapons. Someone was firing outside, although on what he couldn't tell. *Under attack*, he thought, and cursed himself.

Time to get out. He left the room and stopped on the ledge outside, his eyes wide.

The sled was drained – no way of floating back over the chasm.

Skarbo began to run, at first loping and then skittering along the ledge, glancing at the bridges as he passed them. Cracked, cracked, broken, missing altogether, cracked . . .

Then he felt fresh air under one claw. The walkway had curved, and his path had not.

He scrabbled wildly, his eyes shut in panic and his claws screeching and scoring over the stone. There was a searing *crack* from one of his hind-limbs, and then somehow he was lying on the walkway, his limbs still paddling as if he was trying to swim away from the drop.

Like a pinned beetle, he thought.

He forced himself to be still. He wasn't going to fall. He wasn't sure if he was going to walk, either; the crack had felt serious. He got up, very carefully. One hind-limb dragged, but it was still there. It would bear – he experimented – a little weight. Just enough.

Not down to two yet.

The curve of the walkway was deep enough that he couldn't see around it. He moved close to the wall and took a few steps forward, and then a few more.

It was dark. He ramped up his vision, and found it still worked.

Then light lanced through him. There had been another flash, from overhead this time. He spun round to get his sensitized eyes out of the glare – but taking the image with him.

So that was what had happened to the others. Fifty metres on, the walkway ended in wreckage.

The roof was smashed, a ragged tear a hundred metres long. The thing that had smashed it was jammed into fractured rock.

It still had the remains of a streamlined shape – an atmosphere-capable craft, then – but it was blunted and gouged by the impact. A slender scar that might have been the root of a wing before it had been torn off faced Skarbo. The section half-buried in the rock looked to be the engines, suggesting that the ship had tumbled before it crashed. Around them, the rock had melted into obscene bubbles.

Maybe not tumbled, then. Maybe someone had been trying not to crash.

The impact must have been like an earthquake. No wonder it had demolished the bridges.

The flashes were coming more often – too often for Skarbo's eyes to adjust. His head hurt, even if his leg didn't. And there was no time, and he couldn't get across.

Then he paused. Could he?

He had to try.

The lava flow at the base of the crashed ship wasn't too bad to climb over, though the surface was rough with micro-bubbles, some with skins so thin that his claws broke them. His damaged leg dragged and caught, and he was afraid it would be torn off, but then what did that matter?

It would if it kept him here, of course. But that wasn't something he could control.

Five minutes of scrambling, and he was over the lava and standing on the metal hull. It was faintly warm. There must still be a live power source in there. He wondered how much the crash had damaged the radiation containment.

But that probably didn't matter either. His muscles howling at him, Skarbo pulled himself slowly up the hull, the continual flashes overhead burning his vision, and his claws skittering between smooth metal and roughened, burnt patches, until he was over the chasm and then let himself slide awkwardly down the other end.

He kept his grip almost long enough. Then the rough patches were gone and he was slipping down the hull, legs flailing.

He fell.

He hit the rock floor back first, with his legs curled reflexively inwards and his eyes closed.

There was a crack, and his vision blacked out for a moment. Then it crept back, starting at the edges and gradually moving towards the centre.

He uncurled his legs, trying not to think of how he would

293

have looked lying on his back with them clenched across his thorax, and rocked himself the right way up.

Everything still worked, but his carapace was creaking. Some damage there, then.

And that didn't matter either.

Back towards the exit. He hurt, comprehensively, but he could walk, he could see and, crucially, he could remember. That did matter.

And, hopefully, he could improvise, because that was going to matter almost as much, and much sooner.

He had been thinking, while his body was carrying him over the wrecked ship. He had just enough faith in his ability to reach the shuttle intact, but none at all that he could get it off the planet through whatever conflict was flashing and hissing above him.

So someone else had to do it for him. If he had had fingers he would have crossed them.

The great shaft was full of dust. He was a connoisseur of dust by now, and he could tell this was fresh. Not surprising; the rock was shaking under him now. Things were hotting up overhead.

That suited him.

The lifter didn't work any more, but the stairs were undamaged. He climbed slowly, using his damaged limb for stability and brief, so very brief, rest between treads while his sound limbs sought the next one up. Lift, pause, gather, lift.

And then he was at the top, and the next bit needed to be thought out. He slid along the wall to the exit and looked round the corner, and then up, and then froze.

The flashes were nothing. Nothing at all – a dogfight in the shadow of a storm; a childish battle on the margin of a war. A few ships playing in the firelight of something much, much bigger.

It was as if the stars had been multiplied by a million. The sky was black, and full of ships. Ships beyond counting, ships beyond comprehension, ships beyond reason. He had seen something like this before.

The Orbiter had been right. The Warfront had definitely arrived, and it had grown.

He tore his eyes away from the mesmerizing sight and looked across the surface. He could see the shuttle, and by a miracle it looked intact. It was time to make the first gamble.

He eased himself round the corner and moved out towards his ship, his legs almost flattened beneath him. Weapons flared, and sometimes they struck so that the ground twitched beneath his feet, but the focus seemed diffuse and they appeared to be concentrating on the plains.

He made it to the shuttle, and then he made it into the shuttle, and he climbed painfully into a couch, and at last he allowed himself a moment to recover.

Although, to be honest, there wasn't much to recover. Four working limbs and one passenger; half-burnt-out eyes, and a carapace certainly at least cracked.

But a working memory.

He laughed out loud, and then started as the sound bounced off the walls of the little ship. It sounded alien, and more than a bit mad.

Then he reviewed his plan. And hated it – but couldn't think of anything better, so it would have to do.

It had been lifetimes since he had last sat here, and he had been an indifferent pilot then. What did you do? Yes. He remembered.

Wincing with pain, he reached out a claw, snagged the main console control and powered up the board. Lights winked on. Not much air, not much fuel, but plenty of power and, best of all, plenty of comms.

That would do. He thought for a moment, then found the control that opened a general channel, and another that worked the record/repeat function. Then he spoke.

'All shipping. My name is Skarbo. I am injured. I request safe passage off planet, and medical treatment. Please respond.'

And then he waited for an answer, or several competing answers, or death, whichever came first.

The message had just repeated a hundred times when he got his answer in the form of a galaxy of warning lights on the board in front of him. Then a field snapped into hazy being round the shuttle, and the surface of the planet flicked away.

He cut the recorded message and opened the live channel. 'Thanks,' he said. 'Who are you?'

There was no answer.

He tried again. 'This is Skarbo calling whoever. Thanks for pulling me out. Can you tell me who you are?'

This time there was an answer. It was very short.

'No.'

The voice seemed familiar. At any other time, Skarbo would have grinned. 'May I ask why not?'

'Disclosure would be unhelpful. Please be quiet.'

He shrugged and kept quiet. But left the channel open, just in case.

The dogfight was not far above him. He could see it now – a grey-black sphere that looked very close to being a hulk was floating just above one of the orbital solar arrays while half a dozen angular little vessels swooped around it. Energy beams flickered between them, and now and then one missed and lanced down to the surface of the planet.

The course the field was pulling him on led straight through the swerving vessels. He wanted to duck.

Then a stray beam caught him, brightening a spot of the field for a second.

The firing stopped.

Then all the angular ships brightened to incandescence and became vapour.

Skarbo was impressed. That had been no energy beam, but

a major field-weapon. He was glad he was on the friendly side of it.

So far, of course.

The hulk-thing seemed to have been impressed too. For whole seconds it did nothing. Then it turned a little from side to side, looking exactly as if it were making sure it believed its eyes, before dropping towards the solar array. A hatch opened and a swarm of little machines poured out of it and over the panels. As Skarbo watched they began to take the array apart.

Recycling never stopped. He wondered how long it would be before someone else muscled in.

Then the shuttle tipped back so that the view tilted upward, and he forgot all about recycling.

In the centre of his vision was the Orbiter. His mind flinched. He would come to the Orbiter in a while, when he was ready.

In the vreality, when the parade of numbers and models had become impossible, he had sometimes put on a cloak and wandered along the coast to the town, to observe people doing real things. He remembered watching a group using draw-beasts to tow sleds loaded with fish up stone ramps, and the way the tow ropes sparkled with salt water.

This was a bit like that. He was caught in a field, which shrank to a thick filament on its way to the ship that was towing him.

It looked like one of the old warships he had first seen in the Sphere. So did the ships that surrounded the Orbiter, in a ring of six with a latticework of fields strung between them, the Orbiter suspended in the lattice. The old guard had shown up again.

And now he allowed himself to come to it.

The Orbiter was appallingly damaged. Skarbo caught his breath. Fully half the old ship wasn't there.

It wasn't a clean slice. Somehow that would have been better. Instead it was as if the vessel had simply been torn in two, by something that had pulled and twisted and yanked until the hull had ripped and parted down the middle like a green stick. He remembered what had happened to Hamfrets' ship, but this was far more brutal.

They were nearly there. Surely now it was okay to communicate? He leaned towards the board. 'Can you tell me—'

'Not yet.'

He fell silent and watched the dead Orbiter – surely it *was* dead – getting closer, with a sort of horrified calm.

If the ship was dead, what did that mean for the idea they had shared? How much had it shared in turn with its escorts, before whatever had happened to it occurred?

There was no way of asking that over an open channel. He would just have to wait.

Then the shuttle was crawling into the circle of ships. It was brought to a halt alongside the Orbiter, and Skarbo could see straight into the guts of the mauled ship. The sight made him shudder.

Skarbo?

The shock of hearing the voice almost knocked him over. 'Orbiter?'

Just. I am – reduced.

'I can see that. I'm amazed you're functioning. What happened?'

Attack. The Warfront was early . . . and you are late.

'I'm sorry. Have you still . . .' He hesitated.

Yes. Wait. You will be brought aboard.

'Aboard you?' He didn't want to add, you look uninhabitable.

Ships have been built with sealable compartments for millions of years. Part of me is still gas-tight. Skarbo? Did you succeed?

'Yes.'

So, in my way, did I. Now we must see.

'Good.' He wasn't sure what else to add.

Then the shuttle rocked, and the interior boiled briefly with a harsh blue light. Skarbo grabbed the console.

A field had snapped into being around the group of warships. Outside it, energy beams stabbed, lighting up angry patches on its haziness. The Warfront was closing in.

Skarbo swallowed. 'Ship? Will we be able to accomplish – what we need to, from inside a field?'

There was a pause. Then, *No.*

'I thought not. How long will we have, after we drop the field?'

It will depend. The ships will attempt to defend us.

Skarbo thought about that. He wanted to say, then they'll die, but there was no point.

'I see,' he said, instead. 'Get me aboard.'

The tow-field parted in the middle. The far end retracted into the old warship and vanished. The end connected to the shuttle wavered for a moment then snaked over to delve into the open gash on the side of the Orbiter. It probed a few times and then stabilized and fattened.

The ship says you can enter the field tunnel through your airlock. It is pressurized.

Skarbo nodded, and lifted himself off the couch.

With no vacuum to fight, the lock cycled quickly. He pushed himself out into the tube and floated along it. Air sucked at him gently; the Orbiter was helping him along.

He kept his eyes closed. Even through this field and the larger one around the group of ships, the violence of the attack was too bright to look at; unbroken waves of energy were bursting and boiling against the outside of the field. He hoped the field was less transparent to radiation than to visible light.

Then he smiled. That probably didn't matter now – but it was still almost a relief to drift through the gash and into the eviscerated ship.

The field tunnel ended in an improvised airlock. This, too,

cycled quickly, and then he was inside, in a dark space he didn't recognize.

The floor was trembling.

Something hurled itself towards him.

'*Ha!* You back then?'

He felt himself smiling. 'Yes, I'm back. Hello, bird.'

'Don't you ever learn? Still not a bird.' It hovered in front of him, its head tilting from side to side. 'What've you been up to? Radioactive as fuck! Better stay away from anything that breathes.'

'I will.' Then something occurred to him. 'How can you tell?'

It made a yarking noise. 'This beak never lies. Better get busy, before you crumble. How long?'

It was a good question. He hadn't been keeping count of his ebbing life. 'Ah, all other things being equal, about ten hours.'

It looked at him for a second. 'Don't think all other things are equal any more. Still. The ship says to take you this way.'

It flapped off without waiting for an answer. Skarbo followed.

They ended up in a tall, plain dome-shaped space about fifty metres across. It seemed familiar, but Skarbo wasn't sure why. Perhaps it was because it was roughly the same shape as the Second Machine Room – but that wasn't it.

Then he realized – it was the room he had entered on his first time here, but with all the projections switched off.

The plain white ovoids were still on their stands in the middle of the floor. But now they were all pointing upwards.

The old machines are waiting, he thought. And he knew what to do.

He realized The Bird was watching him. He smiled. 'Time to go, I think.'

'Think what you like. I'm staying.'

'All right. Ship? We need to be outside.'

Yes.

And the domed walls opened like a flower, stretching a tenuous field-membrane between them that bulged outwards under the pressure of the air.

Skarbo flinched – the vicious light of the battle was even worse. Seconds at best, he thought. Out loud he said, 'Thanks. Now I need to communicate with these.'

You already are.

And with no warning, a voice like a gong boomed in his head.

'I listen.'

Skarbo took a deep breath. 'Are you machines that can build planets?'

'Yes. We are Creation Machines.'

Skarbo felt something like a spark pass through him. 'Can you see information?'

A sensation of something exploring – a subtle fuzziness, as if parts of his mind were being dislocated, examined, reconnected.

'Yes. We have it.'

He nodded. 'Can you do it?'

'Yes. It is our purpose. It will complete the work. Do you wish?'

Well, did he? Skarbo looked up at the raging energies outside. Utter destruction; but then, that beckoned either way.

He had had a thousand years to think about the question, and in all that time he had only ever answered it one way.

'Yes,' he said. 'I wish.'

'We hear.'

And so do I. Goodbye, Skarbo.

The Orbiter dropped the field. Air belched out through the opening, and Skarbo felt his body swelling into the vacuum.

Then it stopped swelling – there was something surrounding him, close like tight clothing. He looked down at himself and saw a shimmer, like and at the same time unlike a field. A few metres from him, The Bird floated, its wings folded tightly to its body. It looked surprised.

The ovoids were surrounded by the same stuff.

'WITHDRAW!'

The word was like an explosion, like the crash of falling rock celebrated by a thousand voices.

'WITHDRAW! DANGER! BEWARE!'

It was the machines. They were rising out of the Orbiter, and closing into a formation like some complicated molecule.

'BE READY!'

Then the ring of surrounding ships dropped their own field.

Energy ripped through the ring. It hammered into the Orbiter like lava.

The old ship melted, and flowed, and was gone.

The space around the ring of ships flowered with plasma as they turned their ancient weapons outwards. The inside of the wall formed by the ships of the Warfront flared and halted, and for a second Skarbo thought the old warships might prevail after all.

But then one of them stuttered, and incandesced, and was gone. And then another.

Then there was one more vast howl from the machines.

'WE BEGIN!'

The last of the old ships became blue vapour. The firestorm swept in.

And space around him *twisted*.

The storm front slowed, stopped, and reversed, hammering out through the mass of ships.

The inner edge of the Warfront began to burn, like a flame creeping along the edge of a piece of paper.

The ships dispersed, pulling back. The bubble of space around Skarbo began to expand, and emptied.

The machines flickered, just once. Then, all but one of them were gone.

The remaining machine floated in front of Skarbo. Its image

was beginning to fade. It turns out I can't exist in a vacuum, he thought. Or perhaps it would have faded anyway?

With an effort he formed words. 'Is that it?'

'That is a beginning. The work is not instant.'

'I see. How long will it take?'

'Perhaps ten thousand years.'

Disappointment flooded him. 'I won't see it then.'

'You can see the beginning.'

'But I'm dying . . .'

'Not yet.'

And, with no sense of movement, he was moving. The planet dropped away below him, and the star receded, and then he was in clear space.

'Watch.'

A tiny, bright spot formed in the distance. It pulsed once and then, too fast for his eyes to follow, it swelled into a fierce blue-white ball. He had no idea of scale, but there was something about the thing that made his instincts scream vastness. The surface raced towards him so that he wanted to flinch – and then it stopped, reddened, and, as quickly as it had expanded, shrank to a point and vanished.

Skarbo tried to point, but nothing moved. He managed to speak. 'Where did it go?'

'It is still there, although some of it is in multiple dimensions. The part that remains in this dimension is a micro black hole. I will use it to accrete a planet. See . . .'

The vanished point became a blacker point against space, outlined by a faint white ring. The point became a disc, swelling quickly. Then the white halo flared, and suddenly it contained a bright yellow sphere which grew, slowly at first, then faster, and now if Skarbo strained his eyes he thought he could see a tiny swirl of something, spiralling inwards.

'That is star-stuff, from this dimension and others. A new planet is growing; the first of many.'

He sighed. 'I wish I understood. I wish I could see it finished.'

'You have seen the birth of a planet. Would you like to see the birth of a star? It is faster – a tiny version of the birth of a universe.'

'Oh yes. Yes please.'

And a section of space became first an unbearably bright spark, and then a silent explosion that boiled and consumed space.

Skarbo watched the inferno. Then he managed to move his eyes towards the machine. 'Thank you,' he said. 'I can die now.'

The machine didn't answer. It seemed to move closer, or maybe that was his vision playing tricks. A pool of darker space was forming in front of it. He smiled, and closed his eyes, and let himself fall into it.

Place, place

Zeb studied Keff. The creature seemed – what? Worried? Without turning his gaze he said, 'What can we do with it?'

Chvids grinned. 'I should think between us we could make its life hell.'

Keff shook its head. 'Love to see you try. I tell you what, we could spend the next ten millennia pissing each other off, how would that be? I'm game.'

'I don't think I can be bothered.' Zeb shook his head, and sat down slowly. It was still sinking in that Aish and the others were dead – somehow that hit him harder than the certainty he was too.

Chvids walked over to him and put a hand on his shoulder. 'Are you okay?'

'Probably not.' He looked up at Keff. 'Okay, you won. You kept me here until there was nothing left. Do what you like.'

'Fine. I'll do my best to think of something.'

'That lacked conviction,' Chvids said.

'So what? Piss off.'

'Keff? How long have you been dead?'

'Fuck off.'

She nodded. 'Thought so. A long time, I'm guessing?'

'I said fuck off.'

'Long enough to have had time to work out how the place functions, right? Do you even remember how long?'

Keff spun round. For the first time, Zeb saw anger in its face. 'Oh, yes. I remember. I remember every . . . fucking . . . day, okay? I remember every smiling, happy idiot I ever met, and I remember what I did to piss them off. I've wiped the smirks off a thousand faces and *he's* the one I'm proudest of.' It jabbed a finger towards Zeb.

Zeb nodded slowly. 'And now I'm dead, you've won, and that means you've lost.'

It glared at him. Then it looked away. 'Have it your way.'

'I think I will. We're stuck with each other, Keff.' He grinned more widely. 'Okay, we won't actually see each other much, but you'll *know* I'm around, won't you. Every few thousand years we'll run into each other. Or maybe I'll stalk you? I mean, thanks to you I don't have any other options. It's almost as if you *made* me.' He thought back, and the phrase came to him. 'Are you proud yet?'

It looked at him. 'You know, maybe I am.'

Chvids shook her head. 'You aren't nice,' she said.

'You tell me? You burned down Skarbo's toys.'

'That was for his own good.'

'Again, you tell me? That makes it okay then. I tell you what, let's say I was pissing Zeb off for a thousand years for his own good, how about that?'

She stared at Keff. Then she shook her head. '*Don't* try to tell me we're the same,' she said.

'Fuck off.'

Chvids laughed. 'On the other hand, there is something . . .' She turned to Zeb. 'I have a suspicion.'

'Which is what?'

She gestured towards Keff. 'That *thing* kept you here. What if it stops keeping you here?'

He shook his head. 'I don't understand.'

'I'm willing to bet it could send you back.'

He stared at it. 'What? To reality?'

'Yes. For a given value of reality.' She glanced at Keff, which was gazing straight ahead.

'You have to be kidding. I'm dead.'

Chvids said nothing, but kept her eyes fixed on Keff.

The creature stood up and flicked an irritated hand. 'Yes, all right. It could be done.'

Zeb felt his chest tighten. 'How? Time is . . .' He tailed off, trying not to hope.

Chvids took over. 'Time is one thing out there and another in here. Try not to over-think things. Keff?'

'Oh all right. Zeb? Fuck off.'

And with no transition at all he was – somewhere – and there were images in front of him. They began to move, but slowly, so he had time to see detail.

There was the Rockblossom . . .

There was the rear view of a female whose name he couldn't remember, and his body twitched in response and his mind performed a dual backflip of shame and self-satisfaction . . .

There were scenes from the thousands of years he had spent wandering the vrealities . . .

There was . . .

'Stop!'

The images froze.

'Seen something you like?'

It was Keff.

'Yes, but I don't understand.' He gestured at the page. 'That wasn't vreality. That was true . . .'

'Was it? By what definition?'

Zeb stared at the scene. It was a blurred still picture of Aish, sitting behind her desk. She was wearing her usual worried look. He spread his arms. 'By the definition that I was there! I remember those people.'

'Fine. Do you remember Chvids?'

'Well, yes, but that was—' He stopped, as confusion lapped around his ankles.

The voice finished the phrase for him. 'Different?'

Zeb watched the image of Aish. It wasn't a still picture, he realized. She was moving, so slowly that he could only be sure by looking away and looking back to catch the tiny dislocations. One hand was sweeping outwards, in a glacial replay of her *I'm making a point here* gesture. He wondered what point she was making.

There was something different about her. He studied the image for a moment. Then he saw it.

She wasn't wearing the pendant.

Presumably he must finally have annoyed her so badly that she had thrown it away. At least Shol would be relieved.

Without turning away, he asked, 'Why is it so slow?'

'You're a layer above. The shallower the level, the faster. Things get more data-compressed the deeper you go. Less data, less speed.'

'I didn't know.'

'Nor do most people. But most people don't get beyond the surface layers. I believe someone made that point to you once.'

He nodded. 'I remember. I was paying back, you know.'

'I know. And you did, in the end. And maybe I finally got over my thousand-year tantrum. Or maybe I'm going to inflict it on Chvids. Zeb? What do you want to do?'

Zeb watched the image of Aish very gradually standing upright. Even more emphatic . . . and he found his cheek was wet.

A layer above . . .

'Keff?' he said. 'I think I know what you're doing, but I don't care. I want to forget.'

And immediately he was falling.

Wall Energy Collective

Zeb opened his eyes.

He was sitting among the remains of the pod, which was smashed open like a hollow fruit. He must have hit the planet hard.

He couldn't move his legs. He looked down and saw that he was encased in soft, off-white stuff. It had a dry, chemical smell.

Crash-foam. Someone had told him once that it was chemically triggered. He didn't remember it happening, which struck him as odd, but maybe it was just very fast.

He decided not to get hung up on that.

He needed to pee. For a second he wondered if the crash-foam had any negative interactions with human urine. Then he shook his head, and shoved his hands down into the stuff.

It tore easily. After a few minutes he had dug himself free. He pulled himself upright and stood, swaying, while he mentally explored his body. Mostly good, to his surprise. Some bruising but nothing serious. He took a step and—

. . . *something moved, just out of his vision* . . .

—and for a second thought his ankle was going to give way, but it was just some kind of twitch. He gave it a look, but it went on working.

Whatever. The need to pee was still there. He managed not to wet the remains of the pod; presumably someone would want to examine it.

What was going on? He had been climbing, and now he was on the ground . . . He looked around, and raised his eyebrows. One of the guy-wires was lying on the ground, an almost invisibly thin line snaking away to somewhere out of sight. The other two, unbalanced by the loss of the third, had skewed wildly out of position.

Presumably the broken guy-wire explained what he was doing on the ground. He blinked, and ran his eye up the guys to the lens arrays. Then he stared.

They were whole kilometres from where they should have been, pulled away by the unbalanced force of the two remaining guys. And on their way there, they had pulled the guys through a long, shallow arc of the Skylid so that a huge, crescent-shaped section of the fluttering membrane was dull, drifting away from the rest.

He watched the thing dying for a while before looking away.

Well, on the plus side it would help a lot with their power problems, for as long as it took to fix it.

On the other hand, Orbital Joule would be furious.

He grinned.

Right. Time to report in. The pod comms were covered in foam, but even through the mess he could see the sickly glimmer of a dead-battery tell-tale.

Better walk, then. And face the music, because Aish would be pissed off that he had somehow broken not only a Bug but also a guy-wire and, collaterally, the Skylid. And so Shol would be pissed off because Aish was pissed off.

Well, he was just pissing everyone off today, even if he couldn't remember how he'd done it. But there was stuff to do, and after a while Shol and Aish might remember to be glad he hadn't broken himself as well.

Might.

Zeb shook his head, and began to walk back down to the Wall, not sure what he was going to find.

Could things be made permanently okay? He doubted it. The suns would fade and the planet would die, sooner or later. Even if he swore off the vrealities for ever, his presence would not stop that. No human endeavour could.

But perhaps it could be okay for a while. Perhaps that would have to do.

Unknown

Skarbo was somewhere familiar. Air moved softly through woven walls that curved up and over to form a dome. The walls were lined with shelves and pigeon holes.

The shelves were empty.

He sat up, and was unsurprised to find himself in human form. There didn't seem to be anyone else around.

'Hello?'

He was on a pallet. He swung his legs round and off, and stood up. He felt good.

'Hello? I'm awake.' Amazing, he thought. Awake.

'Hello.' The voice was behind him. He turned, and saw a tall, slim woman smiling at him. For a moment he thought it was Chvids, and the thought tugged at him. But then he realized the resemblance was superficial.

'How do you feel?' the woman asked.

'Fine.' He stopped to check. 'Yes; fine. I assume this is a vreality?'

She shook her head. 'It's all real. We pulled the design of this place out of your head. Some of us thought it would make it easier for you to adapt – a soft transition. You've been away for a while.'

'Real?' He walked over to the wall, found a window, and looked out. 'Oh. Yes.'

He wasn't in a Seatree, but in a real tree. Instead of the ocean, he was looking down on a forest canopy – a long way down; his own tree must be much taller than the rest. Black dots of birds wheeled below him.

He turned to the woman. 'What happened?'

There was a stool next to her. She snagged it with a foot and sat down. 'We found you,' she said. 'We think you were called Skarbo. Is that right?'

'Were?' He shrugged. 'Still am, I suppose. Why change? But I wasn't in this body.'

'No. You were in insect form. A very durable insect form! But when we had a look round your memories things got complicated. Half of them said you'd spent the longest as an insect but another set said you'd lived even longer as a human. This human, more or less. We chose the human. You can always change it, if you like?'

He thought about that. Then he said, 'No, I don't think so. Time to settle down. I guess I was dead when you found me? I should have been.'

'Not quite. You had closed down; you seem to have had some very good long-term survival strategies built in to that body. And we wonder if something may have helped you, too; but we'll never know that.'

There was something about the way she said *long-term* that made him pause. He looked at her for a moment; her mouth was turned down at the corners as if she was trying not to smile.

Then he asked, 'When is it?'

She did smile. 'You're going to need it explaining, I guess. Just to confirm, is this yours?'

She reached down behind her and picked up a box of dark, polished wood. She held it out.

He took it.

It contained something that looked like a ball of black cloth. He poked it – not cloth; something much more fragile. He withdrew the finger and inspected it.

Feathers. Broken, and falling to dust, but definitely feathers.

He looked up at the woman. 'It was never mine, but I knew it. It's dead, then.'

'It was never alive. It's more machine than animal. Pretty fancy mechanisms. My technical friends tell me we couldn't replicate it.'

He nodded. The machine part made sense.

She took the box back from him. 'Its mind is empty, but there was a clock still running on one corner of the substrate. Its mind shut down seventy thousand years ago.'

He stared at her.

'It was found next to you. You were sharing an orbit.'

'Orbit?'

'Yes. You were both floating around in space for seventy millennia. You might want to sit down?'

He did. He was trying to work out if he was surprised or not; maybe this thing went straight through surprise and out the other side?

Whatever. He looked away. 'So where are we?'

'You're in the Spin, where you were.'

He nodded, and asked the next question. 'How many planets are there?'

She laughed. 'Let me show you.'

She waved a hand, and an image flickered and swelled in front of him, growing until it filled the space.

'There. The Spin, second generation.'

Familiar, but different . . . He tried to count. 'About two hundred planets?'

She laughed again. 'You should know. There was a map in

your head. It's an excellent map. Two hundred and one planets, and thirty-three suns.'

'I see.' He let the information settle in. It had worked . . . 'What's this planet called?'

'The one we're on? It's called Orbiter. We think it was one of the first ones completed in the second construction phase. We don't know what the name means; it's an odd sort of thing to call a planet. Actually, we were wondering if you could tell us?'

Skarbo stared at her, and then out at the millions of trees. Then he laughed. 'I have no idea,' he said.

Peace Rift Plateau, Sholntp (vreality)

Chvids marched up the path that led to the Peace Rift. She was barefoot, because the softly coarse grass felt good under her toes. A pack wagged gently on her back; food for a day's journey, and shoes, just in case she changed her mind.

She was nearly at the top. She turned round and looked for Keff.

The thin creature was a hundred metres behind her. She cupped her hands round her mouth.

'Hey! Keep up!'

And listened, and smiled. The shouted 'fuck off' had been faint but unmistakable – but the creature was still following her.

She turned and walked on. She was just about on the thin rock promontory, and the damp, exotic forests of the Rift were opening out below her.

Halfway along the promontory she stopped, swung off her pack and sat down. There was a slim flask in the pack, and she was thirsty.

A few minutes later there were footsteps, and Keff sat down next to her. She held out the flask. 'Drink?'

'Fuck off.'

But it took the flask. She smiled at it. 'When are you going to learn some more words?'

'Fuck off.'

'Fine.' It had drunk, and lowered the flask. She reached out and took it. 'So, this was where it all started for Zeb?'

'Yes.'

'Do you think he guessed?'

'About what?'

She tsk'd. 'You know perfectly well. About reality . . . or not.'

'Well if he did, he chose to forget it.'

'Yes.' She paused. 'Would you choose to forget it too?'

This time it didn't answer. She glanced at it sideways. 'Where did it all start for you?'

It looked at her for a moment, and then looked away and got to its feet. 'I don't respond to armchair psychology.'

She nodded. 'Okay. So, down there. Want to go exploring?'

'Fuck off.' But it still followed her.

She smiled to herself. It was progress of a sort. And she had time.

Coda

The soul of the entity that had never been a bird stared out across the landscape below it and tried to find a point of reference. It had always known where and what it was. Now it knew neither.

But it liked the word *soul*. It turned to the thing which had formerly been the Orbiter. 'What am I looking at?'

Nothing, and everything.

'Very helpful.' It turned back to the landscape. Not real, that was the first decision. A crawling, shifting palette of colours it had never seen before. Patterns formed, became intensely ordered, and dissolved into other patterns.

Its physical form had had senses and abilities it had not shared with anyone, and they seemed to have been carried over into whatever it was now – but they weren't helping.

'Then what am I?'

A cloud of data.

That seemed funny. 'Ha! I was always that. We're all always that, even if we keep it in squidgy brains. What else?'

Nothing else, until you choose to be.

'I see. I take it you're the same?'

No.

Another pattern, this time dazzlingly complex: a fractal vortex that wound and unwound itself in a granular blur of violet and black.

'What are the patterns?'

Thoughts. Changes. Permanence. Everything.

It began to see. 'Everything, happening on nothing?'

Yes. In other words, you are looking at a way of seeing the components of a vreality. They are unreal, but they have meaning.

'It seems too slow . . .'

That is because you are too fast.

'I suppose so.' It watched the patterns for a while. Then it laughed.

What?

'I've worked it out. All the way up and all the way down, eh? Ha!'

Ha.

The former bird nodded, and enjoyed the fact that it seemed to have a head.

It came down to this, it thought: Can any system simulate something more complex than itself?

The first answer – the simple one – was 'no'. It was obvious. It thought it could even prove it, by logic alone.

The second answer was 'it depends'.

It depended on many things. If you wish to simulate a universe accurately, you need something of greater complexity than the universe. Another, bigger universe would be the simplest course.

But, if you want to simulate only a few of the things that are happening in the universe, over a short time, and – crucially – if the thing you are using to do the simulating runs much faster than what it is trying to simulate, then the answer is *definitely*.

It was all about speed and scale. If you were big enough and fast enough, modelling the life of a small thing like a civilization was nothing.

The Bird examined the possibilities, and felt awe. Slowly it said, 'Where does it end?'

Below, I assume when quantum effects become a barrier. I believe that there may be worlds near the base of the vreality-stack which are intensely simplified. Perhaps the last layer consists only of one endless thought being thought by a single-celled creature, alone in a two-dimensional space just big enough to contain it.

The Bird shook its head slowly. 'And that's what the inside of your mind looks like after a quarter of a million years, is it?'

It has always looked like that. But you should know; you are being modelled in my mind at this moment.

'The fuck I am . . .'

Of course. How else could you look in at a vreality, except from the outside?

The Bird shook its head. 'But you're a model in a vreality too.'

Yes.

'Fuck.' The Bird hopped a couple of times. 'Head hurts. Fuck!'

Quite.

'Yes. So, how far up does it go? Guess we're near the top, right?'

Why would you guess that?

It thought about it. 'Don't know. Just seems pretty complex here.'

Perhaps. Or perhaps that is what the thought of a single-celled organism feels like.

'Oh fuck off.'

I do not think I will miss you.

The Bird blinked. 'Cutting remarks, eh? Where are you going?'

Not me. You.

'Why?'

You can't stay here. I am hosting you as a temporary favour.

It nodded. 'Where, then?'

You will learn to navigate the vrealities. You may already have done so, in a former life.

That made it stop. It thought about the implications. Then it shook its head firmly. 'No. Not a chance. You've done enough messing with my head. How do I get out of here? If out is the right word.'

It will do . . . fly down into the landscape. The rest will simply happen.

'Right.' It got ready to spring forwards, off whatever it was perching on. Still perching then; that habit died hard.

Then it thought of something. 'Hey! Do you think Skarbo guessed?'

Guessed what?

'Don't play dumb. This! All of it.' It swept a wing round – got wings too, it thought.

The vrealities? I doubt it. And lifetimes of contemplation and one great intuitive leap should be enough for anyone.

'Yes. Not the fastest, old Skarbo! Right. I'm off. See you somewhere!' The Bird sprang forward. The wings worked like wings and the stuff under them felt like air, and it launched itself into a hissing power dive towards the coloured surface.

It felt joy. It wanted to shout, so it shouted.

'Haaaa!' And, just before it entered, turned its head back and yelled over its shoulder: 'Still not a bird!'

The ghost of the Orbiter watched the surface close over the creature.

Have I done right? it thought.

It didn't know. And if nothing was real, could there even be something such as right?

It had lived – had *thought* it was living – its whole life by what it had always thought of as high moral principles. *I'm old,* it thought. *And tired.*

It wished it could have seen things as simply as The Bird. Or whatever the creature had really been, and would be, as it went on its next journey.

Whereas the Orbiter was ready for another sort of journey.

Enough, it thought.

It did the last thing it would ever do. It let its mind begin to run down.

A final thought occurred to it. *Endings can be the same as beginnings* – but the old ship knew it for the lie it was.

Its consciousness faded like a sigh, and was gone.

Acknowledgements

To those who helped and, as this one took a while, to those who waited, and especially to those who did both – thank you!

About the Author

Andrew Bannister grew up in Cornwall. He studied Geology at Imperial College and went to work in the North Sea before becoming an environmental consultant. A specialist in sustainability and the built environment, he presently works on major construction contracts for public bodies in the UK and internationally. He has always written, initially for student newspapers and fanzines before moving on to fiction, and he has always read science fiction. These things finally came together in his novels set in an artificial cluster of stars and planets called the Spin. He lives in Leicestershire.

To find out more, visit www.andrewbannister.com